Weddings by DeWilde

Since the turn of the century, the elegant and fashionable DeWilde stores have helped brides around the world turn the fantasy of their "special day" into reality. But now the store and three generations of family are torn apart by the separation of Grace and Jeffrey DeWilde. As family members face new challenges and loves—and a long-secret mystery—the lives of Grace and Jeffrey intermingle with store employees, friends and relatives.

For weddings and romance, glamour and fun-filled entertainment, enter the House of DeWilde....

PAPERBACK TRADE INN
145 E. 14 Mile Rd.
Clawson, MI 48017
(248) 307-0226

Dear Reader,

As I sit down to start a new book I always hope that this will be one of the stories where there is a special spark of magic, a spark that brings the characters inside my head vividly to life for the reader. Magic can't be forced, but fortunately, from time to time the miracle happens and everything comes together: the pieces of the plot all fit perfectly and the characters remain among the most interesting people I've ever met.

The two novels reprinted in this volume had this special touch of magic for me. Each story has its own unique romance, with a traditional happy ending, but in addition there is an overarching love story that deals with the breakup of Grace and Jeffrey DeWilde's marriage of over thirty years and their struggle to find each other again. Since they also have a worldwide business empire to run, their marital problems get played out on a very public stage, with economic consequences for thousands of employees—a fact that makes the path toward reconciliation even bumpier.

I'm so glad that Harlequin has brought these two separate stories together in a single volume. In *Shattered Vows*, jewelry designer Lianne Beecham and her boss Gabriel DeWilde find unexpected happiness together. Michael Forrest and schoolteacher Julia Dutton are a great example of opposites who attract in *I Do, Again*. And throughout both stories Grace and Jeffrey DeWilde are struggling to put their thirty-two-year-old marriage together again.

I hope you will enjoy reading about these three couples as much as I loved writing about them.

Sincerely,

Jasmine Cresswell

JASMINE CRESSWELL
The DeWilde Affair

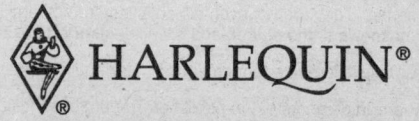

TORONTO • NEW YORK • LONDON
AMSTERDAM • PARIS • SYDNEY • HAMBURG
STOCKHOLM • ATHENS • TOKYO • MILAN • MADRID
PRAGUE • WARSAW • BUDAPEST • AUCKLAND

If you purchased this book without a cover you should be aware that this book is stolen property. It was reported as "unsold and destroyed" to the publisher, and neither the author nor the publisher has received any payment for this "stripped book."

THE DeWILDE AFFAIR

ISBN 0-373-83585-X

Copyright © 2004 by Harlequin Enterprises Ltd.

The publisher acknowledges the copyright holder of the individual works as follows:

SHATTERED VOWS
Copyright © 1996 by Harlequin Books S.A.

I DO, AGAIN
Copyright © 1997 by Harlequin Books S.A.

All rights reserved. Except for use in any review, the reproduction or utilization of this work in whole or in part in any form by any electronic, mechanical or other means, now known or hereafter invented, including xerography, photocopying and recording, or in any information storage or retrieval system, is forbidden without the written permission of the publisher, Harlequin Enterprises Limited, 225 Duncan Mill Road, Don Mills, Ontario, Canada M3B 3K9.

All characters in this book have no existence outside the imagination of the author and have no relation whatsoever to anyone bearing the same name or names. They are not even distantly inspired by any individual known or unknown to the author, and all incidents are pure invention.

This edition published by arrangement with Harlequin Books S.A.

® and TM are trademarks of the publisher. Trademarks indicated with ® are registered in the United States Patent and Trademark Office, the Canadian Trade Marks Office and in other countries.

Visit us at www.eHarlequin.com

Printed in U.S.A.

CONTENTS

SHATTERED VOWS   9
I DO, AGAIN   257

To Grace Allison, so glad you're here!

SHATTERED VOWS

CHAPTER ONE

GABRIEL DEWILDE STORMED into his father's office and slammed the door shut behind him. "What the hell is this all about?" he demanded, thrusting the solicitor's letter onto his father's desk. "If this is your idea of a joke, I don't find it funny."

Jeffrey DeWilde continued to stare out of his office window, apparently fascinated by the view of gray slate rooftops awash in spring rain. "It isn't a joke," he said finally. "Grace has left me."

He sounded no more than mildly regretful, as if he were commenting on the fact that this morning at breakfast he'd run out of his favorite brand of marmalade. Gabe ran his hands through his long, light brown hair and paced the room. He felt as if he'd walked into the familiar surroundings of his father's office only to discover himself free-falling into an alien universe.

"Left you?" he repeated, the simple words incomprehensible when applied to his mother. "She can't have left you. You've been married for thirty-two years!"

"But she has left me." Jeffrey's stark response reverberated in the oak-paneled quiet of the room. "She moved out to a hotel on Friday night. I don't know which one."

Gabe shook his head, trying to restore his sense of reality. "None of this makes the least bit of sense! You and Mother always seemed to have the ideal marriage. Neither of you ever gave any of us the slightest hint that you were having problems.''

Jeffrey still didn't turn around. "Some things are too painful to discuss, even with your children. And perhaps the hints were there if you'd been willing to look for them."

"No, of course they weren't. We didn't have a clue—" Gabe broke off, suddenly remembering the Sunday morning last month when he'd arrived unexpectedly at Kemberly, his parents' home in Hampshire. He'd found his mother red-eyed and alone. She'd insisted her problem was nothing more than allergies, caused by the spring pollen. Wanting to be convinced, Gabe had accepted her explanation without pushing very hard for another. In retrospect, he cursed his willful blindness.

Angry with himself, he took out his frustration on his father. "Your children aren't supposed to be mind readers," he said. "Damn it, Dad, you should have warned us what was going on."

"What would you have expected me to say? I wasn't sure how...the situation...would be resolved."

"Well, I certainly didn't expect you to wait until Mother had left and then order the family solicitor to send us an official announcement that the two of you had separated! Ramsbotham's letter reads like an announcement from Buckingham Palace about another royal marriage on the rocks. We're your children, for God's sake, not company employees! How do you think Kate and Megan are going to feel when they get their copies of this bombshell? They're miles away. They can't even come and talk to you."

"I'm sorry." Jeffrey's apology was clipped. "In the

end, everything happened rather suddenly. I tried to phone you last night but you were out, and I suppose I felt a somewhat cowardly sense of relief. I did manage to talk to Megan in Paris early this morning, but you know I've never been good at explaining emotional...things. That's your mother's department. She always does this sort of thing so much better than I do. I rely on her—"

Jeffrey got up abruptly but didn't seem quite sure what to do next. He opened the heavy drapes to their fullest extent, then pulled them back to their original position. He sat down in his chair once more, his back to Gabriel, and resumed his contemplation of Bond Street in the rain.

He cleared his throat, started to speak, stopped and started again. "Grace has returned to San Francisco. She left yesterday morning, so I expect she's there by now and settling in to...wherever she plans to stay. I'm quite sure she'll be in touch with you soon, Gabriel. It's me she wants to divorce, not you or your sisters. You know how much she loves you all."

Divorce? Good God, were his parents really talking about getting a divorce, not just separating for a while? The more his father explained, the less Gabe understood. This entire conversation would have been ridiculous, a splendid example of black comedy—if it hadn't been so sad. He knew deep in his bones that his parents had once been happy together. Children didn't need to understand adult emotions to be aware they existed, and Gabe had always known his parents had not only liked and respected each other, they'd been deeply in love. Awareness of his parents' love for each other suffused all his childhood memories. Where had all that love gone? If Jeffrey and Grace couldn't make their marriage last, Gabe wondered if any couple could.

"How can you let Mother divorce you?" he asked. "Can't you fight this? Surely you can work out your problems, whatever they are? Good Lord, after thirty-two years there must be some groundwork left to build on. You love each other!"

Jeffrey didn't answer, didn't even move, and Gabe pleaded, "Dad, look at me, for God's sake! Make me understand what's happened. The two of you have always been so happy together!"

"Obviously not happy enough to persuade your mother to remain here in England," Jeffrey said.

"But why has she gone to San Francisco? What in the world is she going to do there?"

"I don't know." Jeffrey shrugged. "San Francisco is her home, after all. And Kate is there."

"Kate's only there until she finishes university," Gabe said tightly. "Mother's home is here in London, with you. Her work is here, her friends are here. Her whole adult life. Why is she doing this to you? To us? How could she just...walk out?"

Jeffrey finally swung his chair around and faced his son. An outsider might have thought his thin, aristocratic features expressionless. Gabe knew better. His father's hazel eyes normally gleamed with laughter, displaying a rueful appreciation of the world's follies, and his own. Today his gaze was cold and bleak, his mouth compressed into a tight line. Whatever the reasons for this stunning rupture in his parents' marriage, Gabe could see at a glance that his father hadn't wanted it and was shattered by Grace's abrupt departure. Jeffrey might sound cool and collected, but inside, Gabe suspected, his father smoldered with feeling.

"A marriage involves two people," Jeffrey said with the same unnatural calm. "When it ends, you can safely bet that both partners contributed to the breakup."

Had he misjudged his father's mood, after all? Gabe wondered. "Are you telling me this was a mutual decision? That you both wanted your marriage to end?"

"I'm certainly not blameless in all this, but the truth is that your mother seems to feel our marriage was a mistake from the beginning." Jeffrey drew in a sharp breath. "At the moment, I think she wants to be as far away from me and from London as possible."

Gabe noticed that his father hadn't quite answered the question. No doubt because he was too honorable to throw all the blame on his wife. His estranged wife, Gabe thought bitterly. "If it's taken her thirty-two years to discover she made a mistake, couldn't she have waited for a couple of months to see if things got better again?"

"Apparently not."

Gabe felt a flash of white-hot anger on his father's behalf. And on his own. He'd always felt a deep affection for his mother, admiring her boundless creativity and the light, whimsical touch she injected into the most mundane aspects of life. Her abrupt departure felt like a personal betrayal. Whatever her reasons for leaving his father, they didn't excuse her flying out of the country without a word to anyone. Why hadn't she called him to say goodbye? To explain why she needed to abandon everything she'd spent a lifetime working to build?

For the past couple of years, Gabe had been the only one of the three DeWilde children living and working in London, and the respect he felt for his mother had increased as he grew to appreciate the heavy workload she carried and the importance of her unique contributions to the DeWilde organization. Her abrupt departure left him disoriented, with the reliable boundaries of everyday life suddenly fluid and uncertain. Her silence left him feeling both rejected and oddly bereft. And if he was feeling bereft, Gabe reflected, it was hard to imagine what his father must be suffering.

"My mother has responsibilities," he said harshly. "Even if she's decided to throw away her husband and family, there's the business to think about. She does remember that she's executive vice president of DeWilde's, doesn't she?" He picked up the solicitor's letter and stabbed his forefinger at one of the many obscure sentences. "What does this mean, for heaven's sake? 'Various financial matters of a personal and business nature continue to be a subject for discussion between your parents.' Elaborate, please."

Jeffrey steepled his fingers and stared down at them as if he weren't quite sure that they still belonged to him. "Grace says that she has no interest in the future success or failure of DeWilde's." He realigned his fingers and stared at them again. "Her official letter of resignation was waiting on my desk this morning. She wants to sever her connections to the stores, as well as her marriage to me."

Jeffrey's voice remained uninflected, but Gabe realized that his cool, courteous and seemingly calm father was hanging on to his control by the merest thread. Not only was Jeffrey personally devastated by his wife's flight, he was fully aware of the serious implications for the business. Stock market analysts might admire his firm control over the bottom line and his ability to cut costs while maintaining the highest levels of service in all the DeWilde stores, but anyone who'd been closely involved in the day-to-day running of the company's five international stores knew how vitally important Grace was to their success. She was recognized throughout the organization as a creative whirlwind, swirling around the solid pillar of Jeffrey's business acumen, breathing life and color into her husband's fact- and number-oriented decisions.

Grace's retailing instincts were unsurpassed on either side of the Atlantic. She had a sixth sense that told her months ahead of the competition what sort of weddings next year's brides would be planning, and she also seemed blessed with a seventh sense that told her exactly how to display and market DeWilde merchandise so that it fulfilled every bride's fantasy of that perfect wedding—and glamorous honeymoon. With a sense of definite foreboding, Gabe realized that his mother's hasty departure had not only destroyed a marriage but could also have a devastating effect on the continued success of the DeWilde stores. With the current upheaval in the retail market worldwide, this was not the moment to have stock market analysts raising questions about DeWilde's capability to remain an industry leader.

"How do you want to handle this with the management group?" Gabe asked. He glanced at his watch. "We have a few hours before the store will be open in New York. But somebody needs to call Ryder Blake in Sydney right away. And we have to talk to Paris, too. Or is Megan handling things over there? And Monaco. Who else have you spoken to here in London? How many people already know that Mother has gone?"

"Nobody," Jeffrey said.

Gabe bit back a frustrated expletive. Grace's departure must have thrown his father for an absolute loop.

In normal circumstances, the departure of a key executive would have meant that Jeffrey had spent most of the weekend on the phone, making sure that his managers were fully aware of the situation, discussing tactics and strategy, preparing his people so that they would be ready to hit the ground running on Monday morning. Gabe began to realize the enormity of the problem he was facing. Losing Grace was bad enough, but DeWilde's couldn't afford to lose Jeffrey's input, as well, not when they had major expansion and renovation plans in the works.

He drew in a deep breath. "If nobody knows about Mother's resignation, you need to call a management meeting right away. You'll need to start assigning people to cover her current areas of responsibility. Mother has four department heads reporting directly to her in London, and she acts as the merchandising consultant for all five stores." It was ridiculous to be reminding his father of such basic information, but Gabe was afraid that at this precise moment Jeffrey needed all the help he could get. "Do you want her people to report to you for the time being? And if not, how do you want to structure things?"

"I haven't thought about it," Jeffrey said. "We don't have to deal with that today, do we? At the moment, all anyone needs to know is that Grace has left the company and won't be coming back."

"Dad, I'm sorry, but that's not true and you know it." Gabe's shock was beginning to fade, and he decided that perhaps the most immediate and effective way to help his father was to ensure that Grace's departure had as little negative impact as possible on DeWilde's. "This insane decision of Mother's doesn't just affect the family, it affects the company, too. If word about her leaving leaks out in the wrong sort of way, it could have a disastrous effect on company morale, not to mention our share price. Quite apart from any problems with the stock market, we need to handle the internal announcements just right or we're going to have a hell of a lot of unhappy employees.''

"Grace is gone," Jeffrey said, his voice icy. "How do you propose we dress that fact up to make it sound positive?"

"I've no idea, but perhaps someone else in the management group will have something constructive to offer. At the very least, we ought to take steps to avoid having the news spread by whispers and rumors. You need to call our PR consultants and institute some instant damage control. Have them draft an announcement about Grace's departure, emphasizing in as upbeat a way as possible that we have people ready and waiting to step into her shoes. And you need to be ready to field the blizzard of phone calls we'll start to get as soon as the press release hits the financial wire services. You also need to decide who's going to take over the international merchandising functions. I can handle things here in London, but I have no international experience to speak of. Adam in Marketing is good, but he doesn't have any of Mother's natural—"

"I can't do this," Jeffrey said, standing up and gripping the edge of the desk. His face was white. "Gabe, I'm sorry. I thought I could handle coming into the office today, but I can't. I have to get out of here for a while. Please, take care of things for me." He strode to the door of his office and walked past his secretary's desk to the lifts, ignoring the astonished stare of Monica and Gabe's plea for him to wait a minute, or at least to take an umbrella.

"Is he going out in this downpour?" Monica asked, tapping a pencil against her computer keyboard without any awareness of what she was doing. "Oh, dear, I do hope he hasn't forgotten that Sir Walter Kenyon is scheduled to arrive in twenty minutes."

"He may well have forgotten," Gabe said. "Either way, it's probably best to cancel Sir Walter, at least for today. Try to postpone the meeting until next week, will you?"

Monica picked up the phone to make the call. She grimaced faintly as her conversation ended. "Sorry, Gabriel, but Sir Walter left fifteen minutes ago. There's no way to reach him and put him off."

"Damn. Do you know if my father arranged for anyone else from DeWilde's to attend the meeting?"

Monica glanced at her desk calendar. "Rupert Findlay was supposed to join them," she said.

"Makes sense. Rupert's the chief financial officer and Sir Walter's a banker. Well, Rupert will have to take care of things. Since he was scheduled to attend the meeting, anyway, he probably knows what my father planned to discuss. Call Rupert and warn him he's going to be on his own with Sir Walter, will you?"

Gabe started to leave, but Monica called him back. Normally the perfect model of the circumspect executive secretary, she couldn't hide her concern. "I hope you won't think I'm pushing into private places, Gabriel, but your father hasn't seemed himself for the past several weeks. Is something wrong?"

It was humiliating to learn that Jeffrey's secretary had noticed something amiss when he hadn't, Gabe thought. He'd been a damn sight too caught up in his own affairs these past two months. While he'd been running around London with Julia Dutton, trying to convince himself he'd found the woman who would make him the ideal wife, his parents' marriage had been crumbling into ruins right under his self-absorbed nose.

There seemed no point in attempting to hide the truth from Monica. Grace would soon be conspicuous by her absence. "My parents have separated," he said. "Grace has already left England and gone back to San Francisco. She has family there." He tried to make it sound rational, as if a brother and a smattering of cousins were sensible reasons to abandon a husband of thirty-two years and a dazzling career with one of England's most famous and successful stores. "And, of course, Kate's at Stanford, finishing her residency," he added lamely.

"I don't understand." Monica flushed with distress. "Isn't Grace coming back?"

What was the point of pretending? "No," Gabe said. "At the moment, she isn't planning to return."

"Oh, no! I'm so sorry. I never dreamed..." Monica smothered a murmur of distress. "Poor Jeffrey!" She straightened, visibly squaring herself to face the uncertain future. "Well, I can see this is going to be a difficult day for everyone. How would you like me to help?"

"I have to inform the members of senior management that Grace has gone," Gabe said. "Would you call everyone and ask them to meet me in the boardroom in half an hour?"

Monica looked at the clock on her desk. "That'll be nine-thirty. Yes, everyone should have arrived by then. I'll start notifying people right away. I'll make sure they realize this is a must-attend session."

"Thank you." Gabe walked back to his office at such a fast pace he was almost running. He didn't manage to outpace his worries. Life had an annoying habit of creeping up behind you and grabbing you by the throat to make sure you were paying attention. At eight o'clock this morning, he'd thought that the biggest problem he faced was extricating himself from his relationship with Julia Dutton without hurting her feelings. Now, an hour later, his problems with Julia seemed little more than a footnote to the stunning news of his parents' separation. He reflected wryly that he would have preferred a less painful and dramatic lesson on how to put his problems into perspective.

Perhaps he'd originally been attracted to Julia just because she was so different from his mother, he thought, pushing open the door to his office. Julia was sweet, calm, even-tempered and—restful. The contrast with the bubbling, high-speed energy of his mother had seemed irresistible. But why had he needed the company of someone restful? Because he'd subconsciously sensed the note of strain behind Grace's habitual effervescence? Because he'd felt the high-wire tension suddenly stretching between his parents? Why else had it seemed so important to spend his leisure hours with a woman who was the antithesis of his mercurial mother?

The phone rang and he snatched it up, dealing swiftly with a call from a supplier. When he hung up, he started sketching out some alternative management reporting structures. This was his father's job, of course, but since Jeffrey wasn't available, somebody had to reassign Grace's duties, at least on a temporary basis. He worked intently, his concentration rigorously focused. For the next few hours, he wouldn't allow himself to think about the personal aspects of the split between Grace and Jeffrey. He needed to keep his attention fixed on the impact their separation was likely to have on the DeWilde organization.

To put it mildly, this was not proving to be the most enjoyable Monday morning he'd ever lived through. Gabe hoped like hell that the day had exhausted its store of unpleasant surprises.

CHAPTER TWO

WHEN SHE REALIZED there was going to be no letup in the unrelenting downpour of rain, Lianne Beecham decided to blow her week's lunch money on a cab. After all, she was about to become a gainfully employed woman, with a real job and a regular income. Once her first month's salary was deposited into the bank, she'd be rich. Or at least solvent, which was a great deal more than could be said about her situation over the past few months. Free-lance designers didn't have it any easier in London than they did in New York, Lianne had discovered, and she was heartily sick of being a starving artist.

When she won the prestigious Garnet Award last December, she'd hoped that commissions and honest-to-God work for pay would result. Instead of work, she'd received accolades. The *Guardian* had assured its readers that she was a costume jewelry designer with "flair to spare." The *Times,* more soberly, had announced that her creative talents "showed astonishing technical competence and promised to develop into genuine originality."

Lianne was suitably grateful for the positive reviews and rather liked the experience of being a minor celebrity in the incestuous world of high fashion. She just wished that the critical praise could have been accompanied by a few checks, since even artists with flair to spare occasionally needed to do mundane things like eat and pay their share of the rent. If Julia Dutton hadn't been such a sympathetic friend and flat mate, Lianne wondered if she would have been able to hang on in London long enough to land a job.

But her life, not to mention her bank balance, was about to undergo a marvelous change. Lianne paid the cab driver, giving him such a generous tip that he actually smiled. She hauled her portfolio out of the cab and looked up at the imposing entrance to DeWilde's, oblivious to the rain pelting down. Her heart pounded with emotion and she felt hot all over, despite the chilly spring breeze. She was so excited to think she was about to start work behind those hallowed blue doors and elegant Queen Anne windows that she would have danced a jig of sheer delight if the pavement hadn't been so wet and muddy.

The rain wasn't letting up, even for a minute. Lianne made a dash for the store and ran inside, tossing back the hood of her raincoat and letting the streams of water drip off her sleeves onto the iron grates set into the marble floor. After a year in England, she really ought to have learned never to leave the flat without her umbrella, but it seemed that she still retained her stubborn American optimism that, however terrible the weather right now, in a moment the sun would be shining.

Unfastening the buttons of her sodden raincoat, she pushed through the second set of heavy doors and squinted into one of the mirrors positioned on the cosmetic counter just inside the store entrance. She sighed. Yep, she looked just the way she'd feared. Her hair was always unruly. On a rainy day it became a tyrant with an uncontrollable will of its own. She'd tried every hair length known to woman, from a short crop to her current shoulder length. Her hair had defeated the best efforts of stylists on both sides of the Atlantic. Before leaving the flat this morning, in honor of her new job, she'd scraped it into a severe French twist and sprayed every obstinate strand into submission. What she had now, a mere thirty minutes later, were the tattered remnants of a French twist and a riot of chestnut curls framing her face. Before informing Grace DeWilde's assistant that she was here, she'd better find the ladies' room so that she could try to re-create her original elegant style. She wasn't holding her breath, though. From past experience, she knew she probably wouldn't achieve anything more sophisticated than flattened curls at the front and a frizzy knot at the back of her head.

But there was no point in agonizing over her hair, which was simply one of those intractable laws of nature, like English rain, or the vile taste of fat-free ice cream. On this, the first day of her new job, she had plenty more important things to worry about.

Lianne had decided to enter the corporate offices by way of the store itself. Grace DeWilde had given her an extensive tour during one of their preliminary meetings, but Lianne needed to internalize the atmosphere of the display floors so that she could develop her own intuitive sense of who the customers were and what fantasies they carried with them as they walked through the imposing gilded doors and into the Edwardian grandeur of the ground floor. From her own brief experience as a bride-to-be five years ago, Lianne was quite sure that brides, even more than most shoppers, were buying a dream right along with their dress and lace veil.

She looked around her, breathing in a subtle scent of lavender polish, sandalwood and rich satin. The overwhelming impression of dignified, traditional splendor would have been out of place in most retail stores, but DeWilde's had proven that, even on the cusp of the twenty-first century, British women enjoyed planning their weddings in surroundings imbued with the solid virtues of permanence and understated elegance. A woman who had shopped at DeWilde's for her trousseau in the thirties could come back today with her granddaughter and be comfortably aware that she was in the same store. And come back they did, bringing new generations of brides with them. In an ever-changing world, customers seemed to appreciate this oasis of tradition.

Still, despite DeWilde's successful track record, Lianne understood why Grace wanted to introduce certain changes. The dawn of the new century was likely to presage an increase in nontraditional wedding ceremonies, and DeWilde's needed to be prepared for the shrinking of their market base. Magnificent as the handcrafted mahogany counters were, they didn't allow for dramatic or inviting displays of merchandise. The lighting was in desperate need of updating. Space wasn't utilized to its maximum advantage. Lianne wholeheartedly agreed with Grace that the famous ground floor could be given a modest face-lift without destroying its beauty and architectural integrity. Still, change wasn't going to come easy. Lianne smiled to herself, glad that she wasn't the one who would have to fight all the stuffy old die-hard conservatives in the upper echelons of management.

In the years following the First World War, DeWilde's had gradually expanded until it sold everything the bride-to-be might need for her wedding and honeymoon. For the past twenty years, most of the store's profits had come from the sale of wedding gowns, lingerie and high fashion clothes for romantic honeymoons. Whether you planned to spend the first few days of your married life sunning on tropical beaches or climbing ice floes in Alaska, DeWilde's had the outfit you needed. But for all this recent emphasis on clothing, the business had built its reputation originally as a jewelry store. Four generations of women had felt their hearts beat a little faster when the young men in their lives pulled out one of the famous dark blue leather jewelry boxes and opened it to reveal a ring, nestled in velvet, with the flowing gold letters of the DeWilde name stamped on the puffed peach satin lining of the lid.

In the nineties, of course, men and women were more likely to come and select an engagement ring together, but the tradition of the real leather box and the real velvet lining persisted. It was one of the luxurious touches that distinguished DeWilde's from its rivals and kept the store ahead in the cutthroat world of modern retailing.

Lianne lingered for a few moments, admiring the dazzling display of engagement and wedding rings, all set with the finest quality gemstones. Although her own interests lay in the realm of costume jewelry, which was considered an offshoot of the fashion industry rather than the world of gemologists and goldsmiths, she often drew her inspiration from the creations of Victorian jewelers, particularly those who had worked at the sumptuous courts of the Indian maharajas. In addition to a line of exquisitely crafted rings set with semiprecious stones such as amethysts and aquamarines, she noticed that DeWilde's had a small display of antique rings for couples who wanted to bring a touch of nostalgia into their marriage. One in particular caught her fancy, an exuberant floral design with tiny diamonds at the heart of each flower, the pink gold a much deeper color than was currently fashionable.

"Is there any way I might help you, madam?"

"No, thanks." Lianne gave the formally dressed man standing behind the counter a cheerful smile. "I'm just looking, but some of these antique engagement rings are so pretty it makes me wonder if marriage might not be so bad after all. That floral design is especially lovely."

He returned her smile, his warm manner belying the high, starched collar of his shirt. "It is lovely, although the diamonds are smaller than we'd use nowadays. My wife always says it takes a lot of diamonds to make up for sharing your bathroom with a man."

"She's right, I'm sure. Your wife sounds like a wise woman."

"With many diamonds," the salesclerk agreed with mock solemnity.

Lianne laughed and walked on. Making her way around the scattering of early-bird customers, she finally stopped in front of the trademark centerpiece of De-Wilde's London store, an exquisitely mounted display of a tiara from the DeWilde family's famous jewelry collection. Protected by an octagon-shaped case of bulletproof glass, the tiara glowed with subdued radiance against its cushion of navy blue velvet. Beneath a cleverly focused spotlight—and a dozen electronic security devices—the strands of diamonds and pearls twisted in serpentine opulence. A descriptive note explained that the provenance of the tiara had never been reliably established, but it was reputed to have been worn by the Empress Eugénie of France on the day of her wedding to Louis-Napoléon in 1853. The empress had lived to a ripe old age after her husband lost his throne, and she'd died in England during the 1920s, so it was quite believable that on some occasion when they'd needed ready cash, Eugénie's heirs had quietly sold the tiara, and it had eventually made its way into the hands of England's most famous family of jewelers.

Lianne stared at the piece for several minutes. She'd seen it before, of course, on previous visits, and she found the subtle mixture of color and texture enchanting, the diamonds imparting brilliance, the pearls offering a rounded, milky contrast to the glittering facets of the gemstones. The overall effect should have been absolutely breathtaking. For the umpteenth time she wondered why there was some tiny part of her that felt disappointed, as if this glorious—and priceless—piece didn't quite live up to the allure promised by its design and history.

Turning away from the famous tiara, Lianne glanced at her watch. Ten-forty-five. Time to make her way upstairs to the corporate offices. The last thing she wanted was to create a bad impression by being late. For her first day, Grace DeWilde had suggested that Lianne should arrive at eleven, two hours after the official opening of the corporate offices and an hour after the store opening at ten.

"There's always so much for me to do on a Monday morning," Grace had said, her husky voice an intriguing contrast to her elegant appearance and blond, classic good looks. "And May is such a hectic month for us. All those June weddings coming up, and all the brides wondering if their dresses are going to be ready on time. And, of course, at the corporate level, we're already making major buying decisions for the following year. I'm usually at my desk by eight-thirty. Give me a couple of hours to catch up on the weekend faxes and get a head start on the crisis of the week—whatever it might be!—then I'll be able to give you my undivided attention for the rest of the morning. I'd like to take you around and introduce you personally to everyone. They've already heard all about my plans to revamp the layout of the ground floor and introduce boutique settings for the first-floor bridal salon. They'll be thrilled to know that I've recruited someone as talented as my first in-house designer. Then, after lunch, I'll hand you over to Personnel, and they can take care of all the paperwork.''

Lianne could hardly wait. Even filling out forms in Personnel had sounded appealing, since it would be the final, official stamp on the reality of her new job. She found the ladies' room and made a valiant stab at fixing her hair, then set out to meet Grace DeWilde. Tapping her foot and humming beneath her breath—she absolutely had to find some outlet for her creative energy or she would explode—she took the lift to the sixth floor. After a year living in England, she was finally remembering not to say "elevator." The doors opened into a pleasant lobby, decorated in beige and moss green, with a large reception desk straight ahead. A receptionist, not the security guard Lianne had seen on previous occasions, greeted her with a somewhat flustered smile.

"Hello, may I help you?"

The receptionist was young and she sounded very unsure of herself. Lianne gave her a friendly smile. Perhaps she, too, was a new employee. "I'm here to see Grace DeWilde. Would you let her know that I've arrived? My name's Lianne Beecham."

If she'd announced that she was the Grim Reaper come to cull excess workers, the receptionist couldn't have looked more horrified. "M-Mrs. DeWilde?" she stammered. "You're here to see Mrs. DeWilde?"

"Yes, that's right." Lianne tried another smile, but the receptionist seemed too distraught to respond. Definitely a new hire, she decided. "If you're busy, why don't you just point me in the direction of her office? I seem to remember that I have to turn left at the end of this hallway."

The suggestion that she might intrude into Grace DeWilde's inner sanctum jolted the receptionist into recovering her voice. "Oh, no! I'll have to ring through first. Someone must, um, escort you. So if you'll just take a seat, Miss—"

"Beecham," Lianne supplied patiently. "Lianne Beecham."

"Yes, thank you, Miss Beecham. Please take a seat for a moment, would you, and I'll let Mrs. DeWilde's assistant know that you're here."

It was clearly an order rather than a request. On Lianne's previous visits, Grace DeWilde had come out to greet her in person, a dynamo in human form. Lianne had secretly been hoping that Grace would be waiting to meet her the moment she stepped out of the lift. Foolishness, of course. Grace was much too busy a woman to hang around the lobby, waiting for a relatively insignificant new hire to show her face.

The receptionist seemed to be having trouble locating the person she needed. Lianne hoped it wouldn't take too long to get through all these preliminaries. She wanted to sink her teeth into her new job and get started. She'd been working twelve hours a day ever since Grace made the final offer, and she was itching to get some of her ideas approved. She wanted to find out where her office was, who'd been hired to design the boutique that would showcase her bridal headdresses, how long it would be before her first designs could be put into production. After waiting nine endless days since her final interview, she had exhausted what little patience she had. She wanted everything to happen now, this very second. Amused by her own zeal, Lianne forced herself to sit decorously in one of the comfortable wing chairs situated at the side of the lobby. As an exercise in self-control, she propped her portfolio against the occasional table and flipped through the glossy pages of *Country Life* magazine. She leafed through a gossipy article about who planned to stay with whom for Ascot week and shook her head in disbelief at a photo of a woman called Lady Emmington, who looked like a New York bag lady and had created a garden of such surpassing beauty that even the magazine pictures of it had the power to bring a lump to Lianne's throat. Sometimes she wondered if she would ever understand the English. Every time she started to think she might at last have a handle on what made them tick, she needed only to pick up a journal such as this to know that her midwestern American soul had barely begun to grasp the intricate weave of history, genes and circumstance that had made the citizens of her temporary homeland what they were.

The receptionist finished her hushed conversation, presumably with Grace's assistant. She looked over at Lianne, her earlier uncertainty replaced by a distant, offhand courtesy. "Mrs. DeWilde's personal assistant will be with you in just a few moments, Miss Beecham. We apologize for keeping you waiting."

Lianne found the formality of the receptionist's manner surprising, as well as off-putting. Grace had implied that the DeWilde corporation was run rather informally by British standards, and she'd suggested at their second meeting that Lianne should call her Grace. The receptionist clearly adhered to a different set of guidelines. Restless and suddenly on edge, Lianne gave up on reading the magazine and rose to her feet, pacing nervously.

A handsome, middle-aged woman, neatly attired in a tailored gray suit, came into the reception area. "Good morning," she said to Lianne. Her smile appeared polite, but her body language conveyed the same odd wariness as the receptionist. "I'm Fredda Halston, Mrs. DeWilde's assistant." Her voice thickened, and she cleared her throat. Lianne had the crazy impression the woman was choking back tears. "I'm sorry that you've been kept waiting, but Mrs. DeWilde didn't make any notation on her calendar that you were coming today."

"Isn't Grace in the office?" Lianne said. "I know she was expecting me. She arranged the time herself."

Fredda's smile became a little strained around the edges, then slipped away completely. "Did she? I'm so sorry, but I'm afraid Mrs. DeWilde has been, um, called away this morning."

How strange, Lianne thought. She ignored the flicker of alarm in the pit of her stomach and mustered a smile. "Well, never mind. Here I am, and anxious to start work. Grace and I can get together this afternoon."

"Work?" Fredda repeated. "What are you supposed to work on?"

Lianne began to feel as if she were trying to communicate in a foreign language. Not just American versus English, but something obscure like Pashto or Swahili.

"Bridal headdresses," she said.

She picked up her portfolio, trying not to appear visibly impatient. "Grace explained how busy she is at this time of year, so if you'll show me to my office, I'll get settled in and Grace can introduce me to everyone later on in the day. Perhaps you could point me in the direction of Personnel once I've seen my office? That way, I could get all those boring forms filled out while we're waiting for Grace to get back."

Grace's assistant and the receptionist exchanged what looked like a totally horrified glance. Fredda Halston cleared her throat. "Miss Beecham, this is rather embarrassing, but am I correct in assuming you're expecting to start work here today?"

The flicker of nerves in the pit of Lianne's stomach swelled to a giant, three-alarm blaze. "Grace DeWilde offered me the job over a week ago," she said tightly. "She said she'd get my contract drawn up and ready for my signature when I arrived for work today. I assumed that you would know all about it since you're her assistant."

Fredda Halston's cheeks flushed an agitated pink. "I'm sorry. I'm afraid there's been some sort of mix-up...."

The three-alarm blaze died an instant death. Lianne froze. She could think of only one explanation for Fredda's flustered behavior. "You mean Grace has rescinded her offer of a position as in-house designer?"

"In-house designer?" Grace's assistant sounded like a Victorian maiden hearing a gentleman swear. "Oh, dear. I hadn't realized—" She stopped abruptly. "Look, Miss Beecham, this clearly isn't the place for us to be discussing this. Why don't you come along to my office? At least I can offer you a cup of coffee."

A cup of coffee didn't sound like much of a substitute for her very own office, a permanent job and an in-store boutique dedicated to the display and sale of her bridal headdresses. Lianne trailed behind Grace's assistant on feet turned suddenly leaden. What had happened? Where was Grace DeWilde? She had seemed such a friendly, efficient, reliable person. Lianne just couldn't visualize her casually offering an important job, then equally casually withdrawing the offer. It was especially hard to imagine her leaving a flurried assistant to handle the resulting mess. Had she misjudged Grace so badly?

Fredda Halston led her into a small, cheerful office, with a computer humming on the desk and shelves stacked high with sample fabric books, catalogs and photos of brides, dating back to the 1930s, all outfitted by DeWilde's. "How do you like your coffee, Miss Beecham? Cream and sugar? Black?"

"Let's skip the coffee, shall we?" Lianne suggested. "Frankly, I'm anxious to clear up this muddle and start work."

"This is very awkward," Fredda said, removing a pile of bridal magazines from a chair so that Lianne could sit down. "I'm afraid I've no idea what Grace hired you to do, so I don't quite know who to call. Since she isn't here, perhaps you could tell me what you do...." Her voice tailed away.

"I'm a costume jewelry designer," Lianne explained. "I studied at the London School of Design here in England and at the Pittsburgh School of Art in the United States."

"You're an American, then?" Fredda shrugged apologetically. "Of course you are. Silly question."

"Yes, I am an American, but my father was an officer with the U.S. Air Force and I spent four years in Hertfordshire, near the U.S. military base, when I was a teenager. I've always loved England, and when I finished my courses at the London School of Design, I decided to take a stab at establishing myself on this side of the Atlantic while I was still young enough to take the chance of falling on my face."

"And that's what Grace hired you for? To design costume jewelry for DeWilde's?"

"No, not exactly. Recently, a friend was thinking about getting married and I played around drawing bridal headdresses for her. I became intrigued with the concept of designing for a bride, and I worked up an entire collection, some of it very traditional, some of it anything but. I submitted my designs to Grace, who liked them so much that, instead of just buying those designs, she decided to hire me with a specific mandate to create a line of bridal headdresses that would be presented as a signature collection—*Lianne for DeWilde*. Now I'm here, ready to start work. As we agreed."

Fredda Halston's gaze narrowed. "This is very difficult for both of us, Miss Beecham, but to be honest, I don't quite understand how you had all these discussions with Mrs. DeWilde without my ever meeting you or even being aware of what was going on."

Lianne decided she was becoming more than a little irritated by Fredda's attitude. "As to why Grace didn't mention our discussions, naturally I'm not in any position to comment on that. I'm as puzzled as you are. As to why we never met, that's easy to explain. Grace arranged our interviews for the evening, after the offices were closed. She said it was the only way we'd be able to talk without constant interruptions. I actually went around to her flat in Chelsea in order to make my final presentation and iron out the last kinks in our agreement."

Fredda's phone rang. She pressed a button and cut off the ringing noise, but Lianne saw that the light went on flashing, presumably meaning the call remained unanswered. "And when was that, Miss Beecham?"

Lianne was watching the phone light blink. It stopped, then started again. Fredda studiously ignored it. "I'm sorry. When was what?" Lianne asked, distracted by the unanswered phone. This was a very strange office. She was highly sensitive to moods and atmospheres, and something about the atmosphere of the DeWilde offices was all wrong. In efficient offices, ringing phones didn't get left unanswered.

"Your final presentation to Grace DeWilde," Fredda said. "The one you made at her home. When did it take place?"

"A week ago on Friday. In fact, that was the interview when Grace specifically mentioned your name. She said that you were an administrative marvel, who kept her flighty feet tethered to reality. She made copious notes about the terms of our agreement and said that she would arrange with you to take care of all the paperwork connected with my new job, and that you would notify Personnel and so on."

Fredda's fingers drummed on the desk. When she realized what she was doing, she stopped at once. "I had a raging toothache that weekend, and when I saw the dentist early on Monday morning, he discovered an abscessed tooth that needed immediate surgery. I had a bad reaction to the anesthesia and was out of the office for three days. Then Grace was in Paris on Thursday and Friday of last week, so we only dealt with absolute essentials. I would have thought, however, that Grace would consider it essential to tell me about a major new hire." Fredda's fingers started drumming again.

Lianne began to wonder if working at DeWilde's would be the dream come true that she'd been imagining, even when Grace put in an appearance. She hoped to goodness that the receptionist and Fredda Halston weren't typical of other DeWilde employees. They both seemed—to use a good old Yankee phrase—several cents short of a dollar. Lianne knew only two ways to work. One was in absolute isolation while she created her designs. The other was at top speed as she interacted with her colleagues to refine the designs into maximum commercial viability. If the remaining DeWilde employees were as dithery and slow as Fredda and the receptionist, Lianne would blow a gasket before the end of the first week. She tried to jolt the assistant into action without being downright rude.

"Look, Ms. Halston, I don't quite see what your problem is. Naturally I'm sorry that Grace isn't here this morning, but I'll see her this afternoon, and if not this afternoon, then tomorrow morning. All you need to do is find me a desk, even a temporary one, and let Personnel know I'm here. I'm sure everything else can be straightened out once Grace gets back to the office. When do you expect her, by the way?"

Fredda Halston's face took on a hunted expression. "I'm going to call our merchandising manager," she said. "I'm sure he'll be able to help you, Miss Beecham. I think he's the proper person to handle this."

"Yes, please do." Lianne's enthusiasm for meeting the merchandising manager was genuine, even though he wouldn't be her direct boss. Since her employment was in the nature of an experiment, with implications for all five of the DeWilde stores, Lianne would be reporting exclusively to Grace for at least the first six months. Consequently, they hadn't spent much time talking about the specific management structure of DeWilde's London store. However, London would be the laboratory for their tests, and the cooperation of the merchandising manager would make Lianne's life a great deal easier. In fact, in many ways it would be essential to her success. She could only hope that the merchandising manager would turn out to be someone with a bit more oomph than the two DeWilde staffers she'd met so far.

Fredda tapped a few numbers on her phone and sighed with audible relief when someone answered. "Thank goodness I caught you at your desk," she said, spinning her chair around as if she wanted to look out of the window. Her voice immediately dropped to such a low pitch that Lianne suspected her real purpose in turning around had been to muffle the sounds of what she was saying. Good grief, what was the matter with the woman? How much secrecy did you need to convey the information that a new employee had just arrived and that Grace had screwed up on the paperwork?

Her mood hovering somewhere between disappointed, annoyed and fearful, Lianne stood up and roamed around the room, staring aimlessly at the bridal photographs and absentmindedly arranging a collection of beads and feathers into an impromptu bridal headdress, vaguely reminiscent of a court headdress of the 1920s. She was stepping back to adjust the angle of one of the ostrich plumes, when she realized that Fredda had hung up the phone.

"Gabriel DeWilde will be with us in just a moment," Fredda Halston said. "His office is only three doors down."

"Gabriel DeWilde?" Lianne spun around, still clutching the ostrich plume. "*He's* the merchandising manager? Grace never said." She had no time to gather

her wits, no time to do anything, before Gabriel walked into the room.

For a split second they stared at each other in weighted silence. Then Gabriel closed the door behind him and the spell broke. "Miss Beecham?" His voice caught slightly as he said her name, but he collected himself so quickly Lianne was sure Fredda wouldn't have noticed a thing. He advanced toward her, his features schooled into an expression of careful blankness. His eyes, an unusual color somewhere between green and hazel, displayed nothing beyond normal courtesy. She envied him his capacity to contain explosive memories behind such a neutral facade.

She found her voice. "Hello, Gabriel." No way was she going to pretend they'd never met.

He answered her with a bland smile. "Goodness, Lianne, it really is you. I wondered if it might be when Fredda mentioned your name."

"Yes, it's me." She realized she was waving the ostrich plume like an idiot and hastily set it back down on the shelf. "How are you, Gabe? I haven't seen you in several weeks."

"No, we always seem to just miss each other, don't we?"

"You two obviously know each other already," Fredda said, sounding overwhelmingly relieved. "What a coincidence!"

"Yes, Lianne shares a flat with a good friend of mine, Julia Dutton. But she always seems to be out when I call for Julia." If Gabe made his voice any smoother, it would slide away. "Why don't you come into my office, Lianne, and we'll try to straighten out this muddle. I apologize for the way you've been kept waiting."

She'd known Gabe worked at the London branch of

DeWilde's, of course. She just hadn't reckoned on meeting him the very first morning she set foot in the place. She certainly hadn't reckoned on meeting him without the moral support provided by having Grace DeWilde standing right next to her. Still, the job she'd been offered was a great deal more important to her than the memory of a sexual encounter that should never have happened. She would concentrate her thoughts on seeing him as merchandising manager of DeWilde's rather than the man she'd found so stunningly attractive that they'd made wild, passionate love the first and only time they'd met.

She followed him out of Fredda's office and into his. Her heart was pounding like an overworked triphammer, but that was worry about her job, she assured herself, and had nothing whatsoever to do with any lingering sexual attraction toward Gabriel DeWilde. She wasn't allowed to have sexual feelings for Gabe. Julia Dutton was deeply in love with him. Julia wanted to marry him. And Julia was her best friend in the whole world. End of story.

He sat down behind his desk and gestured to the leather chair on the opposite side. "You're looking... well," he said, his voice curt.

"Thank you." Gabe wasn't looking well, Lianne realized. He looked strained and oddly weary. Beneath the veneer of self-control, she sensed a simmering tension that was perking close to a boil. But it was going to be a lot easier for both of them if she stopped looking beneath the surface and accepted whatever face he chose to present to the world, so she said nothing more. Casual acquaintances weren't supposed to sense each other's moods, and that's all she and Gabe were. Casual acquaintances who'd lost control one night and shared the most incredible, fantastic, wonderful sex Lianne had ever dreamed about, let alone actually experienced.

Gabe met her gaze with no hint of embarrassing memories of sweat-sheened bodies writhing ecstatically on cushions in front of the fire. He sure was doing a better job of pretending cool indifference than she was, Lianne thought. Except, of course, he wasn't pretending. He actually felt nothing more for her than cool indifference. Their one-night stand had been one of those meaningless flings men always seemed to handle so much more easily than women. Presumably he loved Julia and planned to be faithful to her from here on out. She sure as heck hoped he planned to be faithful to Julia, who was the world's sweetest person and deserved only the best.

"You must be thinking you've walked into a madhouse," Gabe said. "The fact is, we've all been thrown for a loop this morning." She saw him draw in a deep breath, as if steeling himself to impart unpleasant news. "My mother has just announced her resignation from DeWilde's and we're all trying to recover from the shock."

"Grace has left DeWilde's?" Lianne repeated stupidly. "But where has she gone to?"

"San Francisco, apparently." This time, the weariness in Gabe's voice was unconcealed. "The financial press has already heard the news, of course, and every journalist in London seems to be hounding us for a statement that we're not ready to give. We can't access half the files on Grace's personal computer because we don't know her access codes, so we're frantically trying to reconstruct her work schedule for the next month, and my father has disappeared, God knows where—" He stopped abruptly, shoving his chair away from the desk as he stood and began pacing restlessly. "I'm sorry, this has nothing to do with you, and I've no idea why I unloaded it onto you. I apologize again."

Lianne had to sit on her hands to resist the entirely inappropriate urge to walk across the room, put her arms around Gabe's waist, rest her head on his shoulder and absorb some of the electric tension crackling from him. With Grace gone, she realized she could probably kiss her fabulous new job goodbye. But bad as the news of Grace's departure was for her, Gabe seemed to be finding it even worse.

"I can understand how upset you must be," Lianne said. "I hope this doesn't mean your mother has discovered she has health problems?"

"No," Gabe said bitterly. "Unless it turns out she's suffering from a sudden attack of insanity."

Lianne decided she wasn't understanding a tenth of what was seething beneath the surface news of Grace's departure. "Where exactly is your mother, Gabe? If she isn't sick, why can't you reach her? Even if she's resigned from the company, she must realize that you need to access her files and records. Can't you call her and ask some of these basic questions?"

"You'd think so, wouldn't you? She's my mother, after all, as well as my boss, so you'd think she'd give me some idea of where she's flown off to."

"You mean you don't know?" Lianne was genuinely appalled. "I thought you said she'd gone to San Francisco?"

"So the rumor has it, but I don't have anything as helpful as an address or a phone number." He laughed without mirth. "God alone knows why she's chosen to flit off to San Francisco. Or maybe my father knows, only we can't find him, either, so it's a bit difficult to ask." He caught himself in midbreath, running his hands through his dead-straight light brown hair in a gesture that Lianne found both erotic and sympathy-inspiring. Since neither emotion was appropriate to their situation, she decided to focus on the only thing that seemed relatively suitable as a topic of conversation with Gabriel DeWilde. Her job. Or rather her vague hopes of salvaging what had once promised to be her job.

"Gabe, this is obviously the wrong time for you to be worrying about taking on a new employee. Would you like me to come back later in the week, when things have quieted down a bit?"

"No," he said, sounding calmer. "I'd like you to stay. Having you here will give me something halfway rational to think about. I thought I would be able to take charge of things and control the way events unfolded this morning, but I've realized I can't do that. I could cover for my mother's absence, perhaps, or for my father's, but I can't cover for both of them. It's not even appropriate for me to try to step into their joint shoes. DeWilde's isn't a family company anymore, it's a public company, with thousands of shareholders, and there are people working here with a lot more experience and seniority than I have. I should leave them to do their jobs, and I should get on with mine. Which happens to be merchandising manager of the London store. And since Grace isn't here anymore, and we have nothing in writing about the terms of your employment, I'm the person who has to decide whether or not to go ahead and agree to the terms she negotiated."

Obviously energized by a new sense of purpose, Gabe sat down in his chair and leaned back, pushing against the arms. "Okay, Lianne, give me the presentation that sold my mother on your ideas, and I'll see if I agree with her.''

If she'd been asked to describe the least favorable combination of circumstances she could imagine for selling her creative ideas, this was it, but Lianne would be damned if she was going to lose the chance of working at DeWilde's if there was any way to salvage it.

She got up and propped her portfolio in the chair where she'd been sitting. "I didn't come prepared to make a formal presentation," she said. "What I have here are the ideas and sketches I've been working on since Grace offered me the job of in-house designer. I'm happy to show them to you, Gabe, but before both of us waste our time, I need to know if you agree with your mother's plans for creating in-store boutiques. If that idea's going to be scrapped now she's gone, then there's no place for me in the DeWilde organization. I'm a designer, not a retailer.''

"I not only approve, I was the person who first suggested the boutique idea," Gabe said. "Grace built on it and developed the concept of hiring our own signature designers for the boutiques. She told me a couple of weeks ago that she'd begun interviewing designers." He frowned slightly. "It's odd, come to think of it, that she never brought me in on the discussions she was having with you."

Grace DeWilde seemed to have been doing a lot of peculiar things over the past couple of weeks, but Lianne kept that observation to herself. Maintaining a tactful silence, she simply unzipped her portfolio and pulled out the first sketch. She used the back of the chair to make an impromptu easel, feeling the familiar sensation of her surroundings fading to gray as her attention focused on her work. Peripherally, she was aware that Gabe had walked around his desk and was leaning against it, eyes narrowed, attention as sharply focused as her own. She felt a huge wave of relief when she realized that, like her, he was one of those rare people able to close his mind to his personal problems while he made decisions connected with his work. Turning back to her designs, she led him with renewed confidence through a concise and lively presentation of her concept for a line of bridal headpieces that would inspire misty eyes and beautiful memories in women aged nineteen to ninety.

Exhilaration filled her when her presentation was finished. The original drawings she'd shown Grace had been full-color, elaborate, designed to impress. They'd been good. These sketches were rough, but they were better—more original and yet simultaneously more commercial. She looked at Gabe, her expression challenging. "That's it," she said, taking down the last of the sketches.

"What were the terms Grace offered?" Gabe asked, his voice crisp, businesslike.

She told him.

His mouth finally relaxed into a small but genuine smile. "You're hired," he said. "Same terms and conditions. I'll get the contract drawn up. Congratulations, Lianne. Welcome to DeWilde's."

CHAPTER THREE

FOR THE SIXTH TIME since he got home, Gabe tried to phone his sister in San Francisco. "Kate, if you're there, will you pick up the phone, for God's sake? Don't you ever check the messages on your damn answering machine?"

A human voice, thick and groggy with sleep, finally answered him. "This had better be good, Gabe. I just came off an eighteen-hour double shift and I have to be back at the clinic in five hours. So if you're calling to chat about the weather, hang up now."

"I'm calling about Mother."

"Mother?" Kate's voice was instantly alert. "Is something wrong?"

"Obviously she hasn't called you. Damn! Didn't you get her letter, Kate?"

"Gabe, in the past thirty-six hours, I estimate I've had four hours' sleep and approximately three minutes of free time. Possibly less. I've no idea if I got a letter from Mother. I haven't checked my mail in days. What's up?"

"She's in San Francisco, I think. I'm not sure." Gabe steeled himself to deliver the bad news. "She's left Dad and handed in her resignation at DeWilde's. She and Dad are talking about getting a divorce."

"*What?*" Kate's disbelief echoed over five thousand

or so miles of fiber optic cable. "A divorce? Our parents? Don't be silly, Gabe, that's not possible."

Gabe drew some comfort from his sister's reaction. At least he wasn't the only one to be caught totally unaware. When he'd spoken with Megan, his twin, earlier this evening, she'd astonished him by saying that she'd known something was bothering Grace and had even wondered a couple of months back if their father could be having an affair. Gabe would have been less startled if his sister had accused the Archbishop of Canterbury of seducing the choir mistress and had told Megan as much. Ever the peacemaker, she'd backtracked at once, but Gabe had been left with the unsettling conviction that Megan, in Paris, had seen more of what was going on in their parents' lives than he had, living in the same town.

"Unfortunately, Kate, it's not only possible, it appears to be true. Ramsbotham sent us each a godawful official announcement, and Mother followed with a letter of her own, which doesn't actually explain much of anything except that she's leaving. But Dad told me she'd taken a flight for San Francisco on Sunday. I thought she might have called you when she landed."

"Hold on and I'll check the answering machine." Kate came back on the line several minutes later. "No, there's nothing. If she's really here, I can't believe she didn't call me."

She sounded hurt, which wasn't surprising. Of the three DeWilde siblings, Gabe had always considered Kate to be the one most like their father in personality. She'd not only inherited Jeffrey's formidable analytical intelligence, she also shared his exceptional sensitivity and his difficulty in expressing his emotions. Gabe sometimes worried about his sister's choice of medicine as a career. He didn't doubt her technical competence for an instant. What he worried about was her too-generous heart, her willingness to shoulder other people's problems and her inability to ask for help when she needed it. She was the type of doctor who would keep taking on other people's pain until she collapsed under the weight of it.

The last thing he wanted to do was add to Kate's burdens. So, in an effort to ease his sister's mind, he made excuses for Grace, at the same time resenting the need to do so. "Mother probably called and decided not to leave a message when she realized you weren't home. She knows how busy you are with your work at the clinic. And you're bound to find the letters once you check your mail. Let me fill you in on what I know so far."

Kate listened in silence to his account of the day's events. He could visualize her sitting cross-legged on the bed, her wiry body taut with energy, her auburn hair a bright contrast to her pale skin. Unfortunately, he could also picture her mouth tightening and her fists clenching as she struggled to orient herself to the dramatic change in their parents' lives.

When Gabe finished talking, a small silence ensued. "It's odd to think of them as a couple in an intense personal relationship, isn't it?" she said finally, her voice not quite steady. "Until this moment I'd never really moved beyond the point of seeing them as Mother and Dad, providers of bedtime hugs when we were small and stern lectures about the dangers of alcohol, drugs and casual sex when we were teenagers. I don't think it ever crossed my mind that they knew anything personally about the temptations of drugs or alcohol, much less sex. Which was amazingly juvenile of me, I suppose.''

"We've never had any reason to analyze their relationship," Gabe said. "At least until now."

"I suppose not, but I feel foolish all the same. Your situation's different, because you work with them, so you probably have a much more realistic mental image of them as people in their own right, not just as parents. I still have the selfish view of a child—they aren't Jeffrey and Grace, they're Mother and Dad, appendages to us kids."

Kate was giving him far too much credit, Gabe thought with wry insight. He carried two separate images of Jeffrey and Grace: one as his parents, and the other as powerful, accomplished mentors in the world of retailing. He'd never really fused the two visions into one coherent whole, and he'd certainly never attempted anything as sophisticated as integrating their personal relationship into his mental picture of them. Like Kate, his image of Grace had a lot more to do with biscuits and milk at bedtime than the fact that she was a vibrant and exceptionally attractive woman. He wondered if she had a lover waiting for her in San Francisco, then clamped down on the impossible thought. He simply wasn't ready yet to deal with the full implications of his parents' separation.

"I know how busy you are, Kate, but if you can spare a few minutes tomorrow, try to track Grace down, will you? Even if she isn't willing to discuss her reasons for leaving Dad, there are a dozen important business issues on which her input is absolutely vital. Try Uncle Leland or Mallory. They're both in San Francisco. They might know something."

"Why would Mother call them and not me?" Kate

asked, her voice threaded with hurt. "I'm her daughter, for heaven's sake. I know Mother sometimes wonders how she managed to produce a daughter without an artistic bone in her body—"

"Kate, I'm clutching at straws," Gabe said, mentally kicking himself for being so tactless. God, if he weren't close to exhaustion, he would never have been so clumsy as to suggest Grace might be in touch with her brother and her favorite niece rather than her own daughter. He might even have remembered how sensitive Kate was about her occasionally tense relationship with their mother. "I'm sure you'll hear from her within the next couple of days. And when you do, please tell her to call me. She has responsibilities to the company, even if she has gone off in some midlife temper tantrum—"

"That's not fair, Gabe. We have no idea what happened between Mother and Dad. For all we know, Dad may have asked her to leave."

"I'm sure he didn't. I've seen him, remember, and he's devastated."

"Just don't rush to make judgments, Gabe. Marriage is a strange relationship. I'm not sure outsiders can ever really understand the true dynamics."

"Maybe not. But that's no excuse for Mother to abandon DeWilde's without a thought to the consequences. We have five thousand employees worldwide. She can get mad at Dad if she must, but she has no right to hold the company and its employees hostage."

"You're right," Kate said wearily. "But you know how Mother is. She has these explosive fits of creative energy, then the practical side of her kicks in and she works like a supercharged beaver to catch up on the details. She'll come around."

"I wouldn't describe running out on Dad and the store as a burst of creative energy," Gabe said.

"I meant that when she calms down, she'll remember her responsibilities and run to put things right." Kate yawned. "Gabe, I'm falling asleep sitting up. I have a hell of a day scheduled tomorrow, and if I don't get some sleep, I'm not going to get through it. I'll be in touch the second I hear anything from Mother, you can count on it. Okay?"

"Okay, and thanks. Schedule a few extra hours of sleep for yourself, and that's an order, squirt."

"God how I hated that nickname! As if it wasn't bad enough to be three years younger than you and Megan, I had to grow up to be the shortest, too!" He was relieved to hear that a note of soft laughter had crept into her voice. She yawned again. "Good night, Gabe. I'll talk to you soon."

He'd barely disconnected his call to Kate when the phone rang again. He snatched it up. "Hello."

"Gabe, it's Monica. I hope I didn't wake you? I realize it's almost midnight."

"No, I'm still awake." He only realized how much he'd been hoping to hear from Grace when he recognized the voice of his father's secretary. "What can I do for you, Monica?"

"Nothing," she said. "I just wanted to let you know that I've heard from Jeffrey. He asked me to tell you that he'll be in the office at eight o'clock tomorrow morning. He said to reassure you that he will be up to speed and absolutely ready to take hold of the reins again."

Gabe ignored a slight pang that his father had chosen to contact his secretary rather than his son. "Did he say where he was calling from?" he asked.

He wondered if he imagined the infinitesimal pause before Monica answered. "I don't know exactly where he is at the moment, Gabe. But he sounded much more his usual self, and I'm sure you'll find him at his desk tomorrow morning, just as he promised."

Gabe warned himself not to imagine undercurrents where none existed. He was so mad at himself for not seeing what had obviously been under his nose for the past several weeks that he was in danger of rushing to the opposite extreme. Monica wasn't withholding information, and he had no reason to feel aggrieved because his father had chosen to deliver a message to his personal secretary rather than to his son. Jeffrey had sent hundreds of messages via Monica in the past, and he would probably send a hundred more in the future. He had no reason to suspect that his father was avoiding him. Or that Monica knew something he didn't.

He drew in a deep breath. "Thanks for passing on the information. It should certainly make things a lot easier at the office tomorrow if my father's available."

"Yes, I'm sure everything will seem easier tomorrow," Monica agreed. "Good night, Gabe, and try not to worry too much. DeWilde's has weathered greater storms than this one. Everything will work out in the end, you'll see."

MONICA'S WORDS CAME BACK to Gabe on Wednesday evening as he searched for a parking space in the crowded streets near Julia's flat. It was probably true that in the end everything would work out splendidly, he reflected. In the end, if you looked at the big picture, everyone would be dead, and the planets would disintegrate into atoms of hydrogen and helium. In the meantime, however, life had to be lived in the here and now, not in some nebulous future. The fact that he and Julia Dutton would one day be subatomic particles floating through the universe did not make it one bit easier to decide what he should do about their relationship now. He liked her a lot. She was pretty, friendly, and he enjoyed her company. He admired her hard work as a teacher, and her talent for domesticity. She was so sweet-natured he couldn't imagine having a real, honest-to-God fight with her. The trouble was, despite this impressive list of virtues, he couldn't seem to fall even the tiniest bit in love with her. The best that could be said about their sexual relationship was that he found making love to Julia mildly pleasant and that he sincerely hoped she did, too.

Three days ago he'd been quite certain that, since he didn't love Julia, he ought not to marry her. Tonight, he wasn't sure what he felt about their relationship anymore. His parents had built their marriage on love and passion. They'd played together, worked together and fought together, all with the fierce intensity of two people who were vitally important to each other. Their reconciliations had been as spectacular as their occasional blazing rows. Not that Jeffrey ever raised his voice, of course. He left all the shouting and storming around the house to Grace. But Gabe had always known that his father's emotions were just as fully engaged as his mother's, even if less visible. Not to mention less audible.

And look what had happened to them, Gabe thought. Maybe, in the long run, marriages worked out better if the two people involved were friends rather than lovers. Maybe passionate love between the sexes was a chimera that would always betray you. And if romantic love was an illusion, maybe that meant Julia was the ideal wife for him: a partner who was more a friend than a lover; a warm, caring mother for the children he hoped to have one day. As for the sex—hell, he was thirty years old. Surely he was getting a bit old to expect volcanoes to erupt every time he went to bed with a woman?

He spotted a parking space and quickly backed his Jag into it. The rain had finally stopped after two days of unremitting downpour, and the branches of the horse chestnut trees lining the street sagged under the weight of damp buds and fresh green leaves. Behind the iron railings that separated the houses from the streets, boxes of tulips and a few late-blooming daffodils made bright splashes of color against the gray flagstone of the courtyards. Julia's flat had been converted from the second floor of a house built in the late Victorian era, which had the shabby-genteel aura of an elderly lady living on a reduced income. The exterior was nothing special, but inside, Julia had converted the flat into an attractive haven from the noise and fumes of the city. When Gabe first saw her place, he'd been surprised to learn that Julia had decorated it entirely herself, and that she'd had no formal training as an interior designer. Much as he admired her dedication to teaching, he couldn't help thinking her natural talents were being wasted. She had a real eye for line and color.

He let himself into the lobby with the key Julia had given him and made his way upstairs. His pulse beat a little faster at the prospect of seeing Lianne Beecham, but he realized that a meeting was unlikely. Apart from one extraordinary night two months ago, he'd never encountered her at the flat, and Julia had mentioned that Lianne led such an active social life that she was rarely at home in the evening. He didn't doubt it. Unlike Julia, who was calm domesticity personified, Lianne was quicksilver, constantly moving, her emotions barely contained, her energy almost palpable.

Although she obviously had a tough inner core of discipline buried beneath the layers of effervescence, Gabe reflected. When she'd made her presentation to him at DeWilde's on Monday, the intensity with which she focused her creative energy had been awesome. Having worked with artists and craftspeople for the past seven years, he recognized that Lianne was the sort of designer who would go far—she not only possessed an inspiring artistic vision, she had a solid grasp of how to turn that vision into a commercially viable reality. He rang the doorbell, bringing his thoughts back to Julia. He'd stopped by the flat on an impulse after putting in a fourteen-hour day at the office, even though he and Julia rarely got together during the week. There was no guarantee she'd be free to spend time with him, or even that she'd be home.

The door opened almost at once, but Gabe's smile faded when he realized that it wasn't Julia who had answered the door, it was Lianne Beecham.

"I came to see Julia—"

"Julia's still at school—"

He and Lianne both spoke at once. Then they both fell silent. Gabe recovered first. "I'm sorry to have disturbed you," he said with excessive courtesy.

Lianne's gaze wandered past him and focused somewhere to the left of his ear. "You haven't disturbed me," she said. "I wasn't doing anything important."

She was wearing jeans and a man's shirt, the sleeves rolled up to her elbows but the shirttails flapping loosely around her thighs. Her hair was piled haphazardly on top of her head, with curls tumbling out of the tortoiseshell clasp that was supposed to hold it in place. She looked untidy, rumpled and almost unbearably sexy. Still avoiding his gaze, she pushed distractedly at a curl that had fallen over her forehead. "Julia didn't say anything about seeing you tonight."

"She's not expecting me. I stopped by just on the off chance that she'd be home." He wondered, even as he gave the explanation, why he was bothering to lie to himself. He'd come here despite the knowledge buried in the back of his mind that Julia was helping her sixth-form French class with the dress rehearsal for their production of *Le Bourgeois Gentilhomme*. He'd come not to see Julia, he realized, but because he wanted—quite badly—to see Lianne.

"Julia won't be home for another couple of hours at least." Not surprisingly in view of their last encounter in this place, Lianne didn't invite him in. Her voice and expression were equally wooden. "There's not much point in waiting for her, Gabriel. She warned me it could be close to midnight before she got back."

"Then I won't keep you. Tell her I look forward to our date on Friday evening, won't you? Seven o'clock."

"Yes. Of course. Goodbye, Gabriel."

He turned to walk away, expecting at any second to hear the sound of Lianne closing the door behind him. For some reason, the sound never came. When he reached the head of the stairs, he stopped and looked back. Lianne was standing just as he'd left her, her hand still on the doorknob, her body strangely rigid. As soon as he turned around, her gaze slid away again.

Gabe spoke to her quietly. "Do you have plans for tonight?" he asked. "Are you going out?"

There was a long pause. "No."

"Come and have a drink with me," he said quickly,

the invitation made before he had a chance to question the wisdom of it. "I saw a friendly-looking pub just down the road and I'm not in the mood to go home just yet."

She finally turned around. "What sort of a mood are you in, Gabe?"

He looked straight into her dark blue eyes, forcing her to hold his gaze. "I'm not sure. You could help me find out."

Color flooded her cheeks. She looked down, staring at her bare feet, as if surprised to discover she had ten toes, all painted shocking pink. "All right," she said at last. "Wait one minute and I'll get a sweater or something."

He discovered that he had been holding his breath, waiting for her answer. He leaned against the wall of the hallway, twisting the gold chain of his key ring, aware of a hot pulse of anticipation pounding in his gut.

Lianne didn't keep him waiting long. She returned, a pair of scuffed brown leather loafers on her bare feet and her jeans topped by a Chinese-style jacket of padded silk in a brilliant shade of green, embroidered with blue and purple flowers at the neck and cuffs of the long sleeves. The ornate style should have looked all wrong with frayed jeans, but he'd noticed before that she had the knack of making whatever she wore look just right for the occasion.

They walked downstairs in silence, taking great care not to touch each other. Gabe tried hard to think of something witty and insightful to say, but the only thoughts that came to mind involved naked bodies and wild sex. He gave up on witty and decided to settle for coherent, or even polite.

His mind remained a cavernous blank into which

jumbled and distracting images of Lianne intruded. The chestnut gleam of her hair in the light of the street lamp. The supple ripple of her silk jacket as she walked. The hint of her perfume on the night breeze. He'd noticed her scent at the office, on Monday. Elusive, barely there, it had been hovering on the periphery of his awareness for two solid days. It was driving him goddamn crazy.

Work, he thought, grasping at the conversational straw. They could talk about work.

"How were your first couple of days at DeWilde's?" he asked. "I'm sorry I didn't have a chance to check with you personally before you left today." As always when he was on edge, his voice became stiffer, his words more clipped. To put it bluntly, he sounded like a pompous ass.

"Everyone's been very cooperative," Lianne said, smiling as she jumped across a puddle. "And you don't need to worry about me, Gabe. Fortunately, Grace had already finalized her decisions on which bridal gowns DeWilde's would be carrying the season after next, so I know exactly what my design parameters are. Right now I'm studying the pictures and the design specs so that I can coordinate my headdresses to the gowns. I'm conferring with Adam to make sure that I keep the production costs within budget. Once I have the designs finalized, I'll organize a presentation for you. But I don't expect you to stand over me and hold my hand just because I'm new. I'm used to working alone, and I understand how frantically busy you must be with Grace gone."

"Do you?" He smiled without mirth. "These past three days I've felt that I've been running like hell just to keep from falling further behind than I was the day before."

"Well, Grace contributed so much to DeWilde's, it would be odd if nobody noticed she was gone, wouldn't it? You miss her even more than most people, I expect. You reported directly to her, after all—and she *is* your mother."

He was surprised to feel a surge of relief at hearing Lianne speak his mother's name in such a normal tone of voice. At work for the past few days people had acted almost as if she'd died. And she still hadn't called him. The worry about her safety and his concerns for the store were beginning to coil into a tight, hard knot of fury at the irresponsibility of her behavior.

Still, he didn't want to think about his mother for a while. That was one of the reasons he'd sought out Lianne, who barely knew her. They'd reached the corner of the road, and he pushed open the heavy door leading into the pub and ushered her to a small corner table.

The lounge was full, and the barmaid looked harassed. "What would you like to drink?" he asked. "I'll get it from the bar. That'll be quicker than waiting for the waitress to take our order."

"A brandy would be nice," she said, sliding along the padded leather seat. "I feel in the mood for something old and smooth and mellow."

Gabe returned to their corner table carrying two V.S.O.P. cognacs. Lianne had taken off her jacket while he was gone and hung it over the chair behind her, and he realized she was still wearing the oversize man's shirt underneath. She'd simply tied the ends in a knot under her breasts so that they wouldn't hang down under the hem of her jacket. She looked up as he approached and smiled at him, her first smile of the evening. Gabe stopped dead in his tracks, feeling the impact of her smile as a physical blow to his gut.

"Your cognac," he said stiffly, sliding into his seat next to her. He stopped a crucial six inches away from her.

"Thanks." She raised her glass to his, still smiling. "Here's to my new collection and the success of DeWilde's first boutique." He wanted to take the glass from her hand, lean across the table and kiss her. Hard. He closed his eyes and took a slug of brandy. He opened his eyes. "Here's to you," he said. "I'm looking forward to seeing your first set of designs, Lianne."

The barmaid walked by carrying a tray laden with tall glasses of beer. Lianne pulled her feet out of the barmaid's path, and her knee collided under the table with Gabe's. They sprang away from each other as if they'd been scalded by boiling water, the reaction so swift and so obvious neither of them could pretend it hadn't happened.

Lianne put her brandy snifter down on her cardboard coaster and folded her paper napkin into a neat triangle. "Julia's my best friend," she said with seeming inconsequence.

Gabe's mouth twisted into an ironic smile. "Mine, too," he said.

Lianne's head jerked up, her eyes flashing. "Don't mock her," she said. "Julia loves you, damn it!"

Gabe's stomach muscles tensed at this confirmation of his worst fears.

"You know nothing about my relationship with Julia," he said. *Stupid pompous ass,* he berated himself.

She laughed angrily. "More than you do, it seems. She thinks you're going to ask her to marry you, Gabe. She's waiting for you to turn up some night soon with one of those nifty DeWilde ring boxes tucked into your pocket."

"How do you know that I don't intend to do just that?"

"And what are you going to promise her when you hand over the ring, Gabe? That you'll love and cherish her—and stay faithful until the next time your wandering eye happens to land on one of her friends?"

He shoved his brandy to one side and leaned across the table, his temper barely under control. "What's making you so angry, Lianne? The fact that I made love to you the first time we met? Or the fact that you were helping me to rip off your clothes so I could do it quicker?"

She jumped up from her seat, ignoring the brandy that spilled all over the table. She grabbed her jacket and walked to the door, shoving her arms into the sleeves as she walked. Gabe caught up with her outside. He gripped her arm and swung her around to face him. "What's the problem, Lianne? Don't you like hearing the truth? Or were you hoping I'd follow you home so that we could try a repeat performance?"

For a moment, he thought she was going to hit him. Not a ladylike slap across the cheek, but a hard, swinging punch to the jaw. Surprisingly, the rage went out of her as swiftly as it had come. She looked up at him, her eyes no longer blue but gray and stormy as the Atlantic. "I wanted you to follow me home," she admitted, her voice low and harsh.

He wished like hell that she'd punched him. It would have been easier to deal with than her honesty. He shoved his hands into his pockets so that he'd be able to keep them from touching her. "We can't pretend we like each other," he said, trading truth for truth. "We barely know each other. What we feel is nothing but sex. Sheer animal lust."

She wrapped her arms around her waist. "Embarrassing, isn't it?"

"Julia is exactly the sort of woman I've always planned to marry."

Her eyes narrowed. "And what am I? The sort of woman you always planned to keep as your mistress?"

He quelled an intense desire to throttle her. Or perhaps it was an intense desire to put his hands around her throat and hold her immobilized while he kissed her. "When I'm married, I don't plan to keep a mistress, Lianne."

"I'm sure Julia will be pleased to hear that."

How could he possibly pretend that he was going to marry Julia when he couldn't even trust himself to walk into Lianne's office for fear of what he might do once he got there? "Come out to dinner with me on Saturday," he said. "Let's get to know each other. As people instead of sexual partners."

"I can't." She turned away and started to walk down the street.

He followed. "I'm seeing Julia on Friday night."

She stopped but she didn't look at him. "What are you hoping to arrange for, Gabe? Conversation and friendship on Fridays, followed by hot sex on Saturdays? A well-rounded weekend of entertainment?"

"Getting mad at me doesn't change the fact that we both want to see each other again. I'm honest enough to admit it, and to say that I'd like to know more about you than the fact that you're stunning in bed."

"Gee, I'm just a bundle of accomplishments, Gabe. You've barely even scratched the surface of my potential as a bedmate."

"How many different ways can I say it, Lianne? I want to find out more about you as a person, not just as a bedmate."

Her voice was like the line of her mouth. Hard and flat. "Are you going to tell Julia that you invited me out to dinner on Saturday night?"

"If you accept my invitation, I'll tell her."

"And if I don't accept your invitation?"

"Julia should hear this first, but whether you say yes or no, either way I'm going to stop seeing her. It's not fair to either of us, especially Julia."

Lianne stopped at the iron gate leading into the courtyard in front of her flat. She made a small sound of acute distress. "If you stop dating Julia, she's going to be really hurt, Gabe."

"I hope that's not true," he said quietly. "But I'm not in love with her, and if I married her, she'd be hurt a lot more in the end."

Lianne pulled a leaf from the privet hedge and shredded it. "I don't know, Gabe—"

"Yes, you do," he said. "We both know." He crooked his finger beneath her chin and tipped her head back until they were looking straight at each other. He didn't put his arms around her or pull her toward him. Except for his finger, he didn't touch her. Slowly enough to leave no doubt about his intentions, he bent his head toward her. She didn't move away. She stood silently, her face drained of color in the streetlight, her hands clenched into fists. In the last second before his mouth claimed hers, she reached up and linked her hands at the nape of his neck, pressing her lips to his in a kiss that ached and trembled with the force of their passion.

When they finally drew apart, Gabe felt disoriented,

as if he'd been swimming underwater and had hit his head on a rock when he surfaced. Lianne leaned against the gate but she didn't say a word. Her gaze locked with his for a long, weighted moment, then she turned and ran up the stone steps to her front door.

Gabe watched until she disappeared into the hallway. Her absence left him feeling hollow. He wondered how in the world he was supposed to wait until Saturday before he talked her into his bed.

CHAPTER FOUR

IT WAS DEPRESSING to discover that you had all the moral backbone of an earthworm, Lianne reflected, then wondered if she was insulting the integrity of worms. She wanted to go out with Gabe but couldn't bear to tell that to Julia, or to witness how her friend would handle the news of Gabe's defection. Julia Dutton wasn't the sort of person who talked a lot about her deepest feelings, but Lianne was quite sure her friend was in love with Gabriel DeWilde, and she had a sickening suspicion Julia would be desolated when she heard that he didn't feel anything for her beyond friendship.

Coward that she was, Lianne decided to avoid the issue by going to a party on Friday night and staying out until she was sure her flat mate would be in bed. What a great friend she was turning out to be, Lianne taunted herself grimly.

Weeks before she met Gabe in person, Lianne had known how Julia felt about him. Her idea of creating a line of bridal headdresses had been developed after she and Julia cheered up a dreary Sunday afternoon by sitting in front of the fake-log electric fire and designing a bridal outfit, complete with a floating silk net veil scattered with seed pearls, topped by a coronet of satin rosebuds—the perfect complement to Julia's fresh features and sweet smile. Julia hadn't admitted in so many words that Gabe was the unnamed groom at this fantasy wedding, but they'd both known quite well that he was the one.

Lianne didn't meet Gabriel DeWilde until a Friday night at the end of March when he'd already been dating Julia for nearly three months. Julia's mother had been rushed to hospital for emergency surgery to remove a ruptured appendix, and nobody had been able to reach Gabe to explain what had happened. When he arrived to pick up Julia for their date, Lianne invited him in and offered him a drink while they waited for news from the hospital.

Her attraction to Gabe had been instant and overwhelming. The two of them had talked for hours, the pot of coffee growing cold, their brandy forgotten. Even after Julia phoned to say her mother was safely recuperating but she wouldn't be home because she planned to spend the night with her father, Gabe hadn't made any move to leave. Worse, Lianne hadn't tried to send him away.

They continued talking and laughing, but the phone call had destroyed the illusion of casual friendliness they had both been clinging to. Their laughter faded and their conversation gradually died away until nothing was left except silence and the desire pulsing between them. A desire that was all the more potent because they'd spent the previous five hours pretending not to notice it.

Lianne had been curled up in her favorite position on the sofa, bare feet tucked under her, sipping her neglected glass of brandy, not because she wanted a drink but because, for the first time that night, she hadn't known what to say to Gabe. Without warning, he leaned toward her, prying her fingers from the snifter and setting it on the table.

"I want you, Lianne," he'd said, his voice hoarse, his hazel eyes no longer dancing with laughter but blazing with fierce passion. "God, I want you."

His words had slammed into her, giving instant shape and focus to her own unspoken desire. Instead of rejecting him, instead of reminding him about Julia, Lianne had moved eagerly into his arms, returning fevered kiss for fevered kiss, hot caress for hot caress. When he'd fumbled with the buttons on her shirt, she'd ripped it off, reaching for him, pulling his head to her breasts, writhing ecstatically in his arms as he suckled her. They'd stood up to take off their jeans and somehow never made it back onto the sofa. Within moments, she'd been a naked and willing captive beneath him on the rug in front of the fire. Within minutes, she'd been making gasping, greedy, passionate love to her best friend's lover.

The experience had been so intense, their lovemaking so explosive, that Lianne still wasn't comfortable thinking about it, especially her own role in what had happened. All she knew was that in the clear light of morning, the magnitude of her betrayal had been painfully apparent. Appalled by her behavior, Lianne had banished Gabe from her thoughts and dreams as well as from her life. He tried to call her only once, and she refused to speak to him. He'd never tried to contact her again, and he'd continued to see Julia on a regular basis.

He often came to the flat to pick Julia up for their frequent dates, but Lianne had turned the task of avoiding him into a minor art form. Julia was a homemaker, ready for marriage, longing to have children. Lianne was consumed by career ambition, with no plans to marry. Clearly, she had no right to disrupt Julia's promising relationship because she'd had an attack of the hots for Gabriel DeWilde. She'd even managed to convince herself that she was delighted Julia's relationship with him seemed to be going well. Her meeting with Gabe at work had blown that little fiction right out of the water. Their encounter on Wednesday night had blasted through the last tendrils of the myth.

Lianne despised herself for putting lust above friendship, but she had discovered over the past few days that she could no longer ignore the intensity of her response to Gabriel DeWilde. Working with him on a daily basis made it impossible for her to pretend that she felt nothing for him. When he'd come to the flat on Wednesday night, she'd been paralyzed, clutching the doorjamb for support, terrified that if she moved she'd invite him in. Not just into the living room, but into her bed. And she'd known with a shocking, unsettling certainty that if she'd made the offer, Gabe would have accepted it. Neither of them would have given another thought to the fact that Julia could return at any minute, much less to the ethics of the situation.

She had no idea why Gabe made her feel this way. Lianne had never considered herself Playmate of the Month material. It was mind-blowing to find herself tumbling head over heels into a relationship based on nothing except sexual attraction.

Lianne believed that men and women needed to like each other if they wanted to develop worthwhile, lasting relationships. Did she like Gabe? The honest answer was that she had no idea. When she was with him, she was too busy controlling her lust to have time to analyze anything else she might feel. All she knew was that she wanted very badly indeed to go out with him.

Go out with him. Now, there was a great euphemism if she'd ever heard one. But it sounded so much better than admitting she wanted Gabe to take her to bed and spend the entire night having hot, fierce, passionate sex with her.

Creeping into the flat at two o'clock in the morning, Lianne was rewarded for her cowardly attempts at evasion by the sight of Julia sitting on the sofa in the living room, very much awake. Why was she surprised? Lianne thought resignedly. She should have known that dear, honest, open-hearted Julia wouldn't chicken out and go to bed before the subject of Gabriel DeWilde had been settled between them. Unlike Lianne, the earthworm, Julia respected friendship and all it stood for.

Other than giving her a splitting headache, the wine she'd consumed at the party was doing nothing for her, Lianne realized. Her betrayal felt every bit as sharp and bitter as it had before she slugged down four glasses of cheap burgundy. Although she and Julia had been complete strangers when Lianne responded to Julia's ad for a flat mate, the two of them had quickly become the best of friends. And now Julia was much more than a friend, she was the sister Lianne had never had and always wanted. If Gabe had hurt her... If she'd hurt her...

Yes? Lianne asked herself cynically. *If you and Gabe have hurt your best friend, what will you do—refuse to go out with him when your entire body throbs with anticipation at the mere thought of being in his company?*

"Julia, I didn't expect to find you still up," she exclaimed, her voice bursting with false cheer. She stumbled into the living room, feeling such a fraud that her natural coordination deserted her, making it difficult to walk without falling over her own feet.

Julia got up and put out a hand to steady her. "Fun party?" she asked with wry good humor. "It looks as if they had plenty of liquid refreshments on hand."

Lianne gave an exaggerated grimace. Better to pretend that she'd had too much to drink than to admit she was clumsy with guilt and nerves. "The party was thrown by some old friends from art school. There was too much booze, too much smoke, not all of it from tobacco, and way too many people trying to convince themselves they were having a decadent time. You know what that's like."

Julia chuckled. "Unfortunately not. I wish I did, but I ran with a very sedate crowd when I was at university. If they'd had their way, my brothers would have demanded two written references and a typed résumé before I was allowed out on a date." She sat down again and started to gather up colored skeins of embroidery wool, tucking them neatly into their special box, which was decorated with a trompe l'oeil pattern she'd painted herself.

Lianne sprawled in the armchair to the right of the fireplace. Unbuttoning her jacket, she sneaked a covert glance at her friend. As far as she could tell, Julia looked her usual pretty, pink-cheeked, brunette self, but Lianne didn't make the mistake of assuming that Julia's failure to show emotion meant that she had no feelings. Julia hadn't switched on the overhead lights, and she'd angled the table lamp so that its beam was directed at her embroidery, leaving her face in shadow so that it was hard to see her features clearly. Intentionally? Trying not to be too obvious, Lianne searched her friend's face, but she couldn't see any sign that Julia had been indulging in floods of heartbroken tears.

"How did your date go tonight with Gabe?" she asked, doing her best to sound relaxed and unconcerned.

Julia smiled slightly as she folded her needlepoint canvas. "Lianne, love, if that was meant to be a casual question, I feel compelled to tell you that you'll never make your living as an actress."

"Okay, so it wasn't casual. What happened tonight, Jules? I need to know."

"Yes, I suppose you do." Julia's voice caught for a moment, but she sounded just fine when she continued. "Gabriel and I enjoyed a very pleasant dinner at the Mirabel. Sometime between the quail eggs and the poached pears, he told me that he liked me more than any other woman he'd ever met. He also said that he was very sorry, but he wasn't in love with me."

"Oh, Jules, I'm so sorry!" Lianne ached with sympathy.

"Sorry, but not surprised, I'm sure. We've both known for weeks that my relationship with Gabe wasn't going anywhere." Julia got up rather abruptly and rummaged between the cushions on the sofa. "Bother! I've lost my embroidery scissors. I have to find them or someone will sit down and impale themselves."

Lianne walked over to the sofa. She reached out and took her friend's hand, abandoning any lingering pretense that this was a casual conversation. She drew in a deep breath. "Did Gabe tell you that he invited me to go out with him tomorrow night?"

"Yes, he told me." Julia straightened, a pair of tiny silver scissors dangling from her forefinger. "Ah, success! Here they are."

Lianne refused to be diverted. "If you want, I'll tell

Gabe I can't go out with him. That I don't want to date him. Not tomorrow night. Not ever."

"But that would be a lie, wouldn't it?" Julia said quietly. "You and Gabriel are very attracted to each other, aren't you?"

Attraction seemed a laughably mild word to describe what she felt for Gabriel DeWilde. But how could she tell Julia that she'd spent the past two nights sweating through dreams so erotic that she'd woken up gasping for air, her skin so sensitized that Gabe could have brought her to climax with a single kiss and a few swift caresses?

Lianne gave the only answer she could. "Yes, Gabe and I are attracted to each other."

Julia bent over, tucking the scissors into her embroidery work box. "That's what I thought. And I certainly don't want to stand in the way of true love."

"But that's the whole point, Jules. We're not talking true love here. We're talking plain old lust. There's nothing between me and Gabriel DeWilde that's worth destroying our friendship over."

"How do you know that something worthwhile and lasting won't develop between you and Gabriel?" Julia asked. "You haven't spent much time with him, so you can't tell how your relationship might develop. Besides, how can you separate lust and love?"

Lianne was surprised into a stiff little laugh. "Well, I guess I'd always assumed that was pretty easy."

Julia shook her head. "I thought I knew the difference, but I'm not sure anymore. If a man and a woman don't feel any lust for each other, then they're just friends, aren't they?"

Lianne wasn't quite certain what that remark meant, but it didn't sound good. "Tell me the truth, Jules. Has

Gabe hurt you? You're trying to make it sound as if this split doesn't mean all that much to you, but I know you too well. I don't believe you'd have dated a man for more than five months unless your feelings were pretty deeply involved."

"Yes, he's hurt me," Julia admitted. "But you needn't look so worried, Lianne. I've been sitting here for the last few hours thinking about it, and I've decided it's my pride that's wounded rather than anything else. I like Gabriel a lot. I enjoy spending time in his company and I know he enjoys being with me. But that's all there is between us. There's no spark of passion, and there really never has been. We've been friends more than anything for the past few months. I hope we can be friends again in the future."

Lianne wanted to be convinced. God, she wanted to be convinced! Julia looked and sounded as if she were telling the truth, but some nagging inner voice wouldn't let her take her friend's words at face value. "Jules, two months ago you had me sketching wedding dresses and bridal headdresses. Two months ago you must have thought there was a spark between you and Gabe."

Julia walked over to the window, rearranging the folds of the rose chintz curtains, curtains she'd sewn herself. She didn't turn around when she spoke. "I'm twenty-nine, Lianne, and I'm tired of teaching French to other people's children. I want to get married and have children of my own. Gabe is good-looking, intelligent, and he has a fascinating job. When I met him, he seemed the answer to any woman's prayer, and especially to mine. Obviously, he's a very eligible bachelor and a kind man. I suppose we could have married and even been reasonably content together. But he wants more than contentment from marriage, and tonight I realized I want more, too." Her voice became husky. "I want passion and lust and unbridled hot sex along with the companionship and the children."

"Hot sex? Jules, I'm shocked!" Lianne was only half joking.

"Are you? You shouldn't be, you know. Why do you suppose I want any less from my marriage than you do?" Julia snapped the lock on the sash window, closing it. "To get back to the subject of Gabe, if you want to go out with him, don't think you have to ask permission from me, Lianne. You don't. Anything there might have been between the two of us is over. Finished. Nothing you do or don't do is going to change what happens between Gabe and me."

If anybody else in the world had been this friendly and rational when their lover had just dumped them, Lianne would have been instantly suspicious. With anybody other than Julia, she would have been sure that all this superficial sweetness and light was covering up some dark and murky feelings. How was it possible that Julia still described him as a kind man? Gabe had been dating Julia for more than five months. Surely the situation called for a little more rage on her part at being unceremoniously ditched because he now wanted to jump into the sack with another woman—a woman who happened to be your best friend?

Of course, Gabe wouldn't have told Julia the whole story, Lianne reminded herself. Presumably Julia didn't know that she'd already been betrayed, not only by Gabe but by Lianne, as well. She wished she could tell Julia the truth. The trouble was, for Lianne to clear her conscience, she needed to make a confession that would hurt Julia, so she was just going to have to carry the burden of her deception awhile longer. Once you left childhood behind, you began to realize that confessing your sins often made you feel a lot better than the person who was forced to hear your confession.

"I think you and I have opposite problems where Gabe is concerned," Lianne said carefully. "Gabe and I seem to generate lots of heat when we're together, but I'm not sure if we actually like each other all that much."

Julia smiled, albeit somewhat wryly. "I wish Gabriel and I could have generated at least a bit of your heat," she said. "But since we didn't, I'm sure it won't be long before I'll be feeling truly grateful that he called a halt before we allowed ourselves to drift into getting married."

"Julia, honest to Pete, you're too good to be true! Why aren't you yelling and screaming at me? Why aren't you stomping around the flat, sticking pins in pictures of Gabe and telling the world that all men are scum?"

"I can't."

"What do you mean, you can't? Sure you can. Look, here's how. Stamp your foot. Shake your fist. Yell. Go on, do it."

"I can't." Julia drew in a quick, hard breath. "You don't understand, Lianne. You find it so easy to express your emotions. I'm afraid to."

"This might be a good time to learn," Lianne suggested. "Start small and work up. Couldn't you try just a quick, ladylike yell? Smash the photo you have of Gabe in your bedroom, maybe?"

"You don't understand, Lianne. I'm afraid once I started, I wouldn't be able to stop."

Lianne's stomach knotted. "Darn it, Jules, I knew it!

Gabe's hurt you, hasn't he. We've hurt you way more than you're willing to admit."

Julia's voice was too calm. "At the moment, I'm still feeling sorry for myself, but I told you that already."

She flicked her neat plait of dark brown hair over her shoulder, then shrugged. "I really fancied myself in a couple of those headdresses you designed. I'm not quite ready to abandon my dream of an autumn wedding, with you as my chief bridesmaid, looking elegant in bronze satin. But that should tell me something, shouldn't it? My desire to float down the aisle in a long white dress is a silly reason to get married. It's an even sillier reason for you to refuse to date Gabriel. He isn't going to fall in love with me, Lianne, and wishing isn't going to change that."

"One day there'll be a wonderful man to fit into your fantasy of the perfect wedding," Lianne said, the cheap wine churning sickly in her stomach. "You'll find him, Jules, I know you will." She wished as soon as she'd spoken that she hadn't offered such false comfort. They were both too old and too wise to buy into the myth that Mr. Right was always lurking somewhere in the wings, just waiting to be greeted and brought onstage. Divorce statistics proved each year that for a lot of women, there was no Mr. Right, and that women routinely settled for something that turned out to be a lot less than the best.

Julia was too polite to point out that Lianne was talking rubbish. She smiled a bit wanly. "If I ever meet him, you'll be the first to know. I'm tired, Lianne, I'm going to bed. Good night. I expect I'll see you tomorrow morning?"

"Probably not," Lianne said. "I have to go into work for a couple of hours first thing. With Grace gone, everyone's so busy I have to grab the people I need whenever I can.''

Normally Julia would have asked a dozen eager questions about Lianne's new job. Not tonight. Looking suddenly weary, she simply nodded. "See you on Sunday, then. Good night, Lianne."

Deeply troubled, Lianne watched her friend go. Julia was lying about her feelings, she realized with unwelcome and painful insight. She was devastated by Gabe's rejection, just as Lianne had feared she would be. Their whole conversation tonight had been a charade, a ploy on Julia's part to ensure that Lianne wouldn't feel guilty. Very cleverly, Julia had expressed just enough regret to briefly lull Lianne into believing she'd heard all of it.

But despite the fact that Julia was suffering a lot more than she was willing to admit, some of what had been said tonight was true. Julia would only be courting unhappiness if she continued to date Gabe, knowing that he didn't love her. Drifting into marriage with him would have been a terrible mistake, guaranteed to make both of them miserable in the long run. However great Julia's misery now, it would be far worse if the breakup had come later, perhaps when there were children in the picture.

Lianne spent the few hours left before her alarm went off lying on a bed that felt as if it were made out of prickly pear spikes, wondering how she was going to look Julia in the eye ever again. Wondering how she was going to get through the fourteen hours remaining before she would see Gabe. Wondering what she would say if he invited her back to his flat. And knowing that where the last question was concerned, she wasn't really wondering at all.

Gabe was drinking his fourth cup of black coffee and slugging through some of his mother's files when he was interrupted by the persistent ring of the doorbell. Irritated at the interruption—his mother's cross-referencing systems were idiosyncratic, to put it politely, and he needed all the concentration he could muster—he strode into the hall and yanked open the door.

A tall, slender woman stood in the hallway, her finger poised over the bell. "Megan!" He stared at his twin sister blankly for a second or two, then swept her inside and gave her a warm hug. "Meg, this is wonderful. Come on inside. When did you arrive?"

"I flew over from Paris this morning." Megan made her way to the living room, tossing her coat over a chair and kicking off her shoes. She didn't sit down but paced restlessly in front of the empty fireplace, her body radiating energy. "Mmm...that coffee smells good. Do you have any left? The stuff they were serving on the plane was even more disgusting than usual."

Gabe shook the pot, testing. "Only dregs. Come into the kitchen and I'll brew us some fresh." He gave his sister another quick hug as they walked into the kitchen, worried by her drawn appearance and almost febrile restlessness. Ever since that bastard Edward Whitney left her at the altar last summer, she'd thrown herself into her work with an obsessive, workaholic tenacity that was great for DeWilde's Paris store but not so good for Megan. "You're looking very dashing, Megan. I think brown hair suits you better than the bleached straw look you seemed to be aiming for last time I saw you."

She grinned. "It's not brown, Gabe, it's luxurious sable, and it's all part of my new businesslike image.

Note the pearl stud earrings, crisp tailored skirt and neat yellow twin set."

"Businesslike is great," he said. "So long as you remember to take the occasional hour off to play."

She wrinkled her nose in a gesture familiar since childhood. "Play? What does that mean?" She turned away quickly, opening cupboard doors with a lot more noise than was necessary. "Where do you keep your cups, for heaven's sake? Why do men never store anything in a logical place?"

He opened a cupboard and pointed to the row of mugs and cups. "Stored with typical masculine illogic right above the place where I unload them from the dishwasher."

She laughed and took a mug, cradling it between her hands. "It's a good thing you're so damned handsome, Gabe, otherwise no woman would put up with you for five minutes."

He felt the hot color steal across his cheekbones and heard the startled intake of her breath. "My God, you're blushing! My sophisticated, jet-setting, ultimate man-of-the-world brother is actually blushing! Does this mean Julia Dutton's finally decided to make an honest man out of you?"

"No, of course not." He spoke sharply because he was so embarrassed. Good Lord, things had come to a sorry pass when an inconsequential remark from his sister could provoke images of Lianne so erotic that his cheeks turned visibly red. "As a matter of fact, Julia and I aren't seeing each other anymore."

"I'm sorry to hear that. She seemed to be a really nice person."

"She is. But she isn't the woman I want to spend the rest of my life with."

"How can you tell, Gabe?" Megan's smile faded. "It's so difficult to understand a relationship when you're in the middle of it, if you know what I mean?"

"Sure I do. But it seems safe to assume that if you can see problems even before you're married, then you'll see hundreds more afterward."

"I've been thinking about that recently," Megan said. She poured herself a cup of the freshly brewed coffee and sniffed appreciatively. "I was so upset and humiliated when Edward left me at the altar. My spirits were wilting faster than my bouquet. But you know what frightens me the most? I realize now that he was right to leave me—"

"Not that way, he wasn't. Not with such a brutally public rejection."

"No, the way he left was wrong, but at least he had enough sense to realize we shouldn't get married. I just got carried along on the tidal wave. You know, once you start planning a wedding, the event turns into this monster with a life of its own. You stop being a couple hoping to spend the rest of your lives together and instead become an entity, the Bride and Groom. I was so busy deciding what music to play when the bridesmaids walked down the aisle, and what color table napkins to have at the reception, that I lost track of the fact I'd have to live with Edward once the guests had packed up and gone home."

"Do you think that's what happened to Mother and Dad?" Gabe asked. "Their wedding was one of the biggest social events of 1964. Do you think they just got swept away by the social juggernaut?"

"And took thirty-two years to notice they'd made a

mistake?" Megan asked. "It doesn't seem likely, does it?"

"No. But nothing about their separation makes any sense. We agreed on that the last time we talked."

Megan leaned against the counter, running the tip of her finger around her coffee mug. "I got another letter from Mother yesterday. Did you?"

Gabe muttered an expletive beneath his breath. Not that it made him feel any better to swear. Nothing about his parents' separation made him feel better. "Yes, I got a letter from Mother," he said tightly. "International express mail, delivered by courier, no less. I wouldn't say it exactly shed any more light on the situation. She's sorry she left so suddenly, but living with Jeffrey had become so painful she simply couldn't bear it anymore. She loves me very much and hopes to talk to me soon. There were a few fancy flourishes, but that's about the gist of it."

"Mine was along the same lines." Megan's hazel eyes, so like Gabe's, were troubled. "That's why I flew over today, actually. Gabe, I have some news that I almost can't believe is true. Kate called me last night. She tried to reach you as well, but you weren't answering your phone."

"I was out until past midnight. What's happened?"

Megan poured herself another cup of coffee. "Mother didn't send Kate a letter, like she did to you and me. She phoned her instead, and suggested that they should meet for lunch. You know how busy Kate always is at the clinic, but of course she realized how important this meeting was, since nobody from the family had spoken to Mother since she left, but she couldn't make lunch, so she called to try to arrange another time. But Mother didn't answer the phone—".

"Meg, stop! My God, you're scaring the hell out of me." Megan was never rambling or incoherent. One of her major skills as a businessperson was her ability to deliver precise, pithy presentations. "The short version, please. How was Mother? Did she look okay? And what did she and Kate talk about?"

"They didn't actually meet, but they had a long phone conversation. Mother sounded more or less okay, according to Kate, although she never once mentioned Dad or their split."

"So what did they talk about?"

"They talked about Mother's plans for the future."

"Which are?"

Megan put down her mug with a slight thump. "Gabe, you're not going to like this one bit, and Dad's going to be so angry I don't even know how we're going to tell him, but as far as I can gather, Mother's planning to open a store in the San Francisco area."

Gabe frowned. "She can't do that," he said. "It's a crazy idea. Quite apart from the fact that it would be very awkward to have a major new venture opening up when she and Dad are barely speaking to each other, DeWilde's is a public company, and any expansion in the number of stores has to be approved by the board of directors—"

"You don't understand," Megan said. "Mother isn't planning to open a branch of DeWilde's. She's planning to open up a store of her own. In competition with DeWilde's."

The idea was so preposterous—so treacherous—that for a moment Gabe's mind went blank. "That's not possible," he said finally. "Kate's misunderstood. She must have. Mother would never open a rival store."

"Kate has an IQ somewhere around 160," Megan

said wryly. "She spent three hours listening to Mother outline her plans. I think we can rely on Kate's information. Which is that Mother intends to open a bridal store somewhere in the Bay Area, modeled on the concepts that have made DeWilde's famous in five countries. When they finally said goodbye, Mother left to meet with a real estate agent. They were going to spend the afternoon looking at prospective sites for Mother's new store."

For the past several days, Gabe's feelings toward his mother had been in turmoil. Bewilderment and childish hurt had mixed inextricably with sympathy for his father and a more adult regret that his mother had felt unable to turn to her son for advice or comfort. Megan's news changed everything. Gabe could accept that his parents' marriage had run into trouble. He could even accept that marital problems might drive his mother back to San Francisco for a period of adjustment and reflection. He couldn't think of a single reason, other than spite, that would motivate her to launch a rival store in San Francisco.

His already turbulent feelings boiled over and coalesced into hard, icy rage. "Then we'll have to make sure she doesn't succeed, won't we," he said. "There isn't room in this world for more than one chain of DeWilde bridal stores, and Grace knows that better than anyone."

Megan put out her hand, resting it on his forearm. "She's hurting, Gabe, can't you see that? She's opening a store because it's the only thing she knows how to do. Losing herself in plans for a major new project is the only way she can find to ease the pain of being separated from Dad."

"She should consider coming home and discussing

these matters with Dad like a mature adult," Gabe said coldly. "If you speak to her, you might point out that confronting the situation rather than running off would be a much more effective way of easing this pain you insist she's feeling."

"You could tell her yourself," Megan said. "Gabe, right now I really think she needs to hear from us. Pick up the phone and give her a call. The right words from you might persuade her to put her plans for a San Francisco store on hold."

"If she'd wanted to speak with me, she knew exactly where I could be found," Gabe said. "Which is more than I can say about her. I still don't have a phone number for her."

"I have one. Kate gave it to me. Mother's been staying at a hotel and has only just found an apartment-hotel, so she didn't have a permanent phone number to give us. Let me get my handbag and I'll give you—"

"Give it to Dad," Gabe said. "He's the managing director of the DeWilde Corporation. He's the one who should deal with this situation. Along with the lawyers, of course."

"But you're her son," Megan protested.

"Yes," Gabe said icily. "I wonder if Grace is going to remember that at any time in the near future?"

CHAPTER FIVE

LIANNE WASN'T LATE for her date with Gabe, but he was already seated at the table when she arrived at Bruges, the restaurant where they'd agreed to meet. He stood up to greet her, his manner courteous enough, but the tension radiating from him so powerful that she could feel it pricking her skin, setting off little mini-shocks like malfunctioning electrical wiring. Oddly enough, for the first time since she'd met him she had the impression that the tension was only partly sexual, and only partly caused by her.

On the point of asking what was bothering him, she realized that she had no right to probe for such personal information. This was the first time they'd been out on a date together, and for all that she knew his body so intimately, the two of them weren't friends. In some ways, they were barely acquaintances. Aside from those few magic hours in her flat when they'd seemed to talk about everything in the universe, the only intimacy they'd shared was sex. And tonight Gabe didn't seem to want to share even sex with her. The barriers he'd erected against her were as visible to Lianne as the dark, tailored elegance of his Savile Row suit or the subtle, abstract design of his Grieves and Hawke tie.

She sat down opposite Gabe, answering his polite questions with mechanical fluency and quelling a bitter disappointment that was out of all proportion to the reality of what was happening. She'd expected Gabe to be a fascinating, sophisticated companion, and he didn't let her down. Lianne herself was no slouch in the social chitchat department. That was one thing you could say for growing up on military bases around the world. It sure taught you how to spend an evening jabbering eloquently about nothing in particular.

The restaurant Gabe had chosen was a new one, tucked away in an unlikely side street near Piccadilly. The chef was Belgian, the food scrumptious and the service impeccable. All this and Gabriel DeWilde sitting across the candle-lit table being charming. Any sensible woman would have been in heaven. Lianne was in hell.

Aching with misery, she talked about nothing with worldly aplomb. Gabe talked right back. No embarrassing moments of silence were allowed to develop. When all else failed, they discussed the wine and the details of the menu. She discovered that they both preferred artichokes to asparagus, and that they both considered the Grand Cru Montrachet that Gabe had ordered to be one of France's finest wines. She refused dessert with a smile. She refused coffee with another, even bigger smile. Gabe barely managed to conceal his relief. He paid a very large bill and they walked outside, only to discover that it had started raining.

What else, Lianne thought wryly. The perfect finish to a disastrous night.

"I'll drive you home," Gabe said. He sounded as if he would more willingly have volunteered to sit in a torture chamber and have rats gnaw on his toes.

She wasn't sure how much longer she was going to be able to hold on to her bright and cheerful smile. "Please don't bother, Gabe. I can easily get a cab."

But of course she couldn't. It was eleven o'clock on

a Saturday night and it was raining, which meant she could almost as easily have found a camel padding through the streets as a cabdriver looking for a fare.

"We could ask the restaurant to call for a minicab," she suggested, when ten excruciatingly long minutes had passed by without success.

"No, this is ridiculous." He grabbed her hand. "Come on. My car's parked just around the corner. And the rain seems to be letting up for a few minutes. Let's make a dash for it."

They ran, dodging puddles, with Gabe holding her hand so that she'd know which way to run. They reached his car slightly damp and slightly breathless. "I'll get the door for you as soon as I find my keys," Gabe said, sounding more natural than he had all night. "Watch out for the traffic. That red car on the other side of the road is parked illegally. There isn't much room left for anyone else to get by."

He'd just retrieved his keys from the inside pocket of his jacket when a van drove past, sending a spume of chilly water shooting toward them. Lianne instinctively jumped back in an effort to avoid the mud spray, bumping against Gabe because there was nowhere else to go. Her hair bounced against his cheek. Her hands splayed out against his chest. Her hip nudged his thigh. His arms shot around her, steadying her. They both froze, chest to chest, knee to knee, hearts beating in unison.

Oh, my God, Lianne thought. Oh, my God.

Gabe stared down at her, his eyes darkened by awareness and a kind of desolate resignation. His mouth twisted into a grim smile. "We almost made it, didn't we?"

She didn't—couldn't—answer. Her heart was racing

so fast her lungs couldn't seem to keep pace. With slow deliberation, Gabe bent his head until his mouth covered hers. He kissed her with a ferocious passion that paid not the slightest heed to the fact that they were in a public place, on a street where cars were whizzing by, inundating them with dirty water. Lianne kissed him back, mouth open, body welded to his. A part of her stood to one side, shamed by her mindless passion, recognizing the bleak truth that tonight's dinner had proved conclusively—if proof were needed—that she and Gabe shared absolutely nothing except some strange body chemistry that triggered instant mutual desire.

He was fully aroused and she was shaking when he broke off the kiss. His gaze locked with hers. "Spend the night with me, Lianne."

No softening lies, no beguiling promises, just the curt offer of a night of sex. She closed her eyes, shutting out temptation. She had never expected to feel this sort of relentless drive for sexual fulfillment, so she had no mechanisms in place for coping with it. "No." The one-word denial was all she could manage to articulate.

His grip on her arms tightened as if he might refuse to accept her answer. Shockingly, she wished for a split second that he would ignore her rejection and simply bundle her into the car and drive her straight to his flat, refusing to take no for an answer. All the pleasures of mindless sex, with none of the responsibility. For a couple of seconds he neither moved nor spoke. Then he released her, turning abruptly to open the door on the passenger side of his Jag. "I'll drive you home," he said, his voice hard and flat. "Get in."

The traffic was heavy, and the rain started again as an annoying drizzle that distorted depth perception and made driving difficult, but Lianne didn't fool herself that the silence inside the car was caused by the driving conditions. The air around them crackled and sparked with their thwarted desire. Her body was still on fire. Why didn't Gabe say something? she thought, feeling aggrieved.

Perhaps because he was finding it as difficult as she was to think of something appropriate to say. He was thirty years old, long past the stage of needing to bed a woman just so that he could record another sexual conquest in his little black book. He'd spent five months dating Julia, which suggested he was a man who valued friendship as an element in his relationships with women. Since he didn't seem to like her very much, he was probably as embarrassed as she was by the stupid, inexplicable intensity of their sexual response to each other.

"Maybe we should just set aside a weekend to have wild, uninterrupted sex," she said, thinking aloud. "Maybe that way we'd get whatever it is we feel for each other out of our systems and be able to move on with the rest of our lives."

His mouth quirked into a rueful smile. "Isn't that supposed to be my line?"

"Why? Because you're the man? Are you sexist enough to believe that women don't have sexual urges? I'm just as aware of what's going on between us as you are, Gabe. Am I supposed to pretend I haven't noticed that we practically ignite whenever we touch? And that we have nothing much in common except mutual lust—and a good friend we betrayed?"

His hands tightened on the steering wheel. "Julia and I hadn't made each other any promises," he said quietly. "And I think she understands we didn't mean to hurt her."

"She's a much more generous person than I am. And the fact is, we have hurt her." Lianne laced her fingers in her lap and stared at them fiercely, aware that tears were gathering ominously at the corners of her eyes. Damn, she hated it when she went into emotional overload like this! If only she had some of Julia's wonderful British reserve. But all she had was a flaming Irish-American temper, mixed with a liberal dollop of Czech passion, and a British name passed on by a solitary English great-grandfather without any of his stiff upper lip to go with it. She brushed impatiently at the mud splotches drying in hard gray patches on the short skirt of her evening suit. None of them budged. Her expensive new outfit was ruined, she realized, stained and discolored beyond repair. Blinking back tears, she turned to stare out of the car window. Her suit seemed the perfect metaphor for her relationship with Gabe. Destroyed on the first outing.

Gabe turned the Jag into Kensington High Street. Another couple of minutes and they'd be home, thank heavens. Home, where she would spend the night alone. Lianne swallowed hard over the lump in her throat, not even sure why she still felt so depressingly close to tears. Surely the fact that she had resisted a night of meaningless sex was cause for celebration? By tomorrow morning she'd be delighted that virtue had triumphed over hormones and that Gabe hadn't taken her up on that silly offer of a weekend of wild sex.

She wished it would hurry up and be tomorrow morning.

For once, there was room to draw up to the curb right in front of her flat. Gabe parked swiftly and cut the engine.

"There's no need to see me to the door," Lianne

said, already half out of the car. "I'll be fine. The entrance is well lit. Thanks for dinner, Gabe. You chose a wonderful restaurant—"

He got out of the door, slamming it behind him. He intercepted her as she stepped onto the pavement. "I behaved like a major pain in the ass tonight," he said. "I'm sorry, Lianne. Will you accept my apologies?"

She had her bright smile back in full working order. "Of course. Apology accepted. Thanks again for a delicious meal, Gabe. I'll see you at the office on Monday."

He put out a hand, restraining her. "It's no real excuse for my miserable behavior, but for what it's worth, I had bad news about my mother this afternoon," he said.

Lianne swung around in midstep. "Oh, no! I'm so sorry. She isn't sick, is she?"

"No." Gabe rubbed the back of his neck, the gesture weary enough to make Lianne ache to comfort him. "No, she's not ill. Apparently, she's planning to open a bridal department store in San Francisco."

Lianne frowned, puzzled. "A branch of DeWilde's, you mean? Why is that such bad news?"

Gabe laughed without the slightest trace of mirth. "Not a branch of DeWilde's," he said. "If you can believe it, I heard this afternoon that my mother intends to set up a rival store based on the concepts she's perfected over the past thirty years with DeWilde's."

Lianne was shocked. "She can't. Surely she can't do that. She'll never get backers or start-up financing. There must be noncompete clauses in her contract."

"What contract?" Gabe asked bitterly. "When my mother started working for DeWilde's it was a family-owned company, and she'd just married the son of the managing director. I hope I'm wrong, but I don't suppose the thought of a contract crossed anyone's mind."

Lianne shook her head in disbelief. "What does your father say about the situation?" she asked.

"Nothing." Gabe frowned, as if impatient with his own failure to act. "Actually, I haven't told Dad yet. There wasn't time to go and see him unless I canceled our date."

Lianne knew that their date had been the excuse, not the reason, for Gabe's failure to inform his father of Grace's plans. She moved closer, taking Gabe's hand. "You have to tell your father," she said. "Tonight, Gabe, or first thing tomorrow morning. It's going to be much worse if he hears rumors or finds out via the international gossip mill."

"You're right, but I don't know how to tell him. I've been wrestling with the problem for the past several hours since my sister gave me the news. How the hell am I supposed to explain to my father that his former wife is planning to do something that is the equivalent of holding a dagger to his chest and shoving it into his heart slowly, without benefit of anesthetic?"

Lianne winced at the image. "Well, for a start, I'd recommend that you work on finding some less inflammatory language to let him know what's happening," she suggested dryly.

"Whatever words I use, nothing is going to change the basic truth. Which is that my mother plans to open a store that will be in direct competition with DeWilde's."

"That's not quite true, is it, Gabe? If Grace had wanted to be in direct competition with your father, presumably she'd have chosen to open her store in one of the cities where DeWilde's is already operating.

There's no DeWilde store in San Francisco. The only American branch is in New York. DeWilde's may be very famous and prestigious, but I doubt if many San Francisco brides travel three thousand miles across the country to shop in New York."

Gabe drew in a sharp breath. "I hadn't looked at it that way. But I should have. I know our customer base in New York is largely drawn from the East Coast."

"Put it that way to your father. Maybe it'll help to take the edge off Grace's plans just a little."

He looked down at her hand, stroking his thumb across the top of her knuckles. "Why is she doing this, Lianne?" The question seemed to come almost against his will, as if he hesitated to admit an outsider into the intimacy of his conflicting feelings. "My parents have been married for so damn long, and they seemed perfectly content with each other. Astonishingly content, in fact. What happened to them? What went wrong?"

Lianne thought of her own parents, now in their mid-fifties. Their marriage had always been happy, despite the tensions generated by her father's frequent career moves to air force bases often located in obscure parts of the world. She knew other military couples who'd seemed just as much in love as her parents, and yet their marriages hadn't survived the strain of constant separations and transfers, not to mention the looming threat of battles and death. Unlike Grace, Lianne's mother had never pursued a career outside the home, but Lianne refused to believe that it was Grace's career that had caused the breakup of her marriage. Disagreements over jobs and work schedules might be a symptom of a failed marriage, but they weren't likely to be the sole cause. So why were her parents happier than ever as they moved into their fifties, whereas Jeffrey's marriage to Grace was falling apart?

"I can't give you any good answers, Gabe," she said. "I guess if I could I'd be winning either the Nobel Peace Prize or making a fortune selling leather-bound volumes of my secret tips for a happy marriage."

He gave her a reluctant grin. "Some things just seem to get more complicated as we get older, don't they? When I was eight, I knew exactly what love was. It was my father buying me an ice-cream cone at the beach, and my mother sitting on the bed reading *Willy Wonka and the Chocolate Factory.*"

"Seems like a great definition of love to me," Lianne said.

"It was great. Unfortunately, each year since then I seem to understand a little less about what it means to love someone. It's depressing to think I reached my most profound insights on the subject of human relationships at age eight."

Lianne laughed softly. "Don't give up hope, Gabe. Deciding that you know absolutely nothing is probably the first sign of wisdom where love's concerned."

He glanced down at their hands, which were still linked. "Thanks for listening, Lianne. Talking to you has helped put things in perspective. I'll arrange a meeting with my father for first thing tomorrow morning."

"I'm sure that's a good decision."

He carried her hand to his lips, kissing the tips of her fingers with a touch that felt almost tender. "Have lunch with me tomorrow," he said quietly.

She wanted to say yes, but she didn't think she could bear sitting across a restaurant table, eating another expensive meal and exchanging brittle, meaningless conversation. She stared at the back of the hand holding hers. His skin was tanned, and she wondered where he'd been to get so brown at this time of year. There were so many things she didn't know about Gabriel DeWilde, and she realized suddenly that she was hungry to find out more about him. Not just as a sexual partner but as a man, and a potential friend.

"Where were you thinking we should meet?" she asked, her voice constricted, her thoughts flying in every direction.

He paused for a moment. "We could drive into the country and find somewhere by the river...."

"That seems like a lot of driving just to eat lunch."

"Where would you suggest, then?"

She looked up at him, the blood pounding in her ears. "How about your flat?"

He went very still. "I don't cook."

She held his gaze. "I rarely eat in the middle of the day, so lunch isn't a big deal for me."

A smile glinted briefly in his eyes. "You don't eat and I don't cook. It sounds like a date made in heaven, doesn't it? What time shall I expect you?"

Her fingers twisted in the strap of her beaded evening bag. "One o'clock?"

"I'll be waiting."

He gave her directions and she turned to go, scared by the confusing tumult of her feelings, but Gabe pulled her back. He cupped his hands around her face, kissing her long and hard. "Until tomorrow."

"Until tomorrow," Lianne repeated, and ran up the stone steps leading to her front door before she could change her mind. Whether to cancel tomorrow's date or to beg him to take her home with him tonight, she wasn't sure.

CHAPTER SIX

IT HAD BEEN TWO HOURS since Gabe told him about Grace's plans for a new store, but Jeffrey's anger seemed to have increased rather than diminished with the passage of time. Carrying his glass of whiskey, he strode through the elegantly furnished rooms of his flat, trying to find somewhere to sit, somewhere to put himself where the raw ache of his fury might be soothed. The down-filled cushions of the sofas, even the soft, worn leather of the chair in his study, seemed about as inviting as a bed of nails. The rooms echoed with emptiness, mocking him with reminders of Grace's absence, tantalizing him with memories. The elusive hint of her scent was everywhere, too strong to escape, too faint to satisfy.

Last night he'd slept in one of the guest rooms rather than breach the cavernous horror of their silent bedroom. Now he opened the door again, peering into the room as if he expected to be greeted by a tiger who'd missed out on breakfast. There was no tiger, of course, but the sight of the bed he'd shared with Grace was almost as frightening. Its puffy chintz bedspread was immaculately arranged, devoid of rumples and indentations, just as he liked it—the way Grace never managed to keep it, because the bed was her favorite place to sit. Each morning, she would roost cross-legged in the center of a pile of pillows, reading glasses perched on the end of her nose, mug of black coffee in hand, skimming through the newspaper and driving him to distraction when she discarded unwanted pages in a haphazard pile on the floor. Each night, she'd sit in the same spot at the center of the bed, wearing one of those crazy T-shirts that belonged in a college dorm, or one of her hand-embroidered satin nightgowns that belonged in a courtesan's boudoir. Then she'd slowly pull the pins from her trim French braid until her hair tumbled down onto her shoulders in a heavy silk curtain.

God, even now, after all these years, she could still excite him just by taking the pins from her hair and looking at him with a certain teasing light in her eyes. He could remember with bittersweet accuracy how long it had been since they last made love: one month, two weeks and six days. With a pang of regret so sharp it was physically painful, Jeffrey realized he would be willing to give up five years of his life to see his wife again, this very minute, sitting in the middle of the bed and messing up the spread as she brushed the tangles out of her long blond hair. Or even scrawling incorrect answers to the crossword puzzle clues, and laughing when he pointed out her mistakes.

Jeffrey turned away from the too-neat bed, swallowing a hefty swig of whiskey. It burned all the way down into his stomach. Why had he never realized how much he loved watching Grace do a crossword puzzle until it seemed possible that he'd never watch her again?

He closed the bedroom door with a bang and marched back down the hallway. Funny, he'd never noticed until these past few days how damned depressing all that dark walnut paneling could be. He gulped the last of his drink and poured himself another, not bothering to add water or ice. His third whiskey of the day and it wasn't even noon. With a muttered oath, he set the full glass on the trolley and strode impatiently through the drawing room. He'd tried drowning himself in a bottle last week, when Grace finally left him, and he'd already discovered that getting drunk was no solution to his problems. Although, God knew, at the moment there didn't seem to be any solutions.

He pushed open the French doors leading out onto the balcony. He ignored the planter boxes full of bright tulips and budding geraniums and stared across the river to the south bank of the Thames without really seeing it. The rain had stopped sometime in the hours before dawn, and the sun was warm on his face. The roar of buses and cars was muted in this isolated cul-de-sac, the air clear of petrol fumes. A breeze blew in from the distant salt marshes of the Thames estuary, carrying with it the faint tang of the sea.

Grace wasn't even on the other side of the Atlantic Ocean, Jeffrey thought with maudlin self-pity. She was almost three thousand miles farther away, on the shores of the Pacific, closer to Asia than she was to England. And the gap between them emotionally was at least as wide as the physical distance that separated them. He closed his eyes, letting the sun sink into his skin, searching for peace, striving for acceptance. Grace was gone. She wasn't likely to come back. He'd destroyed everything—

No! The howl of pain and regret started so deep inside him that his body shook when he finally bellowed out his denial. Startling the sea gulls flying overhead, he banged his fist on the iron balustrade of the balcony and stormed back into the flat. He grabbed the phone, fumbling for his reading glasses when he couldn't decipher the number written neatly in his Rolodex. Damn, he hated the subtle signs of encroaching middle age. Especially today when he felt so cast adrift, so rootless. Ah, here it was: Grace—San Francisco.

The mere sight of that alien notation was enough to feed several more twigs to the flames of his anger.

He punched in the numbers, aware that it was still early in San Francisco, too impatient to work out the precise time difference. Grace answered on the third ring, her voice thick and husky with sleep. "Hello?"

The sound of her voice made him hot with longing. Though he had no reason to believe she'd flown to meet a lover, he irrationally wondered if she was alone. His hand, suddenly sweaty, slipped around the receiver. Jealousy clawed at his gut, burning and corrosive. He wanted to scream, and so he kept his voice cool, low and utterly controlled—his only defense against total breakdown. "This is Jeffrey," he said. "We need to talk, Grace."

"At three-thirty in the morning? I have nothing to say to you, Jeffrey. We've said it all, many times."

She sounded clipped, cold, indifferent. Grace never sounded that way. She always yelled and stormed and cried when she was upset, forcing him to confront the emotions that he kept buried so deep inside. But today, it seemed, she wasn't going to shout. Apparently she no longer deemed Jeffrey worthy of raised voices or floods of her tears.

He hurt so much that he couldn't bear it, so he let his anger explode. Not in a healing outburst, but in a deadly, ice-cold listing of her sins. "Well, my dear estranged wife, I have a great deal to say to you. According to Megan, you've been very busy in the week since you arrived in San Francisco. Tell me, Grace, just when did you decide that you hadn't punished me enough? When did you decide you needed to turn the screws one more time, just for good measure?"

"I don't know what you're talking about, Jeffrey."

He was too angry to wonder about the faint note of uncertainty in Grace's voice. "I'm talking about the store you plan to open," he said. "The luxury store you plan to start in San Francisco for the Bay area's lucky brides." The rage was welling up inside him, threatening to spill over, so he clamped down, making his voice colder, more punishing than ever. "I understand you intend it to be the ultimate bridal emporium, a supreme rival to DeWilde's. Is there any reason at all for this venture, Grace, other than to irritate me?"

"Oh, the store, that's what you're talking about." She hesitated a moment. "I have to do something with the rest of my life, Jeffrey."

You could come home where you belong. You could come home and be my wife again. His heart cried out the words, but his voice didn't speak them. The temptation to grovel was overwhelming, so he fought it by stoking his anger. Anger that bored more deeply inward with each passing second.

"Let me state my position, Grace, which is also that of the DeWilde Corporation and its board of directors. Any skills you may possess in management, merchandising and retailing were acquired while you were an employee of the DeWilde Corporation. If you attempt to open a store that capitalizes in any way on the expertise you gained while working for our company, or infringes on our trademarks, or utilizes our corporate logo, I shall personally see to it that you are served with enough lawsuits to keep you and your potential financial backers fighting in court for the next several hundred years."

"You can try," she said, and now—finally—she sounded angry. "Good luck, Jeffrey. Have one of your fancy lawyers look up the State of California's laws concerning restraint of trade. I think you'll find that DeWilde's won't have a legal leg to stand on. The fact that you're quoted on the London stock exchange won't help. From the American point of view, DeWilde's is a foreign company."

Jeffrey unclenched his jaw just enough to allow him to speak. "I would remind you that when the DeWilde family took this company public, we signed agreements with strongly worded noncompete clauses in order to protect nonfamily shareholders. You signed that agreement and I intend to see that you honor it. I trust that I have made my intentions, and those of the DeWilde board, crystal clear?"

"Crystal clear, Jeffrey." Her voice was husky, ridiculously sexy, considering what they were saying to each other. "You have many problems when it comes to communication, but lack of clarity isn't one of them. Let me try to be as crisp and succinct as you. Here's my answer. I plan to open a store, and you haven't a hope in hell of stopping me. See you in court, Jeffrey."

He heard her slam the receiver back into its cradle. The sound of silence, of the absence of Grace, echoed in his ear. He realized that he'd handled the situation about as badly as he possibly could have done. He'd killed any hope for negotiation, compromise or explanation. If Grace's plans for a new store hadn't been entirely serious before, they would be now. The phone began to buzz a warning beep into his ear. He hung it up with exaggerated care and walked over to the trolley and his abandoned glass of whiskey.

There were no answers in the bottom of a bottle, Jeffrey reminded himself, his hand curling around the neck of the decanter. True. But there were no answers anywhere else, either. He held the glass to his mouth, tipped it up and swallowed. The throbbing ache of his loss eased just slightly as the single malt trickled with warm comfort down his throat. He tucked the Edinburgh crystal decanter under his arm and weaved a path into the study. The newspaper lay, pristine and unread, on the floor by his chair. The way he'd always told Grace he longed to see it. He kicked it to one side and sank into his favorite chair, squinting at the upside-down headline.

He had, unfortunately, an extremely hard head for liquor, so it looked as if it were going to be a long, unpleasant afternoon. A fitting end to a long and unpleasant week. A rotten end to a marriage that had once seemed uniquely and gloriously happy.

GABE HADN'T REALIZED how much he was looking forward to seeing Lianne until he opened the front door and saw her waiting in the hallway. She managed by some odd alchemy to look both spring fresh and enchantingly rumpled all at the same time. She was wearing jeans, paired with a silk blouse in a soft shade of leaf green. An oversized jacket slid off her shoulders, and her chestnut hair was already beginning to tumble out of the clip that was supposed to hold it in a loose ponytail. He felt a surge of desire, tinged by some other sensation that was warmer, more subtle and harder to identify. Surprisingly, though, the tension that had been tightening in his gut ever since he spoke with his father that morning suddenly loosened.

He smiled at her, glad that she was there and that they had the rest of the day ahead of them. To do what, he wasn't quite sure. He'd been fantasizing about having sex with her ever since he interviewed her at the store, and last night's fiasco had merely sharpened his need. He'd intended to conduct her into his living room, stage a swift, expert seduction and have her in his bed within the hour. Now the plan seemed shallow, the prospect of instant sex not very satisfying.

Confused by his own muddled feelings, he found that his usual repertoire of sophisticated one-liners had deserted him. Since he couldn't think of anything witty to say, he simply smiled and told her the truth. "Hello, Lianne. It's good to see you."

"Hello." She smiled back at him, holding up a small paper bag. "I brought us a present. Two Bath buns, still warm from the oven."

"You baked them yourself?"

She chuckled, her laughter light and happy. "I wish, but my culinary talents don't extend that far. It's such a beautiful day I decided to walk, and I found this wonderful bakery open. So if you can brew coffee, or make a decent pot of tea, I guess we can have lunch, after all."

"Coffee's my specialty," he said, stepping back. "And I love Bath buns. Come on in. If you've walked all the way here from your flat, you must be thirsty."

"It's less than five miles," she said, following him into the kitchen. "And it was perfect weather for walking. The parks and squares look so beautiful at this time of year it seemed a shame to take the tube and miss the views."

Gabe poured beans into the grinder and nodded to a cupboard behind her. "You'll find plates in there."

She set the sweet rolls on the plates and watched in companionable silence while he ground beans for the coffee and set it to brew. "You have an impressive kitchen for a guy who doesn't cook, Gabe."

He smiled ruefully. "When I bought this flat three years ago, I hoped the kitchen would inspire me into becoming an instant gourmet chef. After a couple of disasters, I realized there was more to being a great chef than buying a cookbook and reading the recipes. I signed up for a couple of courses in basic cooking, but I never got beyond the introductory lecture. Some crisis would erupt at work, and I'd be putting in fourteen-hour days again. And the truth is, I eat out so much these days that when I do have a meal at home, a bowl of cereal suits me just fine."

"The pace at DeWilde's seems very fast," Lianne said. "I'm getting used to the crisis-of-the-day approach already. DeWilde's is such a famous store, almost an institution, I'd expected the management to be a bit more conservative."

"According to legend, the organization was very staid until the late seventies. Changes came rapidly then, mostly because of my mother's input. After the company went public in 1986, a lot of the old-timers took early retirement and left. The new hires and the staff who stayed appreciate the loose management structure and the creative freedom we're given to try new ideas. And when you try new ideas, you inevitably get the occasional screwup. Personally, I would never trade the satisfaction I get working for DeWilde's for the leisure time I'd get from a regular nine-to-five job. And I know my parents wouldn't, either, even though they both put in killer hours."

"You miss her a lot, don't you, Gabe? Your mother, I mean."

For a second, while he'd been talking about the store, he'd forgotten that his mother no longer worked at DeWilde's. He was disconcerted by the rush of regret he felt at the reminder of her defection, not only a personal regret but a professional one that he would no longer be working for a woman who was both talented and supremely knowledgeable about the world of fashion retailing.

"I'm sure that Adam will manage very competently once he gets the hang of things," Gabe said, not managing to inject much conviction into his voice.

"Yes, I'm sure he will. How long have you worked at DeWilde's?" Lianne asked, tactfully changing the subject.

"Three years. I was promoted to merchandising manager for the London store five months ago. And why are you looking so surprised?"

"I guess I'd sort of assumed that since you were the DeWilde son and heir that you'd been working there since the day you graduated from college."

He grimaced. "Lianne, you're treading on my ego. Hard. I like to tell myself that I got hired on my merits, not because I'm the boss's only son." He sighed. "Sometimes it feels as if the DeWilde name is this bloody great albatross hanging round my neck, insisting that I carry it everywhere."

"It must be difficult. Have you ever considered working for a rival store?"

"Not only considered it, I've done it. I worked for Bloomingdale's and Tiffany in New York. But in the end, nobody in either of those organizations wanted to promote me to a position with real responsibility, since they all assumed that one day I'd simply go back to DeWilde's, taking all their trade secrets with me. In the end, I swallowed my pride, gave up beating my head against a concrete wall and applied for a job at DeWilde's."

"Why did you have to swallow your pride?" she asked, taking the cup of coffee he handed her and sipping appreciatively.

"Well, I'd left home at seventeen assuring everyone that I was never going to work in the family business. I finally agreed to go to university instead of joining the marines, generously allowing my parents to support me, of course. But once I finished college, I plunged headlong into another attack of rebellion."

"I expect you were wriggling every which way to escape the albatross," she said.

He was surprised at her immediate understanding. "Yes, you're right. I wanted to be around people who'd never heard of DeWilde's, who just accepted me as Gabe, a useful bloke to have near you if you were in a tight corner."

"How did you rebel?" she asked.

"All the usual stupid ways. No illicit drugs, though. I had just enough sense in my testosterone-filled brain to avoid that. But except for the drugs, I tried everything. I made myself so unpleasant to my sisters that they stopped talking to me for the best part of a year. I drank too much, made friends with dangerous men, got involved with all the wrong women. I worked on an oil rig in Texas and on the gas pipeline in Alaska. You could say that I generally wasted an enormous amount of energy proving that my parents couldn't force me to join DeWilde's if I didn't want to. Which, of course, everyone except me already knew."

Lianne took a luxurious bite of her sweet roll and sighed in sympathy. "Lord, I wouldn't want to be twenty again. The world's such a terrifying place at that age, and of course you can't tell anyone just how darn scared you are. Most of all, you can't admit it to yourself. How did your parents react while all this rebelling was going on?"

He grinned. "From my point of view, they didn't really cooperate as well as they should have done. On the rare occasions when I called to tell them I was still alive, they invariably told me that they were thrilled to hear from me, but if I really enjoyed digging ditches in the Arctic tundra or baking my hide climbing rigs in the Gulf of Mexico, then that was absolutely what I should do. Go for it, son, with our blessings. After nine months in Alaska, I got tired of freezing my ass off and having nobody to talk to except the moose, so I decided that business school and an MBA looked like a much better option."

She laughed. "God, growing up is a painful experience, isn't it? I ran away to join an artists' colony in Maine when I was eighteen. But I guess I'm not as stubborn as you. Once winter set in, which was right around the first week in September, I decided that my creative talents were in grave danger of freezing to death along with the rest of me. So I called home and said that maybe I'd consider applying to college, after all. When I told the commune leader I was leaving to catch the next bus home, she shook her head sadly and said that I would regret selling out my artistry to vulgar commercialism. I didn't have the heart to tell her my departure had nothing to do with art. It was the thought of hot water in the shower and a pizza place close enough to make deliveries that lured me away."

Lianne's eyes danced as she talked, and her mouth seemed to quiver on the brink of a smile. Gabe felt his stomach twist with a tug of awareness that wasn't exactly sexual. Much as he wanted to take her to his bed, he realized that what he felt for her had become something more complex than simple lust, a realization that left an oddly discordant note twanging inside his head.

The domestic intimacy of the kitchen suddenly seemed threatening and he wanted to escape. "Come through to the sitting room," he said. "I have a balcony that's about the size of a bathtub, but it's such a lovely day, if I open the doors we'll get a fresh breeze even if we sit inside. We might even smell a whiff of lilac blossoms."

"Sounds perfect." She smiled outright this time, her pleasure sparkling around her like an oversized halo. "On a day like today, it's easy to remember why I decided to live and work in London."

He absolutely was not going to kiss her. He wasn't so besotted that he needed to kiss her just because she smiled. And where had that word *besotted* sprung from, anyway? "Why did you choose London as the place you finally settled?" he asked, his voice carefully cool. "If you wanted the challenge of making it in a European city, why not Paris, or Rome, or Vienna?"

"I guess part of the reason is that in London I more or less speak the same language as everyone else." She set her empty coffee mug in the sink, washing the sugar glaze from her sticky fingers. "But mostly it's because London has always struck me as one of the most beautiful and interesting cities in the world. Of all the places our family lived while I was growing up, I don't think we saw another city that has quite so many magnificent trees and flowers and public gardens. Then there are all the wonderful theaters." Her smile deepened. "And now that I'm an employed person, I can even afford the ticket prices at some of them."

Gabe handed her a towel, taking care to avoid touching her. "I like the theater, too. We should go together sometime. Is there anything special that you like to see?"

"I guess I like straight drama best of all. The more dazzling they make the special effects in movies, the more I realize how much I appreciate a straightforward play, where all the fireworks come from the talent and technical skill of the actors."

"I agree. Did you see *Silent River* at the Barbican last autumn? I found the emotional impact of that stunning."

"Yes, it was." Her cheeks became washed with color. "I cried through most of the last two scenes. I'm a sucker for neglected kids and lonely old folks. The combination of the two did me in."

Gabe found himself wishing that he'd seen the play with Lianne, rather than the elegant journalist he'd escorted, who'd later treated him to a brandy in her flat, accompanied by twenty minutes of rather boring sex and a thirty-minute analysis of the technical flaws in the performance of the male lead. Gabe had wondered if she would subject his performance in bed to the same critical analysis and had decided he didn't much care if she did.

He opened the door to the sitting room, and Lianne looked around appreciatively. "This is lovely, Gabe. Did you decorate it yourself?"

"With the help of some friends in the furniture trade.

The antique pieces in here are all recovered, repainted and refinished castoffs from Kemberly."

"Kemberly?" she asked.

"My parents' home in Hampshire," he explained. "My great-grandparents bought it in the thirties, when they first arrived in England."

Lianne was surprised. "I didn't realize your family had arrived here so recently."

"By British standards, we're fresh off the boat. My father was the first DeWilde to be born here. My ancestors were diamond merchants in Amsterdam and my great-grandparents founded the first DeWilde bridal store in Paris right after World War I. Then, when Hitler came to power in Germany, they decided it was time to protect the family fortune by spreading the risk and opening a branch of DeWilde's in London. That was in 1934."

"And the London store was an immediate, outstanding success," Lianne said.

"Yes, fortunately. So my great-grandfather celebrated his first year's profits by buying Kemberly from a profligate baron who immediately took off to slaughter helpless wildlife in Africa. It's one of those rambling places with its very own secret staircase, and so much storage space in the attics that nobody ever throws anything away. The furniture in this room was probably declared too shabby to use sometime during the last century and got stashed away in the attics until I went up there and found it."

She sighed wistfully. "Now you're making me acutely jealous, Gabe. I always fantasized about having an unknown great-uncle who'd die and leave me a house that had been in the family for generations, one my parents had forgotten existed. Which is probably a reflection of the fact that I never lived anywhere longer than three years when I was a child."

"It must have been hard to move around so much, especially since you had no control over where you'd go and when you'd leave."

She shrugged. "But children never have any real say in where they live, do they? Besides, I was proud of what my father was doing, so I guess that made it easier for me to accept the demands of his career. The hardest part was losing friends. In the end, you learn to protect yourself by not making any friends, and that's the worst of all."

Gabe thought about his stint at boarding school and the security of living, studying and playing with the same group of people for five years. Boarding school might seem like a harsh environment, but in comparison to uprooting yourself every eighteen months or so, he suspected it was a piece of cake. "Were there any places that you really disliked living?" he asked, watching her as she examined a Victorian writing case with almost sensuous pleasure. "Surely there must have been at least a couple that you disliked?"

"There are several places I wouldn't choose to go back to," Lianne said. "But in the end, you can find something positive about almost anywhere if you look hard enough. And I was fortunate that my mother made sure we took advantage of everything the locality offered, whether it was Colorado Springs or the Arabian desert. What I find really surprising is how well my parents have settled down to suburban life in Michigan after all those years of exotic foreign travel."

"Is that where they're living now? In Michigan?"

"Yes, in a cottage right on the shores of Lake Michigan in a town called Benton's Inlet. They've settled in so well you'd think they'd lived there for thirty years at least. Mom's teaching a couple of classes in photography at the local community college, and Dad's opened up a small insurance agency. They seem as happy as clams.''

Gabe wasn't sure that he wanted to hear about middle-aged parents who were blissfully happy. He pushed back the curtains and unbolted the French doors that led to his tiny balcony. He hadn't realized that Lianne had followed him to admire the view and was standing behind him. When he stepped back to swing the doors inward, he bumped into her. Their bodies collided, precipitating them into each other's arms.

He never made a conscious decision to kiss her. One moment they were looking at each other, gazes locked, bodies tense. The next moment his mouth was crushing down on hers, his tongue thrusting against her teeth, desire pulsing hot and heavy in his veins. Her lips opened instantly and she returned his kiss with an eager passion that simply fed his hunger for more. He couldn't seem to get close enough to her, and his hands threaded through her hair, her soft curls winding around his fingers in a silky, teasing caress.

He was awash in the touch and feel of her, drowning in the scent and taste of her. With the tiny part of his brain that still functioned at a rational level, Gabe ordered himself to step back before they ended up making love on the floor for the second time in their brief acquaintance. Even as he was forming the thought, he grabbed her hips and ground himself against the flat, welcoming softness of her belly. Far from being repulsed by the blatant evidence of his arousal, she gave a low, husky murmur deep in her throat, pressing herself even closer to his body. Her blouse slid to the floor.

The satin and lace camisole that she wore underneath revealed the enticing swell of her breasts and the creamy smoothness of her skin. He lowered his head, tracing the curve of her breasts with a trail of hot, open-mouthed kisses.

Her pleasure shivered through him, churning in his veins, intoxicating him. Through the shattering boundaries of his self-control, he managed to latch onto the solid fact that there was a sofa only a few feet behind them. They didn't have to end up making love on the floor, he realized with relief. Fumbling with the buttons of his shirt, he propelled Lianne backward toward the sofa, tumbling with her into the deep down cushions.

Her face was flushed, her eyes brilliant. Even in passion, she didn't appear drowsy or languid, but alive and vibrant and infinitely desirable. Her gaze locking with his, she shrugged her shoulders, twisting with slow deliberation until the straps of her camisole slipped down her arms, revealing her perfect breasts and the hard peaks of her nipples.

Gabe struggled to draw breath. He reached out and touched her swollen lips with fingers that weren't entirely steady. "You're so beautiful, Lianne. God, I want you so damn badly."

She framed his face with her hands, pulling his head down toward her mouth. "I want you, too, Gabe." Her voice was husky, faintly breathless. He wondered why her voice—why everything about her—seemed sexier than in any other woman. Then he kissed her again, and he no longer cared about his reasons for wanting her, only that he did. The world narrowed into a space that held nothing except Lianne, her body cradled beneath his own, warm and curved and inviting.

The sound of his mother speaking was such a shocking intrusion that for a couple of seconds Gabe didn't register that he was listening to the Answerphone and that Grace wasn't actually present in the sitting room, talking to him. Galvanized, he tore himself out of Lianne's embrace and sat bolt upright, realizing belatedly that he'd turned off the ringer on the phone, which was why he hadn't heard any warning sounds before the answering machine clicked in.

His mind was still foggy with desire, and his thought processes seemed slow and cumbersome. There wasn't another human being on the face of the earth who could have caused him to pick up the phone at this precise moment, but his need to speak to Grace was strong enough to cool the heat of his passion, allowing him to reach out and grab the phone before she hung up.

"Hello," he growled, not intending to sound deliberately aggressive, but his body was jangling with need and he didn't have full control over his reflexes. "What do you want?"

Not surprisingly, his mother seemed disconcerted by his roughness. "I'm sorry, Gabe. If I've called at a bad time, I can try you again later."

He wasn't thinking clearly enough to respond to the nervousness in his mother's voice or to consider how she might be feeling. He spoke brusquely, the frustrations of the past few days mingling with his unfulfilled lust. "No, this is fine. Lord knows, if we don't speak now you may decide to take off for the Caribbean and it'll be six months before anyone hears from you again."

Several seconds passed before she answered him. "Gabe, I'm sorry, really I am. I never intended to leave London so abruptly without speaking to you. I did try to phone from the airport, but you weren't home." She hesitated, seeming to search for the right words. "I hope you weren't too shocked when you heard the news, Gabe."

"Shocked? Why should I be shocked?" He didn't even try to control the bitter sarcasm that honed his words to lethal sharpness. "You and Dad have only been married for thirty-two years, so why should I be surprised because you suddenly woke up one morning and decided to leave him?"

"It wasn't quite that sudden," she said. "Things have been—difficult—between us for quite a while."

His father had said the same thing. Gabe's anger faded into puzzlement. "How have they been difficult?" he asked. From the corner of his eye, he saw that Lianne had finished pulling on her clothes. With a tactfulness he appreciated, she went out onto the balcony, closing the glass doors behind her so as to afford him some privacy. "Mother, what happened between the two of you?"

Once again she seemed to choose her words with excruciating care. "I said some things to your father a while ago that he didn't understand...that he misinterpreted."

"What kind of things?"

"Personal stuff. Ancient history, really." Grace's hesitation was longer this time. "Jeffrey was badly hurt. One thing led to another and... Well, the situation just became untenable. We were inflicting so much pain on each other, it was unbearable. That's all I can say, Gabe."

"And is your current situation any better?" Gabe asked incredulously. "Are you happy over there in San Francisco? Have you any idea what you're doing to

Dad? He looks like hell, and he's drinking himself to sleep most nights as far as I can tell—"

"If Jeffrey's drinking, that's his own choice."

"You're forcing him into making that choice."

"No, I'm not," Grace said, her voice diamond hard. "I'm not responsible for Jeffrey's actions."

"He loves you, Mother. He needs you." Gabe swallowed hard. "We both need you. Come home."

"Gabe...don't ask that, please."

He refused to hear the note of desperation in her voice. "You don't have to come back to live with Dad, but you need to come back to work, Mother. You have responsibilities to the store and to all the people who work for DeWilde's. However bad things are between you and Dad, I don't understand how you can run away from your professional obligations like this."

"I can't work with Jeffrey," Grace said flatly. "Gabe, you don't know what you're asking."

"Then explain to me. Make me understand, for God's sake."

"I can't," Grace said again. "Try to see things from my point of view. This is a rough time for me, and I guess I'm asking for your understanding. I need to know that you're willing to accept that I had good reasons for what I did, even though I can't necessarily explain those reasons. I need your support right now, Gabe. I really need it."

Hurt and bewilderment made him cruel. "Support for what?" he asked. "Support for your insane decision to open a rival store in San Francisco? If that's what you're hoping to get from me, then I can tell you here and now that you're not going to get it."

He could almost hear her flinch. She drew in an audible breath. "Sometimes, you know, you sound frighteningly like your father."

"I take that as a compliment."

Grace's voice was harsh with sudden weariness. "Let's not argue, Gabe. I've found an apartment overlooking the Bay, and I want to give you my new address and phone number. I'll be moving in next weekend."

Gabe wrote down the information that his mother gave him. "Thanks for the number," he said. "Although I'm not sure what we have to say to each other at this point."

"You're my son, and I love you," Grace said. "I can think of lots of reasons why I'd like to talk to you. I hope very much that you'll soon find just as many reasons to call me. I'm still your mother, Gabe, even if Jeffrey and I aren't living together anymore."

"It seems to me that conversation might be a little difficult," Gabe said dryly. "You don't want to talk about Dad, and I sure as hell don't plan to talk to you about DeWilde's. Not when you're threatening to open a rival store."

"A bridal store in San Francisco is hardly a threat to the DeWilde retail empire," Grace said. "Be reasonable, Gabe. What am I supposed to do with myself for the next thirty years? Sit at home and knit socks?"

He wanted her to spend the next thirty years in the same way that she'd spent the last thirty—with her husband. But he was too much his father's son to tell her that she was the heart and soul of their family and that he didn't know if he would ever be able to visit Kemberly again if she wasn't there to welcome him. Much as Gabe admired and loved his father, he had always known that Grace was the anchor of their family's relationships. Without her at the center, all of them would be adrift.

"You've chosen to leave DeWilde's," he said coolly, but what he wanted to say was, *You've chosen to leave me.* "I suppose since you've decided to take early retirement, you'll have to find a hobby, just like any other retiree. I don't see why your hobby needs to be a department store, however."

"I'm not sure why you feel the need to be deliberately rude, Gabe."

He wanted to apologize, but the words stuck in his throat—sharp, jagged lumps of resentment. "Thanks for giving me your new address, Mother. I'll be in touch with you sometime."

He hung up the phone, seething with anger that had no place to go. The concept of his mother as a retiree was not only insulting, it was laughable. Grace was the most dynamic, vital fifty-two-year-old he'd ever encountered, a woman constantly on the move, bursting with creative ideas, laughter never very far from her eyes.

For no apparent reason, an image of Lianne flashed into Gabe's mind, juxtaposed with his image of his mother. Lianne was laughing up at one of her coworkers, sketching improvements to the design of a bridal headdress with deft, nimble fingers. It was a scene he'd observed three or four times in the past few days since Lianne had started work at DeWilde's.

Gabe was suddenly able to identify the subtle discomfort that had been nagging at him whenever he was with Lianne. She and his mother were very much alike, he realized, strikingly so, in fact. Not in looks, of course, but in personality.

If Grace could break her husband's heart after thirty-two years of marriage, it seemed to Gabe that he would be every kind of a fool to embark on any sort of permanent relationship with Lianne—a woman who was endowed with all the same fatal charm as his mother.

And the same unreliability?

CHAPTER SEVEN

AFTER THE DEBACLE of their Sunday date, which ended with Gabe once again freezing her out with polite conversation, Lianne decided never to accept another invitation from him. She simply didn't need the grief in her busy life. It had been difficult enough trying to cope with her too-vivid memories of the night they'd made love, but it was well-nigh impossible to deal with the capriciously changing emotions and unsatisfied desire that the recent dates with Gabe had seemed to produce.

Her overwhelming urge to go to bed with him was disconcerting, to say the least. Looking back over the years at her tepid interest in sex, Lianne wasn't sure whether to bemoan her previous ignorance or curse the fact that her body was now well and truly aware of what all the fuss was about. Rather than analyze her own confused feelings, it seemed easier simply to feel angry with Gabriel DeWilde, who was, after all, the source of that confusion.

After Sunday, the only positive traits she could find about the wretched man were his great body and handsome profile, and the fact that he was darn good at his job. The great body and handsome profile she could train herself not to notice. At least she assumed that one day, when she was well into the bifocal years, she would eventually succeed in watching him walk by without an involuntary clenching of her stomach muscles and an immediate acceleration in her pulse rate.

Gabe's professional expertise was harder to overlook, since she was reporting directly to him, and final approval of the *Lianne for DeWilde* designs had to come from him. Seated across the desk from him on Thursday morning, Lianne watched him work through the cost sheets she'd prepared, aligning her estimates and procurement data with the finished sketches for each headdress, veil and jeweled comb. Every question he asked was insightful. Every comment or suggestion he made was valid. She wasn't sure whether to be struck dumb with admiration, or to be furious that he was always so damned right. She decided that, in the circumstances, fury was much the better way to go. She seethed silently, answering him in monosyllables, delighted to have an excuse to let her resentment build.

"I think that takes care of everything." Gabe pushed back his chair and gave her one of the polite, impersonal smiles he'd been lavishing on her for the past several days.

She returned his smile with a scowl, stacking her drawings and estimates into their appropriate folders in dour silence.

"Is something wrong?" Gabe asked mildly. "Lianne, if you don't agree with any of my suggestions, you must speak up. You're the designer. It's your name that's going on the label of the finished products, and it's important for you to feel happy with the way your designs are developed—"

"Your suggestions were all excellent," she snapped. "I'll have the revised estimates on your desk by the end of business hours tomorrow afternoon. Is that satisfactory?"

"We have until Monday," Gabe said quietly. "Don't work overtime on this, Lianne. You need to take it a bit easier for a couple of days. You're here when I arrive in the morning and you don't leave until seven or eight at night. Nobody can keep up that sort of pace indefinitely."

"Thank you for your concern," she said woodenly. "But I'll have the revised estimates on your desk by tomorrow afternoon."

"Damn it, Lianne, would you stop trying to prove you're Superwoman?" Gabe strode around his desk. "The estimates are due on Monday. Go home tonight at five o'clock. That's a direct order, okay?"

"Yes, sir." She touched her hand to her forehead in a mock salute. "You're the boss, sir."

The next thing she knew, her back was flat against the wall and Gabe's hands were splayed on either side of her head, his body fused with hers from shoulder to thigh. "You're driving me crazy," he said, grinding the words out between clenched teeth. "Totally damn crazy."

"Don't give me too much credit," she snapped.

He didn't bother to answer, just slammed his mouth over hers, his kiss hard, demanding, almost brutal. His hands were hot against the bare skin of her rib cage. It was a moment before Lianne realized that he'd tugged her blouse out of her skirt and thrust his hands underneath her camisole. Another moment before she realized that the shock of reaction she felt was pleasure, not outrage. She closed her eyes, letting the impact of his touch explode into every cell and fiber of her being.

He finally lifted his head, but he didn't move away. His breath came swiftly. His eyes glittered. Color darkened his cheekbones. She wondered if she looked as thoroughly and completely aroused as he did.

"Come back to my flat," he said. "Now."

She braced her hands against the wall to prevent her knees from buckling. "No."

"You want me."

"Yes." She kept her gaze locked with his. "I wanted you on Sunday, too, and look what that got me."

A grim smile flickered across his face. "Trust me, Lianne, this time I won't send you away."

She stiffened. "You're right about that, Gabe. You won't send me away, because I'm not going anywhere with you. Especially not into your bed. You've blown your last chance with me."

"I screwed up," he said. "Lianne, I'm really sorry. There's not much I can do except apologize for the way I behaved on Sunday. I let problems within my own family interfere with our relationship."

"And how about on Wednesday?" she asked. "Are you apologizing for that, too? And then there was that delightful little outing on Saturday, since we're reminiscing about past encounters. I'm not a masochist, Gabe. I like to have fun on my dates. So far, fun has been spectacularly missing from our relationship."

Jeffrey DeWilde's voice carried from the doorway. "Gabe, if you could spare me a moment out of your busy schedule, I need you in my office. Immediately, please."

"Yes, sir. I'll be with you in a moment." Gabe moved away slowly, giving Lianne a couple of seconds to straighten her clothes. He turned around to face his father. "I was just inviting Lianne to join us at the theater tonight. She's been kind enough to agree to come with us."

Jeffrey's patrician gaze flicked briefly toward Lianne, and she resisted the urge to run her fingers up and down the buttons on her blouse to make sure they were all closed.

"How very good of you to fill in at such short notice," Jeffrey said with cool irony. "But I gather the invitation my son extended was quite—enthusiastic. I'm delighted you'll be joining us." He stepped back into the corridor without waiting for her to reply. "Gabe, in my office. Now."

"Give me two minutes, please." Gabe closed the door behind his father and swung around, leaning against it. Lianne didn't give him the chance to speak. She exploded.

"Of all the despicable, lowdown, dirty tricks, that has to be the worst! What was all that garbage you fed me the other day about how oppressed you felt by the DeWilde name, and how you hated people to think you'd take advantage of it? I can't believe you actually stooped to using your father's position in the company to coerce me into accepting an invitation from you. Well, it won't work, Gabe. I'm not coming."

"You've every right to be angry—"

"Don't you dare patronize me! Damn right I'm angry—"

"Let me explain. It's the opening night at the Royal Shakespeare for their new production of *Richard II*. It's a gala performance in aid of the new pediatric cancer unit at the Great Ormond Street Children's Hospital. My mother was chairwoman for the benefit and my father's filling in for her at the last minute. Even if you don't want to spend time with me, the fact is you'd be doing my father a real favor if you'd come. I think it will help him to get through a difficult few hours if he has people around that he's forced to entertain. He needs to think about something other than the fact that Grace organized all of this and she isn't here to enjoy the success of her hard work."

Some of Lianne's anger faded, but she wasn't about to let him off the hook that easily. "I don't respond well to intimidation, Gabe, however much sugar coating you slap over the top."

"If it makes you feel any better, there'll be half a dozen other people in our party. You don't have to speak to me all night if you'd prefer not to."

"Is that a promise?"

"It's a promise."

"On those terms, it seems a shame to miss out on a great opportunity. Thank you. *Richard II* is probably my favorite of Shakespeare's historical plays."

"Then I'll pick you up at six-thirty," Gabe said quickly. "It's a black-tie affair, by the way." He left the room before she had time to point out that it would be a great deal easier to avoid speaking to him if she took a cab.

"Ah, Gabriel, I'm glad that you finally found yourself free to join us." His father's greeting carried a sardonic note that Gabe found oddly comforting, perhaps because Jeffrey's habitual irony had been so conspicuously absent since his wife's departure.

"Sorry to have kept you waiting, sir."

"Yes, you appeared to be working with quite remarkable intensity. I trust your—project—was brought to a successful conclusion?"

"More successful than might have been expected," Gabe said wryly, his gaze flicking to the other occupant of the room—a tall, dark, powerfully built man who stood silently by the window.

"Good. Well, now that you're here, I'd like to introduce you to Nick Santos. He just arrived on this morning's flight from New York." Jeffrey gestured to the man by the window, who stepped forward, right hand outstretched, left hand holding his briefcase. "Gabriel."

An impressive man, Gabe thought, shaking Nick Santos's hand and wondering who he was and what he was doing in Jeffrey's office. "Welcome to London," he said. "Did you have a good flight?"

"Uneventful." Nick's voice was deep, his accent hard to pinpoint. "In the circumstances, uneventful was about the best I could hope for."

"That sounds ominous. Is there a problem?" Gabe asked, looking from Nick to his father.

"You could say that." Jeffrey's voice was dry. "Nick brought me something from New York that I want you to see." He got up, depressing the intercom button as he walked around his desk. "Hold my calls, Monica, please. I don't want to be interrupted for the next half hour."

He crossed to the door of his office and turned the key in the lock. Then he drew the drapes and switched on the overhead lights. Gabe frowned, puzzled and a little alarmed by such strange behavior. His father had seemed more at peace with himself and the world for the past day or two. Gabe hoped that peace hadn't been illusory or the first signs of an impending breakdown.

His office arranged to his satisfaction, Jeffrey sat back down behind his desk. "All right, Nick, I believe we're now ready to relieve you of your baggage."

Nick walked silently to Jeffrey's desk. The briefcase he held in his left hand was one of the aluminum styles advertised as indestructible by the manufacturer. Gabe's eyes widened when Nick pulled up the sleeve of his conservative business suit and revealed a set of workmanlike steel handcuffs that attached the case to his wrist.

For the first time a faint smile flickered in Nick's dark eyes. "I sincerely hope you have the keys to unlock these cuffs, Mr. DeWilde. Otherwise we're going to need a blow torch."

Jeffrey opened his desk drawer and took out a small key on a heavy chain. "I have it here." He leaned across the desk and unlocked the cuffs. Nick caught them expertly, as if he'd worked that maneuver many times before. Then he gently set the aluminum case in the space Jeffrey had cleared in the center of his desk. "Do you want to open it, Mr. DeWilde?"

Jeffrey shook his head. "No, go ahead. You brought it here, you do the honors."

The briefcase was closed by two numerical combination locks. Nick took thirty seconds or so to align the tumblers. Then he pressed the latches and lifted the lid of the case.

Jeffrey gave a small murmur of satisfaction, but Gabe was stunned into silence. He stared in blank astonishment at the glittering tiara nestled on a custom-designed bed of padded blue satin. Braided rows of sparkling diamonds refracted the glow of the overhead lights, creating a rainbow of fiery color. At the front of the tiara, six teardrop pearls—famous for the exquisite symmetry of their shape—shimmered in opalescent splendor, each suspended from a four-carat diamond of superlative brilliance and clarity.

Since he'd walked past the real Empress Eugénie tiara when he came into the store that morning, Gabe realized he must be looking at a copy. But what a magnificent copy! He picked the tiara up and examined it more closely, wishing he had his loupe with him. He'd been around gems and jewelry all his life, and he'd never seen a fake of this caliber. Frowning, he set the tiara back in the case and looked at his father.

"Is it paste?" he asked. "Or were there two tiaras made for Empress Eugénie?"

"No, there's only one Empress Eugénie tiara," Jeffrey said.

Gabe held the tiara closer to the light. "The workmanship is extraordinary. If I didn't know better, I'd swear these pearls were genuine. It must have cost a small fortune to make an imitation this good, even using zircons instead of diamonds. Why would anyone bother?"

"It isn't paste," Jeffrey said, reaching inside his drawer and handing Gabe a loupe. "Look for yourself and you'll see. Not only are the stones real, this is the original Empress Eugénie tiara. The one and only genuine article. I authenticated it myself four weeks ago."

"My God!" Gabe screwed the loupe to his eye and stared at approximately three-and-a-half million pounds' worth of gems and history perched on his father's desk. "How did it get up here?"

"I brought it with me from New York," Nick Santos said. "It made for a wakeful night, knowing that I had nearly six million dollars' worth of famous jewels manacled to my wrist."

Gabe set the loupe down. "You brought it from New York?" He stared at Nick, hardly able to believe his ears. "Bloody hell, Dad, the executives at the insurance company would have a collective heart attack if they knew we'd taken the tiara out of the display case. Lord alone knows what they'd do if they heard it had made a trip to New York and back again!"

"The insurance executives wouldn't give a damn if they knew we had it sitting here on my desk," Jeffrey said. "And they wouldn't care if Nick had dropped it into the middle of the Atlantic." He gave a wintry smile. "The tiara isn't insured."

The niggling fear that his father was teetering toward a breakdown returned to haunt Gabe. He spoke with careful calm. "Of course it's insured, Dad. Your father put the entire DeWilde jewelry collection into a family trust sometime way back in the fifties, and we use two companies to insure the collection—Global Associates and Commonwealth International, remember? I'm not sure which company has this particular piece on their books—"

"Commonwealth International thinks the tiara is insured by Global, and Global thinks it's insured by Commonwealth," Jeffrey said. "Actually, it's insured by neither company for the simple reason that until six weeks ago I had no idea the tiara still existed. I assumed it had been broken down into its component parts decades ago."

His father sounded in full command of his faculties. In fact, Gabe thought that he looked rather more cheerful than he had at any time since the devastating announcement of Grace's departure. "Dad, we have fifteen thousand pounds' worth of electronic surveillance equipment sitting downstairs in the middle of the store, guarding the Empress Eugénie tiara. We had that equipment installed because the insurance company demanded it."

"Well, that's what I told people when we arranged for a new storewide security system. But actually, I spent all that money on elaborate electronic security devices for the tiara because it made the setup downstairs look more authentic, as if we really had something to protect. In this day and age, nobody would believe we had a three million pound tiara on display unless we also had some very visible security."

Gabe went cold. He was beginning to understand—and wished he wasn't. "Dad, you can't possibly be telling me that the tiara we have on display downstairs is a fake?"

"That's exactly what I'm telling you," Jeffrey said, confirming Gabe's fear. "The tiara we have on display in the store is an expensive, well-made fake, with a 22-karat-gold setting, but not a genuine gemstone anywhere in the entire piece."

Gabe sat down abruptly. "Let's start this story from the beginning, shall we? All of a sudden I feel as if we're speaking a different language."

"This may take a while," Jeffrey said. "Do you have any meetings you need to reschedule?"

"Nothing until this afternoon."

"Then the first thing to make clear is that everything we say here this morning is to remain strictly confidential for reasons I'm sure will soon become apparent. I plan to fill Megan in on what's happening at lunch tomorrow, since she'll be here for the gala tonight."

Gabe would have sworn that he didn't so much as glance toward Nick, but the American picked up instantly on Gabe's unspoken question. The man obviously had great instincts. "I'm a private investigator," he said. "Your father approached me last month and asked me to make some inquiries for him regarding the provenance of the tiara you see sitting on his desk."

"Nick came to me with the highest possible recommendations," Jeffrey said. "He was a lieutenant with the San Francisco Police Department until a couple of years ago, and he's been very successful in solving some high profile cases since then. Anyway, apart from you, Megan and Nick, I see no reason to involve anyone else in the situation, at least for the moment."

"Shouldn't we alert the board of directors—"

"No." Jeffrey shook his head. "The jewels are owned personally by the DeWilde trust, so this is strictly a family matter, although—unfortunately—I think it's a family matter that might have an unfavorable impact on the reputation of the company, not to mention the share price. Nick has been hired by me personally, not by the DeWilde Corporation."

The DeWilde organization recently seemed to be suffering from more than its share of "family matters" that threatened to impact the share price, Gabe thought ruefully. "If it's strictly a family matter, shouldn't we tell Kate?" he said.

Jeffrey steepled his fingers. "There's absolutely nothing she could do about the situation, and she's under so much pressure with her studies right now that there seems no reason to burden her with extraneous problems she can't hope to resolve."

"All right," Gabe agreed. He glanced at his father, and Grace's name flashed silently between them. Neither of them spoke the name out loud, but it reverberated between them nonetheless. Was Grace the reason why his father didn't want to bring Kate into these discussions? Because she was in San Francisco and might say something to her mother? Did his father's mistrust of Grace now extend that far? Gabe wondered bleakly.

"We're going to have to hash over a fair bit of family history, so let's get started," Jeffrey said, glossing over the tense moment. "Do you ever remember hearing anyone mention my uncle Dirk DeWilde?"

"Yes, but I can't remember much about him," Gabe said. "Wait, wasn't he Grandfather's older brother? He founded the DeWilde store in New York, but he died in the Second World War, or something like that. There are several pictures of him at Kemberly. He was very good-looking, if I'm remembering the right person."

"That's the one," Jeffrey agreed. "As you said, he was my father's elder brother, and the major heir to the various DeWilde enterprises. But he didn't die in the war. He disappeared a couple of years later, sometime early in 1948, I believe."

"You believe?" Gabe said. "Don't you know? I mean, it's rather difficult to mislay an uncle."

"You would think so, wouldn't you?" Jeffrey said ruefully. "But deciding exactly what happened nearly fifty years ago isn't as easy as it sounds, especially since Dirk's disappearance was always treated as a family secret of the highest order."

"Had he done something horribly scandalous?"

"Possibly. Or possibly not." Jeffrey sounded resigned. "Nowadays, what with the gossip journals, tabloids and TV talk shows, it's almost impossible to put ourselves back into the mind-set of people who believed that there was no family scandal too small to cause social ruin, or too huge to be swept under the rug. Incredible as it may seem, I can't find out precisely when Dirk disappeared, or even if he had a good reason for disappearing. I don't know if he ran away because of strictly personal reasons, or if he was fleeing two steps ahead of the law after committing some terrible crime. All I know is what my father chose to tell me when I became managing director of the London store, which was astonishingly little."

"And what did your father tell you?" Gabe asked, intrigued by this introduction to a family mystery.

"Basically my father explained that Dirk had always been a man with a restless spirit, and that he seemed to find it exceptionally hard to settle down into the routine of running the New York store after four years of working as a battle-hardened Marine Corps intelligence officer, with hundreds of lives hanging on the outcome of his missions. According to my father, Dirk struggled along for a couple of years after the war, but he allowed a lot of important business to slide. Then, in April of 1948, he handed in his resignation as president of the American branch of DeWilde's and sent a notarized letter to my father saying that he was relinquishing all rights to the DeWilde family property, including the inheritance due to him under his parents' will. Then he disappeared."

"What do you mean, he disappeared? Presumably we're not talking *pouf*, in a cloud of colored smoke."

"I don't know what I mean precisely." Jeffrey sounded frustrated at giving the same unsatisfactory answer he'd given before. "Transatlantic phone calls in those days cost an absolute fortune, so my father sent a few cables asking his brother to clarify what was going on and where he could be reached. Dirk didn't respond, but as far as I can tell, nobody paid much attention at the time. They knew he had a restless spirit and assumed he'd taken off on an extended vacation and would eventually return."

"Somebody must have worried about the business aspects of his disappearance," Gabe pointed out. "What about DeWilde's, New York? When Dirk left, who was minding the store?"

"That's when your great-uncle Henry was sent to

take charge," Jeffrey explained. "But right from the start, Henry seems to have been overwhelmed by the day-to-day tasks associated with running the store. He'd stepped into a crisis situation, and he certainly didn't spend any time searching for his missing brother." Jeffrey looked disapproving, as he usually did when the New York store was mentioned. "With Henry supposedly in charge, DeWilde's Fifth Avenue location quickly went from being the most profitable of our stores to being the least profitable."

Having worked at both Tiffany and Bloomingdale's in Manhattan, Gabe was well aware of the problems DeWilde's still faced in the competitive New York retail market, and the antics of Henry's large brood of children didn't help to improve the situation. Sloan DeWilde, Henry's son, was nominally in charge of running the store, although he'd never shown much interest in the place. He had plenty of talent and an incisive, clever mind. But so far, nobody had been able to find the key that would unlock Sloan's talents and persuade him to apply himself to the demanding task of making the New York store profitable.

Still, this wasn't the time to deal with the problems of DeWilde's Fifth Avenue store. "What happened when Dirk didn't come back from his supposed vacation?" Gabe asked.

"From what my father told me, it seems that serious efforts to find out where Dirk had run off to weren't started until the family received a letter from him saying that he was well and happy, but he had no intention of returning to the stranglehold of the DeWilde family business ever again."

Gabe felt a moment of empathy with his long-vanished uncle. He could certainly understand why Dirk might have felt the need to distance himself from the oppressive weight of family duties and obligations. "Where was the letter posted from?" he asked. "Surely that would have been a good place to start looking for him?"

"It was posted in Hong Kong, and naturally, that was the first place the family searched for him. My father hired a Pinkerton's detective early in 1949, and he spent almost two years looking for Dirk. They never found a trace of him, and in the end, my father gave up and called off the search."

"How old were you in 1948?" Gabe asked his father. "Seven? Eight? Don't you remember hearing anything about your uncle's disappearance at the time it happened?"

"Unfortunately not. I'm sure it was discussed, but perhaps not in my presence. Or else anything I may have heard must have passed in one ear and out the other. I don't even remember being curious about the fact that he'd disappeared. You have to realize that he'd been living in New York, so I'd never met him personally. Uncle Dirk was simply a name to me."

"And I suppose you were still very young to understand the ramifications of his sudden disappearance."

"Yes, but quite apart from that, the war created a lot of very strange circumstances, and Dirk's disappearance just seemed part and parcel of the general madness. The situation in our family was especially strange because we had so many different nationalities within the same generation. In fact, to give you an example of the oddities of our family heritage, my father and my two uncles all fought in World War II, but they each fought for a different country."

"I remember Grandfather Charles talking about

that," Gabe said. "Henry was in the Royal Air Force, wasn't he? Dirk was in the U.S. Marine Corps, and Grandfather Charles joined the French army. I'd never really stopped to think how bizarre that was. How in the world did it happen that way?"

"The day after Britain declared war against Nazi Germany in 1939, my father was packed off to Brazil by his parents, specifically so that he wouldn't be called up to active duty. He had a history of rheumatic fever, and my grandparents decided his heart would never stand the strain of military service. That didn't sit too well with him, since Uncle Henry was already training to fly fighter planes for the RAF and my father didn't intend to be outdone by his little brother. So after the fall of France in 1940, he defied my grandfather's orders to stay in Brazil, sneaked back to England with my mother, and signed on to fight with the Free French Army, which was being organized by General de Gaulle."

"Why the French army, though?"

"You have to remember that he'd been born in France, and he was trilingual in French, English and Dutch. And the medical exam probably wasn't as stringent as it would have been for the British army because General de Gaulle was desperate for volunteers. He needed all the men he could recruit."

"What about you?" Gabe asked. "Had you already been born when Grandfather Charles joined the army?"

"No, I was born three or four months after he'd shipped out on some secret mission to North Africa, so for the first five years of my life, I grew up not sure whether I actually had a father. When he did finally return from the war, from my childish perspective, it was as if he'd just arbitrarily popped up out of nowhere, and for a couple of years I was always waiting for him to vanish again, just as inexplicably as he'd appeared."

Gabe shook his head. "Good Lord, Dad, I bet all the child psychologists would have a field day hearing about that setup. The war must have played havoc with an entire generation of children's psyches."

"I'm sure it did. That may be why the disappearance of Uncle Dirk aroused so little interest on my part. It was simply part of the pattern I considered normal. I expected people in my family to vanish and reappear with no apparent rhyme nor reason. Just as I expected houses to be standing one day and destroyed by a bomb the next."

Gabe's grandfather, Jeffrey's father, had been dead for several years. But his grandmother was still alive, an active eighty-year-old with a keen wit and the energy of many women half her age. No wonder Grandmother Mary had always struck him as a woman of endless courage, Gabe thought. She would have needed an indomitable spirit to raise her son with bombs raining down nightly and no idea whether her husband would survive to see the child he'd fathered.

"I can't even begin to imagine how families learned to carry on for weeks or months at a stretch with no idea if the people they loved were alive or dead," Gabe said.

"And as if six years of wartime uncertainty weren't bad enough, you have to remember that conditions didn't normalize in 1945 just because the fighting finally stopped," Jeffrey said. "All across Europe there were thousands of prisoners to be repatriated, millions of soldiers to be returned to civilian life, whole cities to be rebuilt that had been wiped off the map, factories to be converted from producing weapons to producing consumer products. There was such a profound sense of relief that the bombs had stopped falling and the guns weren't firing anymore that we tend to gloss over the fact that there was absolute chaos over most of Europe for at least another three years."

Nick looked thoughtful. "I hadn't considered that," he said. "Once Dirk decided to disappear, it would have been a lot easier to succeed in 1948 than it would be nowadays, especially with his international background."

"That's very true," Jeffrey agreed. "Virtually every country in Europe had missing records, and officials in countries that had been under Nazi rule often deliberately falsified their records. Not to mention all the confusion caused by people fleeing in front of the advancing Soviet armies of occupation. Hundreds of thousands of people couldn't prove their citizenship, and the authorities more or less had to take their word as to who they were and where they'd come from. If Dirk went back to Europe, he could easily have claimed that his birth certificate was destroyed. With only a little finagling, he could have acquired a new passport and documentation in almost any name he pleased."

"It's possible that he changed his name," Gabe conceded. "But surely there's also the possibility that he disappeared because he died. Aren't you discounting that rather too casually?"

"He's almost certainly dead by now," Jeffrey said. "Either that, or he's an old man well into his nineties. But my father and Uncle Henry were both convinced that he voluntarily chose to disappear in 1948. To his dying day, my father never expressed any doubt at all that Dirk was alive and well somewhere. He just didn't know where."

"I've run some checks of my own," Nick Santos said. "And I haven't turned up any evidence of foul play. Working with some old documents your father found at Kemberly, I managed to discover that Dirk maintained checking accounts with two banks in New York. Both accounts were closed within hours of each other on April 24, 1948, giving Dirk a combined payout of $2,700. Which was a lot more money in 1948 than it is today, of course. His bank account in London was closed a month later, on May 20. The last check drawn on his London account was for £1,352, payable through a corresponding bank branch in Hong Kong."

"Hong Kong again!" Gabe exclaimed. "That's where Dirk's final letter came from, isn't it? And, Dad, didn't you just say he fought in the Far East during the war?" Gabe's imagination took flight. "Maybe he fell in love with a Chinese woman during the war and went back to marry her. God knows, it wouldn't have been easy to make an interracial marriage in those days, so perhaps he decided to cut his ties and live with her in peaceful obscurity."

"My father considered that possibility," Jeffrey said. "But if Dirk set up residence in Hong Kong, with or without a wife, he covered his tracks well. As I told you, Pinkerton's sent one of their Far Eastern specialists out there in 1949, and they couldn't turn up a trace of him."

"All this is very interesting," Gabe said. "But I can't imagine why we need to keep his disappearance a secret now, fifty years later. These days it would be considered a definite social plus if we announced that Uncle Dirk had had the courage of his convictions and defied cultural and racial prejudice for the sake of love. And I certainly don't see the connection between Uncle Dirk's disappearance and the fact that we have fifteen thousand pounds' worth of surveillance equipment downstairs guarding a fake tiara that's worth less than the equipment beaming down on it."

"There's a very direct connection," Nick Santos said grimly. "There seems to be a strong likelihood that Dirk DeWilde stole some of the family jewels before he fled to places unknown. Six pieces, in fact, including the Empress Eugénie tiara, the most famous and valuable piece in the entire collection."

Gabe whistled softly. "Good Lord, I should have realized. Of course! He gave up his share of the DeWilde inheritance and helped himself to the family jewels in exchange."

"Unfortunately, it's not quite that simple," Jeffrey said. "We don't know for certain if Dirk stole the missing jewels."

"What?" Gabe stared at his father in disbelief. "And nobody took steps to find out for sure?"

Jeffrey smiled. "It's incredible, isn't it? But fear of scandal seemed to override every other concern in those days, and finding out the truth would have been so messy, requiring people to open a lot of cupboard doors where there were very bony skeletons. Dirk had already been gone for almost three months when several pieces in the London collection were scheduled for a routine inspection and cleaning. In those days, the cleaning was done by an old family friend, an elderly jeweler who'd worked with my grandparents in Amsterdam and had emigrated to London just before the start of the Second World War. He came to my father with the stunning news that the tiara he'd been given for cleaning was a copy—a first-rate fake, superlatively well crafted, but a fake nonetheless. You can imagine the consternation that ensued. The jeweler was sworn to secrecy—he's dead now, of course—and my father personally made an inspection of every piece in the collection, including the items normally kept in New York and Paris. He discovered that there were five other pieces, in addition to the tiara, that were copies."

"There doesn't seem to be much of a mystery about what happened," Gabe said. "Doesn't it seem logical that Uncle Dirk decided to supplement his retirement benefits by helping himself to the family jewels?"

Jeffrey smiled wryly. "I don't know," he said. "My father estimated that during the three months between Dirk's disappearance and the discovery of the missing jewels, thirteen people had access to at least one of the missing pieces. Four people had access to all six of them—my father and his brother Henry in London, his sister, Marie-Claire du Plessis, in Paris, and his brother Dirk in New York."

"Even so, surely Dirk is the logical suspect," Gabe said. "Your father knew he hadn't stolen the jewels. There was no reason for Henry or Marie-Claire to steal them. Which leaves good old Uncle Dirk as the guilty party."

"You're leaping to conclusions," Nick said. "Your Uncle Henry enjoyed a very expensive life-style, and his income was tied directly to the profits of the store he ran. Which, as your father has pointed out, wasn't very profitable. He could obviously have benefited from the extra income the jewels provided."

"But Uncle Henry married money," Gabe objected. "Aunt Maura comes from the Connecticut Kellys, and her family has oodles of money. They aren't quite on a level with the Gettys or the Rockefellers, but Henry didn't need to steal jewelry in order to keep a private plane, drink French champagne every night and smoke Havana cigars after dinner."

"Henry didn't marry Maura until 1956, years after the thefts," Jeffrey said. "And my father always suspected that Henry knew more about Dirk's disappearance than he let on. In fact, I think my father was more suspicious of Henry than he was of Dirk."

"That would explain some of the hostility I always felt simmering between Grandfather and Uncle Henry even as a little kid," Gabe said. "And I certainly never understood why he was so hostile toward our cousins."

"Possibly it was because they are, by and large, as lazy and hedonistic as Henry himself," Jeffrey said austerely.

Gabe captured a gleam of laughter in Nick's dark eyes that vanished almost as soon as it came. He bit back a smile of his own. On the subject of hard work, knuckling down to business and treating life seriously, his father had a tendency to be somewhat pompous.

"It's also possible that two or more people were working together on the thefts," Nick pointed out. "There are four people who each had access to more than one of the missing pieces. By joining forces, it turns out that any combination of them could have stolen them all. And, surprisingly, your great-aunt Marie-Claire might have had a motive. She was once very much in love with a man called Armand de Villeneuve, who chose to leave Paris almost at the same time as Dirk disappeared from New York. As you may know, Armand de Villeneuve eventually turned up again as the founder of a very successful textile company in Hong Kong. And your father tells me that nobody knows where his start-up capital came from."

He did indeed know of Armand de Villeneuve, Gabe

thought grimly. And Philippe de Villeneuve, Armand's son, who seemed to bear a determined grudge against the DeWilde family. "I think it's ridiculous to ignore all these links to Hong Kong and pretend they're just coincidences," he said. "But no matter who stole the missing jewels, I still don't understand why we have a fake tiara enshrined in bullet-proof glass downstairs, and why Nick just brought the genuine, long-lost Empress Eugénie tiara across the Atlantic from New York. What was it doing there? And, Dad, if you dare say 'I don't know' one more time, I think I may do you a mortal injury."

Jeffrey smiled, the first genuinely amused smile Gabe had seen in ten days. He felt a surge of relief. If puzzling over a fifty-year-old mystery could keep his father from obsessing about Grace, Gabe hoped the mystery would take another fifty years to solve. "I'll answer the first part of your question," Jeffrey said. "We have a fake tiara on display downstairs because your grandfather had no idea how he could announce that the real one had been stolen without immediately casting suspicion of theft on all three of his siblings."

"At least if he'd spoken up, there'd have been more chance of unearthing the real thief," Gabe said, unconvinced by his grandfather's rationale. "And there's a strong probability we wouldn't be scrambling around wondering what happened to Uncle Dirk fifty years after the fact."

"True, but there was another, more profound, reason for my father's reluctance to reveal the theft. All through the war, even during the height of the blitz, DeWilde's prided itself on keeping the Empress Eugénie tiara on display, just as it had been ever since the day the London store first opened. That gesture of defiance generated tremendous amounts of favorable publicity for the store. And what was more important, Londoners came to regard the tiara as a symbol of hope and beauty in a world that was singularly short of both. With those memories fresh in everyone's mind, can you imagine how upsetting it would have been if my father had announced in 1948 that he was sorry, but he'd just realized the tiara was a fake?"

"That might have been a reasonable decision in 1948," Gabe said. "But we've had almost half a century since then to break the sad news."

"Once my father initiated the deception, the whole embarrassing situation just snowballed," Jeffrey said. "I didn't hear the true story until fourteen years ago, when I became managing director. At that point, we were beginning negotiations to take the company public, and it certainly didn't seem appropriate to announce to the world that DeWilde senior management had practiced a thirty-four-year-old fraud on the general public. The fact is, Gabe, the longer the deception went on, the more impossible it became to rectify it. Hence the godawful mess we found ourselves in when a jeweler called me from New York three weeks ago and said that, as far as he could tell, he'd just been offered the chance to buy the Empress Eugénie tiara."

"Is that why you flew to New York with such urgency that you had to miss Mother's birthday?" Gabe asked.

"Yes, and she thought that I was going to mee—" Jeffrey broke off in midword, bleakness returning to his eyes. "The jeweler agreed to keep our negotiations secret for forty-eight hours but no longer. I had no choice but to go."

His mother had obviously been deeply hurt by Jeffrey's absence on her birthday. Gabe wondered why in the world his father hadn't simply explained the truth of the situation to Grace, but with Nick in the room he didn't like to ask such a personal question. "You were able to confirm on that visit that it was the genuine Empress Eugénie tiara?" he asked, hoping to bring his father's attention back to the mystery and away from Grace.

"Yes," Jeffrey said. "We have the original descriptions of the major stones. We also have technically enhanced insurance photographs dating back to 1926, when your great-grandfather Max bought the tiara as an anniversary gift for his wife. There's no doubt that the tiara sitting on my desk is the tiara that Max bought from Eugénie's heirs."

Gabe frowned. "If the tiara has survived almost fifty years, then it seems as if whoever stole it didn't take it for the money, after all. Otherwise, surely it would have been broken up and sold years ago."

"You would think so," Jeffrey agreed. "Nick, you told me on the phone that you'd made some headway in discovering how the tiara ended up being offered for sale at Blackstone's in New York?"

"Yes, sir, and I think you're going to be surprised," Nick said. "Apparently the tiara was on prominent display in the window of a well-known Australian jewelry store, where it was spotted by a visiting American who'd just won six million dollars in the Florida state lottery. He bought it for his wife, who decided when she got back to the States that she didn't have all that many occasions to wear a diamond tiara and would rather have a yacht instead. Her husband sold it to Blackstone's Miami branch, where it was finally recognized as so nearly identical to the Empress Eugénie tiara, famously kept on display in DeWilde's London store, that Mr. Blackstone, Sr., called you to find out if he was dealing in stolen property."

"What did you tell him, Dad?"

"I told him very little," Jeffrey said dryly, "and Mr. Blackstone, a jeweler of infinite tact, was kind enough to ask only sufficient questions to make sure that he was not involved in a crime. Then he sold me back my own property, at a price that would have bought the English Crown Jewels in 1948. Now that I'd acquired the tiara, the next problem was what to do with it. I couldn't just pack it in my suitcase and bring it home with me. The damn fake we have on display downstairs precluded that option. How was I supposed to explain to Customs that I was bringing home a tiara that officially was already safely installed behind plate-glass security on the ground floor of DeWilde's?"

"So you hired Nick."

"Yes." A trace of color momentarily darkened Jeffrey's cheeks. "As I told you earlier, he came very highly recommended."

"I'm a good friend of Allison Ames," Nick said. "We once worked together on a case that involved breaches of security at an American electronics company with a major telecommunications branch in France."

"Who is Allison Ames?" Gabe asked blankly.

"She owns the security firm of Alliance de Securité Internationale," Jeffrey said smoothly. Too smoothly, Gabe thought, scrutinizing his father with suddenly heightened intensity. Jeffrey was looking at Nick and seemed unaware of his son's searching gaze. Or was he deliberately avoiding Gabe's eyes? Some sixth sense told Gabe that he had stumbled onto a name that his father would have preferred to remain unmentioned.

Jeffrey turned to the detective, not giving Gabe a chance to ask any more questions. "Nick, you say the tiara was on prominent display in an Australian jewelry store with an international reputation. Now, that's a mystery in itself. I can't imagine how any jeweler of repute ever bought the tiara in the first place. I wouldn't have thought there was an experienced jeweler anywhere in the world who isn't familiar with the piece. What's the name of the store?"

"H. Morgenstern and Sons," Nick said. "I understand that Harry Morgenstern, the original founder of the store, is still active in the business despite the fact that he's in his eighties."

"Morgenstern...Harry Morgenstern..." Jeffrey stared unseeingly into the distance. "Hmm, that name's vaguely familiar, and Mr. Morgenstern's reputation used to be excellent, if I'm remembering the right man. We've even done business with his store, before Ryder opened a branch of DeWilde's in Sydney. Mr. Morgenstern emigrated from Germany to Australia in the thirties, getting his family to safety two steps ahead of the Nazi storm troopers. Have you managed to find out how he acquired the piece, Nick? If we knew that, we could decide whether or not to trust him with the information that five other pieces are still missing."

"I can't get him to talk to me," Nick said. "I've written, faxed and phoned. So far, although I've spoken to three different assistants, I've never yet managed to speak to Harry Morgenstern himself. In fact, I decided it would be much better if I went out to Sydney and dealt with him in person, if I have your permission to authorize the expense, Mr. DeWilde. That way, I'll be on the spot if he suggests any leads that need to be tracked down in a hurry."

"Excellent idea. How soon can you go?"

"Tomorrow?" Nick suggested "Provided there's room on the London to Sydney flight, that is."

"Ask Monica to book your ticket. She has friends at all the airline reservation desks. And she'll find you a quiet room in a comfortable hotel for tonight, too."

"In the meantime, what are we going to do with the tiara?" Gabe asked.

Jeffrey pointed to his wall safe, hidden rather obviously behind a portrait of Maximilien and Anne Marie DeWilde, the matriarch and patriarch who had founded the DeWilde family fortune in Amsterdam during the previous century. "That's the safest place I can think of—at least without causing a great deal of speculation."

Nick walked across the room and examined the safe. "Any serious jewel thief would be able to crack this in less than five minutes," he said.

"But first the jewel thief would have to know there's something in there that's worth stealing," Jeffrey pointed out. "Besides, I don't see that I have any alternative until I can work out a plan for switching this tiara with the fake downstairs."

Nick grinned. "You should hire Allison Ames. She's a whiz at that sort of thing. Better than any cat burglar I've ever encountered."

"I'd prefer not to bring another outsider into this," Jeffrey said austerely. "Fortunately, I have access to all the security codes protecting the display case downstairs. It shouldn't be too difficult a task to switch tiaras one night soon. In the meantime, this safe will have to do." He closed the tiara into its carrying case and walked quickly over to the safe, putting the case inside and locking the safe door.

"There, it's done." He turned around, permitting himself a small smile. "That felt very good," he said. "After almost fifty years of wandering in the wilderness, Empress Eugénie's tiara is back where it belongs."

CHAPTER EIGHT

BY THE TIME she'd changed her outfit four times, Lianne was willing to concede that she wasn't behaving like a woman who planned to ignore her escort for the entire evening. Tossing aside her bra, she discarded the ivory stockings she'd worn with the last dress she'd tried on and wriggled into a pair of iridescent black panty hose. Scowling into the mirror, she stepped back into the plain black silk crepe sheath that was the first dress she'd put on thirty minutes ago. She zipped it closed before she could change her mind yet again.

She turned sideways and squinted at herself from the new angle. Now that she'd taken off her bra and panties, at least the lines of the darn dress were smooth, and the couple of pounds she'd lost over the past ten days had resulted in a satisfyingly flat stomach. But wasn't the dress too short and too lacking in glitter for a black-tie affair, even with the fancy stockings? And there seemed to be a heck of a lot of bare skin in the space between her chin and her breasts. Sighing—she knew that tonight, nothing was going to look quite perfect enough to meet her impossible standards—she sprayed herself with a light cloud of perfume and slipped into her highheeled black evening shoes. This was it. She was not going to humiliate herself by changing yet again.

At least her hair, by some miracle, was deciding to cooperate. For once, the unruly mass of curls had allowed itself to be tamed into a semblance of upswept sophistication, and she rather liked the effect of the few wisps that had already tumbled down to coil haphazardly against her neck. She clipped on a pair of outsize crystal earrings that she'd designed and made herself. They were long enough to touch her bare shoulders, and she decided not to wear any other jewelry, not even a watch, so that their impact would be all the more powerful.

She picked up her black evening purse from the bed and walked into the sitting room. Julia was correcting student papers, and she looked up with a smile when Lianne walked into the room. She gave a gasp of heartfelt approval. "Wow, Lianne, you're going to knock 'em dead. That dress looks stunning." She grinned. "Of course, the great body inside doesn't hurt the effect."

"Thank you." Lianne couldn't think of anything else to say. If her date had been with anyone other than Gabriel DeWilde, she knew quite well that she and Julia would have spent the past hour together, examining the joint contents of their wardrobes, pooling the resources of their cosmetic and jewelry drawers, laughing and joking as they made their final choices. She twisted her purse awkwardly, with hands that weren't quite steady.

"Gabe's late," she said, then flushed as she always did whenever she had to say his name to Julia. Her friend was as sweet-tempered and pleasant to be around as ever, but Lianne could never set aside her conviction that Julia was suffering from the breakup a great deal more than she let on.

"Traffic's horrible at this time of night," Julia said with apparent tranquillity, putting down her pen and pushing aside the pile of student essays. "Gabe's very polite, so he wouldn't keep you waiting unless it was unavoidable.''

Gabe certainly had elegant and sophisticated manners, Lianne thought, and perhaps with Julia his behavior had always been scrupulously polite. However, polite was about the last word she would have used to describe his attitude toward her. For about the thousandth time, Lianne wondered what in the world she was doing, pursuing a relationship with a man for whom she seemed to feel nothing but an urgent desire to tear off his clothes and tumble into the nearest bed. This from the woman who had always sworn that it was more important to like the men you dated than to lust after their bodies.

The buzz of the outer doorbell sounded loud in the silence of the sitting room. "That'll be Gabe," Julia said. "Shall I let him in?"

"Thanks. I'll get my coat."

When she came back from the bedroom, Gabe was already at their front door. He was talking softly to Julia, and Lianne didn't even try to hear what he was saying. But she couldn't help noticing the warmth in his eyes and the gentleness of the smile he was giving Julia. He took her hand and cradled it briefly within his clasp. Lianne's throat tightened with misery. Oh, God, if only Gabe would look at her like that just once, instead of with his usual heated mixture of passion and contempt.

She didn't say anything. As far as she knew, she made no sound. But Gabe sensed her presence, and his head jerked up, the tenderness in his gaze vanishing instantly. She'd never seen him in evening dress before, and the impact of his presence quite literally took her breath away.

For a second, the room was heavy with silence. Then

he spoke. "I'm sorry I'm late," he said, his voice cool, the apology perfunctory. "Traffic's particularly grim tonight, so we'd better hurry."

She'd told him that she wasn't going to speak to him, and although she'd never intended to stick to such a ridiculous vow, his attitude didn't inspire her with any immediate desire to change that plan. She swept past him without another glance, only turning back to say goodbye to Julia.

"Enjoy the play, both of you." Julia smiled and waved cheerily. "David Weldon's supposed to be wonderful as Richard II. Hurry up now, or you're going to miss the opening curtain." She shut the door rather suddenly.

Lianne headed for the stairs, but Gabe stopped her. "Wait," he said. "Let me help you put your coat on. It's chilly out tonight."

Lianne stopped walking away, but she didn't answer or look at him. He took her coat and helped her put it on, his hands brushing with tantalizing softness across the nape of her neck as he adjusted the collar. He turned her around until she was facing him. His face was expressionless, his gaze agate hard. "You're beautiful," he said, his voice harsh. "So beautiful that when you came into the sitting room just now, it was as if somebody had slammed a fist straight into my gut."

Lianne started to shake. She felt the heat rise into her cheeks and she briefly closed her eyes. She didn't reply, not because of her stupid announcement that she'd only attend the play if she didn't have to speak to him, but for the simple reason that she couldn't find the breath to stumble through a coherent sentence.

Gabe sighed and brushed his thumb across her trembling lips. "I know. You're coming out with me under duress and you're not speaking to me." His eyes gleamed with sudden amusement. "Of course, a policy of stony silence does have its disadvantages from your point of view."

He bent his head and kissed her with ravaging thoroughness. When they broke apart, he was actually grinning. "That was delightful, thank you. I wonder how many more times I'll be able to kiss you tonight before you decide to break your vow of silence and tell me to go to hell?"

She stared at him, appalled and simultaneously fascinated by the idea that had just taken root in her pitiable, sex-starved brain. If she continued not to talk to him, would he continue to pursue her? She met his gaze head-on, then turned without saying another word and walked out to his waiting car.

THE PLAY HAD BEEN magnificent, the charity gala itself a smashing success. Mingling with the actors and guests of honor at the champagne reception following the performance, Gabe chatted up a dowager Dame of the British Empire and secretly watched Lianne. She had the sort of sparkling personality that made her the center of attention even when she wasn't doing anything more than standing around, looking ravishing. But tonight she wasn't just standing around. She was dazzling anyone who moved within her glittering orbit, tormenting him by engaging in witty, insightful conversation with every single member of their party except him. He'd been watching her most of the night, torn between longing and fury, which seemed to be pretty much his constant emotional state when she was anywhere near.

In many ways, Lianne had proved herself the perfect date, enthralled by the play and not at all intimidated by the high-powered gathering of guests in his father's box. She'd been charming to his father, knowing exactly where and how to draw the line between the social situation in which they found themselves tonight and the fact that tomorrow Jeffrey DeWilde would once again be the managing director of the company she worked for. During the two intermissions, she'd not only been charming, she'd been actively helpful, deflecting questions about Grace and—on at least one occasion that Gabe had witnessed—protecting Jeffrey from the curiosity of a wealthy donor with a great deal more money than tact.

She'd been equally charming to Megan, who'd flown over from Paris for the night to act as a stand-in for her mother. In fact, there was only one person who hadn't been the recipient of Lianne's bountiful dispensation of charm, and that was Gabe himself. He watched in a silence that was steaming rapidly toward the boil as one of his father's guests brought Lianne the glass of white wine she'd requested. She accepted it with a delightful smile and some teasing comment that set the guest, a prominent pediatrician not known for his good cheer, simultaneously chuckling and preening. The idiot was actually sucking in his stomach and smoothing his hair over his bald spot. Did she have to flirt so outrageously with every damn male in the entire theater? Gabe asked himself. Didn't she realize that the man had a wife and grandchildren, for God's sake? It seemed that she did, because within minutes she'd cleverly steered the doctor back to his wife and was talking animatedly to Megan. What could she possibly need to say to his sister that was so all-fired consuming that she had no time to spare him so much as a glance? Enough was enough, Gabe decided, glaring so fiercely at the dowager that she immediately doubled her promised donation.

He had just enough self-control left to thank the elderly Dame for her unexpected generosity and escape without giving offense.

With the expertise gained at a hundred charity balls and gala functions, he managed to make his way across the crowded room without getting waylaid again.

"Megan, I've barely managed to see you all evening," he said as he came up to his sister. Despite his best efforts, his gaze fixed hungrily on Lianne.

Megan gave him a faintly amused glance. "We did spend most of Saturday together, Gabe."

"But I'm sure you still have a lot to say to each other," Lianne interjected smoothly. "Twins are supposed to be inseparable, aren't they?" She smiled at Megan with genuine warmth. "I've so much enjoyed meeting you," she said. "If I may, I'd like to take you up on your offer of a tour of the Paris store next month. I'm hoping that my designs will be at the point that production can take over sometime within the next three weeks."

"I'll look forward to seeing you," Megan said. "I know several wonderful places to have lunch, a little bit off the beaten tourist track. By the way, have I mentioned how impressed I was by the preview you sent me of your designs for the *Lianne for DeWilde* collection?"

"You have now. Thank you." Lianne's smile was strictly for Megan. "Excuse me, please," she murmured, studiously avoiding Gabe's fulminating gaze. She slipped away to talk to the actor who'd played the role of Henry Bolingbroke—a handsome newcomer who looked a damned sight too interested in Lianne's cleavage, as far as Gabe was concerned.

Megan's hazel eyes were brimming with laughter. "Gabe, my pet, I think it might be a really good idea if you stopped staring at her as if you were a drowning man and she was the last lifeboat in the entire ocean."

"She?" he demanded, dragging his attention back to Megan with excruciating difficulty. "Who?"

"The same woman you've been glaring at all night long," Megan said, laughing outright this time. "The same woman who has been doing one of the most splendid jobs of driving a man crazy that I've seen in a long time."

He muttered something unrepeatable. Megan laid her hand consolingly on his arm. "Gabe, you're my twin, and I love you, so I'll betray the sisterhood and let you in on a secret. Lianne couldn't possibly have managed to avoid you so consistently all night long unless she'd been watching you as closely as you've been watching her."

He brightened, then sank back into gloom. "There's no reason for her to watch me except that she's determined to avoid me. She despises me."

Megan bit her lip to keep back the laughter. "I'm not totally convinced that you've assessed her feelings with complete accuracy, Gabe. I hate to betray yet another secret of the sisterhood, but I doubt Lianne chose that outfit because she wanted to make an impact on the chairman of the British Medical Society."

"What do you mean?"

"You can trust my judgment on this, brother dear. Lianne isn't wearing anything but skin under that dress."

"She's not wearing anything?" Gabe said, his voice hoarse.

Megan shook her head. "Nothing. Unless you count panty hose."

Gabe swallowed hard, fighting the urge to run to Lianne's side and throw his jacket over her shoulders before the idiot who was staring down her dress came to the same interesting conclusion as his sister. He started to storm across the foyer, but Megan restrained him.

"If you talk to her now, Gabe, one or the other of you is going to explode. Wait until you're somewhere more private before you confront her with how you feel."

"I don't know how I feel," he muttered, embarrassed when he realized that he sounded as immature and petulant as he felt. "I just know I can't stand to be around her, and it's worse when we're apart."

"I'm sure a few hours in bed together would help to clarify the situation for both of you." Once again, Megan sounded amused. "If you'd like to hear the opinion of a mere bystander, I'd say that both of you are in a near-terminal state of mutual lust. Get that out of the way and the pair of you might—just possibly—discover what else you have going as a couple."

Gabe glowered at her. "When did you get to be so damn smart?"

Megan sighed. "Where other people's feelings are concerned? Years ago. As far as my own feelings go, I still haven't a clue."

"That bastard Whitney really did a number on you, didn't he, Meg."

"I wish I could blame everything on my late, unlamented fiancé, but a lot of this is coming from me and has nothing to do with him. At this point, I'm not sure that I even want to get seriously involved with another man, ever again. Work can be just as all-consuming as a love affair, and the results are usually a heck of a lot more tangible and rewarding.''

Gabe would have answered except that he noticed his father had crossed the room to speak to Lianne. The damn-fool idiot actor who'd been peering down her dress looked disappointed. Good. Whatever Lianne said to his father set both men to laughing. Seeing Jeffrey look reasonably relaxed, Gabe was almost willing to forgive Lianne for her sins, which, to be fair, amounted chiefly to driving him crazy because she was too attractive to be ignored.

"Dad's asked me to stay over tomorrow until lunchtime," Megan said, interrupting Gabe's train of thought. "He says he has something important to discuss with me, family business that affects the company." She paused, her voice darkening with concern. "Is it about Mother, do you know?"

"No, I don't think so. I expect it's about the DeWilde jewelry collection."

"The jewels?" Megan sounded surprised. "Oh, Lord, I do hope Dad doesn't want to organize another one of those international exhibitions. The insurance company drives me insane with the precautions they force me to take whenever those darn jewels are moved out of the store."

"No, I don't think he's planning anything like that. Not for the moment, at least. But he should be the person to tell you what's going on. It's a long story and this isn't the place." Gabe frowned as a memory from the session with his father and Nick Santos tugged at his mind. "Meg, on a slightly different subject, have you ever heard of a security firm called Alliance de Securité Internationale?"

She thought for a moment. "No, I don't believe so. From the name it sounds as if they're headquartered in France. Why? Is Dad thinking of hiring them?"

"Not as far as I know, although the name came up because Dad's hired a private investigator who was recommended to him by the president of Alliance. Or at least I think that may be why he hired this particular man. Alliance itself is a small outfit, from what I gathered. The president, or the owner, is a woman called Allison Ames."

Megan suddenly went very still. "She's about our age? Blond, slim, striking dark blue eyes? Very athletic?"

Gabe turned and looked at his twin. "I don't know. To the best of my knowledge, I've never set eyes on the woman. Her name came up in conversation this morning."

"With Dad?"

"Sort of. Indirectly." Gabe glanced across at his father, who was still talking to Lianne. "Dad looked—uncomfortable—when her name was mentioned, as if he wished Nick Santos hadn't mentioned the connection."

Megan didn't answer for several moments. "No, I don't know her," she said finally.

Gabe shot her a quizzical look. "So who's the blond, blue-eyed woman you thought she might be?"

"I was confused," Megan said. "She's nobody."

Gabe might have pursued that slightly ridiculous answer further, but after an entire evening during which Lianne had kept herself permanently surrounded by people, she was finally alone. He hurriedly kissed his sister's cheek. "Gotta dash, Meg, love. Call me next time you're coming to town. Stay at my flat and we'll do one of our night-on-the-town specials."

"Sounds great. We haven't done that in ages, and we used to have fun, didn't we. You have a date, Gabe." Megan pulled him back as he started to walk away. "Since you're my favorite brother, here's a word of wisdom in your ear. Count to ten before you say anything to Lianne, okay?"

"I'm your only brother. But trust me, I'm going to be the soul of tact." Gabe strode purposefully across the room.

GABE WAS COMING, striding across the damned foyer as if he owned it. Having ignored her for the entire evening, he thought he could now claim her like a suitcase abandoned in Left Luggage. God, he had to be the best-looking, most magnetic man in the entire room, not excluding the actors.

Lianne drew herself away from the column she'd been leaning against and he stopped in front of her, glaring through the lock of light brown hair that had fallen forward into his eyes. "Are you wearing anything at all underneath that damn dress?" he demanded.

She spoke her first words of the night to him. "Go to hell, Gabe."

"I'm already there," he said tautly.

"Enjoy the fires." She turned and walked away, genuinely wanting to escape from him, and wanting equally for him to follow her. She closed her eyes and clutched the stair rail, aware of dizzying elation surging through her when she heard his footsteps follow in her wake. She'd spent the entire night trying to provoke him into precisely this mood of outraged male sexual aggression, but now that she'd achieved her goal she wondered if she was going to be able to handle the results of her success.

Silence, thick and dark with anticipation, blanketed them again as they walked downstairs. Her anticipation as well as his, Lianne admitted to herself. He retrieved her coat from the cloakroom attendant and tipped a parking valet to retrieve his car. He drew her into the shadows of the sheltered portico to await the arrival of his Jag and pulled her roughly into his arms, his mouth ravishing hers, his body pressed impossibly close.

"Lianne, come home with me." He murmured the words against her mouth, the stark statement more an order than a request.

The fiasco of their Sunday date was still painfully clear in her memory. Doubts returned, crowding in, cooling the fever of longing. Could she trust him enough to open herself to the possibility of yet another rejection? Worse yet, if they ended up in bed together, was she ready to cope with the emotional consequences of having sex with a man who didn't seem to like her? What if they indulged in another night of passionate lovemaking and he simply walked away from her as he had done once before? She was ready to admit that what she felt for him was more—much more—than simple sexual attraction. Gabe didn't seem ready to admit any such thing.

Everything in her that was rational said that she should protect herself and insist on being driven straight home. But when she looked up at Gabe, the yearning she saw in his normally controlled features made her heart skip a beat. Without speaking, he lowered his head just enough to close the tiny gap between their mouths. He kissed her again, this time with such aching, desperate hunger that her answer gradually became inevitable. With a sense of reaching a foregone conclusion, she surrendered—not to his passion, but to her own. She gave a small, incoherent murmur of assent, then clasped her hands behind his neck, holding his mouth tight against her own, returning his kiss with all the fierce longing she'd been struggling to suppress for the past several days.

They were both breathing hard when they broke apart. Lianne had consumed no more than two glasses of wine, but her surroundings refused to stay in focus. The parking attendant drove up, and she stumbled to the car in Gabe's wake, already so aroused that she barely registered their journey through the deserted streets of the City and into the West End. He parked the car right in front of his block of flats, beneath a large sign that warned this was a tow-away zone. She knew this ought to be cause for concern, but she couldn't concentrate long enough to remember why.

They blundered into the lift and he slammed her against the wall, ripping off his tie with one hand while he shoved her velvet evening coat open with the other. He caught her chin, tilting her head back, his face stark with the fierce concentration of sexual desire. His mouth came down on hers, hot and demanding, the thrust of his tongue almost savage. She locked her arms around him and felt his erection pulse against her belly. Her heart started to pound at twice its normal speed. Her nipples peaked, and the aching sensation in her womb made her knees go weak. She clung to him, the rock-hard solidity of his muscles the only firm points in a world that seemed ready to dissolve into a misty gray cloud.

A rush of air and the sound of doors gliding open

made her blink. Before she could fully register the fact that the lift had arrived at the fifth floor, Gabe had swept her into his arms and carried her to the door of his flat. He put her down while he searched for his key, then picked her up again without saying a word, walking through the door and slamming it shut behind him with his foot.

Her coat and his jacket were shed somewhere in the hallway. Their shoes got lost at the entrance to his bedroom. Already his skillful hands were unfastening the zipper of her dress, caressing her skin, seeking her breasts. Without asking, he carried her to the bed, dropping her onto the mattress and following her straight down onto the pillows. He pushed aside the straps of her dress, shoving the top down below her waist so that her breasts sprang free.

His breath caught on a harsh sigh, and he set his mouth over her nipples, suckling and caressing her with a craving so intense that waves of answering need immediately surged through her. She wanted to touch him, she wanted to be naked beneath him, to hold him naked in her arms, but her hands couldn't move fast enough to satisfy the urgency she felt. Her fingers grappled with the onyx studs that closed his evening shirt, desire making her clumsy.

"Here, let me." Gabe tore at his shirt, ripping out the studs. Stripped to the waist, he braced himself over her, his eyes glittering, his face taut with sexual arousal. "I want to bury myself so deep inside you that you can't feel anything in the world but me." His voice was harsh with passion, dark with need.

"I want you, too," she said.

"Do you?" His mouth twisted into a self-mocking smile. "Do you know what wanting means, I wonder?

I didn't hear a single word of the play tonight," he said. "I spent the entire evening trying to decide if you were really wearing as little underneath that damned dress of yours as it seemed."

"Now you know," Lianne murmured.

"Yes, now I know."

In a flash, Gabe had dispensed with their remaining clothes. Lianne's breath hissed out as he lowered the weight of his body onto her. Passion exploded deep inside her, a wild burst of energy that ate up reason and caution. There was only now: this moment, this man, and this all-consuming mutual need. Lianne locked her arms around him, her fingers tangling in his hair, her mouth opening beneath his. She writhed against him, the sensations he aroused so powerful that she wasn't sure whether she felt her pleasure or his, her need or his. His kisses were hot, fierce, elemental. Her body vibrated against his, ready for his possession even before his hand reached down and parted her thighs.

His touch was almost more than she could bear. Lianne moaned softly. Her skin felt unbearably sensitive, too fragile to survive the intensity of her pleasure. The drumroll of her heartbeat pounded in her ears, and she clutched his shoulders, needing to anchor herself against the buffeting storm. A pulse throbbed deep in her womb, beating to a rhythm she had felt only once before in her life, the night Gabe first made love to her.

Desire and need were building so quickly, spiraling together, demanding to be appeased. When it finally came, Gabe's penetration of her body was an exquisite relief. Lianne felt herself falling, tumbling headlong toward a climax that was utterly out of her control. Her entire body tensed, then imploded, and she crashed down into the blissful darkness of release.

GABE LAY WAKEFUL, watching the first pale fingers of dawn thread through the blackness of the night sky. Beside him, Lianne slept, exhausted from their hours of lovemaking. He turned onto his side so that he could see her. She slept with the same restless intensity that she did everything else, her hair tumbling over the pillow, one arm flung out, the other curved in toward her waist.

He let his fingers comb through the long, chestnut richness of her hair. A couple of her curls wrapped around his fingers and clung fast. Instead of shaking his hand free, he tightened his fingers around the soft strands, gripping them in his fist. He closed his eyes, shaken by the intensity of the feelings that rocked him. Before he could stop himself, he'd bent down and buried his face in the mass of curls spread out on the pillow.

Unbelievably, he felt desire stir within him. Despite all their hours of sex, there was an ache deep inside him that hadn't been assuaged. Lianne stirred, still sleeping, and the sheet slipped down to her waist. Unable to resist, he reached out and laid his hand over her breast. She made a tiny snuffling sound and rolled onto her side toward him, trapping his hand beneath her breast. The ache inside him intensified. He wanted to hold her close. He wanted to ravish her, protect her, care for her. He wasn't sure that he ever wanted to wake up again without finding her lying beside him.

And that thought scared the living hell out of him.

Very gently, he brushed his thumb across her nipple. She woke up, just as he'd known she would, her flesh sensitized to his touch. Her eyes flickered, drowsy with sleep, sated with sex. Sated with him. She took one look at his expression and her eyes widened, darkening to an impossibly vibrant blue in the feeble predawn light. She recognized what he wanted—needed—and she gave a sleepy groan.

"Gabe, you can't be serious!"

He said nothing. He wasn't at all sure he was capable of speaking without saying something he knew he'd live to regret. For answer, he grasped her wrists and held her hands over her head, leaving her entire body vulnerable to his gaze. And to his touch. Swiftly, silently, he lowered his head to her breasts.

The desperate, pounding urgency of their first coupling was gone, but Gabe felt impelled by a need that was both more subtle and more profound than anything he'd felt earlier in the night. He made love to her with all the expertise at his command, exploiting everything he'd learned during the previous few hours about giving her pleasure, summoning all his skill to take her to a pinnacle she'd never known before. When she climaxed, he held her shuddering body in his arms and poured himself into her, the intensity of his own release so violent that he collapsed for a few seconds on top of her, unable to move.

When he could think again, he realized the ache was still there, throbbing deep inside him, waiting to be soothed.

Lianne stroked her hands very gently down his spine, holding him to her, not protesting the burden of his weight. "I love you, Gabe," she said softly. "I thought maybe you should know that."

Her words were like arrows, winging their way straight to the ache inside him, piercing the wound, lodging inside the pain, intensifying it a hundred times over.

He stared down at her, silenced by the enormity of

his vulnerability. Lianne touched her hand to his face in a caress that scraped across the rawness of the wound she'd inflicted. "It's all right, Gabe, you don't have to look so stricken. You're not required to say anything in return, you know."

He finally found his voice. "I don't know what love means," he said. "All I know is that I want you more than I've ever wanted any other woman."

Even as he spoke, he knew that he wasn't telling the truth. He did know what love meant—it was what he felt for Lianne.

And the thought that he loved her scared him half to death.

CHAPTER NINE

FOR SEVEN DAYS IN A ROW, the clouds and mist that so often veiled San Francisco had been burned away by the heat of the late spring sun. Grace stood at the magnificent picture window of her newly rented luxury apartment and wished stubbornly for rain. The sun seemed a cruel mockery of her mood, a taunting, in-your-face declaration that summer was fast approaching and life was busy renewing itself after the winter hibernation.

Except that she was still stuck in the depths of emotional winter. Her life had been shattered with no possibility of renewal, her grief so profound that some days it required almost superhuman effort to drag herself out of bed and into her clothes. She'd made it a little test for herself, to get dressed every day, put on makeup, do her hair in its usual neat style and go out somewhere. She forced herself to run some errand, no matter how meaningless, no matter how much she resented the intrusion of the outside world into her protective cocoon of grief.

Realizing that she was in danger of sinking into a state of clinical depression, she'd deliberately rented an unfurnished apartment just so that she'd be compelled to buy furniture and household goods. Which had been a good idea in theory, she thought, glancing ruefully around her almost bare living room, except that her sense of taste and style hadn't vanished along with her energy. Since she couldn't make herself buy something unless it really appealed to her, her total furnishings so far amounted to a bed, an antique dressing table and the sofa in the room where she was standing, plus such bare necessities as telephones and a few items for the kitchen.

Grace wandered aimlessly to the sofa, picked up one of the cushions and plumped it vigorously. Pillow clutched in her arms, she stared unseeingly at the spectacular view. Even now, when she'd taken the final step of putting more than five thousand miles between her and Jeffrey, she still couldn't quite accept the reality of their separation. It didn't seem possible that only last Christmas—five short months ago—they'd been content and happy. Ecstatically happy.

No, naively happy, Grace thought. We always got along so well together that we had no mechanisms in place for resolving problems. At the first major test, our marriage fell apart.

Most people who got divorced after years and years of marriage wouldn't be able to identify the precise set of circumstances that had caused the breakup. Usually it was some combination of too many rows, the boredom of overfamiliarity, the grating irritation of intimacy without love. But Grace could pinpoint the exact moment when her marriage began to self-destruct. It had been on New Year's Day, at two o'clock in the morning, when she and Jeffrey returned from a New Year's Eve party that they'd both found tedious in the extreme.

Jeffrey had yawned as he tugged off his black tie, returning it with his usual meticulous care to the special niche in his tallboy where it belonged. He slipped the studs out of his starched shirt, dropped them into their custom-designed walnut box, and fiddled with the heavy gold cuff links that had once belonged to his grandfather.

"Here, let me help you." Grace slid off the bed, where she'd been lying fully clothed, too sleepy and, perhaps, a tiny bit too full of champagne to get undressed. Jeffrey obligingly stuck out his wrist and she wrestled with the recalcitrant cuff link, which point blank refused to slide out through the designated slit in his shirt cuff.

She swore with unladylike vehemence, and Jeffrey grinned, tipping up her chin and dropping a kiss on the end of her nose. "Gracie, my love, you're drunk."

Nobody except Jeffrey was ever allowed to call her Gracie, but when he said it, her heart always gave a tiny little leap of love. "I am not drunk," she said, enunciating with care, mortally offended by the suggestion. "The hole in this sleeve is too small for the cuff links, that's all."

He chuckled. "If you say so. I wouldn't blame you if you were drunk, anyway. That was a hideous party, wasn't it?"

"Mmm." She gave up on removing his cuff link and decided to take off his shirt instead. When his top half was satisfactorily naked, she rested her cheek against his chest, sighing contentedly and letting his shirt dangle from her hand. "New Year's Eve parties always strike me as rather sad."

"Why is that, my love?"

"You know, a frantic attempt to pretend that time and fate aren't both marching on, dragging us with them, willy-nilly."

"Very profound," he said, absentmindedly stroking her hair. "However, I doubt if most of the guests tonight were devoting much energy to philosophical reflections on the meaning of life. They were simply trying rather too hard to have a good time and making themselves ridiculous in the process."

Grace was getting tired of holding Jeffrey's shirt. She tossed it vaguely in the direction of the bathroom and the laundry hamper, despite the fact that his cuff links were still attached to the sleeves. Jeffrey winced but didn't say anything.

She smiled to herself at the silent wince and ran her hands approvingly over his chest. "Did I ever tell you that you have just the right amount of hair on your chest, Jeffrey?"

He grinned. "No, I don't believe you ever did."

"Chest hair is very important in a man," she said with the earnestness of the mildly drunk. "I can't bear those men who look like gorillas, but I think male models who shave it all off look even sillier, don't you?"

"I can't say I've ever devoted a great deal of thought to the subject," Jeffrey said, retrieving his cuff links from the discarded shirt and tucking them into their box. "But I'm flattered that my chest hair meets with your approval, since I know your taste is impeccable."

He took off his trousers and hung them neatly over the clothes valet, despite the fact that the next day they would be going to the cleaners. No woman should be required to live with such a guy, Grace thought. She deserved a place in heaven for tolerating his persnickety ways. Lord, he was impossible! And she loved him just about to distraction.

Desire curled softly through her veins, as familiar and welcome as a favorite pair of slippers. She turned her back to Jeffrey, dipping her head forward, holding her hair up with her arm. "Would you undo me?" she said. "I can't reach the zipper."

A gleam appeared in Jeffrey's hazel eyes. He slid the zipper slowly downward, and her dress fell in a pool at her feet, revealing the interesting fact that at fifty-plus, she could still manage to wear a strapless evening gown without a bra underneath. Standing behind her, he bent his head and pressed a kiss to the nape of her neck, his arms coming around her to cup her breasts. "God in heaven, Gracie, but you're so beautiful I only have to look at you and I want to make love."

That was certainly great to hear. She twisted in his arms, smiling. "I guess we're allowed. Since we're married an' all."

His eyes darkened, and he slanted his mouth across hers with an urgency that was both gratifying and arousing. She kicked off her shoes and walked with him to the bed, their kisses becoming rapidly more impassioned. They tumbled onto the bed, their bodies adjusting instantly to the rhythms they'd made their own. Jeffrey made love to her with satisfying fervor, but also with a caring and tenderness that had become vitally important to her over the years. She supposed that one day the heat of their lovemaking would have to cool, but when they were lying together, locked in each other's arms, it seemed impossible to imagine a life that wasn't sweetened by the pleasures of their passionate sexual relationship.

Afterward, they didn't fall immediately asleep as they often did. Jeffrey stretched out his arm, and she lay nestled against his shoulder, blissfully and utterly happy. Perhaps because it was the first day of a new year, he seemed in a reminiscent mood. "Do you ever regret that we didn't have more children?" he asked, running his forefinger over the faint scar of her hysterectomy.

"I think it bothered me more when I was younger." She smiled into the darkness, her hand resting over his. To her, the scar was a reminder of the ups and downs they'd shared together, and come through safely. The growth in her uterus—barely caught in time—had been one of the very definite downs, the fears and the pain of the surgery made easier to bear by Jeffrey's unwavering love. "Now I just want grandchildren, lots of them, as soon as possible."

"It would be nice, wouldn't it? To see another generation coming into the world. And I'm sure all three of our children will make spectacular babies."

She laughed. "No bias in that remark, of course. Why did you suddenly ask me about having more children? Are you wishing we'd had another baby? If you are, my darling Jeffrey, you can't possibly be remembering what hell it was when they were teenagers."

"Trust me, I can remember every excruciating moment. No, for some reason, it just flashed into my mind that when we got married, you informed me you wanted at least six children."

"I said a lot of incredibly stupid things in those days, Jeffrey. Fortunately, I got smarter as I grew older." She laughed again, yawning as she felt sleep creep up on her again. "I guess there have to be some compensations for the pangs and aches of encroaching middle age."

"You're not middle-aged. The rest of us are getting there, perhaps, but not you." He rolled onto his side, gazing down at her, his expression so warm and tender that she felt an absurd impulse to cry. Jeffrey was such a reserved man. Grace cherished the knowledge that only with her did he ever manage to let down the incredible barriers of his self-control and just be himself. Even with the children, much as he loved them, he was rarely totally relaxed. He had never managed to give himself permission to let them see his flaws and his weaknesses, as well as his strengths.

He took her hand and carried it to his lips. "I love you, Gracie. I love you more than I ever dreamed it would be possible to love someone."

"I love you, too." She cupped his face between her hands, drawing his head down and kissing him softly. She found herself wondering why fate had been so kind to her, and so cruel to other, far more deserving people. "I can't believe how much I've grown to love you, Jeffrey."

For a second, she felt him tense. Then he relaxed and smiled. "Now, if I were an overly sensitive sort of fellow, I'd be getting worried. I might even think you sounded a bit surprised to realize you actually loved me."

She laughed. "Well, I wouldn't go that far." After thirty-two years of marriage, it seemed safe to confess the truth—a gift of honesty to show her husband how foolish she'd been when she was younger, and how deeply she cared for him now. "The truth is, Jeffrey, I didn't love you nearly as much as I should have done when we got married."

His hand stilled, resting on the curve of her thigh. "Well, I can understand that. You were incredibly young, years younger than Katie is now. All our emotions are fairly hormonal at that stage in our lives."

"No, that wasn't it." Suddenly it seemed important to make him understand the truth. "Looking back on it, I can barely recognize myself in the self-absorbed young woman I was in those days. I married you for all the wrong reasons, Jeffrey, and I don't deserve the good fortune that made everything turn out so wonderfully right.''

"Why, exactly, did you marry me, Grace?"

She must have been more tipsy than she'd realized. In retrospect, that was the only reason Grace could come up with for her total and complete failure to hear the betraying chill that had edged Jeffrey's question.

"I married you because you were Jeffrey DeWilde," she said. "The most eligible bachelor in London and the catch of the season." She chuckled suggestively. "You were also, of course, absolutely fabulous in bed. I'm sure that must have had something to do with my instant decision not to let you wriggle away from me."

"And I'm sure the fact that I had money didn't hurt."

She heard the cynicism in his words. Fool that she was, she'd interpreted it as cynicism that mocked the young, twenty-year-old Grace, not cynicism that mocked her, his wife, the woman who now loved him with every fibre of her being.

"It sure didn't," she admitted, sharing his disdain for the thoughtless, shallow woman she'd been. "To be honest, it was simply wonderful to find myself part of a family that actually had the funds to live up to their public image."

"In contrast to your own, no doubt."

With destructive honesty, she agreed with him. "Absolutely. My brother's done such a fantastic job of restoring the Powell family fortunes that it's hard to remember what it was like for us when we were growing up. The Powell family name was a force to reckon with in San Francisco society. The problem was, my parents scarcely had two cents to rub together." She shuddered.

"I loathed all the scrimping and saving and getting into debt, just so that we could turn up at the right functions, with the right people, wearing the right clothes."

Grace had never wished her parents were richer. She had simply wished they would drop out of the social circle they could no longer afford. She assumed that Jeffrey would understand. After all, he'd lived with her for thirty-two years. He couldn't help but know that maintaining her social position was slightly less important to her than the color of underwear Scotsmen wore under their kilts.

"I can see that I must have been the ideal prospective husband," Jeffrey said. "Rich, socially acceptable, and so incredibly stupid that I didn't realize I was being married for my position and my money."

Too late, Grace finally registered the appalling truth that Jeffrey hadn't really understood a word she'd been saying. Or at least, he might have understood the individual words, but he'd totally failed to grasp the meaning or significance of what she'd been trying to explain. Horrified at the misunderstanding, Grace had hurried to correct his mistaken impressions. Jeffrey had been polite and listened attentively. After an hour of frantic attempts to clarify everything she'd said, Grace realized that he was still mired in his original misconception. Jeffrey had heard that Grace married him for money and position. The thirty-two subsequent years of learning to love him—with a love that was deeper and more enduring than she could ever have imagined—counted for nothing. The more subtle truth, that even as a young woman she'd been looking for security rather than wealth and social acceptance, totally escaped him.

In the weeks that followed, Grace realized she'd dealt

her marriage a mortal wound. But in the end it was Jeffrey who delivered the final blow.

The phone rang and she ran to grab it from its temporary perch on a built-in shelf. It might be Jeffrey calling to say... To say what? That the past three months were a hideous mistake? That he still loved her? Surely to God she was past that stage of wishful thinking and willful self-delusion. Grace wrapped her arms around her waist, tucking her hands against her body, forcibly keeping them away from the receiver.

The answering machine clicked in. "Mother, this is Megan. I'm sorry to have missed you—"

"Hello, Meg." Grace picked up the phone, rather proud of the steadiness with which she managed to speak. She gave a passable imitation of a carefree laugh. "I was rather busy, so I was hiding out behind the machine. You know how that is."

"I hope I didn't interrupt something important. I just called to chat." Megan sounded wary, unnaturally polite. All three of her children had sounded that way since she and Jeffrey split up, as if she'd suddenly turned into a person they didn't know and weren't sure how to handle. Except Gabe, who seemed to have decided that he'd handle the problem by not speaking to her at all.

She'd really messed up with those farewell letters, Grace thought, and Jeffrey, of course, had only made the situation worse by instructing the family solicitor to inform the children of her departure in yet another letter.

She should have stayed in London long enough to call Gabe, although God knows what she could have said to explain the inexplicable. Still, with the wonderfully clarifying vision of hindsight, she realized she should have phoned and made up some sort of a story, a rationale that justified her behavior without exposing her to the shattering humiliation of her children's pity. But at the time, it hadn't seemed to matter much whether she called Gabe from London or waited until later, when she hoped to be feeling calmer and marginally less wounded.

And, in truth, she hadn't been prepared for the swiftness of the final break with Jeffrey, despite the months of mounting anguish. After a week of stony, tension-filled silence, the prospect of spending another night in his bed had come to seem unbearable. She was worn out with too many nights of waiting and wondering if he would come home, dreading where he might have been and what he might have done during all those long hours of separation. Her fears, her heartache and her rage had all mingled in one giant explosion, and after their final hideous confrontation, she could think of nothing except escape. The need to find some bolt hole where she could run and nurse her wounds in private had overwhelmed any other considerations.

"Mother, are you still there? Shall I call back? I must be interrupting something important."

"No, you're not interrupting at all. I'm delighted you called." Having claimed to be hiding out behind the answering machine in order to work, Grace tried to think up some plausible task she might have been engaged in. What could she pretend to have been doing? "I was just working on a tentative floor plan for my new store, but I'd much rather talk to you." She injected a note of cheer into her voice, hoping Meg wouldn't notice its brittleness.

"Oh, Lord, Mother, I was hoping you'd forget about that idea of opening a store," Megan said. "I realize you have far too much creative energy to sit at home doing nothing, but are you sure you want to go ahead with this particular plan? You know how many problems we're having with DeWilde's in New York right now, and Dad and Gabe are both angry—"

"These days Jeffrey always seems to be furious about something," Grace said, not quite managing to filter the bitterness from her voice. "I may as well give him a genuine cause for complaint. Not that I can see any reason why a bridal store here in San Francisco would have the slightest impact on DeWilde's Fifth Avenue store, except in Jeffrey's overfertile imagination. Brides in France may travel to Paris to shop for their trousseaux and their wedding gowns, and the same for English brides traveling to London, but American women shop for their wedding gowns in their hometowns. My store here in San Francisco is going to open up a new market, not siphon off DeWilde's existing customers."

As Grace spoke, the idea of opening her own store, which had been nothing more than a weapon to use against Jeffrey, a wild caprice thrown out without any coherent plan or serious thought behind it, suddenly began to take shape. A tiny knot of excitement uncurled in the pit of her stomach as she contemplated the possibility of days crammed with enough activity and decision-making to fill the bleak emptiness of her life. She could take all those exciting ideas that the DeWilde board of directors had refused to approve and use them as the foundation for a store that would bear the exclusive stamp of her own personality. And by golly, she'd make it a success. Jeffrey might think that she was old and undesirable, but she'd show him she still had what it took to make a store zing.

"Dad's never going to accept that you're opening a store for any reason except to annoy him and undercut

DeWilde's.'' Megan sounded subdued. "Mother, honestly, if you could see him... He's terribly unhappy, sort of all withdrawn into himself—"

"I really have no interest in hearing about your father's moods and behavior," Grace said, closing her eyes to shut out the tormenting images that Meg's words evoked. "To be brutally frank, I don't give a damn whether Jeffrey approves of my plans or not. We're separated. I'm planning to file for a divorce shortly."

That was true, wasn't it? How could she claim to want out of her marriage if she took no legal steps to end it?

She drew in a deep, calming breath. "Any business activities I choose to engage in are strictly my own concern, Meg. Surely you can understand that."

Megan's voice tensed. "We were all hoping that you and Dad might work things out—"

Grace had finally reached the point where she refused to allow herself to hope. She'd spent the past few months hoping, and after a certain point, the burden of optimism had become too heavy to bear. "There is absolutely no chance of a reconciliation," she said.

"But, Mother, why not? What happened? None of us understands what's going on. You and Dad always seemed so happy—"

"I don't want to talk about it." Grace heard her voice crack with ignominious despair. "Please, Meg," she whispered. "Don't ask me any more questions."

"No, of course not. Mother, I'm sorry, I didn't mean to upset you. Oh, heavens, Mom, are you crying?"

"No," Grace lied. "You know I only cry when I'm happy, or hopping mad about something. Look, let's not talk about my plans anymore. Let's talk about you. Have you done anything exciting lately?"

Meg gave a short laugh. "Gosh, Mom, I've been working too hard to have a social life. Let's see, I flew across to London to attend the gala benefit for the children's hospital on Thursday, and that's about as close as I've come this month to an exciting date."

"I'm glad you went. Was the gala a success?"

"A smash hit. The reviews for the play were wonderful, and we raised a lot of money for the hospital."

"That's terrific news. Did we reach our..." She stopped and rephrased the question. "Do you know if the targets the fund-raising committee set were reached? The goals I proposed—that the committee proposed—were rather ambitious."

"We exceeded the targets by a comfortable margin. The hospital's chief of staff was walking around the foyer afterward wearing a smile of dazed gratification. Everyone said the arrangements were wonderful. You received lots of compliments in your absence." Meg's voice softened. "You were missed, Mom, and not just by the members of your fund-raising committee."

Grace suppressed a pang of regret that she hadn't been there to see the culmination of several months' hard work, and to enjoy a gala night of celebration in the company of the twins she was so proud of. But she couldn't allow herself to get emotional over every loss from her old life or she would, quite literally, go mad. "I'm glad it was a success," she said. "Did you meet anyone interesting? There must have been dozens of eligible men around."

Megan gave an exaggerated sigh. "I take it that's one of your usual veiled requests for information about the state of my love life?"

Grace perked up. "How in the world did you guess?" she asked teasingly. "I thought I was being so subtle!"

"Sure you were. Like an oversized sledgehammer."

Grace actually laughed. "Okay, I'll give up on subtle and simply beg for information. I admit that I keep hoping to hear you've met some wonderful man who's worthy of you. Not just for your sake, although you're the sort of woman who would make a great wife, but for selfish reasons, too."

"I know, Mom, you're itching to plan my wedding. But I have to warn you that after my experience with Edward, I'm not exactly a prime candidate for another full-scale DeWilde wedding with all the trimmings."

"Planning your wedding would be fun, but that's not the only reason I wish you'd get married." Grace leaned against the back of the sofa. She kicked off her shoes and tucked her toes under one of the cushions, relishing a pleasant and unexpected feeling of relaxation. "I'm becoming selfish as I get older. Your father and I have reached the stage in our lives where we're flat-out jealous of all our friends who are grandparents. We want some grandbabies of our own to spoil."

As soon as the words were out of her mouth, Grace was appalled. Her subconscious mind had tricked her, linking her with Jeffrey again as if they were still a couple. It seemed that the moment she relaxed and dropped her guard, a new trap appeared on the path ahead, ready to spring closed and inflict fresh pain.

Megan would normally have rushed to point out that your parents' wish for grandchildren to cuddle was not one of the smartest reasons for embarking on the hazardous seas of matrimony. But she must have realized that Grace's reference to Jeffrey was an unwelcome slip of the tongue, because she tactfully glossed over the entire subject and went back to talking about the gala.

"Gabe came to the theater with a smashing new woman in tow," she said. "Leggy, gorgeous, hair to die for and a bundle of energy. Every man in the place watched her with his tongue hanging out. Come to think of it, you must know her, because you're the one who hired her for DeWilde's. Lianne Beecham. You remember her, I'm sure."

"Of course. So Gabe came with Lianne, did he?" Grace gave a brief chuckle. "Heavens, I wish I could have seen them together. I must say that when I was interviewing Lianne, the thought crossed my mind that she was exactly the sort of woman who was calculated to drive Gabe to distraction one way or another."

"You were right." Laughter colored Megan's voice. "At the moment, I'd say she's driving him to distraction just about every which way."

"I called Gabe a couple of times this week," Grace said. "I haven't heard back. I think he's decided not to return my calls."

"Oh, dear. I'm afraid he's really angry with you," Megan said after a tiny pause.

Grace had been so caught up in her own misery since she came to San Francisco that she was only just beginning to summon up enough objectivity to step back and analyze the situation from her son's point of view. "We always worked so closely together that I guess he's feeling hurt because I chose not to confide in him. He'll come around eventually when he realizes how difficult it is for parents to discuss their marriage with their children."

She spoke with more optimism than she felt. Divorce didn't just end a marriage, as she'd seen over and over again with her friends. Unfortunately, the fallout tended to be toxic and had an unpleasant habit of destroying the relationships of everyone touched by it. She prayed that her excellent rapport with her children would survive the ending of her marriage unscathed.

"I'm sure he will," Megan agreed. "He's a sensible person, so eventually he'll realize he's behaving like a total ass. There was one other thing, Mother." Meg had always been hopeless at deception. Her attempt to sound casual was so transparently forced that Grace knew immediately that her daughter was about to broach the real point of her phone call.

"What's that, honey?" Grace asked, playing along.

"We've had a couple of minor security problems here at the Paris store, and I have a suspicion that someone in middle management has sticky fingers."

"Oh, Lord, that's always such an unpleasant problem to deal with."

"Yes, it is. We need to hire an outside consultant to make recommendations for improvements to our security systems, and also to catch the thief, of course. Someone recommended a small company called Alliance de Securité Internationale. The owner's a woman called Allison Ames, and I believe she did some work for the London store a few months ago. I wondered if you had any opinion about her and her company. The project I need her to work on is very sensitive, for obvious reasons. As you can imagine, we don't want to accuse an employee unless we're absolutely certain he or she is guilty."

Grace gripped the phone so hard that her fingers hurt. "Have you discussed this company with your father?" she asked, amazed to discover that her voice still functioned.

"Yes. He says that he has no professional knowledge of Allison Ames or the company. He reminded me he was in Australia, working with Ryder, when she completed her work with DeWilde's in London. He says he never met her."

Grace stared straight ahead, seeing nothing beyond the scarlet curtain of rage that had fallen in front of her eyes. She fought to keep control over her voice so that she wouldn't humiliate herself in front of her daughter. When love had vanished, pride and self-respect were all you had left. She was tired of weeping, Grace realized. Tired of mourning. Tired of regretting her mistakes. She didn't want pity from anyone. She wanted revenge.

"I'm not the person to ask," she said, astonished by the seeming tranquillity of her voice. "As merchandising VP for DeWilde's, my concerns were limited to questions of stock and display. If your father remembers nothing about Allison Ames..." Somehow she said the name without choking. "If your father has no comment, then the person to question would probably be Freddie Trevelyan. He's directly responsible for security in the London store and must have been responsible for hiring Ms. Ames's company."

"I'll talk to Freddie, then." Megan sounded uncertain.

"Personally, I'm a believer in using one of the large consulting firms," Grace said. "Nowadays, as you know, security is mostly a question of high-tech electronic systems, and I think the larger firms tend to have experts with a broader range of experience. But Ms. Ames may be an outstanding exception to the rule, of course. I wouldn't know."

Grace forced herself to exchange a few more pleasantries with her daughter before saying goodbye and hanging up the phone. She wasn't sure who was deceiving whom. Meg's story about needing to hire a security consultant might be true, but it wasn't the reason that she'd mentioned Allison Ames and Alliance de Securité to her mother. Grace would bet on it. Megan was merchandising manager for the Paris store, and she was no more involved in the routine administration of security matters than Grace had been.

The mere sound of Allison's name was enough to propel Grace into a state of full-blown fury. After spending most of her waking hours for the past two weeks staring listlessly into space, she was seized by a rage that felt almost refreshing in contrast to the debilitating inertia that had held her captive ever since she'd arrived in San Francisco.

Damn Jeffrey's lying soul to hell, she thought, pacing from kitchen to living room and back again. How dare he claim that he'd never met Allison Ames? The fact that the man she'd lived and slept with for thirty-two years had the capacity to indulge in such all-encompassing deceit made her question the very foundation of trust on which her life had once rested with such seeming security.

Grace paced from the living room to the bedroom to the room that would one day be a cozy den and through to the kitchen. The spacious apartment suddenly seemed too small to contain her fury. She stormed back into her bedroom, threw herself in the middle of the bed and reached for the phone. Of course it wasn't there, because she didn't have nightstands. Damn it, tomorrow she was going to buy nightstands. Somewhere in a city the size of San Francisco there had to be a pair of nightstands she could learn to live with. She hung over the edge of the bed and retrieved the phone from the floor, dialing the number of their London flat before she could wimp out and change her mind.

The answering machine clicked in. "This is Jeffrey DeWilde. I'm unavailable to answer the phone at the moment, but leave a message and I shall return your call at the earliest opportunity."

She knew he was there, could sense his presence at the other end of the line as clearly as if he were speaking to her. "Jeffrey, pick up the phone," she said. "Damn it, Jeffrey, do it—*now.*"

"Grace, I'm here."

She closed her eyes when she heard the cool familiarity of his voice. The usual wave of pain started to wash over her, but she refused to surrender to it. "Are you alone?" she asked.

His voice chilled. "Yes, I'm alone. Do you care?"

"No." She willed her answer to be true. "What I do care about is my relationship with my children. I have no intention of allowing you to turn me into an object of derision in front of them, which seems to be your current intention."

"I've no idea what you're talking about, Grace."

"Then I'll spell it out for you, Jeffrey. I've just had a long phone conversation with Megan, and next time you're trying to scrounge work for your mistress, don't send her anywhere she's going to come into contact with my children. I won't have your sleazy little whore worming her way into my family. There, is that clear enough for you?" She brushed away her tears with the heel of her hand, determined not to let him hear a single sob. She was so sick of being torn apart by the intensity of her feelings while Jeffrey retreated deeper and deeper into dignified reserve.

"Allison isn't a whore—" Jeffrey stopped abruptly,

but she'd heard the burst of protective anger in his voice, and it damn near killed her to accept that Allison Ames could rouse his emotions from their perpetual deep freeze, but she couldn't.

"This conversation is inappropriate and ridiculous," Jeffrey said, all trace of his anger suppressed.

Why not? Grace fumed. He was talking to his wife again. It was only mention of his mistress that had the power to inflame him.

"I gather from your wild outburst that someone at DeWilde's Paris has considered the possibility of hiring Alliance de Securité for a security check," he went on. "I assure you that I had no knowledge of such a proposal and certainly did nothing to promote or encourage it in any way."

"You're such a soul of rectitude, aren't you, Jeffrey. I wonder why I find it so damned hard to believe your protestations of innocence."

"Unless you have something useful to say, Grace, I have many other demands on my time at the moment and I need to curtail our conversation." With faint but discernible irony, he added, "You'll appreciate that I'm somewhat short-staffed at the office at the moment."

"I'm surprised you haven't hired a replacement for me already."

"I'm currently reviewing several interesting résumés."

"With Allison Ames to warm your bed and a new merchandising VP for DeWilde's, you'll be cozily squared away, won't you, Jeffrey?"

"What do you expect?" Surprisingly, she'd provoked him into another flash of temper. "I can't just sit around and worry about the fact that you chose to leave me and abandon your responsibilities to DeWilde's. Although you apparently find the concepts of loyalty and obligation difficult to understand, I have a responsibility to my shareholders and to the many fine people who work for DeWilde's."

"Oh, I understand perfectly, Jeffrey. How could I not? With my new store that I'm planning to open, I'm already knee-deep in obligations."

"What does that mean, precisely?"

She hadn't the faintest idea. She'd simply been engaged in another of their totally stupid sessions of parry and thrust, wound and retreat. "Which part of my statement didn't you understand, Jeffrey? I'm planning to open a new store here in San Francisco, you know that. Naturally, that requires me to enter into various legal contracts and negotiations."

"You can't possibly open a store," Jeffrey said. "How in the world are you going to get financial backing for such a major venture?"

"I thought I'd try a bank," she said sarcastically. "I'm quite sure that my brother will be able to give me some helpful introductions." Since her brother, Leland Powell, was the president and CEO of a corporation with vast holdings in real estate and several retail enterprises, the suggestion was credible.

Jeffrey gave a scornful laugh. "I think your brother has far too much business acumen to assist in finding loans for a venture that's bound to fail. You don't have the financial knowledge or the overall management skills to successfully launch a major new store. You have no way to raise the necessary capital, Grace."

It was the scorn in his voice that did it. "Of course I can raise capital," she said. "And if need be, I can provide the start-up capital myself."

"Impossible—"

"Not at all impossible," she said. "I plan to sell my stock in the DeWilde Corporation."

She had no idea what she'd been going to say until the words were actually spoken. The silence that greeted her statement stretched interminably, but she didn't question for a moment that Jeffrey was still on the other end of the transatlantic line.

Hah! she thought gleefully. She'd finally come up with a threat that pierced through the steel armor he'd wrapped himself in.

"The family's shares in the DeWilde Corporation are held in an irrevocable living trust," he said finally.

"The family's shares are in a trust," she agreed. "But mine aren't. Remember, your father was so thrilled when we got married that he made me a wedding present of what now amounts to five percent of the total stock in DeWilde's. For tax reasons, my shares were never included in the trust. I plan to sell them, Jeffrey, and use the money to start my own store here in San Francisco."

She had barely given the shares a thought since the day she received them from Charles DeWilde—until now. Suddenly, she realized that she wasn't joking, that she wasn't bluffing, and that she had the power within her grasp to exert some small measure of control over her life again. It was a heady, intoxicating sensation. "I plan to instruct my stockbroker to place my shares on the market ten days from now," she said with a coolness that almost matched her husband's. "If you would care to suggest an alternative source of capital for the down payment on my new store, please feel free to contact me. Anytime."

"You can't be serious!" In normal circumstances, the icy rage in Jeffrey's voice would have been terrifying. Today, lingering rage over his unfaithfulness with Allison Ames protected Grace from hurt.

"Is this some form of blackmail?" Jeffrey exclaimed. "Are you suggesting that I should bribe you with God knows what to prevent you from selling several million pounds' worth of DeWilde stock? You know that if you place your block of shares on the market, you'll exert an enormous downward pressure on the share price for DeWilde's."

Good. He was worried. She smiled. "That's exactly what I'm suggesting, Jeffrey. I'm sure it's a very worrying prospect for you."

He started to expostulate.

Grace hung up the phone.

CHAPTER TEN

THESE DAYS, when he thought about Allison Ames, Jeffrey couldn't quite remember what she looked like. He knew that she was blond and blue-eyed, and that she had a slender, trim body, but if he'd been asked to pick her out of a police line-up of women with similar coloring and features, he had a terrible suspicion he wouldn't be able to do it. Even in his current state of mingled fury and maudlin self-pity, it struck him as beyond ironic that he'd destroyed his marriage by having an affair with a young woman whom he would now find difficult to recognize.

He'd met Allison during one of his frequent business trips to Paris, a couple of months after Grace's humiliating admission that she'd married him not because she loved him but because she valued his name, his money and his position. Jeffrey supposed that some other men might have been able to handle such a confession with casual aplomb. He had been shattered. As far as he was concerned, Grace had undercut the very foundations of their relationship and rocked him to the center of his being.

Having spent the first five years of his life wondering why his father never came home, even though his mother insisted that he was well and safe, Jeffrey had grown up with a deeply rooted suspicion that he might not be worthy of love. The war hadn't been over long before he'd been old enough to recognize that his father's absence had been a matter of necessity, not of choice, and that his mother's daily claims that "Daddy" was alive and safe had been prayers, not statements of fact. Even so, there was a part of him that never overcame his early childhood fears.

By the time he finished university and acquired a reputation as one of Oxford's most eligible bachelors, his dazzling success with women had in some ways simply underscored his insecurity. He was smart enough, and perceptive enough, to notice that women were attracted to the DeWilde name and fortune almost as much as they were attracted to Jeffrey, the man. Being a mere human with no aspirations to sainthood, he took advantage of the offers of sex and guarded his emotions with fierce intensity.

Grace had seemed the glorious exception to the general rule. He'd met her while he was doing graduate work at the London School of Economics and she'd enrolled for a semester at King's, one of the other London University colleges. He fell head over heels in love at first sight, captivated by her bubbling energy, her artistic talents, the ease with which she made friends. In short, by all the things she was that he so markedly wasn't. After they made love for the first time, he knew that he would never want to marry any other woman. He took her home to Kemberly to meet his parents, and they were as captivated by her as he was. He proposed, on his knees, in the rose garden at Kemberly. Grace had accepted his great-grandmother's engagement ring, a sapphire surrounded by diamonds, with tears in her eyes and a kiss so tender he could still feel it in his dreams.

Fool that he was, he had never doubted that he and Grace were both making a love match from the day he proposed until the moment when he lay in his bed, with Grace in his arms, and listened to her say that she had married him because he was Jeffrey DeWilde, the rich and eligible bachelor.

Ever since that night, he'd been having difficulty sleeping. He always stayed at the Hotel Bristol when he was in Paris, and the staff there had become accustomed to his frequent late-night excursions. The night Allison came into his life, they simply nodded to him and murmured polite greetings when he came downstairs at one in the morning wearing sweat pants, a ski parka and sneakers.

He'd left the hotel, intending to take a brisk stroll through the nearby streets, hoping to exhaust himself physically so that sleep became inevitable. He'd barely reached the intersection with Rue de la Paix when he saw a woman, dressed much as he was, running toward him at a spanking pace.

What a crazy hour to be out jogging, he thought, watching her with detached admiration, enjoying the athletic fluidity of her movements. Gabe and Megan had both run on their university track teams, so Jeffrey was accustomed to estimating running speeds on sight. He calculated this woman was doing close to a seven-minute mile, which was almost competitive standard for some of the longer distance runs.

She was less than twenty yards away, her stride relaxed and easy, when a car turned out of the side street at cross angles to her, its headlights on full power.

Jeffrey could see her with perfect clarity in the beam of the car lights, but she was momentarily blinded. She blinked and lost her stride at precisely the same moment that a cat shot out of a side alley where it had been rummaging among the dustbins. Allison and the cat both met in midstride. The cat escaped unharmed, definitely using up one of its nine lives. Allison lost her balance and sprawled full-length on the pavement.

Jeffrey was at her side in seconds. She was cursing eloquently and creatively in American-accented English. He was surprised to discover she was American. She'd looked so at home, he'd assumed she was French. Besides, there was a certain indefinable Parisian chic to her appearance, even in a jogging suit.

Relieved that she hadn't been knocked unconscious, he introduced himself and offered his help. She insisted she wasn't badly hurt, but he could tell from the way she was rubbing her ankle that she'd given herself at least a mild sprain. She was covered in mud and grit, sneezing because she was violently allergic to cat hair, and annoyed that she wasn't going to complete her eight-kilometer run in thirty minutes, as she'd intended.

Jeffrey prided himself on his physical fitness, but he sighed a bit when he thought of the youthful energy involved in planning to run six miles in half an hour. He should introduce her to Gabe, he thought. They could run marathons together, and his son would probably enjoy the uninhibited vigor with which she expressed herself.

When she finally hauled herself to her feet with Jeffrey's help, she told him that her name was Allison Ames. She explained that she lived in Monte Carlo, but she was staying for the week with friends who had an apartment about four miles away.

"Come back to my hotel and we'll ask the concierge to call you a cab," Jeffrey suggested. "You can't walk to your friends' apartment with a sprained ankle." Unable to restrain his paternal impulses, he gave her a mild scolding. "You're fortunate something much worse didn't happen to you than a sprained ankle. It isn't safe for a young woman to be out running alone at this hour of night, not even in this part of Paris.''

She smiled. Looking back, Jeffrey remembered that she had a lovely smile, and the perfectly straight teeth that only expensive American orthodontics could produce.

"It isn't safe for a young woman to accept invitations back to a man's hotel, either," she said, sounding amused rather than alarmed.

Horrified, Jeffrey had dropped the supportive arm he'd automatically placed around her waist. He quickly stepped back two paces. "My dear young lady, I assure you I had not the slightest intention of suggesting anything even remotely improper." As always when he was nervous or upset, his vocabulary became slightly old-fashioned, his way of speaking stilted and much too formal.

She flashed him another one of her nice smiles, her voice warm and self-confident. "Oh, well, in that case, I'm delighted to accept your offer of help. Thanks."

He was relieved that she didn't seem to be the sort of woman to read sexual harassment into the most innocent of actions, but he didn't risk holding her around her waist again. He extended his arm, offering help but not forcing it on her. Allison leaned her weight on his arm, and they'd stumbled along together. It wasn't far to the hotel—that was why he'd suggested taking her there—but they couldn't walk very fast because of her injury. To avoid an awkward silence, he'd explained that he lived in London but he often came to Paris on business. To reassure her that his intentions were strictly honorable, he also mentioned that he was married and had three children, two of them twins who were probably as old as she was.

Allison hadn't said much, no doubt because she was in more physical discomfort than she was willing to admit. Jeffrey admired the stoicism with which she endured the painful walk back to the Hotel Bristol. He also admired the fluent French in which she explained her predicament to the concierge once they got there. Guillaume had been all concern and insisted on showing *mademoiselle* to the ladies' powder room so that she could refresh herself before embarking on the cab ride home.

When Allison emerged from the ladies' room, Jeffrey was surprised to see how attractive she was once she was spruced up. She'd brushed her shoulder-length blond hair and washed the dirt from her face, revealing the fact that she had rosy cheeks and an absolutely perfect complexion. He also noticed that her eyes were a vivid blue, rather like Grace's. At the memory of his wife, he'd felt his mouth tighten and his smile fade. Thinking about Grace was as natural to him as drawing breath, but he resented the constant intrusion now that he knew the truth about her feelings toward him.

With one of the Gallic flourishes he reserved for favored customers, Guillaume had crossed the lobby to announce that the cab he'd summoned was now at *mademoiselle*'s disposal. Allison had thanked him in her perfectly accented French. Then she'd shaken Jeffrey's hand, thanking him, too. He'd been flattered by the obvious admiration in her gaze, the admiration of a woman for a man she found desirable. As she entered the cab, he realized that she'd probably come out without any money, and he borrowed two hundred francs from the concierge, giving it to Allison and refusing to take no for an answer.

"You don't want to wake up your friends," he said when she protested that there was no need for him to be so generous. "It's almost two o'clock in the morning. Please, I insist that you take it. Make a donation to your favorite charity if you feel you must pay me back."

Afterward, he wondered if it had been that casual gift of two hundred francs that triggered everything that followed. Would Allison have called the next day and invited him to dinner if she hadn't felt indebted to him for the loan of her cab fare? Would he have been smart enough to refuse her invitation if he hadn't been able to pretend that Allison was offering nothing more than an innocent thank-you for the loan of what amounted to less than twenty pounds?

He'd agreed to meet her at La Lune Ascendant in Montmartre, and had told himself that he shouldn't apply the standards of the sixties to behavior in the nineties. Asking him to dinner was no more than a courtesy, as far as Allison was concerned. After all, he reminded himself, she was younger than Gabe and Megan and undoubtedly saw him as a decrepit father-figure. He shouldn't read sexual overtones into a situation where none existed.

Looking back from the ruins of his broken marriage, Jeffrey admitted that if the two hundred francs hadn't provided him with an excuse to accept Allison's invitation, something else would have done. The fact was, he'd been ripe for an affair. His marriage had become a wasteland. His ego was bruised and aching. His sex life, once an incredibly beautiful part of his relationship with Grace, was now nonexistent. For the first two months of the new year, he and Grace had barely made love at all, even though a part of him desired her as much as ever. The final humiliation had come a couple of weeks before his encounter with Allison, when he'd tried to make love to Grace and hadn't been able to. "Temporary" impotence was not something that a fifty-five-year-old man could take lightly, because there was always the dreadful fear that "temporary" might soon slide into permanent. He added his inability to perform sexually to the long list of sins he was attributing to Grace.

Allison had made him feel young, potent and desirable. She'd also made him feel guilty as hell, even though he assumed that she was a young woman who was in the habit of enjoying multiple casual affairs. After two months of stolen weekends in Paris and midweek encounters in various discreet London hotels, he'd realized that she wasn't at all in the habit of having casual affairs, especially not with a married man. Appalled, he'd taken immediate steps to end their relationship. Which was when he'd made the even more shocking discovery that Allison wasn't sleeping with him because she enjoyed illicit sex with older men but because she thought she was falling in love with him.

It was odd, Jeffrey reflected, that a major part of Allison's appeal had been his assumption that she didn't care very much about him—the exact opposite of what he wanted from his relationship with Grace. About the only redeeming feature of his behavior during the entire affair had been that he'd broken off all contact with Allison the instant he realized her feelings were deeply involved. He'd even gone to considerable lengths to convince her that he was the sort of heartless, philandering bastard who didn't deserve a single moment of her regret.

The last, bitter irony of the whole situation was that Grace had discovered the name of his mistress and the details of where they'd been meeting on the very weekend that he ended the affair. She had been furious at his betrayal, whirling through their apartment, throwing things, crying.

Jeffrey, of course, had been his usual inarticulate self, incapable of explaining to her how he'd stepped onto the slippery slope that led to his unfaithfulness. The louder Grace had stormed and yelled, the further he'd retreated into stony, uncommunicative silence—until the fatal moment when his control broke completely and he told her that he never wanted to see her again.

Which had led to the cosmically absurd circumstance that in the very week when he broke off all contact with Allison Ames and planned to grovel at Grace's feet, begging for her forgiveness, his wife had walked out and left him. At his behest.

The gods, Jeffrey imagined, must definitely be laughing.

THE MEETING HE'D CALLED with his top managers that morning had been surprisingly productive, Jeffrey concluded, poking his head around the door of Monica's office to let her know that he was going out for a quick lunch.

Ten days had come and gone, and so far his stockbroker was reporting that there was no sign of any large block of DeWilde shares coming onto the market. Jeffrey wasn't as reassured by this news as he might have been. These days, he couldn't judge Grace's motives and plans any better than a rank outsider. At best, he was afraid that her decision not to sell her shares simply meant that she had no immediate need for capital. At worst, he feared that she was deliberately tormenting him, dangling the ever-present possibility of their sale in front of him as a constant reminder of the power she retained to hurt both him and DeWilde's.

He wasn't imagining Grace's feelings of enmity toward him. A San Francisco attorney had recently sent him a three-page letter, very brisk, very blunt and very American, outlining the terms of the no-muss, no-fuss Nevada divorce Grace was prepared to offer him. Jeffrey hadn't shown the letter to Ramsbotham yet, he'd been too embarrassed, but he hadn't needed a solicitor in order to interpret the terms of the letter. Grace, it seemed, was willing to leave him with Kemberly and his shirt, possibly a pair of socks or two. Everything else, including the London flat, was to be hers.

In some ways, though, the letter had been a blessing in disguise. He could finally stop pretending to himself that tomorrow Gracie would come home. Energized by the knowledge that she was gone and DeWilde's was vulnerable, he'd steeled himself to expose the sorry state of his failed marriage to senior management and had told them bluntly that Grace was likely to use her block of company shares as a weapon in their divorce negotiations, or even as collateral to raise capital to finance her plans for a new store.

Gabe had been furious to learn of his mother's plans. If Jeffrey had wanted to find some tactic to alienate his son from Grace, he realized he could hardly have devised a better one. But, thankfully, his bitterness toward Grace hadn't yet corroded his sense of common decency to the point that he wanted to poison her relationship with their children. Grace had always been, and still was, a loving and wonderful mother. It pained Jeffrey that Gabe had decided to be so partisan, to place the blame for the breakup so totally and completely in Grace's lap.

The rest of management had, of course, taken the news less personally. They'd been surprisingly swift to come up with creative ideas to shore up the strengths of DeWilde's and to mitigate the effects that dumping such a large block of shares might have on the ability of the company to raise its own necessary investment capital.

Monica was already making arrangements for a conference call with Sloan DeWilde in New York and Ryder Blake in Sydney so that Jeffrey could update them on the situation and get their feedback on some of the ideas proposed at this morning's meeting. All in all, Jeffrey thought, this had been about the most productive day he'd had since Grace left him. Now that he'd finally accepted the sad truth that he wasn't going to wake up and discover Grace sleeping peacefully beside him, he had to stop wallowing in self-pity and get on with his job—which was the running of the DeWilde empire.

A surge of energy jolted through him, and he realized he had no desire to sit in a crowded restaurant and bolt down a meal when he wasn't hungry. It was another lovely spring day, after a week of showers and gray skies, so he decided to stroll along Bond Street and check the window displays of some DeWilde competitors before returning to the pile of paperwork waiting on his desk.

He was halfway through the arcade when he noticed a woman staring into the window of Asprey's, one of London's oldest and most prestigious jewelry stores. He recognized the rich chestnut color of Lianne's hair before he consciously registered who it was viewing the window display with such total absorption. Since the night Lianne had attended the play with his son, Jeffrey had been more aware of her presence in the office and had come to enjoy the occasional brief exchange of pleasantries with her. She was one of those sunny, extroverted people who almost always seemed to have something cheerful or interesting to say.

She was examining the display in Asprey's windows with the same vibrant intensity that she seemed to bring to every aspect of her life. It was almost, Jeffrey thought, as if she looked with her whole body and not just with her eyes. She was oblivious to passers-by, and it would have been quite easy to walk past her unnoticed. Jeffrey surprised himself by crossing over and standing next to her.

"What are you admiring?" he asked, without any other greeting. "The swan brooch? It's splendid workmanship, isn't it?"

"Not the brooch," she said absently, so caught up in what she was doing that she accepted his presence next to her almost as if they'd arranged to meet. "Look at the design of that emerald and diamond necklace at the side there. Now imagine that magnified about three times and twined around tiny silk orchids. Wouldn't that make a perfect bridal headpiece for a woman who's in her thirties and who's trying to find something romantic to wear for her wedding that doesn't look as if it was designed with an eighteen-year-old debutante in mind?"

He looked at the necklace, which years of training enabled him to say was of high quality workmanship and pleasing design. His imagination was definitely not up to the task of visualizing the stones magnified, reproduced in crystal and wound around silk flowers. "I haven't the faintest idea," he said, amused by his own inadequacy. "I'm afraid my creative talent is invisible even under the most powerful of microscopes."

She turned around and finally noticed—really noticed—who he was. "Mr. DeWilde!" She smiled at him as if she were genuinely pleased to see him. "I'm sorry. I wasn't paying attention, except peripherally. I have a hole in my collection where I ought to have two spectacular designs for older first-time brides, and I'm becoming marginally obsessive about what I'm going to do to fill the gap."

Jeffrey returned her smile. He suspected Lianne was the sort of woman whose smiles were always returned. He deliberately pushed away the thought of Grace, the only other woman he'd known with the capacity to make everywhere seem brighter just because she was there. He cleared his throat. "Delighted as I am to see one of my employees slaving away during her lunch hour, could I tempt you away from visions of bridal headgear and ask you to drink a cappuccino with me? There's an excellent coffee bar not five minutes' walk from here."

"I'm a coffee-holic, so I would love that. Thank you." Like Grace, she managed to sound enthusiastic without gushing.

"Did you enjoy the production of *Richard II?*" he asked as they fell into step together. "I thought they put on a pretty fair show myself. Outstanding direction from Sir Tony."

"Yes, I enjoyed it very much. I love Shakespeare's historical plays. Better than the tragedies, to be honest."

"Why is that? Do you know?"

Her forehead wrinkled. "I think it's because the histories are action-oriented, which suits me perfectly. I'm not good at dealing with hesitancy and indecision, which is what the tragedies all hinge on. Midway through Hamlet's umpteenth soliloquy wondering what he should do next, I'm sorely tempted to yell out that he should stop contemplating his navel and get a life."

Jeffrey laughed. "You have a point, but if that's the case, I wouldn't have thought that Richard II would appeal to you. He isn't exactly a model of decisive action."

"Oh, I don't know. I don't mind suffering with people who have real problems. Richard strikes me as noble and worthy, betrayed on all sides by men who are too thick-skulled and insensitive to see the pitfalls ahead of them. Henry Bolingbroke had tunnel vision. So he just charged forward and, of course, rode successfully over the pitfalls because he didn't even know they were there. And then his side won, darn it."

"It was probably better for England that they did. Henry made a good king."

"And Richard wasn't brutal enough to take charge of all those squabbling nobles, was he?" She looked momentarily saddened, totally caught up in the lives of people who'd been dead for approximately six hundred years. "There's absolutely nobody like Shakespeare for reminding you that life is frequently unjust."

"And invariably messy," Jeffrey agreed, opening the door to the coffee bar. "We're here," he added.

Lianne stopped on the way in to sniff a tub of violets on a street vendor's stall. "I love spring in London," she said as they sat at a table by the window. "On a day like today, I suffer from the very best sort of amnesia and totally forget how much I loathed all those dreary wet weeks in February and March."

"London's pleasant at this time of year, but the country is even lovelier. I'm going down to Kemberly this weekend, why don't you come and join me? I'm not a gardener, but even I can tell that the gardens are spectacular just now. I'll ask Gabe if he can drive you."

As soon as he issued the invitation, Jeffrey questioned whether he'd taken leave of his senses. Go to Kemberly this weekend? Where had that idea sprung from? Only a short while ago he'd been convinced that he would never be able to visit Kemberly again, that the reminders of Grace's absence would be too unbearably painful.

He wondered at what point he'd realized that the pain he felt was buried within his own psyche and would go with him everywhere. Which meant that a weekend at Kemberly was going to be no more—and no less—painful than a weekend spent anywhere else.

But quite apart from his own ambivalence, he wasn't at all sure why he was choosing to interfere in Gabe's personal life. After twenty-five years of rigorously refusing to get involved in his children's love affairs, a policy which had started when Gabe attempted to show his devotion to a nursery school playmate by constantly taking her crayons, this hardly seemed the appropriate moment for him to be playing the role of matchmaker. Lord knew, he was the last man in the world to pretend that he understood what made two people into suitable mates for each other. Just because Gabe had been stalking the hallways of DeWilde's corporate offices like a bear awoken too early from hibernation and unable to find food didn't mean that Jeffrey had any reason to intervene. If Gabe wanted to get together with Lianne, presumably he was more than capable of making his own arrangements.

Their coffees arrived and Lianne stirred the milk froth on hers with far more concentration than the task required. Jeffrey, whose sensitivity to other people's feelings was a great deal better developed than his ability to express his own, realized that his invitation had thrown her into a quandary.

When she finally lifted her gaze from her cappuccino, he could see there was a little flush of color staining her cheeks. "Thank you for asking me," she said. "But I'm not sure if I should accept. I enjoy Gabe's company and he enjoys mine, but I don't think he'd like to take me to Kemberly. I think he might find my presence there rather...intrusive."

Jeffrey decided he could make a reasonably good translation of that cryptic response. At a guess, it meant that Gabe thoroughly enjoyed having sex with Lianne, but he'd made it plain to her that he wasn't thinking in terms of marriage, commitment and introductions to his family. His son, Jeffrey reflected, was a fool.

He put down his cup. "My dear, Gabe isn't extending this invitation to you, I am. To put it bluntly, we're simply asking Gabe to be the chauffeur."

She smiled a little at that. "Well, when you put it that way, how could I refuse? Thank you, Mr. DeWilde. I'd love to accept your invitation to spend the weekend at Kemberly."

CHAPTER ELEVEN

SHE SHOULD NEVER HAVE told Gabe that she loved him, Lianne thought, staring at the hedgerows rushing by the car window without really seeing them. Even though she'd been scrupulously careful never to repeat her mistake, the damage had been done. Gabe hadn't been ready to hear anything about her feelings the night of the gala, and he still wasn't now, more than two weeks later. Unfortunately, when he'd taken her into his bed that night, her defenses had been so depleted by the stunning impact of their lovemaking that the fateful words had slipped out before she could stop them. Almost, in fact, before she'd realized their truth.

She stole a glance at Gabe's unrevealing profile and sighed. Her own face sometimes seemed to be a fast-moving TV screen of everything she was feeling, a window straight into her heart, whereas Gabe was a master of the controlled, reveal-nothing expression. Except, of course, that the very blankness of his features betrayed the fact that he was concealing emotions he didn't want to share with her, a deprivation that Lianne was beginning to find hurtful.

She couldn't fathom why it was that their relationship disturbed Gabe so much, but she knew his refusal to acknowledge their attraction for each other went beyond the standard reluctance of an eligible bachelor to give up his freedom and make a commitment. For some reason, Gabe didn't trust the chemistry that sizzled between them. Sometimes she almost had the feeling that he actively resisted the idea that the great sex they'd shared might develop into something more lasting.

For the past two weeks, the boundaries of their relationship had barely changed. They had discovered when Gabe got ready to drive her home after the night of the gala that his car had been towed from its illegal parking spot in front of his flat. Muttering curses beneath his breath—curses that Lianne considered quite mild, considering the circumstances—he'd summoned a taxi to take her home. As she started to step up into the cab, he'd pulled her back and held her close while he murmured how important the night they'd just shared had been to him.

Lianne believed he had been sincere, but from that moment until this he'd made no further mention of his feelings or how he viewed their relationship. Their frequent dates fell into a rigid pattern, carefully controlled by Gabe. Basically, they amounted to nights of blistering hot sex, preceded by formal outings where she and Gabe were invariably surrounded by other people.

He'd invited her to attend two plays and to accompany him to the opening of an art exhibition at a friend's gallery. He'd taken her to a rare concert given by Enya, for which tickets were almost unobtainable, and she'd twice joined him as his partner at fund-raising banquets for causes connected to the preservation of various historic buildings. She teased him that he harbored a secret desire for the whole length and breadth of England to be done out with flats and shopping malls disguised behind fake Georgian Revival facades. He'd grinned, only slightly shamefaced, and told her that every man was entitled to one eccentricity.

Lianne wondered why it was that when you fell in love with a man, even his foibles seemed endearing. She was enchanted by the fact that Gabe, who on the surface appeared every inch the international sophisticate, cherished a sentimental attachment to quaint thatched cottages and village gardens full of hollyhocks and snapdragons.

When contrasted with the memorable occasion of their first date, Lianne supposed she could say that their relationship had inched forward. Gabe had finally progressed from spending the entire evening glowering at her, as if daring her to have a good time, to the point where he now took obvious pleasure in her company and the ease with which she fitted into the circle of his friends. But she couldn't fail to notice that he never invited her to spend the evening at his flat, comfortably doing nothing, and that he always had some excuse as to why he couldn't join her when she suggested a Sunday morning at the zoo, or browsing through the Victoria and Albert Museum, or any other informal outing that would have required lots of one-on-one interaction.

This weekend had been shaping up as typical. She'd known for several days before Jeffrey invited her to Kemberly that Julia was going to stay with her brother's family for three days. Taking advantage of her friend's absence, Lianne had invited Gabe to come to the flat and share Chinese take-away food, followed by a night watching rented movies.

"I'll even let you have one of the bags of microwave popcorn that just arrived in my mother's latest care package from the States," she'd teased him. "Since you spent all those years in America, you must recognize that a movie isn't really a movie without popcorn, and I can supply the real thing.''

He'd smiled and admitted that popcorn made even the worst movie almost bearable, but he hadn't agreed to come and spend the evening alone with her. Lianne could guess exactly how the weekend would have turned out if Jeffrey DeWilde hadn't forced the issue. At the last minute, Gabe would have found some concert, or dinner party, or charity ball that he needed to attend, and he would have asked her to accompany him. Anything so that he could see her, and have sex with her afterward, without venturing into a situation where there was the danger of long, quiet conversation and real intimacy. If she were forced to be honest and describe how Gabe felt about her, Lianne would have said that he liked her, but wished he didn't.

The sexual attraction between the two of them burned as fierce and strong as ever, but Lianne was beginning to feel the strain of sex that wasn't underpinned by emotional commitment. When Gabe had called at her flat this morning to pick her up, he'd made no effort to hide the desire that flared in his eyes the moment she opened the door. As soon as she confirmed that Julia had left for the weekend, he'd swept her into his arms and kissed her with a passionate thoroughness that left both of them aching and breathless.

They'd stood in the tiny entranceway, staring at each other in wary silence. Gabe might not be willing to acknowledge the stresses in their relationship but he wasn't a fool, and Lianne was sure he recognized them and knew that she was hurt by his elusiveness.

"We don't have time to make love," Gabe said finally. He was close enough that she could feel he was already aroused.

"No, we don't." Her denial carried not a shred of conviction, even to her own ears. It was one thing to wish that there was more than sex between the two of them, another thing altogether to deny the potency of their mutual attraction. She drew in a shaky breath. "Your father asked us to be at Kemberly in time for lunch. We need to leave right now if we're going to get there before one."

He bent his head, preparing to kiss her. "You've no idea how fast I can drive."

She turned away, avoiding his kisses but not moving out of his arms. Typical wishy-washy behavior when she was with Gabe, and utterly unlike her usual decisive self. "The speed limit..." she mumbled, furious with herself for wanting him, despite everything. Furious with him for assuming she was always available to fulfill his sexual needs. "The police come out in force on Saturday mornings."

Gabe looked at her, and his hazel eyes took on a lustful gleam. "I'll pay the speeding ticket," he said.

Arrogant bastard, she thought angrily. She steeled herself to say no. She knew she ought to refuse to open her heart and her body to him again until he was ready to take both halves of the package. But he swung her up into his arms and walked swiftly to her bedroom before she managed to summon up the necessary resolution.

His expression was savage as he looked down at her. "Damn it, Lianne, how in hell do you do this to me?"

"The same way you do it to me," she said, and for the first time there was a thread of bitterness in her words.

He didn't answer, just tumbled with her onto the bed, groping for the buttons of her sweater as she reached for the zipper of his slacks. Desire built so quickly, Lianne felt a flash of fear. How could she cope with the passion that blazed out of control at the mere touch of Gabe's lips on her breasts, or his fingers between her thighs? She'd never felt this way in her entire life, either about sex or about a man, and the intensity of her response scared her.

By the time Gabe entered her, she was wild, but so was he, driving into her with surging force. Lianne shook with every thrust. She struggled for breath, her rasping moans mingled with Gabe's as they raced toward the shimmering moment of release. Her nails scraped at his back. Her body arched off the bed, bowstring taut with anticipation. Above her, Gabe tensed, then plunged into her one last time. On cue, her body destructed into a thousand shooting stars of pleasure.

Gabe collapsed on top of her, oblivious to the world for at least a minute. Just long enough for Lianne to burrow her head into a pillow and fight back the betraying tears. She had been making love to Gabe. He had been having sex with her. She'd felt the deliberate withholding of his emotions in every fiber of her being. She wasn't sure how much longer she'd be able to tolerate the physical fireworks without any affection to give meaning to the dazzling display.

GABE'S VOICE BROKE the silence that blanketed the car, bringing her abruptly back to the present. "We're almost at Kemberly," he said. "The house sits on the crest of a slight hill, so you'll get a good view of it as soon as we turn the next bend in the road."

"I'm really looking forward to seeing it," Lianne said, putting aside the uncomfortable memories. "In fact, I'm looking forward to the whole weekend."

She was speaking the truth. Despite everything, it was wonderful to be out of town for a few hours, and she'd been enjoying the riotous green of the countryside ever since they left the motorway. She rolled down the window so that she could breathe in the good smell of fresh-mown grass and the occasional sickly sweet waft of silage for feeding to the dairy cows. She enjoyed living in London, and she relished the challenge of working in the competitive European fashion market, but the real reason she had chosen to leave the States was because, as a teenager, she had grown to love the English countryside, and that love had never left her. Her secret dream was one day to own a house or a cottage that had been built some time before the dawn of the twentieth century.

Even so, even knowing how much she loved old houses and old English manor houses in particular, she wasn't prepared for the surge of emotion that flooded her as they rounded the bend and Kemberly came into view.

Built at the crest of a rise, it was an early Georgian mansion whose baronial owners had been too poor and too profligate to indulge in endless modernizations. Consequently it had survived unscathed in its original flawless state, avoiding the Victorian passion for fake medieval turrets, the Edwardian craze for imperial embellishment and the early twentieth-century penchant for stringing telephone poles and electrical wires with a complete disregard for aesthetics.

The design of the house was simple, a central core and two angled wings, all facing onto a courtyard. The walls of Cotswold stone were mellowed by age and further softened by the rough, hand-hewn cast of the individual stones. Tall, graceful Queen Anne-style windows were teamed with incongruously wide Elizabethan sills, on which sat window boxes filled to bursting with spring flowers. The yellow and purple jonquils and hyacinths appeared almost indecently brilliant, overflowing their containers and splashing sensuous color against the pale golden stone. Flagstone steps led down through formal terraced gardens to a sloping lawn and a sheltering copse of beech and sycamore trees. The sun, apparently determined that Lianne should see the house at its most spectacular, slanted across the tops of the trees and illuminated the front portico in radiantly clear light. To add the final touch of enchantment, a cuckoo called out, repeating his summons a half dozen times, as if in welcome.

Lianne looked at the perfection that was Kemberly, and the artist within her fell instantly and irredeemably in love. Speechless, she stared straight ahead, unable to move, while her overloaded senses drank in the sights, sounds and smells of the blossoming flower beds and picturesque house.

Gabe drew the car to a halt in the middle of the cobblestoned circular driveway. The slippery, uneven surface was probably an accident-in-waiting on a wet winter's day, Lianne thought wryly, but the cobblestones looked so wonderfully right that she could understand why the DeWildes had chosen not to replace them. Gabe got out of the car and came around to open the door for her. For once, Lianne scarcely noticed the careful way in which he avoided physical contact with her, since her gaze was riveted on the house. Gabe was still preoccupied with getting their overnight bags from the boot of the car when Jeffrey DeWilde came out and greeted them both with a smile that, Lianne saw, was a touch strained around the edges.

"Glad you made it in time for lunch," Jeffrey said, shaking her hand and giving his son a friendly pat on the shoulder. "Mrs. Milton's been cooking up a storm, she's so pleased to have people visiting here again. I trust you've both brought hearty appetites with you or she'll be disappointed."

He misses his wife, Lianne thought immediately, not sure how she had read that message behind the jovial words of Jeffrey's greeting, but quite sure that she had. Weekends, she supposed, must make Grace's absence more conspicuous, without the hurry and bustle of the office to disguise the loneliness. Jeffrey always seemed so self-possessed, it was easy to forget that appearances could be deceiving. In truth, the better she got to know Gabe, the more Lianne realized that a controlled facade not only could mask a tumult of emotion but usually did. Jeffrey's feelings, like Gabe's, were probably all the more powerful because they ran so still and so deep.

She felt sorry for Jeffrey and wished she knew him well enough to put her arms around him and give him a hug. Since hugs were out of the question, she compromised by returning his smile with all the friendliness she could muster.

"Thank you so much for inviting me here this weekend," she said to him. "Kemberly's cast its spell over me already. If the interior of the house is even half as beautiful as the grounds, you've won a slave for life, Mr. DeWilde. All you need do is promise me time at Kemberly, and your wish will be my command."

His eyes, so like Gabe's, gleamed with affectionate amusement. "Dangerous words, Lianne. I shall certainly remember them." He turned to his son. "Traffic must have been heavy. You're a little later than we expected."

Lianne felt the heat rush instantly to her cheeks, but Gabe didn't blink. "We were delayed setting out," he said coolly.

"Ah." The amusement in Jeffrey's gaze deepened. Appalled as she was to have her early morning activities so readily guessed at, and by her lover's father, no less, Lianne was almost willing to bear the embarrassment in exchange for the lightening she sensed in Jeffrey's mood. "Mrs. Milton decided that Lianne should have the blue guest room," Jeffrey added.

Gabe finally smiled at Lianne and her stupid heart immediately skipped a beat. "You should be honored," he said to her as the three of them strolled toward the house, stopping from time to time to admire an especially colorful flower bed. "It usually takes at least a cabinet minister before the redoubtable Mrs. Milton is prepared to open up the blue room."

Jeffrey laughed his agreement. Then bleakness returned to his gaze. "Mrs. M. has been sadly deprived of guests to impress with her skills these past few months," he said. "If she had her way, you'd both be eating four meals a day, all served on antique china and tables smothered in starched damask tablecloths."

So the break between Jeffrey and Grace hadn't come out of the blue as Gabe assumed, Lianne thought. For the "past few months," it seemed the DeWildes' usual pattern of entertaining at Kemberly over the weekends had been disrupted. She had never for a moment believed that Grace had walked away from her marriage on a sudden whim, and Jeffrey's words seemed to confirm that there had been trouble in the marriage for some time before the final break.

"I'm honored, of course, to be on Mrs. Milton's 'A' list, but what's so special about the blue room?" she asked, hoping her question would banish the bleakness from Jeffrey's eyes again.

"Probably nothing." He chuckled. "Rumor has it that the Prince Regent was the first guest invited to the house after it was refurbished in 1826, and that he not only won three thousand guineas from his host playing whist, thus sending the poor baron into instant insolvency, but he also entertained the baroness in his bedroom that night, leaving significant lingering doubt as to whether the son and heir born nine months later was actually the progeny of Baron Kemberly or a by-blow of the Prince Regent. I've never been able to find any document that confirms the legend, but all the locals insist that during their night of passion, the prince commended the baroness on her splendid new blue wallpaper and that subsequent ladies of Kemberly always chose a blue decorating scheme for that room in honor of the prince's compliment."

"My mother likes to point out that if the Prince Regent had time to comment on the wallpaper, he and the baroness couldn't have been having very much fun," Gabe said. He stopped abruptly, seemingly annoyed with himself for introducing his mother's name into the conversation.

Jeffrey looked at him intently, then spoke with surprising mildness. "Your mother lived in this house for more than thirty years, Gabe. She's been mistress of it for the last twenty. You're not going to be able to come here for the weekend and never mention her name or remember her presence."

"No, of course not. I'm well aware of that." Gabe's voice was colorless and his expression neutral. "This house is the ultimate expression of my mother's personality. She loved it here." Without missing a beat, he added, in the same bland tone, "If you're ready, Lianne, I'll take you upstairs."

"Good idea," Jeffrey said, sending another assessing glance in his son's direction, but deciding to make no more personal comments. "Perhaps you could unpack after lunch, though. Mrs. Milton is doing something elaborate with puff pastry and would like us to eat as soon as possible."

Gabe dutifully escorted Lianne upstairs, but left her as soon as he'd shown her into the blue room, which was as lovely as she'd imagined it would be, with furniture dating from the Regency period, an elegant Greek Revival fireplace and a captivating view. The windows faced the rear of the house and looked out over sloping lawns and a meadow bordered by a meandering stream. Sheep grazed on the far bank of the stream, and in the distance she could see a farmhouse and the spire of the village church. The scene was so idyllic it might have been the template for a Victorian print entitled Home Sweet Home.

The idyllic views were going to have to compensate for a lot this weekend, Lianne thought ruefully, hurriedly combing her hair and fixing her makeup in the modern bathroom that adjoined her room. It was almost as if seeing her here at Kemberly had brought all Gabe's ambivalent feelings into focus, to the point that he was having trouble being civil to her, much less loverlike. So much for her crazy, secret hope that being with her at Kemberly would make him start thinking in terms of commitment and permanence and all those other words he seemed to be avoiding with such fierce determination.

After a lunch that was as delicious and overabundant as he'd predicted, Jeffrey suggested a brisk tour of the gardens to walk off the effects of too much gooseberry pie topped with far too much Cornish cream. He did most of the talking during the walk, explaining the history of the house to Lianne, and how his family had bought it in a bad state of disrepair in the mid-thirties.

"My grandparents barely had time to finish the basic structural repairs when the Second World War broke out, and, sadly, they were killed during a bombing raid only months after I was born, so I never knew them, even though I was born here at Kemberly, and lived here until my father came home from the war."

"What happened after the war?" Lianne asked. "Didn't you continue to live here?"

"No." Jeffrey smiled. "My mother, Mary, is a very remarkable woman. She was the daughter of an English country squire, and she had the most traditional upbringing you could imagine. You'd have expected her to be enchanted with Kemberly, which is the quintessential English country house, and to spend all her time here, wearing droopy cardigans and trotting around with a wicker basket, snipping the heads off dead delphiniums and knitting booties for her grandchildren."

That description actually evoked a chuckle from Gabe. "You'll have to meet my grandmother," he said. "She's in her eighties, smokes like a chimney, using one of those long, jeweled cigarette holders like Marlene Dietrich, and she loathes the country with a fierce passion. She says only those people whom God has blessed with a twisted sense of humor could possibly want to live near cows and chickens. She has a flat in London and an apartment on Park Avenue in Manhattan, and she commutes across the Atlantic as the whim takes her."

"She's in New York at the moment," Jeffrey said,

his mouth curving into a grin as he thought of his mother. "She says all the best plastic surgeons are in New York, and she's thinking of having a nose job."

"Fortunately," Gabe said, "she's having difficulty finding a doctor willing to perform elective cosmetic surgery on a woman in her eighties."

Lianne laughed, delighted at the affectionate pictures they were painting of an obviously remarkable woman. "How fortunate that her husband didn't insist on living in the country and making her play the role of lady of the manor," she said. "Your father must have been a very understanding husband."

"Superficially they weren't well-matched at all," Jeffrey told her. "My father, Charles, was hard-driving, work obsessed and very conservative in his manners and appearance. But in his heart of hearts, I've gradually come to believe he was just as much of a rebel as my mother. In typical British fashion, at least for those days, I was packed off to boarding school soon after my seventh birthday, and my parents joyfully removed themselves to London, where they bought a flat in Knightsbridge and lived a very sophisticated, glamorous life. Except during the long summer holidays, when they dutifully removed themselves to Kemberly for my sake. When Grace and I got married, my parents were delighted to find that we finally had a woman in the family who was longing to live at Kemberly. They formally deeded the house to us as a gift on our tenth wedding anniversary."

"So Megan, Kate and I grew up here," Gabe said. He shrugged his shoulders, a touch self-conscious. "It's crazy when you think of it. My mother's American, and Dad is the first generation in his family actually to be born in England, and yet I feel as if I have roots at Kemberly that stretch back forever."

"I can easily understand how that would happen," Lianne said. "I traveled around so much when I was a kid I soon realized it was feelings that bound you to a place, not how long you'd lived there, and certainly not where your ancestors came from." They'd been climbing a steep incline back toward the house, and she turned to catch her breath and look at the patchwork quilt of fields and village buildings behind them. Gabe turned to look with her.

"Despite your grandmother Mary's proclamation about cows and chickens, I imagine for most people it would be very easy to grow roots here," she said to him. "The past has barely been glossed over with a few modern touches, so you only have to dig a little way down and you can attach yourself to all the richness of Kemberly's history. I envy you your connection to this place, Gabe."

He was, as usual, maintaining a careful few inches between her body and his, because Gabe only ever touched her in passion, never in friendship. But as she finished speaking, he reached for her hand and slowly carried it to his lips, kissing the tips of her fingers with more warmth than he'd shown her in weeks of torrid sex. Silently, she looked up at him, her blood thrumming loud in her ears. What she saw in his gaze made her heart beat faster. Oblivious to his father a few yards away, he bent his head and brushed a slow, gentle kiss across her mouth.

Jeffrey continued to walk tactfully ahead, but Lianne was too conscious of his presence, and she reluctantly drew away from Gabe's embrace. "We'd better catch up with your father," she said, her voice sounding as shaken as she felt. She had just about learned to hang together and function when Gabe was offering her nothing but sex. If he started to offer her tenderness as well, her sanity was rapidly going to become a lost cause.

Gabe released her, but he held her hand in his and tucked it through his arm, walking with her in a silence that for the first time ever simply felt companionable. The spell Kemberly cast was truly potent, Lianne reflected, if it could mellow even Gabriel DeWilde.

They caught up with Jeffrey as he reentered the formal gardens. He was standing beneath a curved trellis that led into a walled and sunken garden with a stone-flagged lily pond at its center and rose bushes planted all around the edge.

"This is where I asked Grace to marry me," he said, walking slowly to one of the wooden seats, angled to give a pleasant view. "She brought this garden back from virtual ruin. Some of the roses she rescued are varieties that date from the eighteenth century and can't be found anywhere else."

"It's beautiful," Lianne said. "But everywhere here is beautiful."

"That's all Grace's doing. She transformed Kemberly from a cold barn of a place into a real home." Jeffrey cleared his throat, blinking rapidly. He gestured toward the arbor, deliberately drawing their attention away from himself. "I'm sure you can imagine what a spectacular sight this is in summer, when the dog roses are in full bloom over the walls and the trellis. Of course, at this time of year, the early buds are barely beginning to form."

Gabe paced restlessly around the paved perimeter of the lily pond, his eyebrows drawn back down into the scowl he'd only recently abandoned. Lianne sat next to

Jeffrey. Acting on an impulse she didn't allow herself to reconsider, she reached out her hand and laid it over his. "She'll come back," she said quietly. "Nobody could build a home as warm and welcoming as Kemberly and then abandon it. Not permanently."

Gabe made an impatient sound. He skimmed a tiny pebble across the top of the lilies. "My mother did just that," he said harshly. "She upped and left, and flew to San Francisco, abandoning my father, and Kemberly and anyone else who happened to be in the way of her new, self-appointed path to fulfillment."

Jeffrey stared at the rich black earth of the rose beds. Slowly, his fingers curled around Lianne's, accepting the clasp of her hand. "No," he said at last. "That's not quite what happened." He drew in a long, unsteady breath. "Grace left because I drove her away."

Behind her, Lianne felt Gabe freeze into shocked silence. When nobody spoke for several seconds, she said tentatively, "You could always ask her to come back, Mr. DeWilde."

Jeffrey gave a wintry, self-mocking smile. "No, I couldn't," he said. He removed his hand from Lianne's clasp, but swiveled on the seat to meet her gaze. "I'm a man without much courage. And like a lot of cowards, I suffer the consequences of my own fears. I forced Grace to leave because I was afraid of her power to hurt me. Which is rather like chopping off your arm because your finger is bruised." He watched a dragonfly land on a lily leaf, and his voice shaded into deeper irony. "To my profound amazement, I'm discovering that a missing arm hurts more than a bruised finger."

"I don't believe you're a man without courage," Lianne said quietly.

"Thank you," Jeffrey said. "But that's because

you're one of those people who is fortunate enough always to see the very best in others. I used to find that tiresomely naive. Now I consider it a major strength." He stood up, brushing nonexistent lint from the immaculate creases of his twill slacks. He looked at his son. "In some ways, Gabe, you're too much like me. Don't make a fool of yourself by amputating your arm because you're afraid that one day—years from now—you may have a bruised finger."

"What point are you trying to make?" Gabe asked, his voice clipped. "I've never been good at solving riddles."

Jeffrey's mouth twisted into a faint smile. "Then I'll make my advice crystal clear. You, Gabe, are currently behaving like a blithering idiot. I will therefore point out that you're not me, and Lianne isn't Grace. If the two of you get married, you're not doomed to repeat your parents' mistakes. Or our successes, for that matter."

Having reduced both of his listeners to openmouthed silence, Jeffrey nodded courteously to Lianne and swung on his heel. "I have some paperwork I need to catch up on, so if you'll excuse me, I'll leave Gabe to entertain you. Dinner tonight is at seven-thirty. I've asked a few of our neighbors to join us, so I'll see you both then." He walked off, his stride lithe and energetic, but his shoulders hunched and his hands thrust deep into the pockets of his tweed jacket.

Lianne stood and watched him leave, her face burning with embarrassment. Gabe came to stand in front of her. Surprisingly, he didn't look either annoyed or embarrassed but rather amused. "My father has the most infuriating capacity for hitting the nail squarely on the head," he said.

"Which particular nail were you referring to?" Lianne asked with unusual tartness. "The fact that he called you a blithering idiot?"

"Especially that." Gabe put his arms around her waist, drawing her slowly toward him. "But more specifically to the fact that I've spent the past several weeks running away from you because I was too much of a coward to do what I really wanted to do. Which is to tell you how much I love you, and ask you, please, to marry me."

Her breath constricted in her throat, but she turned away, uneasy at his instant capitulation to his father's bidding. "Gabe, you don't have to do this. We're a hop, skip and a jump away from the twenty-first century. This may come as hot-breaking news to you, but it's been a hundred years or so since dutiful sons proposed marriage because their fathers told them to."

"Now you're being foolish," he said. "Totally absurd, in fact." He drew her back to the seat and sat down, taking her into the shelter of his arms and dropping a light kiss onto her hair. "Of course I'm not asking you to marry me because my father told me to. I'm in love with you, Lianne, crazily in love. That's why I want to marry you."

"You've never expressed the slightest interest in marrying me until one minute ago."

He hesitated for a moment. "These have been a rough few weeks for me, Lianne, watching the breakup of my parents' marriage. The truth is that my feelings for you got badly mixed up with the way I was feeling about their separation." He shrugged, self-conscious at revealing his uncertainties. "Most of the time recently, I haven't been sure what I felt about anything. Somehow, it never seemed to be quite the right moment to suggest getting married."

"I can understand that," she said. "But I have the impression something a lot more personal was going on between us than just the generalized backwash of your parents' situation. Sometimes when we're together, I get the feeling that you're actively struggling not to like me. This morning, for example, in the car. You hated the fact that you were bringing me to Kemberly. I could feel it as clearly as if you'd said the words out loud."

"Well, my father was right about a lot of things just now, including the fact that I was scared. I didn't hate the idea of bringing you to Kemberly, I was scared of it."

"But why? Scared of what? I've never thought of myself as an intimidating person."

He drew in a deep breath. "I was scared by how much you remind me of my mother," he admitted. "Not in looks, but in personality. You have all her exuberance, her creativity, her capacity for grabbing life by the throat and getting the best out of it. I always think of myself as being more like my father, with my emotions held on such a tight rein that I'm often in danger of choking myself to death. Seeing you here—seeing how completely you fit in…" He stumbled to a halt and started over. "It seemed to me that if my parents couldn't make a go of their marriage, the two of us would be tempting fate if we tried. We'd be juggling problems that were so similar to theirs, and if they couldn't succeed, how could we?"

"And a few words from your father could make you change your mind, just like that?"

"Not in the way you're imagining," Gabe said, failing to hear the quiver of anger in her voice. "My father is normally a very private man, and I think the reason he told us as much as he did about the breakup of their marriage was because he wanted me to see that I've been misjudging my mother. He wanted me to realize that she didn't wake up one morning and decide to fly to San Francisco on a whim, that there were all sorts of complicated undercurrents at work that contributed to the breakup."

"And because your mother didn't precipitate the split with your father, now you've decided that it's safe to ask me to marry you? That because Grace didn't behave in the way you feared, now you can trust me to be a good wife?" Lianne's entire body was shaking with the force of her fury. She scrambled to her feet. "Thank you, Gabe, for asking me to marry you. The answer is no. I'm not interested in being some psychologically twisted substitute for your mother."

She pulled away from him and ran toward the house, but he caught up with her and dragged her around to face him. "It isn't you I don't trust," he snarled. "It's myself."

"And your father's suddenly inspired you with a burst of confidence in your own judgment?" she demanded with biting sarcasm.

"Yes, damn it, yes! He made me realize that I can't bear the thought of spending the rest of my life without you, and to hell with the problems, real and imagined. I want to marry you because I love you, damn it! Because life with you is a rainbow of color and without you it's nothing but gray shadow."

"Very poetic," she said. "It's a great act, Gabe, but it's too late for protestations of undying affection. I don't want to marry you."

He slammed her against the wall, palms flat on the

bricks, imprisoning her between his arms. "Then live with me in sin, I don't care. But don't try to tell me you're ready to give up this." He slanted his mouth across hers, his kisses searing, almost cruel.

No, she didn't want to give up the sex. But she didn't want to marry a man at his father's bidding, either, however well-meaning Jeffrey's interference had been. "You're right, Gabe," she said wearily. "Sex with you is fabulous. Gives me a real high. So when you next want sex, call me. I'm available. But I'm not going to accept any more invitations to concerts and plays and charity balls. And I'm especially not going to accept invitations to spend the weekend at Kemberly. Let's not pretend there's anything more to our relationship than there really is."

He looked confused, angry, unsure of himself, light years from his usual cool self. "You told me two weeks ago that you loved me."

"Yes, well, some things are better left unspoken. Or forgotten once they've been said."

He stepped away from her, but only far enough to reach into the inner pocket of his jacket and remove a small, dark blue box with the familiar DeWilde logo stamped in gold on the lid.

He held it out to her. "I bought this the morning after we made love—after the gala," he said. "I've been carrying it around with me ever since, trying to find the words to go with it."

Lianne didn't move, so he took her hand and dropped the box into her palm, curling her fingers around it. "It's probably too late," he said. "But I wish you'd open it."

She looked down at the ring box, almost unable to believe what she was seeing. This had to have been

Gabe's own idea, nothing to do with what his father had just said. Throat tight, she pressed the tiny gold latch and watched the lid spring open.

Nestled in a bed of velvet, with the traditional puff of peach satin as a backdrop, was the Victorian ring she'd admired on the day she started work at De-Wilde's.

Slowly, she drew the ring out of the box. The tiny diamonds at the heart of the golden flowers sparkled in the sunlight. "How did you know I liked this ring?" she asked, voice low, not quite even.

"Harry Pierce, the salesman, told me you liked it." He cleared his throat. "I wish you'd keep it, Lianne, no strings attached, of course. It suits you perfectly, and I'd like to think of you wearing it."

The workmanship was exquisite. Even so, it had probably been one of the least expensive rings in the entire DeWilde store. Lianne's heart turned over with love when she looked at it and knew that Gabe had had the sensitivity to choose something so absolutely right for her. "You'd better put it on," she said, holding out her left hand.

Gabe perked up a bit at that. "Er...which finger?" he asked.

"You choose," she said softly.

"That's easy," he murmured. He slid the ring onto her engagement finger, then carried her hand to his mouth and pressed a burning kiss at the place where the band met her skin. "I love you, Lianne. More than I know how to express. If you marry me, I promise that I'll do everything in my power to make you happy."

She touched the ring, smiling at him, her eyes misty. "Actually, Gabe, you just did a pretty good job—of expressing yourself, and making me happy."

He grinned, still faintly self-conscious. "Yes, well, I heard you can always buy a woman's affections with diamonds."

"Or with great sex," Lianne said. "You should keep that in mind for future reference."

He took her into his arms, crushing her against him. "Then I've got it made," he said. "How many men can you hope to find with their own private supply of cost-price diamonds and the best damn sex outside of the *Kama Sutra?*"

"Not many," she said, her breath catching. "I'm sure there can't be many."

CHAPTER TWELVE

3:00 P.M.: INSPECT possible office space with Rita Shannon. Tossing her purse and car keys onto the kitchen counter, Grace made the entry in her calendar and underlined it. Rita Shannon was her newly hired assistant, and she was already proving herself invaluable, a hard worker with creative energy to spare. And Grace certainly needed competent administrative help. She was getting inundated with work, meetings and commitments—and it felt terrific!

She poured herself a glass of ice water and drank thirstily. Inspecting potential sites for her new store was hot and tiring work, but she was loving every minute of it, despite the fact that she was no closer to finding something suitable than she had been ten days ago. Today, she'd been shown a building that was ideally located. Unfortunately, it was almost derelict, but she supposed it might, with extensive renovation, be made viable as an upscale bridal store rather than the failed health club it currently was. She would take her architect to look at it tomorrow and see how much money they were talking about to do the job properly. She was determined not to ruin her concept for the new store by skimping on the up-front expenditures.

She checked her answering machine, which was crammed with messages from three different real estate agents, an interior design architect who had heard rumors of her plans to open a store, her bank, her brother, and even one from Kate, who for once didn't seem to be working back-to-back shifts and wanted to meet for dinner.

Grace wrote down the messages, smiling as she turned the pages of her calendar and saw that every day for the next couple of weeks had at least one meeting scheduled. She smiled again, even more happily, when she turned to September and saw the red-letter notation for September 21.

Gabe and Lianne's wedding.

Three months almost to the day and her beloved Gabe would be a married man. Among the many changes his engagement had produced was the minor miracle that Gabe was speaking to her again. He'd phoned personally to tell her the wonderful news that he and Lianne Beecham were engaged, and although he hadn't initiated any more conversations, he'd at least answered the phone on the two occasions during the past month that Grace had called him. If she could just get him to accept the fact that her plans for a bridal store in San Francisco would have no impact on DeWilde operations...

Realistically speaking, convincing Gabe that she had no plans to undercut DeWilde's was likely to be a gradual task, and in the meantime, the days were marching inexorably toward September and his wedding. They really didn't have enough time to arrange the perfect ceremony and reception, but with a little bit of hard work and cooperation from all the parties involved, Grace thought she should be able to pull off something spectacular enough to do justice to the occasion. If she'd hand-picked the woman she wanted Gabe to marry, she couldn't have come up with anyone more perfect than Lianne, and she wanted the ceremony that celebrated their union to produce memories both Lianne and her son would treasure for a lifetime.

Humming, Grace walked into the bedroom, casting an approving half glance toward the sleek lines of her all-in-one headboard and nightstands. The hideous phone conversation with Jeffrey last month had proven liberating in the end, cutting her loose from the paralysis that had gripped her in the first few weeks of their separation. Riding high on a burst of fury, she'd rushed right out and spent a small fortune on furniture, which was still being delivered on an almost daily basis.

The memory of her painful conversation with Jeffrey—the last one she'd had, since he'd chosen to remain totally silent on the subject of Gabe's engagement—was no more than a minor irritant, a sore spot she could comfortably bandage over. These days, she could sometimes go for hours at a stretch without giving her husband so much as a passing thought. She assumed that one day in the not too distant future, she'd discover that she had survived an entire twenty-four hours without thinking of him at all. And that would be the day on which she finally worked up the courage to file for a divorce.

She tossed her linen jacket over the back of the swivel rocker in the corner of her bedroom and dropped her earrings into a ceramic pot on the top of her dresser. Having lived most of her adult life surrounded by antiques, she'd decided to make a complete break with the past and furnish her San Francisco apartment with the latest in contemporary, high-tech style. So far, her bedroom was the only room for which all the furniture had been delivered, and she loved every piece of it. Moreover, the alien and glossy freshness of her apartment was inspiring her with a cornucopia of ideas for the new store.

In her mind's eye, she was already building an image of her store, and she saw display areas with lots of soaring glass and polished chrome, softened by intimate display nooks and specialty boutiques decorated in warm, feminine colors, so that brides trying on wedding gowns would be able to visualize themselves against both soaring, public spaces and the intimacy of their honeymoon suite.

Oh, yes, Grace thought, kicking off her high-heeled sandals and walking toward the bed, her San Francisco store was going to become an immediate landmark in the retailing industry. And it would owe nothing, absolutely nothing, to the stuffy, antique splendor of DeWilde's. The concept would be entirely hers, all Grace and nothing of Jeffrey. Definitely not even a smidgeon of Jeffrey.

She sat cross-legged in the center of the bed and reached across to press a command button on the electronic keypad built into her nightstand. A small door in the headboard slid open, and a shelf projected itself forward electronically to offer her the telephone. When the shelf was fully extended, a little spotlight illuminated the dial. She grinned with childlike pleasure as she lifted the receiver, wondering in amusement how any furniture designer ever came up with the idea that customers would pay money to have their phones glide in and out on a useless electronic tray, and knowing full well that she'd fallen for the lure and would never again be entirely happy with a bedside phone that didn't have its own secret niche to slide into at the push of a button.

It was already ten-thirty at night in London, but Grace assumed Lianne would still be up. Pulling her checklist of wedding questions out of the bedside drawer, she dialed the number of Lianne's London flat. So far, the list was depressingly clean, unsullied by a single checkmark indicating task accomplished, which was worrisome, to say the least. She mustn't forget to ask about bridesmaids, Grace thought, scribbling a notation as the phone started to ring. Sometimes choosing the right bridesmaids' dresses could be more difficult than finding the perfect wedding gown....

"Hello." A sleepy, distracted voice finally answered the phone.

"Lianne? This is Grace. How are you, my dear? I hope I didn't wake you."

"Grace? Oh, how nice to hear from you. No, you didn't wake me. It's...um...only ten-thirty."

"Good, I'm so glad I managed to reach you. We have so much to talk about, and with the eight-hour time difference, it's difficult to catch you at home." Grace crossed her legs and tucked a pillow behind her back, getting comfortable. "I'm longing to hear all your plans for the wedding. Gabe really didn't seem to know anything when I spoke with him last week, but then men never manage to cope very well with wedding plans, do they. I remember Jeffrey was absolutely useless when we were trying to decide—"

Damn! She'd been doing so well in the Jeffrey department today. She broke off sharply and began again. "Well, let's get down to the most important question first. Have you decided yet whether you're going to be married in town or at All Saints in Kemberly?"

There was a long pause before Lianne replied. "Actually, Grace, my parents seem to feel that it would be a very good idea if Gabe and I got married at the Unitarian church they attend in Benton's Inlet. They like the minister a lot and they think I'll like him, too."

"Benton's Inlet? In Michigan?" As soon as she spoke, Grace realized that she'd said Michigan as if it were located somewhere between the dark side of the moon and the planet Jupiter. "Well, of course I realize that the bride's family traditionally chooses where the wedding is going to take place, but Gabe has so many friends in London, and I'm sure you do, too. Not to mention all our friends, people we ought to invite because of their connection to DeWilde's..."

"My parents have a lot of friends, too."

Grace drew in a deep breath, appalled at her tactlessness. "Of course they do, how thoughtless of me. A fall wedding in Michigan will be just lovely, I'm sure. Your mother and I had a long chat on the phone the other day, and I remember that she told me Benton's Inlet is right on the shore of Lake Michigan, which must make for a very pretty setting. And if you and Gabe want to get married on this side of the Atlantic, naturally I'm delighted."

"Well, we still haven't quite decided exactly what we want to do," Lianne said. "As you pointed out, most of our friends are here in London, but my relatives nearly all live in Michigan, and they really want to come and see me get married. Plus my mother is worried about my grandparents. My grandfather is eighty-six years old, and his wife is eighty-seven. My mother knows the plane journey to England would be too much for them, but if I get married here, they'll insist on making the trip. Which is a bit of a dilemma."

"I can see how it would be. But rather a nice dilemma in a way. How splendid that your grandparents are still alive."

"Yes, my father's mother is alive, too, but she's in much better health than my mother's parents. I'm very fortunate." Lianne's voice sounded hollow.

"Well, if you and Gabe decide to tie the knot in Michigan that will make travel plans a lot easier for Kate and me!" Grace was determined to look on the bright side.

"Don't book your plane tickets yet," Lianne cautioned. "Gabe and I are still discussing all the various pros and cons. There's a lot to take into consideration."

Grace bit her tongue and managed, with heroic effort, not to point out that with only three months to go, she and Gabe needed to stop "considering" and make a decision one way or the other. Lianne was a dear, sweet girl, but she obviously didn't grasp the time constraints they were working against. Three months was scarcely more than the blink of an eye when you were trying to plan a formal wedding. In fact, it would be impossible if it weren't for the DeWilde connection and the contacts Grace had within the industry. Until the church had been selected, no arrangements could be made for the reception. And until the venue for the reception had been decided upon, no caterers could be selected. And without caterers, no menu could be finalized. Not to mention the thousand other details that would have to be taken care of—the band, the flowers, the photographers, the video people.

And then there was the urgent need to get invitations engraved and addressed in plenty of time for busy people to clear their schedules and plan their travel itineraries. Especially, Grace thought, if guests from England and France were going to have to get themselves to an obscure place like Benton's Inlet. And how about Ryder Blake in Australia? Gabe would probably want Ryder as his best man, and with his hectic work schedule, Ryder would need to know whether he was supposed to be flying to the States or to England.

However, she had always sworn she would never turn into one of those dreadful, bossy mother-in-laws, Grace reminded herself, much less one of those mothers who was so busy organizing the wedding to her own taste that she forgot about minor details like the wishes of the bride and groom. She decided that a tactful change of subject was called for.

"Have you chosen your dress yet?" she asked. "This is a good year in terms of style and workmanship, isn't it? The manufacturers seem to be deemphasizing the glitter and paying more attention to subtle details like the cut and fall of the dress."

"You're right, the selection was great." Lianne finally began to sound enthusiastic. "I had a hard time making my final choice, but I'm really pleased with the one I picked in the end. It's quite a simple design, ivory satin with long sleeves and a scandalously low neckline."

A bubble of the bright laughter that Grace always associated with her daughter-in-law-to-be finally warmed Lianne's voice. "I'm going to buy one of those new superbras that they're advertising everywhere and see if I can't walk down the aisle with some real, honest-to-God cleavage beneath my modest lace veil. That'll be a real wedding present to myself."

Grace laughed. "I shall remember to take special note of the cleavage. I'm sure it will be spectacular! Please have one of your bridesmaids take a picture when you have your fitting and send it to me by express mail. I can't wait to see exactly what you've chosen. And, Lianne, I'd be thrilled if you'd allow me the very great pleasure of buying your dress for you. Think of it as a little extra wedding gift from me."

There was a moment of tense silence before Lianne responded. "Grace, thank you, you're so kind, and I do appreciate your generous thought, but...um...Jeffrey has already offered to pay for my dress and I accepted."

"No problem," Grace said, managing—she hoped—to make her response sound light and carefree. "You'll simply have to indulge me when I next come over to London and we'll buy something wonderful for your honeymoon. Where are you going, by the way? Or is that a secret?"

"It's a secret. Although I will tell you that I vetoed Gabe's first suggestion of a yak trip through Kathmandu." Laughter returned to Lianne's voice. "I suggested he should stop striving so hard for originality and start thinking more along the lines of in-room hot tubs and twenty-four-hour room service. He came up with Las Vegas. It took him a couple more tries, but I think he's finally managed to get it just right."

Grace refused to remember her own honeymoon in Rome, with hot, blissful days exploring the wonders of the ancient city, and cool, blissful nights discovering the wonders of making love to Jeffrey. She wouldn't think about the afternoon, sipping espresso in the Piazza San Bartolomeo, when Jeffrey had bought a slightly wilted rose from a street vendor and handed it to her with a shy, self-conscious smile. And she'd made the astonishing discovery that she was falling head over heels in love with the man she'd married for all the wrong reasons.

Her honeymoon in Rome was more than thirty years in the past, the love she'd shared with Jeffrey dead and forgotten. These days, her husband didn't care enough about her to pick up the phone to talk about plans for their only son's forthcoming marriage—

Grace ruthlessly cut off her descent into self-pity, knowing from bitter past experience that it was a most self-destructive path to take. "Well, it's been great talking to you, Lianne, although I can't exactly say we finalized any plans." Grace tried not to let even a trace of impatience color her voice. "I'll look forward to hearing from you as soon as you and Gabe make up your minds exactly where you're going to have this great event."

"Yes, of course. I'll be sure to call."

"When you next see Gabe, give him my love, won't you?"

There was an infinitesimal pause. "Yes, I'll tell him. Er...when I see him."

Oh, Lord, Grace thought wryly. *Gabe's there with her, which is why she sounded so sleepy and distracted when I called.*

"Well, I must run," she said, deciding it was definitely time to get off the phone. "My schedule is jam-packed for the rest of the day, and it must be getting toward your bedtime."

"Yes." There was a tiny catch in Lianne's voice and Grace had a sudden, embarrassingly vivid image of what might have caused it.

"Nice chatting with you, Lianne," she said quickly. "Goodbye."

LIANNE HUNG UP THE PHONE and rolled over in bed, swatting with mock annoyance at Gabe's marauding fingers. "Your mother guessed," she said accusingly. "It was extremely embarrassing. She guessed you were in bed with me."

Gabe nibbled delicately on his fiancée's earlobe. "Did she? Somehow I don't think that will be the first hint she's had that we're not going to our marriage bed in a state of virginal purity."

Lianne sighed. "Honestly, Gabe, the way things are going right at the moment, I'm beginning to have serious doubts about whether we'll ever make it to our marriage bed."

He sat up, his smile wiped away in a single instant. "What do you mean? Are you suggesting that you don't want to marry me after all?"

She shook her head. "No, of course not. How could you even think that? But, Gabe, you've been so busy at work, I don't think you realize what's going on. This wedding ceremony is turning out to be a nightmare of major proportions. I honestly don't know how we're going to get through it."

"How so? What's the problem?" He grinned. "I've heard a rumor that DeWilde's is a really good bridal store, with contacts to help you take care of every detail in planning the perfect wedding."

She didn't crack even a small smile. "It isn't one problem, it's dozens of problems, and none of them the sort that can be solved by DeWilde's or any other store. Your mother isn't talking to your father and vice versa, and either one could file for a divorce at any moment. That's just for starters. Then there's Julia, my best friend, the person in the world I most want to have as my maid of honor. She's in love with you, Gabe. There's no point in trying to ignore that fact any longer."

"Are you sure?" he asked, frowning. "Honest to God, Lianne, I never said a word about marriage to her, never even hinted at it. And she always seems perfectly cheerful whenever we happen to meet. You know, like a friend, a good friend."

"She's way too cheerful, that's the problem. She's lost half a stone in the past two weeks, and she smiles with such desperate determination every time she sees us together that I want to cry, even if she doesn't."

He took her hand, lacing her fingers with his. "I'm really sorry if I've hurt Julia. I sure as hell wish I hadn't. But I'm in love with you, and we can't decide not to marry just because it upsets Julia. That makes no sense at all."

"True. But I'm going to go all through the service knowing that my best friend's heart is breaking, and that I'm putting her through several hours of unrelieved torture by asking her to watch us get married."

"You couldn't ask someone else to be your chief bridesmaid?"

Lianne shook her head. "I've thought about it, but that would be worse. At least now she still has her pride. If I don't ask her to be my maid of honor, she'll know exactly why I didn't, and it sort of forces everyone to confront truths it would be much more comfortable to keep covered up."

"Yes, for once I don't think honesty is the best policy. You're right—it's a problem," Gabe said.

Lianne grimaced. "You ain't heard nuttin' yet. We've barely started on the list of problems. There's the whole issue of my family. My mother and father have discovered approximately two hundred aunts, uncles, cousins and miscellaneous relatives who are going to be mortally wounded if they can't come and dance at our wedding. Which they can't afford to do unless we have the ceremony in Michigan."

"Well, that's easily solved. We'll get married in Michigan."

"Gabe, I could hear your mother grinding her teeth to stop herself from having apoplexy when she heard that might be where we would have the ceremony. My parents are thinking picnic tables in the church hall, and your parents are thinking caviar and champagne, followed by a four-course dinner catered by England's finest chefs."

"The picnic sounds just fine to me."

"Does it? What about all our friends? They're here in London. I don't think they want to fly to Michigan for a barbecue. As for your sister Kate, she was excruciatingly polite when I called and asked her to be one of my bridesmaids, but I know she was secretly worrying about how in the world she was going to find time to fly to London. Or Michigan, or wherever the heck this wretched ceremony is going to be."

"You've left out Megan," he said, settling back against the pillows and beginning a languid tasting of the hollows at the base of her neck. "What's Megan's complaint to add to this litany of pending disaster?"

"Nothing," she said. "Megan is so relieved your mother has another family wedding to plan that she's ecstatic. She's hoping everyone will lay off for a few months and stop trying to fix her up with some man or another. She thanked me profusely for taking the spotlight away from her."

"There you are, then," he said. "At least we're making one member of the family happy."

"That leaves about 295 people in the other column."

"Then I guess this is where you draw in a very deep breath and accept that you can't please everyone."

"Not even ourselves?"

"You always please me," he said, his voice deepening. "I'll do my damnedest to return the compliment." He rolled over and captured her hands, holding them high over her head so that he had better access to her body. "Mmm," he said, tasting appreciatively. "You know, I can understand how the vampire legends got started. There's something so incredibly erotic about a woman's throat. Not to mention her breasts and her—"

"Gabe, damn it, you're not listening to me!"

"It's hard to lick and listen at the same time."

She pushed him away, surprised to discover that she was a hairbreadth away from tears. "Gabe, this isn't funny! What are we going to do? By the time this wedding finally takes place, nobody is going to be speaking to anybody! Probably including me to you!"

Gabe sat up, pulling her into his lap and cradling her head against his shoulder. "I'm sorry, sweet, you're really serious about this, aren't you."

"Of course I'm serious. Gabe, this is the sort of situation that tears families apart, creates feuds that last into the sixth generation and leaves the bride and groom so exhausted that they take the first two years of their marriage to get over the horrors of the wedding."

"You exaggerate, my love. I'm sure it wouldn't take us a day over six months. We have such great communication skills."

She smiled weakly. "Gabe, what in the world are we going to do?"

He put his hand under her chin, tipped back her head, and kissed her gently. "Don't worry," he said. "The important thing is that we both know we want to spend the rest of our lives together. It shouldn't be impossible to solve the problem of how we actually get married."

When he smiled at her, she could believe that he was capable of anything, even devising a way to marry her without hurting the feelings of either set of in-laws. She sighed and nestled closer to him. "Sometimes that DeWilde arrogance of yours comes in really handy. You sound so self-confident, I almost believe you."

He kissed the end of her nose. "You should believe me. Trust me, darling, this is all going to work out just fine, you'll see."

EPILOGUE

THE DOORMAN STOPPED GRACE as she hurried toward the elevators after a day filled to bursting with appointments, meetings and discussions with lawyers. "Mrs. DeWilde, a package has arrived for you. We put it in the fridge in our storeroom, so it would keep cool."

"Thank you," Grace replied absently, her thoughts split almost evenly between tomorrow's meeting with one of her brother's bankers and the fact that neither Gabe nor Lianne had seen fit to call her in almost two weeks. She was trying to hold on to her patience, but their failure to fix on a place for their wedding was progressing well beyond inconvenient and moving into downright inconsiderate. It was too late to phone England tonight, but first thing tomorrow morning she was going to call Gabe and read him the riot act.

The doorman came out from the storeroom carrying a large wicker basket, wrapped in cellophane and tied with long streamers of silver ribbon. "Can you manage it, Mrs. DeWilde? There's nobody else covering the door or I'd carry it upstairs for you."

Grace took the basket and hefted it in her arms. "I can manage, thanks. Fortunately, it's not too heavy." She poked apart the cellophane wrapping while she waited for the elevator. "Mmm...Dom Perignon," she said, seeing the magnum of champagne nestled in a bed of fake white straw. "Not to mention a box of chocolate truffles and a carton of imported Italian sugared almonds. It all looks very expensive." She smiled at the doorman as he held open the elevator door for her. "Somebody's sure anxious to make a good impression. I wonder what they're trying to sell me?"

The doorman grinned. "Whatever it is, take your time deciding. That way you may get another basket of goodies."

"Great advice," Grace said as the elevator doors slid closed.

Her apartment was blissfully cool and quiet after the hot, noisy day. Grace set the gift basket on the center island in her kitchen, along with her purse, and untied the streamers of silver ribbon. Pushing aside the cellophane, she reached for the enclosed gift card at the same time as she pressed the playback button on her answering machine. Listening to the first message, she slit open the gift card, which was unusually large and bulky. And probably came complete with attached sales pitch, Grace thought cynically.

The gift card didn't come with a sales pitch but with a letter. Grace started reading. The second phone message never made it past the first three or four words. With a strangled gasp, she hit the pause button on her answering machine and stared in blank disbelief at the letter. Blinking as if faulty vision were the problem, she read through the lengthy note one more time. It was still signed by Gabe and Lianne. It still said the same incredible things.

Choking back several choice expletives, she grabbed the bottle of Dom Perignon and stormed into her bedroom, shedding shoes and clothes as she went. She ended up undressed as far as her slip, perched in her favorite spot in the middle of the bed, breathing hard, the bottle of champagne nestled at her feet.

She grabbed the phone, dialing London without even stopping to think. "Don't leave the answering machine to pick up," she muttered. "Come on, Jeffrey. I need to speak to you. I really need to speak to you."

"Hello."

"Jeffrey." Her entire body slumped in relief. "Jeffrey, thank goodness I caught you at home. I just got back to my apartment and there was this totally incredible package waiting for me from Gabe and Lianne—"

"Champagne," he said. "And chocolates. Also *confetti*—the traditional sugared almonds at Italian weddings. You must admit that they made their announcement in grand style."

"Good grief, Jeffrey, I can't believe you're sounding so calm!"

"You should have caught me six hours ago when I came home and found my gift basket! You have to remember that I've had a little longer than you to get used to the idea. In fact, I've been expecting your call for the past several hours."

Belatedly she realized that in London it was 2:00 a.m. "Oh, Lord, Jeffrey, I'm sorry to phone at such an ungodly hour, but I had to talk to you. I can't believe it! They've eloped, damn it! Eloped!"

"To Gretna Green, according to the helpful little note they enclosed with my basket of goodies," Jeffrey said dryly. "I'm sure they gave you the same fascinating piece of information."

"How could they?" Grace wailed. "Jeffrey, we would have given them such a beautiful wedding, and instead they decide to run off and get married in some poky little registrar's office in Gretna Green, for heaven's sake!"

"I know. It's monumentally inconsiderate of them. I would have strangled Gabe for you, my dear, but unfortunately, he wasn't available for strangling. And by the time he and Lianne get back from their honeymoon in the Scottish Highlands, I dare say we'll be foolish enough to forgive them."

"Oh, Jeffrey!" Grace hovered somewhere between tears and laughter. "For a family that has a world-famous name for fulfilling wedding fantasies, we don't seem to be doing too well with our own children, do we. First Megan gets left at the altar. Now Gabe and Lianne elope. I shudder to think what Kate will come up with—"

"Better that Megan got left at the altar than that she ended up married to the wrong man. And in the long run, the important thing is that Gabe and Lianne love each other, not whether they got married with a supporting cast of hundreds to watch them."

"I suppose so. But I did so want them to have a special day to remember."

"I'm sure this has been a special day for them," Jeffrey said quietly. "Anyway, Gracie, the deed is done. All that's left for us now is to wish them happiness."

"Damn it, Jeffrey, would you stop being so...so mature about all this? He's our son, our only son. I know it's selfish of me, but I so badly wanted to stand next to you in the church at Kemberly while he and Lianne promised to love and care for each other—" Grace stopped abruptly, appalled at how much she'd unwittingly revealed in that unthinking remark, not only to Jeffrey but also to herself.

Her husband was silent for several long moments.

"Well, I suppose we shall have to make our own impromptu, long-distance celebration as best we can," he said at last. "I haven't opened my champagne. Why don't you get your bottle and bring it back to the phone. Then we'll pop the corks, each pour ourselves a large glass, and toast Gabe and Lianne together."

"I already have the bottle of champagne here on the bed with me," Grace said.

"You're sitting on the bed?" Jeffrey asked, his voice suddenly strained.

"Yes." For some odd reason, a wave of heat washed over her. She swallowed, moistening her dry throat. "Old habits are hard to break."

There was another long pause. "Yes, I've discovered that." Jeffrey cleared his throat. "Do you have a glass, or just the bottle of champagne?"

He knew her too well, Grace thought, knew that she would have stormed to the phone clutching the champagne and—inevitably—forgotten to bring a glass. It was almost as if he were in the bedroom with her. "I don't have a glass, but I'll get one," she said. "The start of our son's marriage deserves to be toasted with something more elegant than a swig from the bottle."

She grabbed one of her new crystal glasses from the dining room and came back to the bed. She picked up the phone. "I'm ready. I have everything now."

"Then open the bottle of champagne and pick up the phone when you've poured yourself a glass."

The cork shot up toward the ceiling with a satisfying pop. Grace poured herself a glass and picked up the phone. "Jeffrey? Are you there? I have a full glass."

"I'm here," he said, "Dom Perignon in hand. And I offer a toast to our son, Gabe, and Lianne, his new wife. May they spend a lifetime together in love, health and happiness."

Grace was suddenly afraid that she was going to cry. "I'll drink to that," she said huskily, and took a quick sip of champagne. "To Gabe and Lianne."

She put down her glass and waited, breath squeezed so tight in her lungs that her chest ached, but Jeffrey didn't ask how she was or what she'd been doing with herself all day. Perhaps he was afraid to, she thought sadly. Perhaps, on a call celebrating the start of Gabe's marriage to Lianne, he didn't want to risk introducing the bitter debris of their own failures.

Finally, he spoke. "Grace, thank you for calling. I'm glad we were able to share a glass of champagne together on such a special occasion, even if it was at long distance."

"We did make three super kids, didn't we, Jeffrey? Whatever else we messed up, we managed to get that just right."

"Yes, we did," he said softly. "We managed to get that just right."

He didn't say anything more, and this time it was Grace who broke the silence. "Well, I know it's late for you, Jeffrey—"

"Yes, it is rather late, and with Gabe leaving so unexpectedly, I'm going to have a hell of a day tomorrow. Good night, Grace. Take care of yourself."

"Good night, Jeffrey. Sleep well."

She hung up the phone and stared unseeingly at the bottle of Dom Perignon. Finally, she squared her shoulders, picked up her glass and tossed back the rest of her champagne in a couple of quick gulps.

"Here's to us, Jeffrey," she whispered. "Here's to us."

I DO, AGAIN

CHAPTER ONE

THE FAMOUS GROUND FLOOR of DeWilde's London store was silent, the lights dim, the glittering trays of jewels covered, the daily throng of customers dispersed. Jeffrey DeWilde prowled among the deserted displays, noting the changes that had been made during the past week and wondering if they were improvements. He admired an elegant arrangement of Spanish leather handbags and Italian silk scarves, raised an eyebrow at the decision to present sterling silver hairbrushes on a bed of purple satin underwear, and paused for a moment in front of the eye-catching booth that now housed the gift registry. Was it really a good idea to bring the registry down from its traditional cramped quarters on the fourth floor and set it up in a prominent position here on the ground floor by the lifts? Jeffrey had no idea, but Gabe seemed to think so, and over the past months, Jeffrey had learned to trust his son's judgment on matters of merchandising.

Until their separation little more than a year ago, Jeffrey and his wife had always made this ritual Friday-night tour together. With Grace at his side, explaining the practical significance of each innovation, Jeffrey had thoroughly enjoyed the hour it took to complete the tour. He'd treated their stroll through the quiet store as a prelude to the weekend, a way for Grace and him to unwind after the frenetic intensity of their work week.

Sometimes, he'd even been able to contribute something useful by tying in what Grace showed him with the overall financial status of the DeWilde retail empire—which included branches in Paris, Sydney, New York and Monaco. Sales figures, wholesale costs, interest charges, overhead and profit margins were always crystal clear in his brain. But without Grace to help him translate that financial picture into more concrete terms of day-to-day retailing, he had nothing to offer when it came to decisions about the choice of merchandise and the way it was displayed.

For the past fifteen months, his Friday-night tour had been little more than an act of defiance—a gesture to prove to himself that everything in his entire world hadn't changed for the worse just because Grace had left him and they were now divorced.

Divorced. As far as Jeffrey was concerned, the word still sounded nonsensical when applied to himself and Grace, although his solicitors had assured him in one of their typically pompous letters that after thirty-two years of marriage and a year of separation, he was once again a bachelor. He'd wanted the divorce from Grace. Five months ago, when she took up residence in Nevada in order to file for divorce, he'd positively craved an end to their marriage, yearning for a surcease of the pain they were causing each other.

He'd been officially footloose and fancy-free since April, and now it was almost August. Fifteen weeks of glorious liberation from the chains of matrimony. Jeffrey let out a crack of harsh laughter. Ah, yes, he was experiencing all the joys of freedom from his miserably failed marriage. He hoped—he really hoped—that in another year or so, the mere mention of the words *di-*

vorce and *bachelor* wouldn't have the power to make him feel suicidally depressed.

"Is everything all right, sir?" One of the uniformed security guards stepped out of the shadows into Jeffrey's line of vision.

"Yes, everything's quite all right, thank you." If you didn't count the frequent desire to throw punches at the nearest wall, everything was just wonderful. Jeffrey swung away, reluctant to submit to the guard's barely concealed curiosity. He would never get used to the fact that his most intimate concerns were a matter for interested gossip by his employees. Not to mention the prurient articles in the tabloids. The gossip magazines seemed determined to treat him as a sex icon for any readers too mature to go into raptures over John F. Kennedy, Jr., an idea that Jeffrey would have found hilariously funny if it hadn't been so embarrassingly wide of the mark.

They were standing next to the octagonal glass case that housed the Empress Eugénie tiara, and his movement away from the guard brought him face-to-face with the dazzling coronet of diamonds and pearls, displayed on an artfully rumpled cloth of scarlet velvet. The cascade of seemingly casual folds formed a perfect contrast to the formal rigidity of the tiara, the rich color adding a voluptuous contrast to the icy brilliance of the jewels. The display setting had recently been redesigned by Lianne Beecham, Jeffrey's daughter-in-law, and its exotic flair carried the unmistakable stamp of her talents.

The tiara was the genuine article, a multimillion-pound piece of history, a costly tribute from Emperor Louis-Napoléon to his much-loved wife, and Jeffrey felt a brief surge of emotion each time he passed the display case and registered the flamboyant sparkle of the diamond clusters and the warm luster of the priceless pearls. The genuine tiara, missing for almost fifty years, had finally been returned to its rightful home almost a fortnight after Grace had left England for San Francisco. The timing, Jeffrey reflected, had been quite spectacularly ironic. He'd regained one of his family's lost heirlooms at virtually the same moment as he'd lost his wife. A hell of a price to pay for a few jewels, however historic.

He pulled himself together, refusing to let his thoughts ramble down that well-worn path of useless regret. "Did you know I'm expecting a courier to deliver something important tonight?" he asked the guard, whose nametag identified him as Bill Babb. "I spoke with your supervisor yesterday to arrange an after-hours security clearance."

Bill nodded. "Yes, sir, everything's been taken care of. Keith is at the security desk, and he's planning to give you a ring as soon as the messenger arrives. I'll escort the visitor up to your office, or wherever it is you want to meet with him."

"My office will be fine." Jeffrey glanced at his watch. "I expect the courier to arrive before seven, which means some time in the next fifteen minutes or so. Let Keith know I've gone up to the sixth floor, will you?"

"Yes, sir. I'll pass the message on right away. Good night, sir."

Back in his office, Jeffrey shuffled through the stack of papers and spread sheets waiting for his attention, then gave up pretending that he was doing any work. He walked across to the bar concealed behind the mahogany doors of a wall cabinet and poured himself a whisky, not bothering to find ice or soda. He let the mellow single-malt Scotch rest on his tongue for a moment before swallowing. He cradled the glass between his hands, but resisted the urge to keep sipping. He'd managed to control the heavy drinking he'd indulged in right after Grace left for San Francisco, but he knew he still depended too much on alcohol to take the edge off his loneliness. Slowly, painfully, in the months since Grace left him, he'd come to realize that it was better to acknowledge what you were feeling, even if it was unpleasant. If you buried your feelings too deeply, eventually the pressure built up until something exploded. In his case, what had exploded had been his marriage.

The debris from that giant explosion still littered his personal landscape, blighting positive emotions and intensifying the negatives. His lack of excitement over the return of the DeWilde jewels was a perfect example of his problem. For the past year, he'd focused with almost desperate intensity on the mystery of the missing jewels and the fate of his long-lost uncle, Dirk DeWilde, who had disappeared at the same time. With the help of Nick Santos, his private investigator, all the mysteries had been solved and the jewels recovered. He'd had the pleasure of meeting two sets of previously unknown DeWilde cousins in Australia, seen a long-standing feud with the Villeneuve family laid to rest, and discovered the reasons behind Dirk's disappearance. Tonight, as icing on the cake, the last of the missing jewels would be returned to him. An occasion for major celebration—except Jeffrey could barely remember why their return had once seemed so vitally important.

The phone rang, providing a welcome interruption to

his gloomy thoughts. He picked up the receiver. "Yes?"

"Mr. DeWilde, this is Keith Jones at the security desk."

"Yes."

"The courier you were expecting from San Francisco has arrived, sir."

"Good. Send him up right away, please."

"Er...yes, sir. Bill is escorting the...courier upstairs now."

The pause before the guard replied had been so slight that in the old days Jeffrey would never have noticed it. But, if nothing else, his separation from Grace had taught him to be more alert to the subtle nuances of people's conversation. "Keith, is there a problem?"

"Er...no. No problem, sir. The courier's papers are all in order. Signed by Nick Santos, like you said." The guard made an odd noise, which he tried to disguise as a cough. "I've released the lock on the lift controls, sir. Bill and the courier are on their way up to the corporate offices. Shouldn't be more than a couple of minutes until they're on the sixth floor. I'm sure you'll find everything in order, sir."

"All right. Thank you." Jeffrey set his unfinished whisky down on his desk and walked across the room to open his office door. Halfway to the door, he realized he was still bothered by the hesitation he'd heard in the guard's voice.

Damn it, something was wrong. The guard had said the proper things, but his tone of voice had hinted at a problem. Far more than hinted, in fact. Toward the end, he'd as good as announced that he was hiding something.

Nick Santos should have made this important delivery in person. Jeffrey had protested when Nick informed him that another courier had been found to bring the jewels from San Francisco to London, and now it seemed as if his sense of foreboding had been right on the mark. The courier was bringing some sort of trouble with him, Jeffrey could smell it.

With heirloom jewels worth millions of pounds about to be transferred into his keeping, he was in no mood to take chances. What if Keith had unlocked the lifts with a gun held to his head? The only way Jeffrey could find out was to go down to the ground floor and personally inspect the lobby, but he was unarmed and untrained, and although he'd once been a bruising tackle on the rugger field, these days he was prone to arthritis in his left knee. Any attempt on his part to play the hero might well precipitate a tragedy. Or a humiliating farce.

He needed professional help. Securicorps had been warned of the imminent return of the DeWilde jewels, so they wouldn't be altogether surprised to get an emergency summons to the store.

Jeffrey strode back to his desk and activated the silent alarm that connected directly to Securicorp's headquarters, feeling better for the knowledge that armed guards would be dispatched immediately to check into any problems. He might be overreacting, but there was no point in waiting for Nick's courier to arrive in his office—trailing armed robbers—before deciding there was trouble brewing. By the time he had proof of what instinct was telling him, it might be too late to sound the alarm.

Jeffrey heard the lift doors open and he tensed, bracing himself for trouble. The thick pile of the carpet muffled the sounds of approaching footsteps, and neither the courier nor his security escort seemed to be talking.

A bad sign. Bill Babb had struck him as the garrulous type.

His office door stood slightly open, but Bill knocked, anyway, simultaneously poking his head around the door. "Your...er...your courier has arrived from San Francisco, Mr. DeWilde."

The guard was visibly ill at ease. Jeffrey gripped the edge of his desk. "Send him in, Bill."

"Yes, sir." Bill sighed with evident relief and sidestepped as if to hold the door open for the person accompanying him.

Jeffrey frowned. "Come in," he said sharply, tired of being played for a fool. "I don't know how you expect to get away with this, whatever you're planning. We have state-of-the-art security...." His voice died away as a woman walked into his office. He realized his mouth was hanging open and snapped it shut.

"Hello, Jeffrey."

He swallowed twice before he could reply. "Grace," he said thickly. "Grace, what are you doing here?"

"Nick allowed me to act as the courier for the return of the DeWilde jewels," she said. The familiar huskiness of her voice curled around him, squeezing all the breath out of his lungs. She lifted a slender aluminum briefcase onto his desk and stood directly across from him, close enough for him to see the flush of color that ebbed and flowed in her cheeks. Close enough to smell the light fragrance of her perfume. She pointed to the briefcase. "I have all four pieces here, waiting for your inspection."

"You've cut your hair." He hadn't meant to say something so irrelevant—so personal—but he was hypnotized by the changes in her appearance. He had seen her only a few weeks earlier, at their daughter Kate's

An Important Message from the Editors

Dear Reader,

Because you've chosen to read one of our fine romance novels, we'd like to say "thank you!" And, as a **special** way to thank you, we've selected <u>two more</u> of the books you love so well **plus** an exciting Mystery Gift to send you — absolutely <u>FREE</u>!

Please enjoy them with our compliments...

Pam Powers

Peel off seal and place inside...

How to validate your Editor's "Thank You" FREE GIFT

1. Peel off gift seal from front cover. Place it in space provided at right. This automatically entitles you to receive 2 FREE BOOKS and a fabulous mystery gift.

2. Send back this card and you'll get 2 brand-new *Romance* novels. These books have a cover price of $5.99 or more each in the U.S. and $6.99 or more each in Canada, but they are yours to keep absolutely free.

3. There's no catch. You're under no obligation to buy anything. We charge nothing—ZERO—for your first shipment. And you don't have to make any minimum number of purchases— not even one!

4. The fact is, thousands of readers enjoy receiving their books by mail from The Reader Service. They enjoy the convenience of home delivery...they like getting the best new novels at discount prices BEFORE they're available in stores... and they love their Heart to Heart subscriber newsletter featuring author news, horoscopes, recipes, book reviews and much more!

5. We hope that after receiving your free books you'll want to remain a subscriber. But the choice is yours— to continue or cancel, any time at all! So why not take us up on our invitation, with no risk of any kind. You'll be glad you did!

GET A *Free* MYSTERY GIFT...

SURPRISE MYSTERY GIFT COULD BE YOURS **FREE** AS A SPECIAL "THANK YOU" FROM THE EDITORS

The Editor's "Thank You" Free Gifts Include:

- **Two BRAND-NEW Romance novels!**
- **An exciting mystery gift!**

Yes!

I have placed my Editor's "Thank You" seal in the space provided above. Please send me 2 free books and a fabulous mystery gift. I understand I am under no obligation to purchase any books, as explained on the back and on the opposite page.

PLACE FREE GIFT SEAL HERE

393 MDL DVFG   193 MDL DVFF

FIRST NAME

LAST NAME

ADDRESS

APT.#

CITY

STATE/PROV.

ZIP/POSTAL CODE

(PR-R-04)

Thank You!

Offer limited to one per household and not valid to current MIRA, The Best of The Best, Romance or Suspense subscribers. All orders subject to approval. Credit or debit balances in a customer's account(s) may be offset by any other outstanding balance owed by or to the customer.

▶ DETACH AND MAIL CARD TODAY! ▶

© 2003 HARLEQUIN ENTERPRISES LTD.
® and ™ are trademarks owned by Harlequin Enterprises Ltd.

The Reader Service — Here's How It Works:

Accepting your 2 free books and gift places you under no obligation to buy anything. You may keep the books and gift and return the shipping statement marked "cancel." If you do not cancel, about a month later we'll send you 3 additional books and bill you just $4.74 each in the U.S., or $5.24 each in Canada, plus 25¢ shipping & handling per book and applicable taxes if any.* That's the complete price and — compared to cover prices starting from $5.99 each in the U.S. and $6.99 each in Canada — it's quite a bargain! You may cancel at any time, but if you choose to continue, every month we'll send you 3 more books, which you may either purchase at the discount price or return to us and cancel your subscription.

*Terms and prices subject to change without notice. Sales tax applicable in N.Y. Canadian residents will be charged applicable provincial taxes and GST.

If offer card is missing write to: The Reader Service, 3010 Walden Ave., P.O. Box 1867, Buffalo, NY 14240-1867

BUSINESS REPLY MAIL
FIRST-CLASS MAIL   PERMIT NO. 717-003   BUFFALO, NY

POSTAGE WILL BE PAID BY ADDRESSEE

THE READER SERVICE
3010 WALDEN AVE
PO BOX 1341
BUFFALO NY 14240-8571

NO POSTAGE
NECESSARY
IF MAILED
IN THE
UNITED STATES

wedding in San Francisco, but tonight she seemed a different person. After a lifetime of styling her hair in a smooth, heavy twist at the nape of her neck, she'd had it all cut off. She now wore it brushed back from her face, except for one thick blond strand that swept forward over her forehead and skimmed the side of her cheek. He felt unsettled at this visible sign of the fact that she'd moved on to a new stage of her life. Leaving him behind in the old rut.

"Kate decided it was time I updated my image." She gave a slight smile. "If Kate noticed a problem, I knew my hairstyle had to be at least ten years overdue for a change." She tucked the wayward strand of hair behind her ear and fiddled for a moment with her sapphire-and-gold stud earring. "Do you like it?"

He stared with hypnotized fascination as her fingers massaged her earlobe. He'd never before realized that earlobes were a part of the female body with major erotic potential. "It's very...nice." He cleared his throat and tried again. "It suits you. Very flattering and modern."

Her voice was low, huskier than ever. "I'm glad you think so."

How was he supposed to respond to that? he wondered. Jeffrey looked away, clenching his fists helplessly. In a business setting, he could command an audience of hundreds, field hostile questions, toss witty asides into the conversation and quell hot tempers with calm reason and good judgment. But with the people he cared about, when he really needed to be fluent, his tongue seemed to stick to the roof of his mouth, too thick and clumsy even to mumble acceptable platitudes.

This was the first time Grace had been in his office since the day she left him. That had been a Friday, too.

A Friday in early May, over a year ago. It was disorienting to see her in such a familiar setting—looking so different. How odd it was that after a lifetime of marriage and more than a year of separation what he felt at this precise moment was neither nostalgia nor regret—not even anger. What he felt was pure desire, the sort of straightforward and consuming physical lust he couldn't remember experiencing since he was in his twenties. He conquered a primitive urge to toss his ex-wife onto the couch and make mad, passionate love to her. Quite apart from any other considerations, he had just enough sense of the ridiculous left to wonder if he'd be able to put his fantasy into practice without his arthritic knee giving out on him.

As always when he was at a loss for words, Jeffrey took refuge in the practical and nonemotional. "Nick shouldn't have allowed you to cross the Atlantic with millions of pounds' worth of jewels in your custody. That's not a job for a..." He'd been about to say for a woman, but he caught himself just in time. Megan, Kate and Lianne had managed to raise his consciousness at least to the point that he no longer gave voice to his prejudices. "That's a job for a trained professional," he amended. "I hope you didn't run into problems with Customs?"

"No, none. I had wanted to fly out the night of Kate's wedding, but I realized the logistics were impossible. Nick arranged for an experienced courier to make the flight with me. He took care of all the paperwork, shepherded me through the maze of Customs regulations and drove me here tonight. But I wanted to have the pleasure of being the person who actually returned the missing DeWilde jewels to you."

He wondered why that had been important to her but

was afraid to ask. Ever since that fateful New Year's Day nineteen months ago when Grace had confessed she had married him without being in love with him, Jeffrey had realized it was dangerous to ask personal questions unless you were absolutely sure of the answer. Still, he couldn't help but be cheered by the knowledge that Grace had deliberately sought him out. She'd spent most of the past year protesting that she needed "space"—an American euphemism that seemed to mean she wanted to be anywhere that her husband wasn't.

Jeffrey recovered enough equanimity to smile with false heartiness. "Well, I suppose I'd better open the briefcase and take a look at the jewels...make sure they've survived the journey."

Grace held up her hand and he saw that the case was fastened to her wrist with a faceted stainless steel chain welded to an engraved and polished manacle. The manacle was lined with padded black velvet and clasped her wrist like a kinky sex toy. He wondered if she'd commissioned the handcuff specially or gone shopping in one of San Francisco's sex boutiques. Neither possibility did anything to lessen his smoldering sexual tension.

"Here's the key to the handcuffs," Grace said, reaching inside the neckline of her navy blue linen suit and pulling out a chain of interwoven threads of gold and silver. She slipped the chain over her head and held out a little silver key toward Jeffrey. "This will open the padlock and the handcuff. Nick told me you already know the numbers for the combination lock on the case itself."

"Yes, I do." Jeffrey took the key, which was still warm from being nestled between her breasts. "Could you...could you hold out your hand? The lock on that handcuff looks quite tricky to unfasten."

"Certainly." She held out her hand, palm upward, and he unlocked the clasp. The manacle around her wrist opened, falling to the desk with a clatter that sounded explosively loud in the oppressive quiet of his office.

Jeffrey stuck his fingers inside his starched collar, tugging to loosen his tie. His office seemed to be suffering from a severe ventilation problem. Grace massaged the inner flesh of her wrist, and he turned away abruptly, keying in the combination that would open the jewel case. Some crucial synapse must have been disconnecting between his brain and his fingers, because it took him four attempts before the locks sprang open. When he finally succeeded, he raised the lid slowly, actually forgetting about Grace's nearness for a second or two when he saw the four exquisite pieces nestled in their custom-designed compartments.

"Thank goodness," Grace said, bending down to examine the jewels. "They don't seem to have moved in transit. Some of the settings are so fragile I was worried there might be some damage."

"No, they were very well protected. Whoever designed the carrying case did a good job."

"Nick and I worked on the specifications together."

Jeffrey lifted out a pair of earrings and held them up to the light. They were almost too heavy to wear, set with priceless Burmese rubies and diamonds. The brooch was a mixture of rubies, diamonds and emeralds, mounted against an unusual background of stark black onyx. Even more stunning was the Dancing Waters necklace, a cascade of diamonds scattered with bursts of sapphires that looked like the blue depths of a mountain river, glimpsed through foaming white water. And last was the Empress Catherine tiara, an exquisite circlet of diamonds, rubies and emeralds, once owned by the Russian empress.

Jeffrey picked up the shimmering necklace and turned it slowly so that the diamonds caught fire in the refracted light. Grace exclaimed in delight and, acting on impulse, he fastened the necklace around the slim column of her throat. "Jewels always look better when they're worn," he said.

Her laugh was soft and breathy as she bent down to catch her reflection in the narrow strip of mirror behind the bar. "True, but I don't think navy blue linen does justice to a necklace like this. Jewels this spectacular need satin and rare Mechlin lace at the very least."

"No," he said. "All they need is the bare shoulders of a beautiful woman like you."

Grace's gaze locked for a moment with his. "Sometimes, Jeffrey, you pay the most astounding compliments."

He smiled wryly. "No, I don't. That was a case of speaking the simple truth and sounding eloquent."

"Perhaps we should test your theory," she said, reaching for the row of tiny buttons that fastened her suit jacket. "I say satin and lace, you say bare skin. Let's see who's right."

She was going to take off her jacket. Jeffrey reminded himself to breathe. She was his wife...his ex-wife...and her body was entirely familiar to him. He must have held her naked in his arms a thousand times.

That mundane fact seemed to have no impact on his pounding pulse and racing heartbeat. Afraid to speak in case he stuttered, he watched her unfasten the buttons of her jacket one by one. She slowly drew the lapels apart and shrugged out of it, letting it drop from her hand onto his desk with casual abandon. Underneath her suit jacket she wore only a confection of translucent peach silk. A camisole, Jeffrey thought dazedly. He remembered that type of wispy top was called a camisole.

Grace pivoted slowly beneath the light, so that the necklace sparked with pinpoints of white flame against the creamy smoothness of her skin. She smiled at him. "Well, who was right?"

With considerable effort, Jeffrey recalled what they'd been talking about. "I was," he said, relieved to discover that the power of speech hadn't entirely deserted him. "Satin and lace would be complete overkill when you have such perfect shoulders."

She laughed and turned a little pink. "Thank you—I think. I'll concede the lace, maybe, but I'm sure I could make a compelling case for midnight blue satin. A low-cut dress, absolutely plain, with a long straight skirt, split at the side to mid-thigh."

Not only could he visualize the dress, he could imagine exactly how Grace would look wearing it. Jeffrey was swept by a wave of longing so intense it hurt. To hell with minor problems like the fact that they were divorced and he was supposed to be rebuilding his life without her. He covered the space between them in a single swift stride and pulled her into his arms.

"God, Gracie, I've missed you so much. It feels like two lifetimes since we were last together."

She spoke against his chest, her voice muffled. "We were together in San Francisco just a few weeks ago—at Kate's wedding."

He shook his head. "We weren't together. We were just in the same place at the same time. That's different."

She didn't reply, but she didn't move away, either. "Gracie..." he murmured, and then gave up on the hopeless task of finding words to express the turmoil of what he was feeling. He bent his head and kissed her passionately, all the pent-up frustrations of the past weeks and months somehow transforming themselves into an urgent need to show her how glad he was to have her here again in DeWilde's flagship store. In his arms, where she belonged.

Their kiss was as warm and familiar as his favorite armchair, as fresh and intoxicating as the return of spring after a cold and dreary winter. She was pliant in his arms, soft and yielding against his body. Her warmth seemed to pour into his veins, renewing his spirit and doubling his energy level.

For a few wonderful moments she returned his kiss with such eagerness that he was disoriented when she suddenly jerked away from him and grabbed for her discarded jacket. "Jeffrey," she muttered. "Look behind you. There are two men standing at your office door. They've got guns."

Guns? He swung around, stepping in front of Grace and wondering frantically how he was going to protect her from a pair of armed robbers. "There are security personnel and cameras throughout the store," he said to the intruders, his voice cold and clipped. "You have no hope of getting out of here with any jewels, and even less chance of escaping from the police."

The two men exchanged glances, and one of them stepped forward, his gun still aimed with unnerving firmness at Jeffrey's middle. "We're not burglars. There seems to be a misunderstanding here. I'm Ron Bradley, with the Securicorps Quick Response Team. This is my partner, Alan Hicks. Identify yourself, please."

Jeffrey glared at the two men who claimed to be security guards. What the hell did they mean by bursting into his office like that? He'd never seen them before and didn't recognize their names, but they were wearing the khaki Securicorps uniform—and then he remembered. Good God, the silent alarm! Grace's unexpected arrival had so scrambled his brains that he'd forgotten all about his emergency summons to Securicorps. How in the world had he managed to forget something so important?

"I'm Jeffrey DeWilde," he said, trying not to sound as idiotic as he felt. Behind him he was aware of Grace scrabbling to fasten the buttons on her jacket, and he heard her smother a tiny gurgle of laughter. He suddenly saw the humor of the situation himself. Hiding a grin, he wondered how many years had passed since he was last caught necking. He turned back to the guards, using his body to shield Grace from their view. "If you'd like to see some identification, I'll have to get my wallet, which is inside my jacket."

"You're claiming to be Mr. DeWilde?" The security guard looked confused, as well he might. "Reach inside your jacket very slowly, sir, and hold out your wallet at arm's length."

Jeffrey held out the wallet. "As you can see, I am indeed Jeffrey DeWilde. I was waiting for the delivery of some valuable jewelry this evening and I had reason to believe there was a security problem. However, I realized within moments of activating the silent alarm that I'd been mistaken. There was no problem."

"But you didn't deactivate the alarm? Or call in to headquarters?"

"No." Jeffrey decided against inventing some plausible excuse to explain that oversight. This was an occasion, he decided ruefully, when his reputation for aloof inscrutability came in useful.

The guard scanned the contents of Jeffrey's wallet. "Everything seems to be in order, sir, but to confirm that there hasn't been any breach of our security systems, would you key in the code that deactivates the alarm signal? Nobody knows that except Mr. DeWilde."

Jeffrey punched in the six-number code and the guard examined a small beeper, watching as an indicator light flashed from red to green. "Thank you, sir. That's the correct code. The alarm has been deactivated."

"Then I won't keep you," Jeffrey said. "Check in with your colleagues at the security desk on your way out. Let them know that my wife and I will be another twenty minutes or so and then we'll be leaving, too."

The guard's eyes narrowed with renewed suspicion. "Your wife?" he queried.

"He means me, I expect." Grace stepped forward and smiled warmly at the two guards. "I'm Grace DeWilde, Jeffrey's former wife. We were married to each other for so long, we sometimes forget that we're divorced now."

Jeffrey was furious with himself for making the mistake of calling Grace his wife, and even more furious with her for the ease with which she glossed over his mistake. The guards, however, seemed reassured by her friendliness. Grace explained that she'd just arrived from San Francisco for a brief vacation in London, and one of the guards immediately started to recount the details of his holiday trip to America the year before.

Typical, Jeffrey thought, deciding to be annoyed. *I have to give the guards a wallet full of proof before they'll accept I'm who I say I am. Grace just smiles, and they're her instant pals.*

"You can report to your supervisor that I was disappointed to discover that it took Securicorps fifteen minutes to respond to my emergency alarm signal," Jeffrey said when a pause finally opened up in the exchange of chatter between Grace and the guards. "I trust that Securicorps will work on improving that response time. If there'd been a genuine robbery in progress, the thieves would be halfway to Land's End by now."

"Yes, sir." The guards stopped smiling and visibly reverted to their stiff, professional selves. "We had problems with heavy traffic, sir."

"We'll talk about it on Monday," Jeffrey said, already regretting that he'd snapped at the guards for no better reason than because he was annoyed with Grace. No, he amended. Because he was annoyed with himself. He waited until the guards had left before speaking to her directly.

"Am I to conclude from your conversation with the security guards that you're planning to spend some time in London?" he asked, inwardly wincing at the stuffiness of his words and the chill of his tone.

In the old days, Grace would have grinned, rolled her eyes and answered his question just as if he hadn't asked it like a pompous ass. In their uncertain new relationship, she hesitated for a moment, then replied in a voice carefully devoid of color. "I plan to spend a few days in England, and then go on to Paris and see Megan and Phillip."

"Would you..." He cleared his throat. "That is, I wondered if you would have time to join me for dinner one night?"

Grace, it seemed, was not in the mood to make things easy for him. "Why do you want to have dinner with me, Jeffrey?"

Damned if he knew the answer to that simple question. Hadn't he wanted the divorce precisely so that there would be nothing left to discuss, no issues that needed to be confronted, no cause to lacerate his soul by sitting across the table from her, feeling their love erode molecule by molecule, heartbeat by heartbeat?

"We were husband and wife for over thirty years," he said stiffly. "We have three children, all of whom got married in the past year. Surely we could find something to talk about?"

"I'm sure we could," Grace acknowledged gently. "But why should we? We're no longer married and the children all seem to be doing just splendidly."

She was quite right. There was no reason for them to get together to discuss three adult, happily married children. Jeffrey spread his hands helplessly. When all else fails, he reflected wryly, try telling the truth. "I don't know why I want to have dinner with you, Gracie, but I do. Very much."

She didn't say anything for a moment or two. Then she reached up and unfastened the clasp of the Dancing Waters necklace and held it out to him. "When you can think why it is that you want to spend time in my company, Jeffrey, give me a call. I'm staying at that new hotel in Knightsbridge, the Goreham. Good night."

She left the room so quickly he didn't have time to say anything more. Jeffrey was left alone in his office with nothing to keep him company except several million pounds' worth of fabulous jewels and the haunting fragrance of Grace's perfume.

CHAPTER TWO

OVER THE PAST YEAR, Julia Dutton had discovered that working herself to the point of bone-deep, mind-numbing fatigue was a pretty good way to disguise the fact that her heart was broken. Unfortunately, living in a state of permanent exhaustion hadn't done a whole lot for her appearance. Adjusting the position of the swivel light over the bathroom mirror, she scowled at her reflection. Not a pretty sight, Julia concluded gloomily. She looked like an escapee from a Casper the Ghost movie, all mournful eyes, scrawny arms and pallid skin.

There was no way she could face Lianne and Gabe looking like this. For them, of all people, she needed to present the illusion of Miss Vitality. Adjusting the light didn't help much; she looked dreadful from all angles. What she needed right at this moment was a fairy godmother willing to wave her wand and bestow instant glamour.

Fairy godmothers being conspicuous by their absence, Julia rummaged around the bathroom cabinet and came up with a year-old pack of rejuvenating facial mask. Not exactly the magic she'd been looking for, but for some months now, magic had been seriously missing from her life.

Piercing the tube, she slathered on the gritty goop, which the packaging blurb promised would transform her pallid complexion into one of pink, glowing beauty. Ten minutes seemed rather a short time to achieve such a miracle, but Julia was willing to believe. While she waited, she plugged in her curling iron and considered hairstyle options. She couldn't remember the last time she'd felt the urge to dress up for an occasion, and the curling iron felt heavy and awkward in her hands.

She shook her hair loose from the clip that had held it up on top of her head while she bathed. At least she wasn't having a bad hair day. Bad everything else, perhaps, but her hair had always been her one redeeming feature. Long and thick, it bounced with health and had a natural shine like polished rosewood, even when the rest of her felt limp and frazzled.

To her surprise, Julia realized that tonight she didn't feel limp or frazzled, despite a tough week at school teaching an intensive summer course in French, and long evenings at home sewing a quilt copied from a 1920s photograph for her niece's third birthday. In a burst of renewed optimism, she got busy with the curling iron, gave herself a few extra curls, and persuaded her fringe to flick away from her face instead of flopping over her forehead.

She squinted dubiously at the result, and hoped she wasn't deluding herself that the effect of the backward flip was slightly wanton. Tonight she was definitely aiming for wanton. She would see Gabe again for the first time in almost four months, and she wanted to look like a woman who had a life. An interesting life, crammed full of exciting, sexy men. She'd be damned if she was going to be on the receiving end of his silent pity anymore. She'd had enough of that to last several lifetimes.

The mere thought of Gabriel DeWilde was enough to

make her cheeks turn hot beneath the clay mask, and she quickly cut off memories that remained too vivid and much too painful. Gabe and Lianne were happily married and expecting their first child next month, and it was time—past time—that Julia got her stupid feelings for Gabe under control. Unplugging the curling iron, she wondered why the Victorians had considered unrequited love so romantic. Personally, she felt there was something ridiculous about a woman whose love life was so pathetic that she couldn't conquer her feelings for a man who'd dumped her more than a year ago.

Being dumped by the love of your life in favor of another woman was not an experience Julia would recommend as enriching. Being dumped in favor of your best friend was an experience she wouldn't wish on her worst enemy. It was a testimony to how close she and Lianne had been in the past that they were still good friends despite Gabe. They saw each other whenever they could get their busy work schedules to coincide, and phoned each other at least once a week. When they met, to overcome the awkward truth that Lianne was married to the man Julia loved, they'd developed a system whereby they tossed casual references to Gabe into the conversation and pretended they didn't notice each other's strain. It was a necessary pretense since they both wanted to save their friendship.

For the past few weeks, though, Julia hadn't needed to pretend very often, because she'd seen little of Lianne and nothing of Gabe. With their baby due in late August, they had been spending most of their weekends in the country, trying to speed up the workmen who were adding a new kitchen and an extra bathroom to the eighteenth-century stone cottage they'd bought soon after their marriage. The previous owners had been a pair of elderly sisters, recently deceased, and the place had been long on charm and short on convenience. The existing bathroom had a wonderful Edwardian claw-foot tub but no hot water. The bedrooms had pretty casement windows but plaster ceilings moldy with damp. As for the kitchen, it had a two-hundred-year-old oak floor—along with a cooking stove that had been the latest word in modernity around the time that Queen Victoria celebrated her Diamond Jubilee.

Julia's fingers had positively itched to get busy working on the interior decoration when Lianne had shown her over the cottage. Interior design had always been an obsession with her, even when she was a child, although she realized her parents were quite right when they told her it was far too unreliable and competitive a field in which to earn a living. Since the debacle of her affair with Gabe, she'd filled her empty weekends touring National Trust houses, enlarging her knowledge of antique furniture and becoming something of an expert on the fabrics and linens used to decorate English country homes over the past three centuries. Her trips had started out as a ploy to avoid brooding, but at some point along the way, Julia realized she'd developed a genuine fascination with the techniques of antique fabric preservation and restoration.

In renovating the cottage, Lianne had frequently asked Julia's advice about patterns and color schemes, since she and Gabe wanted to achieve a workable compromise between comfort and an authentic period look to their house. Then, last week, Lianne had phoned to say that the workmen were finally finished.

"They're gone, they're out of here!" she crowed. "I think I'm ecstatic, but I'm too tired to know for sure!

We have a house in which every room has four solid walls and a dry ceiling."

Julia laughed. "That's not only wonderful, it's truly amazing. But how many of the solid walls are painted?"

"All of them. Every last one. You can't imagine how gorgeous the house looks, Jules. And can you hear the blissful quiet? I'd forgotten what it was like to spend a day without listening to a bunch of workmen all hammering at once and yelling at the top of their lungs so they could hear each other over the noise of their radios."

"You must be thrilled to have the cottage to yourselves. Did Liberty's finish the curtains for the drawing room? I'm dying to see how they look."

"Yes, they're finished and they look wonderful. You were absolutely right that I needed the rose chintz, not that dreary moss green I was looking at. And the Wedgwood-blue wall panels in the dining room are perfect as a contrast to the ivory plaster moldings. I don't know what's happened to my color sense recently. It all seems to have dissolved in prenatal hormones. Thank God most brides still wear white, or DeWilde's would have fired me months ago."

Julia grinned. "I seriously doubt it. It would be tough for them to fire the woman who was voted Designer of the Year by *Brides Magazine*."

"How did you hear about that?" Lianne asked, sounding embarrassed. "Did Gabe tell you? Honestly, he was impossible when the magazine called us with the news. I barely managed to restrain him from putting up a billboard in Trafalgar Square."

Julia kept her voice light. "No, I haven't spoken to

Gabe recently. Megan told me the news. We had lunch together when I was in Paris at the end of last month.''

"You were in Paris? You never said anything." Lianne laughed. "I hope you were doing something scandalous."

"Nothing even remotely scandalous, unfortunately." Julia repressed a sigh. "I was escorting a group of sixth-form students on a tour of the city's cultural highlights. The closest I came to scandal was when I caught two of the girls drinking in the hotel bar at two in the morning."

"That isn't scandalous, Jules, that's just annoying. Damn! I was hoping you'd met some gorgeous man who'd whisked you off to Paris for a weekend of hot sex."

"I don't think I'm the sort of person who inspires men to rush off to Paris for hot sex," Julia said, then immediately wished she hadn't sounded so sorry for herself.

"You're one of the prettiest women I know," Lianne said. "And you have a great body. Fabulous legs. You could attract any man you wanted."

Not Gabe. And she didn't want anyone else. "Thanks for the compliment," Julia said. "But pretty isn't the same thing as sexy, is it?"

"I'd say how sexy a woman is to a man depends more on how she thinks about herself than anything else. Your family has you so convinced you're a domesticated homebody, Jules, that you can't see the truth. In my opinion, you're a package of dynamite, waiting to be ignited by some lucky man."

Julia laughed, albeit a touch wistfully. "The package must be wet, or the fuse went dead or something. You're a wonderful friend, Lianne, but honesty compels me to admit that I have never in my whole life inspired a man with passionate thoughts about hot sex and sinful weekends in Paris."

"How do you know what the men around you are thinking?" Lianne asked. "Are you a mind reader?"

"I don't think a woman needs psychic powers to know when a man is lusting for her body," Julia replied with a touch of irony. "Aren't there supposed to be a couple of more obvious clues?"

"Do you want to inspire men with lust?" Lianne asked, her voice turning alarmingly thoughtful. "I always assumed you were only interested in dating men who were already tamed and domesticated."

"I am," Julia said quickly. And it was true, of course. She wanted to find a decent, honorable man to marry, so that they could settle down to have children and live a nice quiet life together. Some people might find that wish old-fashioned and boring, but it was what she'd always planned for herself. Even if she'd suddenly been endowed with enough sex appeal to rival Sharon Stone—even if she weren't still in love with Gabe—wild affairs wouldn't be on her agenda.

Julia spoke firmly to quash any crazy ideas Lianne might be getting. "We've been friends for a long time now, Lianne, and I know exactly what it means when your voice takes on that thoughtful note. You're mentally reviewing your list of bachelor friends as we speak, trying to decide which one would be most likely to rush me off somewhere exotic for a night of sex and sin—"

"No, no, Jules, of course I'm not." Lianne changed the subject with incriminating speed. "Actually, the reason I'm calling is to invite you down to the cottage this weekend. We're having a few friends join us to celebrate the fact that Gabe and I are no longer sleeping with buckets in our bedroom to catch the rain. Say you'll come. We have to move back to town on Monday so that I can get ready for the baby's arrival, and we're dying to show off the house before we're knee-deep in diapers and midnight feedings. If you need any more persuading, they're forecasting sunshine all weekend, and the countryside's gorgeous right now."

"I don't need any persuasion at all," Julia said. "I'd love to come. I can take a train to Winchester if somebody could pick me up at the station—"

"There's no need to take a train—Edward Hillyard can drive you," Lianne said quickly. Far too quickly. Edward was an old schoolfriend of Gabe's, recently divorced, and this was the third time Lianne had roped him in as an escort for Julia. Obviously, he was the bachelor Lianne had decided to pair her off with, Julia decided, trying to be grateful that her friend had picked on such a solid and respectable citizen. Edward was exactly the sort of man any sensible woman would want to marry. Except his ex-wife, of course. Julia sometimes found herself wondering exactly why Edward's marriage had lasted less than two years.

Lianne rushed on before Julia could say anything. "Edward's already accepted our invitation to come for dinner on Saturday evening. He plans to return to London on Sunday after lunch, so he could take you back with him, too. Why don't I ask him to pick you up about four on Saturday?"

"That's fine with me, but shouldn't you ask Edward first? Are you sure he won't mind giving me a lift?"

Lianne gave an exaggerated sigh. "Honestly, Jules, you're hopeless. And you're the woman who claims to know what the men around you are thinking! Edward is positively dying for excuses to spend time with you, and you ask a question like that. I'll have him call you so that he can tell you in his own words just how thrilled and happy he is to drive you down here.''

Julia quite liked Edward, so she had thanked him politely when he called to repeat Lianne's offer to drive her down to the cottage. Edward was a barrister, fast making a name for himself in legal circles, and he'd seemed both kind and intelligent on the two other occasions Julia had gone out with him. He was also good-looking, and she was hopeful that, with a little effort, she could persuade herself that she found him sexually attractive. Surely to goodness there had to be a few men in the world, other than Gabriel DeWilde, who had the power to make her heart beat faster? With any luck and a little hard work on her part, Edward Hillyard might turn out to be the man who made her forget all about her abortive love for Gabe.

Julia splashed cold water on her face and washed off the mask, which—amazingly—seemed to have left her complexion pink and glowing as advertised. Glancing at her watch on the bathroom counter, she saw that she had only fifteen minutes left before Edward was due to pick her up, and Edward was never late. Unfailing punctuality was just one more of his many admirable characteristics. Julia wondered why she suddenly felt depressed.

Twelve minutes later, makeup done, hair brushed into artful casualness, and skin spritzed with perfume, she stepped into the dress she'd bought specially for this weekend. It hadn't been easy to find an outfit that made the statement, *I'm really glad you and Lianne are happy, but look what you missed out on, Gabriel DeWilde,* but she'd been rather pleased when she discovered this one.

Turning slowly so that she could view the short, tight skirt—well, okay, the very short and very tight skirt—from all angles, Julia realized she might have gone a little overboard with her subliminal messages for Gabe. Given the skimpy dimensions of the skirt, perhaps she hadn't needed quite such a low neckline. Or maybe she should have chosen a more subtle color than in-your-face yellow. Working in a private girls' school, and having grown up with two older brothers who for years had checked her appearance before every date, she tended to buy clothes that were conservative, even for special occasions. The outfit she was wearing tonight could be called many things, she decided, but conservative wasn't one of them.

Slipping into high-heeled black shoes and stepping back to view the final effect, Julia was assailed by the awful suspicion that the dress wasn't sexy and intriguing but simply vulgar. Panicked, she decided to change into her standby outfit, a sober suit in beige linen. If only Edward could be a couple of minutes late for once, she'd have time to make the switch.

She had her new yellow dress half on and half off when the doorbell rang. Edward—inevitably—was right on time. Muttering words her brothers would have been horrified to realize she knew, she shoved her arms back into the sleeves and pulled up the zipper. Naturally, it stuck. And of course the dress was too tight to get on or off unless the zipper was open all the way.

Julia reminded herself that she was not a woman who believed in omens. The weekend wasn't doomed simply because she had to face Edward Hillyard with a half-open zipper. She walked briskly to the door, holding the front of the dress up to her chest. Glancing through the peephole, she confirmed it was Edward and unlocked the door to her flat, greeting him with a friendly smile and inviting her heart to beat just a little faster at the sight of him. Her heart refused.

Julia tried not to be discouraged. She'd introduced Edward to her parents when they met by chance at the theater, and they thought he was wonderful. Her mother had managed to slip his name at least once into every subsequent phone conversation. Julia was trying to see why it was that both Lianne and her family considered Edward so terrific. Her mother had been so charmed by his old-fashioned good manners that she hadn't even blinked when she learned he was divorced.

Julia stepped back to let him into the flat. "Hello, Edward, you're right on time. You didn't have any problems with the traffic, obviously?"

"H-hello, Julia." Edward, usually a man of unflappable temperament, seemed stunned by her changed appearance. So stunned, in fact, that he stumbled over the doorsill and almost fell.

Cheeks splotched with angry red, he tugged at his starched shirt cuffs and smoothed his hair back into place, finding no humor in his near pratfall. Julia overcame an unworthy desire to giggle. "Guests are always tripping on that rug," she lied. "I'll have to move it."

Edward gave a final tug to his cuffs. "No harm done. Silly of me to trip, but I wasn't paying attention to where I was walking." He spoke calmly enough, but his gaze traveled rapidly down the length of her body and stopped at her thighs. His somewhat protuberant gray eyes showed signs of being about to pop out of his handsome head, but he was basically a courteous man and he hastily pulled his gaze back to her face.

He spoke jerkily. "The traffic's building up going toward the motorway. It'll take us a couple of hours to get to Lower Ashington, so we ought to be on our way. Are you ready to leave?'' His Adam's apple bobbed as he swallowed. ''That dress is rather, um...er... It doesn't look very warm. Do you need a jacket?''

With an inward sigh, Julia realized just how unsuited she was to the role of femme fatale. She'd bought this incredible bombshell of a dress and all she'd inspired Edward to say was that it didn't look very warm. His goggle-eyed amazement made her feel silly instead of feminine and sexy, but it was too late to wish that she'd bought a more demure dress, so she forced herself to continue smiling.

''I have a jacket in the bedroom, but I need your help first, Edward, if you don't mind. This is rather embarrassing, but the zipper is caught on the lining of my dress and I can't seem to disentangle it. If we stand directly under the light here, do you think you could loosen whatever's catching and zip me up properly?''

''Er...yes, of course.'' Edward waited while she positioned herself beneath the hall light fixture, then put his hands on her shoulders and turned her around. She jumped when his hands touched the bare skin of her back.

Edward cleared his throat. ''I'm sorry if my hands are cold.''

''It's quite all right,'' Julia said, although it wasn't. She hated the enforced intimacy, the fact that he now knew she was wearing no slip and a sun-yellow bra to match her dress, but she couldn't complain that he was taking advantage of the situation. Far from it. He scrupulously avoided touching her in any way that might be considered suggestive.

''There, that's got it,'' he said after a couple of minutes of careful tugging. ''All done.''

"Thank you very much." She swung around and realized that Edward hadn't moved away. Half a step forward and she would be in his arms. Julia felt momentarily paralyzed. She willed herself either to step briskly backward or to take that crucial step forward into his arms, but her feet remained glued to the area rug, her hands rigid at her sides, her insides churning.

In the end, Edward solved the dilemma for her. He murmured her name on a note of inquiry, and when she didn't protest, he clasped his arms around her waist and slowly bent his head toward her.

He'd kissed her before on a couple of occasions, presumably with modest satisfaction on his part. Julia hadn't felt anything, of course, but that wasn't surprising. She hadn't felt even a flicker of sexual desire for any man since the last time Gabe kissed her. She reminded herself that she was determined to cure herself of her stupid fixation on Gabe. If she concentrated, she was sure she'd finally be able to inject some pizzazz into her response to Edward. Eyes squeezed shut, she tilted her mouth up to his.

His lips closed eagerly over hers. His kiss felt like...nothing in particular. Determined to work up some enthusiasm, Julia imagined that he was Hugh Grant and she was Emma Thompson in *Sense and Sensibility*. She imagined they were succumbing to their love for each other after months of silent yearning. When Julia realized that her mind had drifted off into a mental review of the movie, she decided she'd picked the wrong fantasy. Jane Austen was obviously too chaste to inspire an appropriately passionate response. She needed a more contemporary scenario. How about Richard Gere and Julia Roberts in *Pretty Woman*? Their kisses had been hot enough to melt the celluloid they were filmed on.

Julia concentrated on visualizing Edward as Richard Gere, but her imagination failed her. Edward remained stubbornly Edward, and her blood refused to catch fire or even to send out a hopeful spark or two. His kiss tasted of peppermint toothpaste, which wasn't a bad thing for a kiss to taste of, she supposed, but she wished she could forget about the mechanics and just go with the flow. When she started to obsess about the fact that she couldn't breathe and her nose was going to bump into his if she came up for air too quickly, she decided it was time to do them both a favor and break off the kiss. Belatedly it occurred to her that if she needed to pretend Edward was a character in a movie before she could tolerate kissing him, then their relationship didn't seem destined to scale the heights of passion. At the moment, she reflected wryly, they were doing a better imitation of Mickey and Minnie Mouse than Richard Gere and Julia Roberts.

Edward, ever courteous, let go of her as soon as she pulled back. Surprisingly, he seemed to have noticed nothing amiss with her tepid response. He was flushed and breathing deeply when they drew apart, and Julia felt guilty because she had been left so unmoved by an experience he seemed to have found arousing. What was the matter with her? she wondered despairingly. Had she been born with a defective sex gene that enabled her to feel passion for Gabriel DeWilde and nobody else?

She was having a hard time finding something appropriate to say. Edward, fortunately, was not a man who required his companions to provide their fair share of the conversation. She'd learned on their earlier dates that he could talk more than enough for two. He escorted her down the street to the spot where he'd parked his BMW—Edward could always find parking places—chatting entertainingly about his work week. Julia listened, nodded in all the right places, and wished he hadn't tucked his hand beneath her elbow with such a proprietorial air.

It was after six when they approached the Winchester exit from the motorway, but there was no risk of the light fading before they reached Lower Ashington, since the sky was cloudless and the sun was just beginning to bathe the surrounding fields in mellow mauve light. They rounded the bend in the road by the fifteenth-century village church of St. Thomas and drove through the twilight to Briarwood Cottage.

Lianne opened the door before they had a chance to ring the bell. "Jules!" She wrapped her friend in a warm hug. "You're so skinny and gorgeous, I can't stand it! Your hair looks terrific, your dress is to die for, and I think I hate you. I swear, if I get any bigger, we'll have to hire earth-moving equipment to haul me in and out of bed."

"You look wonderful," Julia assured her. "Glowing with health." She grinned. "Wait till next month and then you'll really find out what huge means. The day before she gave birth, my sister-in-law bore an uncanny resemblance to a beach ball with legs."

Lianne shot her a look of mock fury. "A fine friend you are. Rub it in that I have another four weeks of this torment to go. Just wait until you're pregnant."

"I feel quite safe from your revenge. My sister-in-law insists that giving birth causes instant amnesia."

"Don't count on it, Jules. I'm taking names and making written notes. I'm determined to remember every heartless comment from my so-called friends. What's more, I intend to pay them all back with interest."

Turning to Edward, Lianne held out her hand. "Nice to see you again, Edward. Come in, and Gabe can pour you a drink. Then, once you're fortified with alcohol, we'll expect you to be a dutiful guest and walk around the whole house, making admiring comments while we point out the magnificence of our new electrical wiring and what terrific ball bearings we have on our plumbing fixtures."

Edward smiled uncertainly. "I don't believe plumbing fixtures have ball bearings," he said.

There was a split-second pause before Lianne replied. "No, I don't suppose they do. Never mind, Edward. The idea I'm trying to convey is that you're supposed to be enraptured when we show you all the renovations. If you don't like what we've done, Gabe and I are hoping you'll lie."

"I'm sure we won't need to lie," Julia said diplomatically. "You've worked a minor miracle, Lianne, I can see that already. Did you keep the workmen chained to their hammers or something? Everything looks gorgeous."

"And so do you." Gabe came out of the drawing room and kissed the air to the right of Julia's cheek. "I like your new hairstyle. It's very dashing."

She willed herself to look straight at him and smile. "Thanks, Gabe. I decided it was time for a change."

"A very successful one." He returned her smile with one equally warm and just as impersonal. Julia's stomach performed its habitual somersault. Despairingly, she wondered if she'd still be fixated on Gabriel DeWilde when she was a doddery old woman, wandering from room to room in search of her false teeth. The image was absurd enough to make her laugh, and she murmured something appropriate to Gabe about being delighted to spend the weekend with him and Lianne, before escaping into the drawing room.

Two guests had already arrived. A man and a woman. The woman looked vaguely familiar, but Julia's smile froze as she recognized the man sitting in the window seat recessed into the deep bay window. Michael Forrest! What in the world was he doing here? Oh, Lord, of all the men to have underfoot for the next twenty-four hours, Michael Forrest was absolutely the last one on planet Earth that she'd have chosen. It was bad enough that she had to watch every move to make sure she didn't betray her feelings for Gabe. Now she'd have the added burden of being polite to a man who literally set her teeth on edge. Lianne and Gabe were normally sensitive to other people's feelings, but for some reason they didn't seem to have noticed that she and Michael practically came to blows every time they were in the same room for more than five minutes.

She'd met Michael for the first time a year ago this past spring, when she'd still been dating Gabe. She'd attended a gala benefit hosted by Grace and Jeffrey DeWilde, one of the last events she'd gone to with Gabe as her date. The evening had been ruined by her dawning awareness that Gabe wasn't in love with her—and the unfortunate circumstance that Michael Forrest had been seated next to her. Julia, who considered herself very easy to get along with, had felt her skin prickle with hostility from the first second her eyes met Michael's. He had clearly reciprocated her feelings. Their mutual antagonism had been instant, and noticeable enough to be embarrassing.

Michael had been the focus of attention all night

long, telling a succession of scandalous stories about politicians and Hollywood celebrities that kept the entire table—except Julia—in gales of laughter. Even Jeffrey DeWilde had relaxed in a way she'd never seen before, engaging in a couple of exchanges with Michael that displayed not only Jeffrey's rapier-sharp wit and rather endearing sense of the ridiculous, but also a warmth Julia had never before associated with Gabe's somewhat intimidating father.

Even if there hadn't been that strange, inexplicable tension between the two of them, Julia wouldn't have enjoyed Michael Forrest's company. She wasn't normally judgmental about other people's life-styles, and she didn't care how many women he dated or even that he seemed to enjoy spending his time with people who were notorious chiefly for the reckless pace of their lives. What she couldn't forgive was the fact that Michael Forrest had a son he didn't seem to care about in the least.

As a teacher, she'd seen too many children who were emotionally neglected by their families, and she had no patience with irresponsible parents, especially when they were smart enough and educated enough to know better. Michael Forrest was a prime example of careless fatherhood.

Three years ago his affair with the movie superstar Cherie Lockwood had been the talk of the tabloids. For a few weeks their relationship blazed with a heat and passion that kept gossip columnists supplied with newsworthy items on a daily basis. Then Cherie Lockwood announced that she was pregnant and her affair with Michael heated rapidly to a boiling point. But by the time her son, Storm, was born, the relationship was over. Michael had the grace to acknowledge that Storm was his son, and for a month or two after the birth he spent the occasional weekend with Cherie and the baby. According to numerous media reports, his visits soon trickled away to nothing. At the celebration for Storm's first birthday, an astute reporter pressured him into admitting that the party was only the second time he'd seen his son in more than five months.

Fortunately, Storm's sad story had a more or less happy ending, although not one that shed a flattering light on Michael Forrest. Cherie had recently married Brad Stein, the Hollywood legend who'd directed her first movie. In a town famous for lack of integrity, Brad Stein was the well-known exception to the Hollywood rule. His devotion to his first wife, Terri, had achieved legendary status, and the entire movie industry grieved when Terri died after a brave, decade-long battle against muscular dystrophy.

Cherie and Brad were reported to have fallen deeply in love while she was trying to console him after the loss of his wife. They'd been married quickly and quietly, in a private ceremony notable for the absence of crass Hollywood trappings. Within weeks of their marriage, Brad had started legal proceedings to adopt Cherie's son, apparently without any opposition from Michael. Just a couple of weeks ago, *People* magazine had published a photograph of Storm feeding a bottle of milk to an orphan calf on Brad Stein's Texas cattle ranch. Julia wondered how Michael could bear to see such pictures and know that this wonderful little boy was being brought up by another man.

Despite her dislike of his casual approach to fatherhood, she hadn't been able to forget Michael after that first meeting. His face had lingered unaccountably in her mind's eye, a constant minor irritant that wouldn't go away, and she often found herself scanning the gossip magazines in search of an article about him. Presumably she did this out of a perverse desire to be annoyed, since that was always the state she found herself in after reading of his activities.

He was an American, a cousin of Grace DeWilde's who spent most of his time in Chicago and San Francisco, so she had no reason to expect to meet him ever again, especially after she broke up with Gabe. On a teacher's salary, she didn't frequent many of the dazzling galas, first nights and gallery openings that were Michael Forrest's habitual playground. Somehow, though, in the past three months, she and Michael had suffered the misfortune of ending up as dinner partners on at least half a dozen occasions, all of which had left Julia seething with fury for days afterward.

And now it was happening again. She stopped dead in the center of the drawing room. If she'd been a dog, she was quite sure her hair would have bristled. Michael sent her a look she couldn't interpret, then grinned and rose indolently from his seat. Why did he always look as if he owned the air around him, Julia thought angrily. He strolled across the room, hands stuffed in the pockets of his well-cut slacks, and stopped in front of her. He was at least two feet away, but her space felt crowded, and her nerve-endings jangled.

He bent his head in a mocking salute. "Hello, Julia, my sweet. I guess I'll have to come and do the honors, since you're obviously so delighted to see me that you can't move for sheer ecstasy."

She gritted her teeth—there, it had started already! Before she could come up with something halfway polite to reply, he took her hand and dropped a casual kiss on the tips of her fingers. Her skin prickled in instant outrage. Good heavens, didn't he realize how ridiculous it was for a man to go around kissing a woman's hand in this day and age?

She drew in a deep breath, determined to match his casually ironic manner. "Hello, Michael. What a surprise to find you on this side of the Atlantic. I thought you were still in the States, personally teaching the Dallas Cowboy cheerleaders how to parachute."

He smiled, his green eyes lazily amused. "That was last week," he said softly. "This week I'm planning to lead a life of boring sobriety. Perhaps you'd like to keep me company?"

The implication that she was the ideal companion for someone expecting to be bored wasn't lost on her. Julia glared at him. "The paparazzi won't know what to do with themselves if you're too discreet. They count on you for at least one feature item per week."

"I guess next week they'll have to make do with Chuck or Di." He brushed his thumb across her knuckles, and she realized to her chagrin that he'd been holding her hand all this time. She extracted her fingers from his clasp, her breath coming too fast.

"You're looking great, Jules," Michael said carelessly. "Yellow suits you."

"Thank you." She spoke stiffly, because she never could relax around Michael, but his offhand compliment was oddly reassuring. His womanizing was so notorious that she could probably accept his judgment as that of an expert witness. Since the Cherie Lockwood episode, Michael's name had been linked with half the movie stars in Hollywood, and although Julia realized that every couple featured in the tabloids hadn't necessarily met, much less slept together, the gossip about Michael was so widespread that she supposed there must be at least a grain of truth to it.

"Julia, my dear, I brought you some champagne."

"What? Oh, thank you." Belatedly, Julia registered the fact that Edward was standing right next to her elbow, and that she hadn't the faintest idea how long he'd been there. Being around Michael had all her senses alert to him, to the point that she forgot about other people. Glad of an excuse to break though the web of tension she and Michael always seemed to weave around themselves, she introduced the two men.

"Edward, do you know Michael Forrest? He's Gabe's cousin, and the president of the Carlisle Forrest hotel chain. Michael, this is Edward Hillyard. He went to school with Gabe, and now he's a barrister."

The men shook hands. "Good to meet you, Michael," Edward said jovially. "President of Carlisle Forrest, eh? That's an impressive job title for such a young man."

Michael's eyes narrowed, then he smiled. "I came by it the old-fashioned way. I inherited it."

Edward chuckled. "Well, being born to the right parents is always a good way to go straight to the top."

Michael's smile tightened only a fraction. "So everyone tells me."

"I feel as if I know you already," Edward said amiably. "The scandal sheets keep up with your exploits even on this side of the pond. I must say, Michael, I envy you your exciting life."

Michael bared his teeth. Julia supposed some people might have been misguided enough to think he was smiling. "You're a lawyer, Edward, so I'm sure you know you can't believe everything you read in the papers. The truth is, I routinely put in sixty- and seventy-hour work weeks and have virtually no time for socializing."

Edward chuckled. "I quite understand. And those lovely cheerleaders you were entertaining last week were strictly business, of course!" He grimaced in mock sympathy. "Bad luck, old chap, to have such a dreary job."

"Yes, some parts of my work do seem tedious on occasion."

Edward sensed nothing amiss, but Julia was acutely aware of the tension coiling inside Michael. She realized with a jolt that part of the reason being in Michael's company made her so uncomfortable was this sensation she always had that Michael was deliberately projecting an image that had little to do with the man underneath—and nobody seemed to notice anything wrong except her. The insight was disturbing, but her awareness of Michael's feelings remained acute. Superficially, he appeared relaxed, but she knew he was fighting for self-control as he turned and extended his hand to the woman who'd walked across the room to join them.

"Just in time, Tate darling," he murmured, tucking her hand beneath his arm and pulling her close.

The woman gave him a knowing glance, her eyes full of secret amusement. She leaned against him, her tall and shapely body folding into the curve of his arm with the ease of long-standing intimacy. Julia wondered if the two of them were lovers, then wondered how she could possibly doubt that they were.

"I'm Tate Herald," the woman said, holding out her hand, her smile warm and her voice friendly. "And you must be Julia. It's wonderful to meet you at last. Lianne's told me so much about you. Every time she shows me a piece of furniture or a color scheme in the house that I particularly like, she tells me it was your idea."

"Thanks for the compliment, but Lianne exaggerates the amount of help I've given her," Julia said. "I'm thrilled to meet you, Tate. You'll have to forgive me if I gush, but I'm a real fan of 'Grosvenor Square,' and I admire your acting talent enormously. You've built the role of Rowena Slade into something truly complex and intriguing."

Tate pulled a face, but her cheeks turned pink with pleasure. "Thanks for the kind words. I do try, although there are days when I get a little tired of scripts that seem to be devoted exclusively to finding more and more exotic excuses for me to take off my clothes in front of the camera."

"But, darling, you can't blame the producers," Michael murmured. "You look so exceptionally gorgeous lying on rumpled sheets, wearing nothing but a hungry smile."

Tate laughed. "Well, thank you, darling. It's always nice to get a compliment from a connoisseur. And the regular supply of money makes up for an awful lot of silly scripts." She grinned cheerfully at Julia. "I'm a weak woman, I admit it, but it's so nice to be rich after years of struggling to pay the rent."

"A television series is a good place to get your foot in the door," Edward interjected kindly. "Don't worry, Tate. Perhaps you'll have the opportunity to play some more worthwhile roles later on in your career."

There was an infinitesimal pause before Tate responded. "Yes," she said, her voice bland. "Perhaps I will."

Gabe joined them, carrying a bottle of champagne to

fill any empty glasses and a Scotch and soda for Edward. "Sorry to keep you all waiting," he said. "Lianne and I have put away so many groceries over the past few days that I couldn't remember where we'd stashed the soda water."

Edward took the glass of Scotch and raised it in a toast. "Here's to you and Lianne," he said. "May this weekend mark the first of many happy occasions in your new home."

"I'll drink to that," Michael said, and they all raised their glasses.

"Speaking of Lianne," Tate said, "where is she?"

Gabe grinned. "When I last saw her, she was slandering the ancestry of the ducks she's cooking for dinner. I decided it would be smart to leave her alone until she and the birds come to terms."

"Oh, dear," Edward said. "Is there anything I can do to help? I enjoy cooking and I have quite a bit of experience with duck. Duckling à l'orange is a favorite with my mother."

The man truly was a walking suitcase of admirable qualities, Julia thought. It was sweet that he liked to cook for his mother, and she was a perverse female not to be more appreciative of him.

"Thanks for the offer," Gabe said. "But as a man who has already survived an entire year of marriage, I can safely say that if Lianne wants help, she won't hesitate to let us know."

His words were punctuated by the sound of crashing crockery and a loud groan from the direction of the kitchen. Gabe rolled his eyes humorously. "Well, I guess we could interpret that as a request for immediate help."

The crash was followed by an ominous silence. "I'll

go," Julia said, glad of an excuse to escape from three men who were all, for different reasons, rubbing her the wrong way.

She discovered Lianne leaning against the kitchen wall, eyes half-closed, a broken serving dish at her feet and steaming broad beans scattered over the newly resurfaced oak floor. Alarmed, Julia reached for her friend's hands. "What is it, Lianne? Did you burn yourself? You need to run your fingers under cold water quickly—"

"I didn't burn myself," Lianne said, her voice sounding simultaneously detached and overexcited.

Sensing something wrong, Gabe had followed Julia out of the drawing room. Squashing broad beans underfoot, he strode across the kitchen and put his arms around his wife. "Honey, what's up? Do you need to lie down?" He pressed his hand to her forehead. "Do you have a temperature? A headache? You don't look well, sweetheart."

"Don't I?" Lianne gave a crooked smile and drew in a deep breath. "I don't need to lie down, but I guess we do need to call Dr. Masham. Except he's away for the weekend, and even if he wasn't, he'd be in London, which isn't any use because I'm in Lower Ashington and I knew I should have lined up an obstetrician here, but I was going to do it next week—"

Gabe spoke with deliberate calm. "Lianne, honey, you're not making much sense. You have to tell me what's wrong. Why do you need to call the obstetrician?"

"Well, I've had this nagging back pain all afternoon. I was busy, so I kept hoping it would go away. But it didn't, it got worse. And just now, I had a really strong contraction. It startled me so much I dropped the vegetable dish I was holding."

"A contraction? You had a contraction?"

"Yes." Lianne shivered, although the kitchen was very warm. "Gabe, I think I'm in labor." She looked at her husband with a mixture of panic and excitement. "I guess this is the big moment, Gabe. We're going to have our baby."

CHAPTER THREE

GABE'S EXPRESSION WENT completely blank. Julia was so accustomed to thinking of him as practical and efficient that it took her a few seconds to register that he wasn't staring at Lianne because his mind was weighing options and making crucial decisions, but because he was paralyzed by shock.

Edward had arrived at the kitchen door just in time to hear Lianne's announcement. He clucked in dismay, making vague flapping motions with his hands. "Oh, good heavens!" he exclaimed. "This is so unexpected! Whatever shall we do?"

"You and I are going to take a walk in the garden," Tate said, taking care of his flapping hands by putting another glass of whiskey into them. When he started to protest, she hooked her arm through his and led him firmly in the direction of the back door.

"I'll keep him out of the way," she murmured to Julia in passing. "That seems the most useful thing I can do for now. If you need me for anything else, just give a shout."

If Julia hadn't already been a devoted fan of Tate's, she would have become one in that moment. "Thank you," she said with heartfelt gratitude. "I owe you one."

"Darling, you most certainly do, and I'll be sure to remind you of that at some supremely inconvenient moment." Tate sailed out of the door, dragging a reluctant Edward behind her.

Gabe and Lianne continued to stare at each other like a pair of puppets waiting to be animated. Julia spared a moment to reflect on how strange it was that prospective parents spent months planning for their baby's birth and then invariably seemed astonished when the big moment arrived. She waited for Gabe to take the elementary first step of calling the local doctor, but when she realized that he was showing no signs of doing that or anything else, she spoke up.

"Since Dr. Masham is away this weekend, you probably need to call your GP here in Lower Ashington," she said to Lianne, deftly removing a wooden spoon from her friend's clenched fingers and picking up the pieces of the shattered vegetable dish so that nobody would cut their feet. "You do have a doctor here, don't you?"

"Yes," Lianne replied, not moving.

"If you tell me where I can find his phone number, I'll give him a call and see whether he thinks you should drive back to London or have the baby at the local hospital," Julia prompted. "I don't suppose you've made arrangements to have the baby at home?"

Gabe finally snapped out of his stupor. "Lianne's mother made me promise we'd have the baby in a hospital," he said tightly. "She doesn't trust the idea of a midwife."

"Well, then, you just have to decide whether to go to Lower Ashington or make the drive back to London."

"The local hospital was closed three years ago," Lianne said, her voice high and breathless. "Nowadays, the nearest maternity unit is in Winchester. That's a forty-minute drive from here, and I'm not even sure exactly where in town the hospital is located."

"We can soon find out. Don't worry." Gabe looked so frantic that Julia gave his arm a few reassuring pats—the first time she'd voluntarily touched him since the night he told her he didn't love her. Surprisingly, all she felt was a sisterly sort of desire to calm him down so that he didn't upset Lianne with his panic.

"Gabe, you're worrying too much," she said, giving his hand a final consoling squeeze. "Babies come early all the time, and people who work on maternity cases expect the unexpected. At the moment, we need to focus on getting the best possible medical care for Lianne, whether that's in London or Winchester."

Lianne looked at Gabe, eyes brimming with guilty tears. "I should have made these arrangements weeks ago, instead of assuming we'd be back in London in time for the delivery. I can't believe I was so careless about something so important. I'm sorry, Gabe."

He put his arms around her. "It's my fault, sweetheart, not yours. I was the one who insisted on staying here until the renovations on the cottage were finished."

Lianne smiled mistily through her tears. "But I wanted to be here, Gabe. You know I love this cottage. It's my dream house come to life."

The parents-to-be seemed to have entirely forgotten the somewhat pressing problem of deciding on a hospital in which to have their baby, Julia thought. They stared tenderly at each other, lost in their own little world. She remembered her brother and sister-in-law saying that irrational behavior and the onset of labor went hand in hand, but she hadn't expected Gabe and Lianne, of all people, to demonstrate such classic symptoms of prenatal idiocy.

For some reason, Julia found her gaze drawn to Michael Forrest's. They exchanged amused, faintly exasperated glances.

Michael spoke softly. "It seems a shame to break up their lovefest, but I guess we should inject a note of reality into this discussion."

"I couldn't agree more. See if you have any better luck getting through to them than I did."

Michael tapped Gabe on the shoulder. "Guys, it's great that you're so happy with your new home, but Julia and I would like to concentrate on a couple of more immediate issues right now. Like where Lianne is going to give birth. Which I guess could be right here in the kitchen if you don't talk to us real soon. Could one of you come down to earth for a couple of minutes and tell us the name and phone number of your local doctor?"

Gabe blinked, visibly forcing himself to concentrate. "Yes, you're right. We need to call the doctor right away. Her name's Emily Crane. That's right, isn't it, sweetheart?"

Lianne nodded. "Yes. And we have her phone number pinned up next to the fridge. At least, I think I put her business card there when the workmen left."

Lianne barely finished speaking before she gave a smothered gasp of pain. Her hands fisted and she doubled over, cradling her hands around her swollen belly.

"Oh, my God!" Gabe put his arm around her shoulders, his features twisted with worry. "Are you having another contraction, sweetheart?"

"Mmm." She clung to Gabe, squeezing his hand hard enough to turn her knuckles white. "Gabe, it hurts so much," she whispered.

When the contraction ended, Julia realized that she

and Michael had both been holding their breath in sympathy. They let it out in unison as Lianne collapsed against the counter, panting. Gabe massaged her back and shoulders, but her face still appeared taut with strain. Julia felt a twinge of alarm. She was no expert on the course of normal childbirth, but she was fairly sure that the onset of labor was supposed to be more gradual than this.

Lianne slowly straightened, leaning heavily on her husband's arm as he helped her walk across the kitchen to a chair. "Jules, did you find the doctor's phone number?" she asked.

"Yes, I have the card and I'm dialing the number now this minute. Any special symptoms you want me to report to her?"

Lianne massaged her forehead, as if thinking was an effort. "Just tell her that Gabe's driving me to the hospital in Winchester, and ask her what the admission procedure is, will you? To be honest, I don't think delivering this baby in London is a realistic option. I'm not sure we'd make it that far."

Gabe's hair was already standing on end, he'd pushed his hand through it so many times. "What the hell's going on here? Those last two contractions were only four minutes apart. I thought they taught us in our prenatal classes that labor starts out with contractions that are at least twenty minutes apart?"

"They taught us, Gabe. I guess they forgot to teach our baby." Lianne managed a small smile. "He's obviously going to be a typical DeWilde and do things his own way and according to his own timetable."

Gabe was too worried to rise to the offered bait. He gave his fingers another distracted push through his hair and winced when Lianne shifted uncomfortably in the chair. Sweat was beginning to break out on her forehead, and her face was pale except for two bright splotches of color on her cheeks.

Hanging on to the phone, waiting for the doctor's office to answer, Julia opened her mouth to suggest that Lianne might like a cool cloth to wipe her face, but Michael was ahead of her. He'd already found a clean tea cloth in one of the drawers and wrung it out in cold water. He handed it to Lianne without saying a word, and she pressed it gratefully to her forehead.

"The answering service is paging the doctor now," Julia said. "Relax, Gabe. I'll have instructions on exactly how to get to the hospital and which entrance you should use in just a minute. I'll ask the doctor about any paperwork you might need, too."

The seconds ticked by, freighted with tension. "Is the answering service having trouble finding the doctor?" Michael asked Julia, keeping his voice low.

"No, they know where she is and they asked me to wait on the line. They're paging her now. She's at the theater, but they've used a code to show it's an emergency, so she should respond soon."

"Let me handle the doctor while you pack an overnight bag for Lianne," Michael suggested.

"That's a great idea." Julia paused in the act of handing the phone to Michael. "Or perhaps Gabe should do the packing."

Michael shook his head. "Gabe's useless at this point. He'd probably pack jeans and a garter belt, and forget her robe and toothbrush."

"Lianne might not want me to go through her personal belongings—"

Michael reached out and took the phone. "You're being too considerate, Julia. Our about-to-be Mom and

Dad are in shock and not functioning rationally. Any minute now, Lianne will have another contraction, and Gabe will go berserk. He'll start trying to take charge, but he won't be able to concentrate long enough to get anything done. He'll be running around, tripping over his own feet and bumping into the furniture. Strong, take-charge men who are crazily in love with their wives are always the worst at delivery time. Trust me on this, the only way we're going to get the pair of them out of here in the next half hour is if we make all the arrangements."

"You're right," Julia acknowledged. "I'll go and pack Lianne's bag. It shouldn't take me more than five minutes."

She located the master bedroom with no difficulty, but finding a suitcase proved impossible. In the end, not wanting to waste time, she took her own weekend bag, turned her clothes and toiletries out onto a bed in one of the spare bedrooms and hurriedly restocked the bag with the things she thought Lianne might need. She came downstairs again just in time to see Michael hanging up the phone.

He glanced at her inquiringly and she held up the bulging bag and the two pillows she'd brought down to put in the car for Lianne to rest against. He grinned and gave her a thumbs-up sign. "Great thinking. Lianne should bless you."

His smile banished his usual sardonic expression and gave his face an appealing warmth. Julia's stomach gave an odd little lurch, but there was no time to wonder why. Lianne gripped the arms of the chair as another contraction swept over her.

Gabe barely waited for the contraction to end before he shot into frenzied action. "That's it!" he exclaimed.

"Only three minutes since the last one. We have to get to the hospital right away! This is an emergency!"

He put his arm around Lianne's waist and pulled her to her feet, then pushed her back into the chair. "No, you wait here. Don't move! I'll get the car."

He rushed blindly in the direction of the front door, knocking into a console table and almost sending a valuable Crown Derby jug flying.

Julia grabbed the jug while Michael grabbed Gabe's arm and hauled him back from the door. "Gabe, slow down. You need car keys before you can go anywhere."

"Right. Car keys." Gabe blundered toward the kitchen and Julia shot a warning glance toward Michael, shaking her head very slightly.

He nodded, picking up right away on her worry. "Yeah, well, on second thought, Gabe, why don't I drive you and Lianne to the hospital? That way, I can worry about the traffic, and you can sit in the back seat and hold your wife's hand. Remind her to relax and keep breathing, or whatever it is expectant fathers are supposed to do."

Gabe stared at Michael as if he no longer understood simple English. Michael pulled a set of car keys from his pocket and jiggled them in front of Gabe's nose. "These are my car keys," he said. "We'll go in my car. Fortunately, it's parked right outside the front door so Lianne won't have far to walk."

Gabe nodded, his clumsiness vanishing as he turned to his wife. Tenderly, he helped her to her feet and took the pillows from Julia. "Are you ready to leave, sweetheart? Do you want an extra sweater?"

Lianne shook her head. "It'll be warm enough in the car."

At the front door, she and Julia exchanged hugs.

"Good luck," Julia said softly. "I'm sure everything will be fine. And ask Gabe to phone us as soon as he can tear himself away from the new baby. I can't wait to hear if it's a boy or a girl."

"I'll make sure he calls," Lianne promised. She bit her lip. "I'm just a bit worried because the baby's coming so early. What if something's wrong, Jules? What if its lungs aren't properly developed?"

"These days, doctors are saving babies born eleven and twelve weeks before their due date. Four weeks barely counts as premature. Your baby's just impatient to get out and see the world. You said it yourself, a typical DeWilde." Julia gave Lianne another encouraging hug. "You'd better hurry up and get into the car. Gabe's getting his wild and woolly look again."

Lianne's gaze softened as she glanced toward her husband. "He's excited, that's all. I've been feeling our baby grow inside me for eight months, but Gabe's had no role to play except to stand on the sidelines and watch my body go through changes he could do nothing about. That's hard for a man who likes to be in charge of everything."

"Yes, I'm sure it must be." Julia chuckled. "Tell him he can be in total charge of all nappy changes and any feedings between midnight and 6:00 a.m. for the next three months. That should help to make him feel truly involved in his baby's early development."

Lianne smiled. "You always have the best suggestions, Jules. Oh, I just remembered! Call my mother for me, will you, please? She's had her plane ticket booked for the past six weeks. She's going to be really disappointed that she didn't get here in time for the birth."

"I'll call her as soon as you and Gabe have left for the hospital," Julia promised.

"Call Gabe's father, too, would you?" Lianne hesitated another moment before getting into the car. Then she turned her back on her husband and spoke quickly, almost as if she didn't want him to hear what she was saying.

"Grace is in London, Jules, but I don't know exactly where she's staying. Kate forgot to tell me. Will you find her and let her know that I've gone to the hospital? I really want her to come and see the baby as soon as she can."

"I'll track her down," Julia promised. She knew Gabe had been estranged from his mother for over a year. Lianne had rarely talked about it, except to say a few weeks ago how relieved she was that things were finally improving between her husband and her mother-in-law. Though apparently not enough for Lianne to be sure that Gabe would invite Grace to come and meet her new grandchild.

Julia felt a spurt of unexpected anger toward Gabe. She understood why he'd been upset about the breakup of his parents' marriage. But Grace had left Jeffrey more than a year ago, and it was time for Gabe to get over it. If Megan and Kate could remain on good terms with both their parents, it shouldn't be too hard for him to do the same.

As soon as Lianne was settled against the pillows, Michael slipped into the driver's seat. "I'll leave everything here in your capable hands," he said to Julia, turning the key in the ignition. "And I'll call you as soon as there's any news about the baby."

"Oh," Julia said. "I didn't realize you planned to wait at the hospital until the baby arrives."

Michael's dark eyes glinted with mischief. "Why,

Julia, honey, if I didn't know better, I'd say you almost sound as if you're going to miss me.''

"Ha!" Julia tossed her head, and her hair gave a satisfying swish as she flicked it over her shoulder. "Don't you wish."

Michael sent her a long, level gaze. "Yes," he said finally. "I do."

He drove off in a spray of gravel, leaving Julia to stare, speechless, at the retreating lights of his car.

CHAPTER FOUR

JEFFREY HAD ALWAYS considered that of all his children, Kate was the most similar to him in character. Sensitive, intense, driven and painfully intelligent, she'd inherited all his inhibitions about expressing her deepest emotions. The stormy course of her relationship with Nick Santos was exactly what Jeffrey would have predicted for his youngest daughter. What he wouldn't have predicted was the miraculous blossoming of her self-confidence since her marriage. With a mixture of pleasure and chagrin, Jeffrey was discovering that his daughter no longer hesitated to express her views about subjects she'd previously been careful to avoid.

When Grace had left him and moved to San Francisco, Kate had called to offer him polite sympathy, but she'd given no clue as to what she actually felt about the breakup. By contrast, during their most recent phone conversation, she'd informed him in no uncertain terms that his behavior over the past year had been idiotic.

"You want Mom to come back to you," Kate said. "And yet you can't bring yourself to tell her that simple truth. It's crazy, Dad. You're ruining your life because you're too proud to tell the woman you love that you behaved like a donkey's rear end."

"The situation's more complicated than that," Jeffrey protested. "Much more complicated."

Kate sighed audibly. "No, Dad, it's not complicated

at all. You've spent almost a year and a half doing stupid things for no real reason except to make Mom's life miserable. And then, to crown it all, the pair of you spent a fortune on lawyers, arranging a divorce neither of you really wanted, chiefly because of that stiff-necked pride of yours—"

"You're confusing pride and dignity," Jeffrey said stiffly. "There were factors you aren't aware of that made our divorce inevitable." Pictures of Ian Stanley flashed into his mind: Ian dancing cheek to cheek with Grace, Ian kissing Grace, Ian making love to Grace. Jeffrey slammed the door on that last, excruciatingly painful image. Ian had been his friend for half a lifetime, but he and Ian hadn't spoken since the day Grace filed for divorce. Kate might be wrong about the details of his split from Grace, Jeffrey reflected, but she was dead right about the fundamentals. In the space of one short year, he'd lost his wife and his best friend. If he'd set out to make a major screwup of his life, he couldn't have done much better.

"I'm not confusing anything," Kate said. "We're two of a kind, Dad, and I know from experience that pride makes for empty days and lonely nights, and not much fun in between. The truth is, you rejected Mom's efforts at reconciliation one too many times, and she finally decided you meant what you were saying. Now you want her back, and you realize to your dismay that she isn't sitting around waiting for you to forgive her. That maybe she isn't going to come back unless you grovel. So I guess I'm wondering how long it will take you to come to your senses and start the groveling process."

"You seem to be forgetting that your mother left me," Jeffrey said tautly, the defense reflexive after months of using Grace's flight as an excuse for his own behavior. "I didn't leave her, it was the other way around."

"Dad, what happened to cause the breakup is almost irrelevant, can't you see that?" Kate sounded impatient. "The past is gone, and you can't change it. If I were you, I'd start working on the future instead of obsessively reworking the past. Fortunately, Mom has a generous heart and a great sense of humor. I guess she's going to need both if you ever do the smart thing and beg her to take you back."

Grace would need a sense of humor to take him back? It was one thing to think of the breakup of his marriage as a cosmic tragedy, quite another to think of it as a bad joke. Jeffrey scowled as he recalled the conversation with his daughter. Kate had been wrong in her assessment of his situation, he decided. For a start, his pride wasn't condemning him to empty days and lonely nights. On the contrary, his calendar was chock-a-block full, seven days a week, and not just with business appointments. If he wanted to, he could escort beautiful women to glamorous parties on a nightly basis. He stayed home so much because he preferred solitude, not because he had no alternative. Still, however hard he attempted to rationalize Kate's insights away, her words stung with the annoying prick of truth.

Determined to prove to himself that he was a man still in his powerful prime, rather than a lonely reject who was determined to behave like an idiot, Jeffrey managed to devise a Saturday schedule that promised to be a nonstop round of activity.

He breakfasted with a supplier from Taiwan, did a quick tour of a competitor's new store, had a late lunch with a vice president from the advertising agency to review next year's marketing plan for DeWilde's, and spent the latter part of the afternoon discussing a new look for his London flat with an interior decorator his secretary insisted was the best in London.

By the time the decorator left at five-thirty, Jeffrey was a hair's breadth away from committing murder. He wondered if he could have chosen a worse way to waste a sunny Saturday afternoon than thumbing through swatches of fabric with a woman who wielded her maroon nails like weapons and referred to half the wallpaper samples in any given book as "simply darling." But since the alternative was to continue living in a flat where every nook and cranny reminded him of Grace, Jeffrey suffered through the three hours of torment, and even acknowledged that the problem wasn't so much the decorator's grating personality as his own ambivalence about the fact that Grace was gone from his home, as well as from his life.

Which, he realized, brought him back full circle to the point he'd been at this morning when he set out on his round of frenzied make-work. The knowledge that his ex-wife was in town—that he knew the hotel where she was staying—was like a splinter under his thumbnail, constantly throbbing. To stop the ache, all he needed to do was pick up the phone and call her. But what would he say when she answered? Was he ready to grovel? Would it do any good if he did?

Jeffrey wanted to believe it was a good sign that Grace had personally brought him the long-lost DeWilde family jewels. What else could the gesture mean except that she was trying to bridge some of the emotional distance still yawning between the two of them? When he'd kissed her last night, she'd seemed perfectly willing to respond. But perhaps he'd been mistaken.

God knows, he'd been seriously misreading Grace's signals for most of the past two years.

The harder Jeffrey tried to analyze everything that had happened in his office the evening before, the less he could remember exactly how his ex-wife had behaved. Was he imagining that she'd been deliberately sexy? Perhaps she merely wanted to get things back on a friendly footing with him for the sake of the children. Grace was too kind-hearted to want their strained relationship to mar the harmony of future family gatherings. But then again, she hadn't needed to kiss him with so much enthusiasm if all she wanted was to maintain a polite friendship. Jeffrey clenched his jaw in frustration. Lord, this was insane! He hadn't spent this much time worrying about a simple kiss since the cricket match when he missed his call to bat because he was behind the pavilion kissing the sister of the captain of the opposing team.

In the solitude of his kitchen, with his dinner of packaged soup heating in the microwave, Jeffrey finally acknowledged why he had never asked Grace to come back to him. It wasn't pride that held him back, it was fear. If he didn't ask Grace to come back, she couldn't refuse. And as long as Grace hadn't refused point blank to return, he could cherish the fantasy that one day they would be together again, the nightmare of the past two years wiped away.

Jeffrey watched the seconds count down on the microwave timer. He had every reason to avoid putting his fate to the test, he reflected gloomily. Grace was an attractive, intelligent woman, brimming with warmth and vivacity. He couldn't think of a single reason why she would want to come back to a dull stick like him. What in the world did he have to offer her?

The microwave beeped and he rotated his bowl of soup a precise quarter turn, then pressed the restart button. Once upon a time he'd have said that his marriage to Grace was a true partnership, and that his share of the bargain was to provide rock solid integrity and financial security, a counterbalance to Grace's contributions of beauty, warmth and sheer joy of living. He had destroyed the delicate balance of that bargain beyond repair. His affair with Allison Ames meant that he could no longer lay claim even to sexual faithfulness, let alone rock solid integrity. And Grace had proved with the success of her San Francisco store that she didn't need him for financial security or professional advice. As for the emotional balance he'd always believed he provided, Jeffrey had realized within days of Grace's departure that he needed her warmth a hell of a lot more than she needed his occasional calming influence and commonsense advice.

The microwave beeped again, and he stared at his bowl of bubbling minestrone with a grimace of distaste. The terrifying truth was that for all his wealth and for all his power in the world of business, he had no power at all over Grace. He could go to her and lay bare his soul, beg forgiveness for his adultery and tell her he loved her so much that he was going insane without her. And she would likely as not give him one of her sweet smiles and remind him that she'd already forgiven him for his affair with Allison, but that she hadn't the faintest desire to come and live with him ever again. Being a generous soul, she might even take pity on him and make love to him for old times' sake. Jeffrey couldn't make up his mind whether it would be more terrible to accept her offer or to refuse, knowing that she would never make the offer again.

The phone rang and he grabbed it fast, thankful for the interruption. At this point, anyone, even the maroon-nailed decorator, would be a welcome interruption to his own bleak thoughts.

"Mr. DeWilde?"

The caller was a woman, but she spoke with a soft, attractive voice that was vaguely familiar. Definitely not the decorator. "This is Jeffrey DeWilde," he acknowledged.

"Mr. DeWilde, this is Julia Dutton. You may remember that we've met a couple of times. Lianne used to share a flat with me before she married Gabe."

"Yes, Julia, of course I remember you. What a pleasant surprise to hear from you." She would never guess just how pleasant, Jeffrey thought ruefully. "You're a friend of Michael Forrest's, aren't you?"

There was an odd little pause before Julia spoke again. "Michael and I know each other," she said. "I'm calling from Briarwood Cottage, Mr. DeWilde, and I have some exciting news. Lianne's gone into labor and Gabe's taken her to the hospital in Winchester. He asked me to give you a ring to let you know that their baby will probably be born tonight or early tomorrow morning. He was hoping you might be able to come and meet your new grandchild sometime over the weekend."

Gabe and Lianne's baby was about to make an appearance in the world! Jeffrey felt a rush of exhilaration so intense it caught him off guard. He'd been looking forward to the birth of his first grandchild, but until this moment, he'd had no idea how much. He laughed delightedly, remembering the excitement of the night Gabe and Megan were born, and experiencing some of the same deep-seated sense of wonder.

"Of course I'll come," he said. "What a splendid way to spend the weekend! I'll throw my shaving kit into an overnight bag and drive down right away. I should be there in a couple of hours, traffic permitting."

"I'm sure Gabe and Lianne will be thrilled to see you."

Julia had always struck him as a particularly nice young woman, but Jeffrey could detect a note of discomfort in her voice, as if she were hiding something from him. "Julia, is something bothering you?" His stomach lurched. "If there are problems with Lianne or the baby, I'd much rather hear about them now—"

"Oh, no, nothing like that," she said hastily. "I'm sure everything's going to be fine. I just have a slight problem that I'm not sure…" She paused for a moment. "Mr. DeWilde, this is rather awkward, and I apologize, but Lianne mentioned that her mother-in-law is in London. She wants me to let Mrs. DeWilde know…er… Grace…"

Julia stopped again. She drew in an audible breath and tried one more time. "Lianne wants me to let Grace know that she's in labor, and the baby should be here within a few hours. She would like her mother-in-law to come to the hospital as soon as possible. Unfortunately, I've called half a dozen London hotels already, and Mrs.…um…Gabe's mother isn't staying at any of them. There's no reason why you should know her whereabouts, of course, but I wondered if you might happen to know which hotel she's staying in? Or if she's visiting with friends?"

Perhaps he was feeling so cheerful because of the imminent arrival of his first grandchild, but Jeffrey found the poor young woman's frantic efforts to avoid saying "your ex-wife" almost entertaining. "I'm glad you thought to ask me," he said, a note of amusement creeping into his voice. "Yes, by fortunate coincidence, I know exactly where Grace is staying."

"Oh, super! Could you give me the name of her hotel, please?"

"I'm sure you must have a dozen other things to do besides call Grace," Jeffrey said, barely restraining himself from giving a whoop of glee when he realized that he'd been presented with the absolutely perfect excuse to contact his ex-wife. "Let me take one task off your plate, Julia. Why don't I call Grace and tell her the news?"

"Well, if you're sure you don't mind, that would be a big help—"

"It will be my pleasure," Jeffrey said, with absolute truth. "In fact, Julia, it's only sensible for me to drive Grace down to Winchester. I'm sure she'll want to rush down there the minute she hears the news, and there's no point in her hiring a car to go to exactly the same place as I'm going."

"Wonderful. I'll try to get a message to Lianne and Gabe at the hospital in Winchester to let them know you'll both be on your way shortly."

"Do you have directions to the hospital?" Jeffrey asked.

"Yes, Michael wrote them down. I'll repeat them for you." She gave him clear and concise instructions on how to find the hospital. They exchanged goodbyes and Jeffrey hung up, humming the theme song from the most recent James Bond movie as he poured his unwanted soup down the garbage disposal. He looked up the number for the Goreham hotel and dialed quickly, heart thumping.

Yesterday the DeWilde jewels had come home, and

now his first grandchild was about to be born. Plus, he was going to spend several hours in Grace's company! He smiled broadly as the hotel telephonist answered his call. One way or another, this was shaping up to be quite a weekend.

JEFFREY STRODE ACROSS the polished marble floor of the Goreham hotel lobby. Skirting a fountain that he barely noticed was there, he found the concierge desk with the unerring instinct of a man who had stayed in hotels the world over. "I'm Jeffrey DeWilde," he said crisply. "I've been trying to reach Mrs. DeWilde since half past eight. I rang earlier, and when she didn't answer the phone, someone on your staff was kind enough to check her room and confirm that she was out. I need to get in touch with her urgently, and it occurred to me that she might have asked you to help her with theater tickets, or some such thing."

The concierge checked in a small ledger, then shook his head regretfully. "I'm sorry, sir, I can't help you. Mrs. DeWilde didn't ask us to make any bookings on her behalf. But if you would care to leave another message, I'll make sure that she knows to get in touch with you the minute she returns."

Jeffrey glanced at his watch. Not quite nine o'clock. It would take less than two hours to drive to Winchester at this time of night, and the impatience he felt to get on the road was caused by eagerness rather than any sense of emergency. Since he very much wanted to be with Grace when they met their first grandchild, the most sensible thing for him to do was to control his impatience and remain at the hotel until she returned from her evening's engagement.

"I'll order a sandwich while I wait for her to come

back," Jeffrey told the concierge. "Could you point me in the direction of the coffee shop, or wherever it is you serve light snacks at this time of night?"

"Of course, sir. Our coffee shop and tearoom are located to the rear of the atrium, on my right, behind our indoor garden." The concierge swiveled around to point toward a veritable forest of tropical greenery. He swung back as Jeffrey was on the point of walking away. "I just thought of something, sir. It's possible that Mrs. DeWilde is in our Oak Room restaurant. We've won several awards for our outstanding menu of all-British food, and many of our guests choose to eat there rather than going out to dinner. Since you're heading in that direction, you might want to take a quick look before you order your sandwich and see if Mrs. DeWilde is in the Oak Room."

"Good thought," Jeffrey said. "I'll certainly take a look. Thanks for your help."

Winding his way through a sea of Doric columns, he wondered why an architect would choose to design the lobby of an English hotel to look like a cross between a Roman emperor's palace and a Hollywood sound stage. There wasn't even any design consistency, he discovered on reaching the restaurant. In contrast to the chilly brightness of the atrium, the Oak Room was paneled in somber oak, carpeted in hunter green and furnished with overstuffed leather chairs to look like a nineteenth-century gentlemen's club. The heavy white damask cloths covering the tables glowed with ghostly luminescence against the surrounding gloom. The overhead lights were so dim that Jeffrey couldn't imagine how diners were supposed to connect their forks with their food, much less read their all-British menus.

The maître d' was busy settling a group of eight Japanese businessmen into their seats, and most of the other tables seemed to be filled exclusively with men, without even a token wife or female executive to leaven the masculine atmosphere. Although this seemed the last sort of place in which Grace would choose to eat, Jeffrey decided he might as well make a quick tour of the restaurant before escaping to the coffee shop and ordering a sandwich.

He heard the soft ripple of Grace's laughter before he saw her, and he strode forward, calling her name almost in the same instant that he recognized the man seated beside her in one of the booths along the far wall. Damn it to hell, his wife was eating dinner with Ian Stanley!

Jeffrey halted in midstride, consumed by a white-hot jealousy as irrational as it was fierce. Almost worse than the jealousy was the stark realization that he had no right to question Grace's choice of dinner companion. Perish the thought, but for all he knew, he might be interrupting their engagement dinner. Drawing in a couple of quick, deep breaths, he stepped forward with grim determination, trying to greet his ex-wife and his former best friend with the easygoing courtesy he knew was appropriate. But, as always happened when he was confronted by emotional situations he didn't know how to handle, he froze. The casual words he sought so desperately wouldn't come.

For a tense moment, nobody moved or spoke. Then Grace looked at Ian, her gaze quizzical, and Jeffrey could sense some unspoken question and answer pass back and forth between the two of them. He would have sworn nothing could have made him feel more jealous of Ian Stanley than he already did, but witnessing the silent intimacy of that exchange, he realized for the first time the full enormity of all that he'd lost when Grace left him. Anger and jealousy both disappeared in an overwhelming rush of sadness.

"Jeffrey, please join Ian and me for coffee. We'll ask the waiter to bring another cup." Grace turned to him and held out her hand, the gesture unconsciously appealing, as if she expected him to do or say something hurtful and wanted to prevent a scene. It was a depressing commentary on his recent behavior that she should so obviously feel nervous. "Were you looking for me, Jeffrey, or is this meeting just a coincidence?"

"I was looking for you," he managed to say. "The concierge suggested I might find you here." He fixed his gaze on a knot in the oak paneling and tried to sound polite, instead of sarcastic. "I trust I'm not intruding at an inconvenient moment."

"No, of course you're not. Sit down, Jeffrey. You're so tall looming over us that I'm getting a crick in my neck. Ian and I were just discussing his plans for the rest of the summer."

His plans? Did that mean Ian was expecting to spend the rest of the summer alone, without Grace? Jeffrey willed his legs to bend at the knee and slide into the booth opposite Grace and Ian. He wondered how in God's name he'd ever arrived at the point in his life where being asked to drink a cup of coffee at the same table as the woman he loved and the man who'd been his best friend should seem like a test of endurance equivalent to dipping his fingers into a tub of acid.

But, damn it, he wasn't going to ignore Ian's presence just because he was insanely jealous. Ian was in no way responsible for the breakup of his marriage, and it was past time to stop blaming everyone except himself for the fact that Grace had left him. Jeffrey cleared his throat. "How are you, Ian?" he asked coolly. "Keeping well, I trust?"

Grace and Ian exchanged another of those infuriating silent dialogues. "I'm doing—very well," Ian said. "And as I was just telling Grace, I have exciting plans for next month. I've made arrangements to visit China. I'm going to spend three weeks in a small town west of Beijing."

"How interesting," Jeffrey said woodenly. "Is it a business trip? Does the bank have plans for an investment there?"

"It's much more exciting than that," Grace said. "Ian has been supervising the fund-raising to rescue three hundred orphaned girls whose home burned down last winter. They've built a new home for the orphans, and now he's trying to get permission to build a high school for them. You know that girl babies in China are abandoned at ten times the rate of boys, and very often they receive almost no education, because in country districts the traditional beliefs about female inferiority still hold sway. Ian's been working like a fiend to cut through all the paperwork and government red tape to get this orphanage built, and the provincial authorities have invited him out for the grand opening. It's quite an honor, because the central government usually doesn't like to have foreigners spending too much time outside the official Foreign Enterprise Zones."

Jeffrey would have been only slightly less shocked if Grace had told him Ian planned to spend the next month learning to pilot an alien spaceship. "You're going to spend three weeks in a Chinese village, drawing up construction plans for a school?" he exclaimed, unable to conceal his surprise.

"You could try sounding slightly less amazed, old

chap." Ian spoke with his usual self-mocking irony, but Jeffrey thought he could detect a faint note of hurt behind the seemingly flippant words. "Even frivolous people like me have their occasional bursts of nobility, you know."

"You don't have to convince me of your good qualities," Jeffrey said quietly. "You're the one who always seemed hell-bent on showing the world that you didn't give a damn. I'm surprised you're willing to destroy the image you've always worked so hard to project, that's all."

Ian didn't reply for a moment. "Sometimes life has a way of flicking its tail and catching you unawares," he said finally. "I've learned some valuable lessons about myself over the past year, and I've discovered that I don't want to look back on my life and realize that the most useful thing I've ever done is provide entertaining gossip for my ex-wives."

The past year had taught Jeffrey a lot, too. Not least of the skills he'd acquired in Grace's absence was the ability to hear what was being left unspoken, as well as what was being said out loud. He looked at Grace for guidance, but she seemed intent on rearranging packets of artificial sweetener in a pile around her plate, and she stubbornly refused to raise her eyes.

Jeffrey pushed the floral centerpiece to one side and looked across the table at the man who had been his friend for almost forty years. "What's going on here, Ian?" he asked. "Something's wrong, and not just with the treatment of girl babies in China. What is it?"

Ian smiled, but he didn't meet Jeffrey's eyes. "Nothing's wrong, old chap, quite the contrary. I'm going to China to make sure that the orphanage meets the specifications we agreed on and that corrupt officials haven't siphoned off any of the funds for their private profit. But the trip isn't going to be all work and no play. There will be plenty of free time in which I can indulge all my familiar bad habits. I understand that now the regime has relaxed its dress code, young women have gone back to wearing gorgeous silk cheongsams instead of those dreary Mao suits. I'm looking forward to meeting many beautiful women and making them very happy."

"Don't," Jeffrey snapped. "Ian, I'm your oldest friend. Don't pretend with me. What the bloody hell is going on here?"

For the first time, Ian allowed his gaze to drift upward until it locked with Jeffrey's. "Are you my oldest friend?" he asked. "Funny you should say that. I rather had the impression that we were no longer speaking, at least about anything meaningful. Which would make you my oldest former friend, wouldn't it?"

Ian's words hurt in ways Jeffrey would never have expected. "I've done a great many things over the past two years that were remarkable for their foolishness," he said. "Believing that I could deny our friendship was one of the most foolish. Of course we're still talking to each other about things that matter, Ian. Or at least my part of the *we* is still talking. And you may as well accept that I plan to keep on talking until you start answering. Really answering, as opposed to pushing me away from you by erecting a barrier of smart comebacks."

Ian smiled, this time with genuine warmth. "I'll be damned, Jeffrey, that was almost eloquent. Although, I suspect that it would take somebody who's known you since prep school to appreciate how out of character that speech was."

"Fortunately, you qualify," Jeffrey said.

"Yes." Ian was silent for a moment, then he looked up and grinned. "Since it seems a shame to throw away so many years of putting up with you, old chap, I suppose I'd better accept that we're destined to be best friends forever." He hesitated for another moment, then held out his hand across the table. "Here's to old and trusted friends, Jeffrey, and a lifetime of good memories. Let's shake on it."

Jeffrey grasped Ian's hand, swallowing over a sudden lump in his throat. "You should have given me a swift kick in the pants several months ago," he said gruffly.

"The temptation to do just that was frequently overwhelming," Ian said. "However, Grace persuaded me that you were being so rock-hard stubborn that I risked breaking my toe without bringing you to your senses. And I had no particular desire to sacrifice my toe in a lost cause."

Jeffrey shot a quick glance at Grace, but she still refused to meet his gaze. He sighed and turned back to his friend. "I'll be honest with you, Ian. If you and Grace end up married to each other, I won't see as much of you in the future as we did in the past. I'm not a generous enough man to totally put aside my own feelings and enjoy watching your happiness. That doesn't mean I don't...that I won't always care about you. About both of you."

Grace finally stopped poking at the packets of sweetener and gave an impatient sigh. "I told you weeks ago that Ian and I have no intention of getting married," she said. "For a smart man, you can take an annoyingly long time to get a simple idea into your head, Jeffrey."

"Possibly," he said, thinking how incredibly beautiful she looked in the soft candlelight. "But for thirty-two years I relied on you to keep pounding away until I got the message, Gracie. It's a little difficult to develop alternative coping methods at this stage in my life."

The silence that fell over the table was broken by Ian. "Since the waiter seems to have decided that we're not worthy of a second cup of coffee, I think I may go up to my room and leave you and Grace to discuss whatever business it is that brings you here, Jeff." He rose to his feet. "Grace, darling, I'd love to clamber over those luscious legs of yours, but since your ex-husband is sending dagger looks in our direction, I think we'd better be discreet. Could you stand up and let me slide out?"

Grace stood up at once, but Jeffrey wasn't looking at her. He stared at Ian with new eyes, taking in the gauntness of his friend's cheeks and the way his expensive, perfectly tailored jacket hung from shoulders that no longer seemed broad and strong, but shrunken and horrifyingly frail. He slid out of the booth and stood himself. "Ian?" he said hoarsely, his stomach plummeting. "Ian, for God's sake, stop lying to me. Tell me what's wrong. Have you been ill?"

For a split second, Ian hesitated. Then he shrugged. "Do I look that bad?" He managed a rueful smile. "And to think my doctors are all rather pleased with me."

"Your doctors?"

"God, yes. I've a positive retinue of the creatures. But at the moment, we're all on very good terms with one another. They've postponed my death sentence by several months because I'm responding to treatment so well. One of them confidently expects to win a prize for the paper he's writing about the beneficial effects of the drugs he's dosing me with."

Jeffrey looked from Ian to Grace and back to Ian again. Grace's face confirmed the worst. He didn't insult his friend by pretending not to understand. "How long?" he asked tersely.

"Possibly as much as another year," Ian said. "I told you, my doctors keep postponing the moment of execution, but a year seems to be about the outer limit." He put his hand on Jeffrey's shoulder. "Don't look so shattered, Jeff. I've learned there's a certain satisfaction to be derived from ensuring that you make each hour count. Life takes on a whole new perspective when you're forced to count exactly how many days of it you may have left."

"And I've already squandered four months of the time we could have shared," Jeffrey said. "What idiots we both are, but especially me. For God's sake, Ian, why didn't you tell me when you first got the diagnosis?"

"I wasn't sure you'd be willing to take my phone call, and I wasn't quite feeling in the mood to have my oldest friend refuse to speak to me."

Jeffrey wanted to protest that he would never have given Ian the brush-off if he'd had even a hint that something was seriously wrong, but remembering some examples of his own stupidity during the past year, he was appalled to realize that he might easily have refused to listen to Ian long enough to discover the extent of his friend's problem. Dismayed at how close he'd come to throwing away something of enormous value, he put his arm around Ian's wasted shoulders in a rare gesture of physical affection.

He swallowed over the lump in his throat two or three times before he could speak normally. "I'll phone you next week so that we can arrange to spend some time together before you take off for China. Perhaps you could come down to Kemberly for a couple of days, give Mrs. Milton a chance to show off her cooking, and let me boast about how I've learned to take care of Gracie's rose garden. I want to hear all about this high school you're building. It sounds like an intriguing project."

"I'll wait for your call. And if there's a chance of squeezing a donation out of you, I'll even bring pictures and architectural drawings of what we're doing in Beijing."

Ian smiled, but now that he was paying closer attention, Jeffrey could see that it was costing his friend real effort to conceal his pain.

"Bring the pictures, Ian. Knowing your silver tongue, I'm sure before the weekend's over you'll convince me that it's always been my lifelong ambition to support an orphanage in China. I might as well see the details of what I'm buying into."

Ian grinned. "I'll make a note to bring pictures." He took Grace's hand and carried it to his lips with typical flamboyance. "Good night, sweetheart. By the way, as one of your oldest and dearest friends, it's my duty to warn you that this Jeffrey DeWilde fellow has a shocking reputation with the ladies. Don't let him talk you into going anywhere with him unless you're willing to let him take you to bed."

Grace blushed. "I'll keep your advice in mind, Ian. Good night, sleep well. And thank you so much for a lovely dinner."

"As always, it was definitely my pleasure. Good night, Jeff." Ian strode purposefully across the room, stopping at the maître d's station to pay the bill.

"How long have you known he was dying?" Jeffrey

asked abruptly as he and Grace sat down again at the table.

"Since I was in Nevada, waiting for our divorce to come through."

"You should have told me, Grace."

"He asked me not to, and I respected his wishes. It was the least I could do."

"He's been in love with you for years. You know that, don't you?"

"Yes." Grace had returned to piling up her packets of sweetener. "But Ian is aware that although I love him dearly as a friend, I'm not in love with him."

"It would be a horrible mistake to marry him because you're sorry for him—"

"For heaven's sake, Jeffrey, how many different ways do I need to say it? I'm not planning to marry Ian. He knows it. I know it. Can we please drop the subject?"

"I'm sorry," he said stiffly. "But for once I wasn't thinking about you and me when I gave that advice. I was genuinely thinking about Ian. He would hate to be married out of pity."

"And I don't plan to marry him out of pity or for any other reason." Grace pushed her empty coffee cup to one side and looked up at him questioningly. "You said you were searching for me, Jeffrey. What did you want to see me about?"

Jeffrey felt a return of his former excitement, although it was tinged by sadness for Ian. He reached across the table for Grace's hand, smiling as happiness about the soon-to-arrive new baby overtook his other emotions. "I had a phone call this evening from Julia Dutton Do you know her?"

"Mmm, yes. She dated Gabe for a while, didn't she?"

"Maybe, but it can't have been serious, because I've seen her at a couple of dinners seated next to Michael Forrest. Even I noticed the sexual tension the two of them were generating—"

"Michael Forrest and Julia Dutton?" Grace's eyes lit up. "Now, that's a surprising combination, but oddly enough, it might be a good one. His parents' marriage was so horrible, he used to swear that he'd never marry, and given the way my cousin Maddy behaved toward Michael—"

Jeffrey almost laughed at how swiftly their conversation had wandered off track. It was so typical—so marvelously typical—of the conversations he used to have with Grace. "Gracie, dearest, if we could please stick to the subject—"

"But I thought Julia was the subject."

"No, she's not. Except that she phoned to say that Lianne went into labor earlier this evening, and Gabe wants us to go to the hospital right away so that we can meet our new grandchild."

"Oh, how wonderful! Our grandchild is here! Are Lianne and the baby all right? Is it a boy or a girl?"

"When Julia called, Lianne was still in labor. But by the time we arrive at the hospital, the baby could have put in an appearance."

Grace's entire body seemed to spark with delight. "Oh, Jeffrey, what great news! This is so exciting! My first grandbaby, can you imagine? It doesn't seem possible." She reached for her purse and stood up. "Shall we take a cab together? Then we can have a glass of champagne to celebrate, or even several glasses, without worrying about drinking and driving."

"A cab isn't an option, unfortunately," Jeffrey said. "Lianne and Gabe were spending the weekend at Briarwood Cottage, so Lianne isn't having the baby in London as she planned. Apparently there wasn't time to make the drive back into town, so she's having the baby in the local hospital, which is in Winchester."

Grace's forehead crinkled into a frown. "Everything's going to be all right, isn't it, Jeffrey? I know Lianne's taken wonderful care of herself during the pregnancy, but it's always worrying when a baby arrives too early."

"According to all the reports I've been given, everything's splendid," he said. "But we need to get a move on if we're going to see our new grandchild before he's a day old."

"He? You're such a chauvinist, Jeffrey. I've told you this baby is definitely a girl."

Jeffrey let his mouth curve into a predatory smile. "How much are you betting, Gracie?"

She looked at him thoughtfully. "Are we talking money?"

He shook his head. "Of course not. That's no fun at all. I had something more along the lines of our traditional bets in mind."

He couldn't tell whether she was shocked or not. Her gaze traveled slowly from his face to his chest and then back up again. "All right," she said at last. "We'll bet one hour."

"Two," he said instantly.

She hesitated for a moment. "All right," she agreed. "Two hours."

He couldn't believe it had been that simple. Jeffrey spelled out their bet, just to make sure. "If it's a boy, for two hours you do exactly what I order you to do. Agreed?"

"Yes." The flush in Grace's cheeks darkened. "And if the baby's a girl, for two hours, you'll do exactly what I order you to do."

"It's a deal," Jeffrey said softly. He touched her lightly on the cheek. "I'm sure you remember that I always collect on my bets, Gracie."

"Yes." She turned abruptly, so he couldn't see her face and had no idea what she was thinking. "I need to change into something more comfortable for the drive," she said.

"Of course." Jeffrey overcame the impulse to dance a quick jig. "And it might be wise to pack an overnight bag, in case we decide to stay in Winchester tomorrow night."

Grace turned back to him at that, and her cheeks were flaming. "All right, I'll pack a bag. I shouldn't be more than fifteen minutes."

"Would you like me to help you pack?"

She gave him a flustered, half-amused glance that made Jeffrey's toes curl inside his polished loafers. "Thanks, but I think I'll probably be ready more quickly without your help."

Jeffrey tugged at his collar and discovered he wasn't even wearing a tie. He cleared his throat but his voice still sounded hoarse. "I'll wait for you by the concierge's desk."

Grace pressed the tips of her fingers against his mouth. "Fifteen minutes," she murmured. "I'll join you in the lobby."

CHAPTER FIVE

JULIA ABANDONED HER VIGIL by the phone and ran to meet Michael the instant she heard his car turn into the driveway. "What's the news?" she called, scarcely waiting for him to step out of the car. "How's Lianne? Has the baby arrived?"

"No baby as yet," Michael said, walking with her into the house. "The doctor's giving it another three hours, then if things aren't progressing the way he wants, he may decide to do a C section."

"A cesarean?" Julia pulled a face. "Oh, no, what's the problem?"

"Nothing drastic, according to Gabe." Michael sat down on the sofa and stretched wearily. "Where are Tate and Edward?"

"Gone back to London." Julia glanced at the clock. "They should have arrived a few minutes ago if they didn't run into traffic. Tate says she'll phone you on Monday night. Now, tell me what's happening with Lianne and the baby."

"Gabe wasn't too coherent, but as far as I could understand, Lianne's early contractions were so powerful that the baby moved too rapidly down the birth canal, and so far, the cervix hasn't effaced sufficiently for the baby to be born. The doctor scheduled the C section just to be on the safe side, so that the baby won't have to spend another five or six hours banging the top of its skull against Lianne's cervix."

Julia curled up on the sofa next to Michael, tucking her feet under her. "My sister-in-law had a cesarean, too. If the baby's not in the right position or the labor's not progressing as it should, it seems to be the safest choice."

"That's pretty much what Lianne's doctor said," Michael agreed. "And Gabe seems confident the doctor's making the right decision."

"What sort of shape was Gabe in when you left the hospital? Do you think there's any chance he'll remember to phone us when the baby does finally arrive?"

"I wouldn't count on it," Michael said wryly. "When we spoke, he seemed to be having a hard time remembering his own name. But with luck, his brain will start operating on full power again once the baby's born and Lianne's recovering."

"I still can't believe how he went to pieces!" Julia shook her head. "Men are so useless where babies are concerned."

Michael looked amused. "Actually, I'd heard rumors that we're somewhat essential to the process of baby-making. Are you about to disillusion me?"

"Heavens, no. I wouldn't dream of arguing with an expert."

Michael tensed for a moment, then yawned and flexed his shoulders. "Very wise of you, my sweet."

She turned her head when she realized she was staring at the muscles rippling beneath his shirt. "I wish you wouldn't call me that."

"Call you what?" His voice was lazy; his eyes were anything but.

"My sweet."

"Why not? Aren't you sweet?"

There was a knot twisting tight in the pit of her stomach. "Not particularly. And I'm certainly not yours. You sound so blasted patronizing when you call me that, and I hate it."

He said nothing for a moment, his eyes on hers. "I'm sorry. I never intended to sound patronizing."

The knot twisted tighter. "Then how did you intend to sound?" she demanded. "Sarcastic? Condescending? If so, it worked."

"I've apologized already. What more do you expect me to say?" Michael got up and strode into the kitchen.

Julia marched after him. "I expect an explanation. As far as I can tell, you've been deliberately setting out to needle me ever since I've known you. What's your problem, Michael? What in the world have I ever done to offend you?"

"Not a damn thing." He slammed the fridge door shut and swung around to face her. "Or maybe this," he said, and pulled her into his arms.

The instant Michael's lips touched hers, Julia knew that, at some deeply buried level of her consciousness, she'd been waiting for him to kiss her since the night they first met. He kissed her hard and long, his mouth open, his tongue thrusting aggressively against hers, his hands hot and urgent on her body. She kissed him back with equal hunger, drawing his tongue deeper into her mouth, her skin jumping with little shocks of pleasure everywhere he touched her.

He held her tight. Her arms wrapped around him and clung. She registered a fleeting sense of astonishment that being held by Michael Forrest should seem so incredibly right, but even that hazy awareness soon vanished, burned away by the heat and passion of their kiss.

He unzipped her dress and tugged it from her shoulders. It didn't occur to her to protest. She moved restlessly against him, the blood roaring in her head so loud and fierce that it drowned out everything else, even her thoughts. She only knew that the longer they kissed, the more she wanted.

It was Michael who finally drew away, Michael who stepped back until a gap opened up between the two of them. He rubbed his hand briefly over his eyes, leaning against the door of the fridge, his chest rising and falling as if he'd just run a hard race.

Her body was throbbing with a need that reduced her normal inhibitions to rubble. She wasn't ready for their lovemaking to end, and for once, she was ready to take the initiative in carrying things further. She moved blindly toward him, but he grabbed her wrists and held her at arm's length, forcing her to keep her distance.

"Back off, Julia." His voice was rough. "You're tempting as hell, but I make it a rule never to go to bed with a woman who's in love with another man."

She flinched at his rejection. A dozen conflicting emotions rose inside her, but anger seemed the safest one to allow to the surface. He'd turned away, and she moved, positioning herself directly in his line of sight. "As far as I can recall, I didn't say anything about going to bed with you, Michael, not a single word."

"You didn't need to say the words. Your body was carrying on a very explicit conversation."

Julia shoved her arms into her dress and yanked it up onto her shoulders. Her pulse raced and her heart was pounding. Her breasts still tingled, and her nipples ached because Michael was no longer touching her. It was insane—absurd—that someone she didn't like could have this much of an effect on her. Edward had kissed her only a few hours ago, and she'd experienced nothing more than mild boredom. Michael kissed her and she erupted like Mount Vesuvius. Sometimes, Julia thought, life could be really infuriating.

She glared at Michael, because being cross with him was a lot more satisfying than being angry with herself. He returned her look with a cool, knowing stare, and her stomach gave a treacherous lurch of desire. Her stupid body apparently didn't have enough sense to accept that the man had just flat-out turned her down.

He finished buttoning his shirt, but didn't bother to tuck it back into his trousers. To Julia's supreme annoyance, his resulting appearance wasn't in the least disheveled. Instead, by some subtle alchemy, he managed to convey the impression that well-dressed men this season were wearing their hair rumpled and their shirts hanging over the belt of their trousers.

Meanwhile, she undoubtedly looked a wreck. No lipstick, hair tumbling every which-way, and her dress undone. Julia reached behind her back and yanked at the zip. It glided halfway up, then stuck. She muttered several creative curses about tight yellow dresses, bought for all the wrong reasons, then tugged again. To no avail. The wretched zip wouldn't budge.

Michael popped the top on a can of lager he'd taken from the fridge. "Would you like some help?" he asked.

His politeness scraped on her nerves like a drill on tooth enamel. With Michael, she always seemed to be waiting for the sharp edge of his mockery to poke through the velvet-smooth courtesy. "I can manage," she said curtly, her skin turning hot and then cold at the thought of him touching her again. Amazing how different this hot-and-cold sensation was from the feeling

Edward had aroused when he rescued her from zip failure earlier that afternoon.

The thought of Edward reminded her of Michael's strange comment when he ended their kiss. "Whatever gave you the idea that I'm in love with Edward Hillyard?" she demanded, still tugging at her dress. "Edward and I are barely acquaintances, let alone lovers."

"Edward?" Michael was silent for a second or two, then his gaze locked with hers. "I wasn't talking about Edward Hillyard," he said. "I was talking about Gabriel DeWilde."

Julia's hands froze, then fell to her sides. Gabe. She was so shocked to have forgotten about Gabe that she wasn't even humiliated by the realization that Michael knew of her abortive love affair. When Michael implied that she was in love with another man, why in the world hadn't she realized he was talking about Gabe, she wondered. Why hadn't Gabe's name even crossed her mind?

The answer struck her with the illuminating force of a hammer smashing through a barred and shuttered window. "I'm not in love with Gabe," she said.

She listened to herself speak the incredible words, then repeated them, just to be sure she registered their truth. "I'm not even a tiny bit in love with Gabe. He's an interesting, successful man who happens to be married to my best friend. You're mistaken if you believe anything else."

Michael finished his lager and crushed the can. He gave her a long, assessing look. "You were in love with Gabe."

It was surprisingly easy to admit the truth. "Once. A long time ago. Not anymore."

He tossed his empty can into the trash. "I'm glad you corrected my mistake," he said. He leaned back against the counter and smiled, his manner newly relaxed. "Now, are you sure you wouldn't like to reconsider my offer of help?"

His smile really did have the most extraordinary effect on her. Not least, it seemed, on her ability to understand simple sentences. She blinked. "Your offer of help? What for?"

"With your zipper." He wiggled his fingers. "If you're interested, I have ten certified zipper masters at your service."

"I'll just bet they're certified," Julia muttered, but she clearly wasn't going to get her dress fastened by herself, so she turned around, holding up her hair to prevent it getting caught.

He fastened her dress within a few seconds, his fingers coming into contact with her skin only once, when he had to glide the zip over the hook of her bra. Her body, demonstrating a total lack of good sense, responded with an instant flood of renewed desire. Remembering her indifference to Edward, Julia wondered if there'd ever been a scientific study done that explained how and why a woman could react so differently to the touch of two men, neither of whom she could even see. She supposed there must be some obscure hormonal reason for her response to Michael Forrest, because nothing else explained the effect he had on her.

She moved away the moment he was finished. "Thanks."

"You're welcome."

She wasn't nearly comfortable enough in his company to allow silence to fall between them, so she searched for something to say. Something bland and uncontroversial. Since they were standing in the kitchen, she came up with food. "You probably haven't eaten dinner, Michael, and you must be hungry. Could I make you a sandwich or something?"

"A sandwich would be great, but I can make my own. What about you? Have you eaten?"

"Oh, yes, before Tate and Edward went back to town. It turns out Edward wasn't exaggerating when he claimed gourmet cooking was a hobby of his. He rescued Lianne's ducklings from certain incineration, kept the wild rice warm while he tossed up a fabulous salad, and even helped clear away the dirty dishes when we'd finished eating. Thanks to Edward, we ate a truly scrumptious meal."

"He sounds like a regular paragon of virtue," Michael muttered, pulling a loaf of bread and a hunk of cheddar cheese from the fridge.

"A man without vices," Julia agreed.

Michael put two slices of bread onto a plate and cut a wedge of cheese. "Have you ever noticed how tedious perfect people are?"

She chuckled. "Yes, especially since I met Edward."

Michael looked at her, his expression arrested. "You don't laugh much," he said quietly. "You should do it more often."

"I'll make it a midyear resolution," she said tartly. "Laugh often, even when I'm not amused."

"Keep up with that tightly pursed mouth and haughty squint, honey, and in another few years, you're going to be able to do a damn fine imitation of Queen Victoria."

She should have been offended, but she found herself laughing, instead. Michael was right, she reflected. She did have a tendency to clamber onto her high horse for no particular reason. And he was also right that she should laugh more often. She'd wasted too much of the past year making a catastrophe out of a minor problem. If she hadn't been determined to cast herself in the role of tragic heroine, she'd have recovered from her infatuation with Gabriel DeWilde months and months ago. It was a disquieting realization. One of several tonight, all of which she owed to Michael.

She watched him put together his sandwich. "That looks awfully dry," she said. "Why don't you add some cucumber or something?"

"You want me to mix cheese and cucumber?" Michael wrinkled his nose. "Sounds like a mighty odd combination to me."

"British people eat it all the time."

Michael's silence was eloquent enough to make her smile again. "You're in no position to make rude comments about British cooking," she said.

He put on an injured expression. "I didn't say a word! Did I say a word? No."

She gave him a repressive look. "Your silence spoke volumes, and you, Michael Forrest, come from a country where people pour syrup on pancakes and then put bacon and sausages on the *same* plate as the syrup. Not to mention serving fried chicken with honey. Honey and fried chicken! Don't you dare talk to me about gross combinations."

Michael grinned. "A golden brown chicken drumstick, fried in cornmeal and served with honey and biscuits, doesn't appeal to you, huh?"

Julia shuddered.

"Why don't we do a deal?" Michael suggested. "I'll put cucumber on my cheese sandwich, if you'll have breakfast with me one day and eat pancakes served with real maple syrup and bacon."

"It's a deal," she said, taking the cucumber out of the fridge and searching for a sharp knife to slice it.

He eyed her with justifiable suspicion. "You agreed to that much too easily."

"Not at all. I have no plans to weasel out of the deal." She gave a sly smile. "Although by great good fortune, I don't think there's anywhere in London that actually serves American breakfasts."

"How little you know your own hometown," he murmured.

"I'll take my chances." She quartered his cheese sandwich, now brimming with cucumber, and handed it to him with a smile. "Here you are, Michael. Eat up and admit you were wrong."

He took a small, dubious bite, chewed for a moment, then looked at her with wide-eyed astonishment. "It's not bad!" he exclaimed. He took another bite. "I must be hungrier than I thought. This actually tastes pretty damn good. The cucumber adds crunch."

Julia smiled graciously. She could afford to be generous since she knew Michael wouldn't bother to invite her to breakfast. That thought didn't make her quite as happy as it should have, and she sat down opposite him at the kitchen table, feeling a renewed attack of restlessness.

"Gabe should have called by now," she said. "It's past midnight."

"It seems a long time to us because we're just hanging around, but it's less than six hours since Lianne went into labor. That's nothing, especially for a first baby."

She drummed her fingers on the tabletop. "Yes, I know. The waiting's difficult, though."

He covered her hand with his. "Do you want to go to bed? I can wake you as soon as I hear something."

"Thanks, but I'm too keyed-up to sleep. This is my godchild that's about to make his or her debut in the world."

Michael finished his last bite of sandwich. "Mine, too." His gaze met hers across the table, eyes gleaming. "Does that make us related, do you think?"

"In medieval times, the church used to claim that it did." She made an apologetic gesture. "I'm sorry, ignore that. It's my teacher-reflex kicking in. I have this annoying habit of taking other people's throwaway remarks and responding with a minilecture."

"A sentence is hardly a minilecture," Michael said. "Besides, who told you it's an annoying habit?"

"My brothers," she said ruefully. "They're both engineers, and they tend to explain things much better with charts and diagrams than they do with words. They really dislike it when they make some casual comment or other, and I respond by branching off into a long and usually irrelevant byway that I find fascinating and they find boring in the extreme."

"I'd say that's their problem, not yours." Michael stood up and carried his plate over to the sink. "For two people who are about to become relatives, at least according to ancient church doctrine, we don't know much about each other, do we? Why don't we choose some comfortable chairs in the living room and tell each other our life histories while we're waiting to hear from the hospital?"

Having heard Michael tell plenty of amusing stories about himself, Julia was more than willing to have him entertain her until Gabe phoned. "You go first," she said, following him out of the kitchen.

Michael shook his head. "I'm a traditionalist at heart. Ladies should always go first in this sort of situation." He sat down in a Queen Anne-style wing chair that was conveniently close to the phone.

"Well, all right," Julia said, taking a seat on the sofa. "But this isn't going to take me long. Let's see. I was born in London and I've more or less lived there all my life. I'm thirty, and planning to stay that age for the next three or four birthdays. I have two older brothers, who are both married, and two nieces, who are seriously adorable. I teach French at a private girls' school in Kensington. Now it's your turn."

"In a minute. I think your biography could be expanded a bit. How old are your nieces? Do you spend a lot of time with your family?"

"My nieces are three and five, and we see quite a lot of one another since we all live in the London area."

"Your brothers are both older than you?"

She nodded. "They're thirty-six and thirty-seven. I was the proverbial unexpected afterthought, although my mother swears that she was thrilled to have a daughter after being surrounded by men for the first ten years of her marriage. Nowadays, it's my father who says he's surrounded, what with two granddaughters and two daughters-in-law."

"Do you like your sisters-in-law?" he asked, stretching out his legs in front of him.

Julia plumped up an oversized down cushion and tucked it behind her. "They're very good women, both of them."

"Ah." Michael smiled. "You can't stand 'em."

"I didn't say that," she protested.

"Yes, you did," he said cheerfully. "I know the feeling. I have a brother-in-law who drives me nuts. He's a surgeon, saves lives on a daily basis, but I think he had his sense of humor clinically excised when he was in medical school."

"One of my sisters-in-law has plastic flowers planted in her front garden because real ones are too messy," Julia said. She caught Michael's eye and they both burst out laughing.

"We won't waste any more time discussing our boring in-laws," he said. "Tell me why you became a teacher. Was it something you always wanted to do?"

"In a way. When I was growing up, I was quite sure I wanted to be a teacher. I was accepted at King's to read French—"

"Whoa! Translation time," Michael said. "What does that mean exactly?"

"King's is one of the colleges that make up London University," Julia explained. "And for my degree, I read French—"

He looked puzzled. "Didn't you have to write it and speak it as well, to get a degree?"

She laughed. "Reading French means that the main subject I studied at university was French. It doesn't mean that all I had to do was read French to get a degree."

Michael's frown cleared. "I never heard that expression before. Okay, I understand now. In the States we'd say that when you were in college, you majored in French. Go on."

"I graduated when I was twenty. Then I took a year off, working at odd jobs all over France. I had a great time, especially when I got to the south. We Brits always go a bit crazy when we're exposed to bright sun." Julia smiled at a sudden rush of memories. "I fell madly in love with a handsome Frenchman called Jean-Paul Rossier and almost married him."

"What stopped you?"

"My guardian angel," she said. "Either that, or I got tired of competing with his mother for his attention."

He laughed. "Sounds as if you had a lucky escape."

"Definitely. Anyway, having run away from Jean-Paul and Madame Rossier in the nick of time, I came home to England and took a teacher's training course for a year. When I had my diploma, I applied to teach French at the middle-school level."

"At the school in Kensington where you are now?"

"No, at that point in my life I was full of high ideals about shaping young minds and transforming the world through the miracles of education. I took a job at a state school in one of London's poorest districts." Julia paused for a moment, remembering. "That was a pretty devastating experience. For the first two years I assumed I was a total failure as a teacher. By the end of the third year, I realized I wasn't all that terrible, I just wasn't good enough to compensate for parents who didn't care, and a school system that had provided my students with years of rotten education long before they reached my classroom."

"Did you quit?"

"Not for another year. But it was hard to make my French lessons anything but drudgery when half the students in my class couldn't distinguish between a noun and a verb in English, let alone in a foreign language."

"You can't blame yourself for the failure of an entire system," Michael said.

"Perhaps not. But you know, there were a couple of teachers at that school who managed to inspire their students class after class, week after week, year after year. One of them taught remedial reading, and the other taught history. I saw the miracles that a truly dedicated and talented teacher could work, even with children everyone else had rejected as hopeless. Watching those two old-timers, I realized that I was never going to measure up. With time and patience I could learn to be a competent teacher, but I didn't have the fire inside me that was going to transform me into an inspirational teacher. By the very best standards, I wasn't going to make the grade."

She paused again, wondering why she was telling Michael something about herself that she hadn't confided to anyone else, not even to Lianne. "It was a difficult thing to accept about myself—that I was a second-rater in my chosen career."

Michael didn't insult her with a facile reassurance that she was probably a better teacher than she realized. He steepled his fingers and looked at her over the top. "I guess the obvious question is why are you still teaching? It's not only your students who deserve something better, Julia. You deserve it, too. You have way too much intelligence and guts to waste your time doing something that doesn't command a hundred percent of your energy."

She grimaced. "Have you any idea what the jobless rate is in this country? I may not be a superb teacher, but I'm a good one, and I like the people I work with at Kensington Academy—"

"Those are all excuses for not making a change," Michael said. "They're not reasons."

"They're pretty good excuses," Julia said hotly. "I have to support myself, you know. My father was forced to take early retirement, so he and my mother have just enough income to scrape by. My brothers have young families to think about, and more children on the way. I have a huge mortgage on my flat, and the building society isn't going to be in the least bit interested if I tell them that I can't afford to make any more payments because I'm taking a few months off to beat bongo drums and try to find myself."

"I think it's men who are supposed to beat bongo drums," Michael said. "But I get your point. You can come out of your attack dog mode."

Julia grimaced. "I wouldn't have reacted so strongly, but the truth is, you touched one of my hot buttons." She drew in a deep breath. "I very badly want to make changes in my life, but it's a scary prospect."

"Change usually is."

"Mmm, especially for me." She leaned forward, hands clasped around her knees. "I was brought up to believe that taking risks was irresponsible, that sensible people found a solid career and plugged away at it, nine to five, week after week. But I watched Lianne when she came over here from the States, with nothing much behind her except talent and determination. The truth is that I not only admired her courage, I envied her willingness to stake everything on the slim chance of making a success as a designer. If I'd been in her shoes, I'd have weighed the odds, made a careful analysis of the marketplace and come to the logical conclusion that I had no chance at all of succeeding. Lianne simply had faith in herself and her talent. She knew she was an innovative and creative designer, so she hung on, through one setback after another, until she won the chance to show people how good she was. And look at how brilliantly she's succeeded."

"Lianne also had some help from her friends," Michael said. "She's told me that there were plenty of days when she wouldn't have been able to eat if you hadn't been subsidizing her talent with your hard-earned cash."

Julia flushed. "Lianne paid me back twice over the second she started work at DeWilde's."

"I wasn't criticizing Lianne's faith in herself, or the fact that she relied on you when times were tough. I'm pointing out that even talented people need a helping hand on occasion."

"That's true." Julia smiled. "Well, if I ever discover that I have a secret talent, I'll start looking round for some helping hands. And now you've pried all those confidences out of me, it's your turn."

"You already know everything there is to know about me," Michael said lightly. "You're the person who keeps reminding me that the tabloids carry a running account of my life."

As so often happened, she felt that something in his body language didn't quite fit with the casualness of his voice. Julia examined him thoughtfully, weighing the implausible idea that Michael might actually have been hurt by some of her sarcastic comments about his lifestyle. "There must be a few private moments for you to fill between flirting with cheerleaders and drinking champagne with movie stars," she said, matching his light tone, leaving him free to decide whether he wanted to talk honestly or hold her at arm's length, as she suspected he did with most people who tried to get close. "What do you do when the paparazzi aren't on your heels? Do you go fishing? Deep-sea diving? Listen to jazz? Read Plato? Shakespeare?"

He raised an eyebrow. "Read Plato and Shakespeare? You're joking, right?"

"No," she said quietly. "I'm not joking. Far from it."

"I work," he said abruptly. "Eleven or twelve hours a day, six days a week. Two or three nights a week, I have some function to attend that's geared strictly toward generating maximum publicity for the hotels. Those are the events that usually make a splash in the gossip columns. Sundays, I take off."

"And what do you do on Sundays?"

He looked away. "I spend a lot of Sunday sleeping. Sometimes I try to spend a few hours with a friend, a real friend, not someone who has gossip value for the hotel's PR flacks."

"And..." she prompted.

"I also play the piano," he said, as if he were admitting to a guilty secret. "Chiefly Bach and Mozart. I'm very bad, but nobody has to listen except me."

It occurred to Julia that for a man constantly surrounded by other rich men and beautiful women, Michael Forrest led a lonely life. "Why do you work so hard?" she asked.

He shrugged. "For the past year, mainly out of habit. Until then, I worked my tail off because the prestigious and famously gracious Carlisle Forrest hotel chain was about to slide into extremely ungracious bankruptcy."

She was startled. "I thought the Carlisle Forrest hotels in the States were like the Ritz in Paris, or Claridges in London—part of a tradition that had never lost its luster."

"I can't speak for the Ritz or for Claridges, but as far as our hotels are concerned, when I took control of the company, we were doing a fabulous job of providing all the comforts and services that you might have expected from a superb hotel prior to World War II. We polished shoes and had a maid on each floor ready to serve tea at four in the afternoon, because those were services my great-grandfather had instituted when he built our original hotel in Chicago. If you can believe it, we didn't have a computerized billing system, and most of our hotels only had one fax machine to serve the combined needs of the guests and the hotel staff. We were catering for a clientele that simply didn't exist anymore, and if we hadn't done something to spruce up our image and attract convention business, the entire chain would have gone under. We'd been operating at a loss for more than five years."

"You had to fight the existing management to get the changes you wanted implemented," Julia guessed.

"Yes." Michael got up from the wing chair and started pacing. "Unfortunately, existing management happened to be my father."

"I'm sorry," she said with real sympathy. "Was it very bad?"

"The pits." He shoved his hands into his pockets. "My father had a heart attack the week after I took over his job. He died a year later, and my mother hasn't spoken to me since."

"I'll bet she cashes her dividend check," Julia said tartly.

"You'd win your bet," Michael said. His smile didn't quite reach his eyes. "She's the only person I know who disapproves of my life-style more than you do."

"Until tonight, I had no idea what your life-style was."

"You knew about my relationship with Cherie Lockwood. And about Storm."

"Yes."

"You don't approve."

Julia chose her words carefully. "When you're a teacher, you see a lot of children whose parents neglect them. I don't care what sort of a relationship two consenting adults choose for themselves, but I don't think men or women should have children unless they're willing to be real parents."

Michael hesitated for a moment. "Cherie doesn't want me to spend time with Storm," he said finally. "I would see more of him if Brad Stein didn't strongly object."

She believed him, Julia realized. Astonishingly, she even found herself feeling sympathy for his plight. Her voice softened. "I'm not a complete idiot, Michael. I realized long before tonight that what the gossip magazines write about you probably bears only a glancing relationship to the truth. I'm sorry that my teaching experiences distorted my judgment when it came to your relationship with Storm and Cherie. I should have known there was more to it than the line being pursued by the tabloids. Lord knows, I shouldn't have been so credulous. These are the same journalists who keep reporting that the Loch Ness monster is eating the local milkmen."

"Is she?" Michael asked innocently.

Julia smiled. "With all that good salmon in the loch? I'm sure poor old Nessie's got better taste."

Michael came and stood in front of her. "Thank you for the vote of confidence." He grasped her hands and tugged her gently to her feet. He framed her face with his hands and looked down at her with a rueful gleam in his eyes that she couldn't quite interpret. "You're the most incredibly beautiful woman, Julia. You know that, don't you?"

No, of course she didn't know anything so ridiculous, but Michael sounded almost convincing enough to persuade her. "You make me believe it," she said huskily.

"Believe it all the time, because it's true." He ran his hands through her hair, and she closed her eyes, letting the magic of his touch shimmer through her veins. She wished this night would go on forever. She wished they could meet again, talk again, discover more about themselves and each other. She wished they could make love. Here. Now.

Her eyes flew open. Michael had stopped touching her, but he stood very close, his green eyes dark, almost brooding. She reached up and stroked his cheek before she had time to consider what that oddly tender gesture might signify. "I've enjoyed the time we spent together tonight," she said softly. "Thank you, Michael."

"I'm the one who should thank you. It was definitely my pleasure." He glanced away, then abruptly turned back and looked down at her. "You know, it's damned inconvenient, but I really want like hell to take you to bed."

His words were casual, but the heat in his voice made her cheeks burn. She swallowed, moistening her dry throat. "What's stopping you?"

"The remnants of my conscience." He traced the outline of her mouth with his thumb. "The certainty that we'd end up making each other very miserable."

The fact that she knew he was right didn't lessen the fierce regret that seized her. She realized suddenly that this overwhelming sensation of sharp, sexual hunger was what had been missing from her relationship with Gabriel DeWilde. Belatedly, she gave thanks that Gabe had had the sense to realize the lack before it was too late, even if she hadn't.

Julia tilted her head back so that she looked straight into Michael's eyes. What she saw there made her wonder if the pleasures of making love to him tonight might not outweigh the misery of the inevitable parting in the morning.

He leaned toward her. "Julia..." He murmured her name against her mouth. "God, don't look at me like that."

"All right," she whispered. She closed her eyes, but he kissed her, anyway. He kissed her with a passion that left her shaking, then held her tightly in his arms to still her trembling. No wonder she'd always been so tense and prickly around him, Julia thought. Her subconscious had been smart enough to sense the danger, even if the rest of her had been pathetically slow on the uptake.

Their kiss went on, and this time Michael didn't draw away. The longer they kissed, the faster Julia's inhibitions scattered, and the less she cared about the inevitable reckoning in the morning. Her head pounded with the roar of her blood, and it was a while before she realized that what she heard was a real noise, coming from outside the house.

"Michael..." She dragged herself back to awareness of their surroundings. "Michael, there's a car in the driveway. Someone's here."

He rested his forehead against hers. "Can't we tell them to go away again?"

"I don't think so. They must have seen all the lights are on."

"If it's your friend Edward, I'm not likely to be polite." Michael sighed. "Turn around. I'd better do up that damn zipper of yours again before we have to answer the doorbell."

But the doorbell didn't ring. Instead, an attractively husky female voice called out from the entrance hall. "Hello! Is anyone there? This is Grace DeWilde."

Julia shot an appalled glance at Michael. There was only one reason she could think of for Gabe's mother to make such a noisy announcement. "She must have come in already and seen us," she hissed.

He gave a wry smile. "Yes, I guess she did." He raised his voice. "Grace, come on in. We're in the living room."

Since the floor failed to open and swallow her, Julia made a dash for a dark corner, but Michael clamped his arm around her waist and refused to let her go. "Julia, honey, I think Grace and Jeffrey have probably seen two people kissing before."

"There's kissing and then there's kissing," Julia muttered.

He grinned. "Yeah, and I guess we were definitely doing the latter."

Grace came into the room before Julia could say anything more. She'd changed her hairstyle since the last time Julia had seen her, and the shorter cut made her face look softer and younger. Or perhaps it was just her glowing happiness that made her look so youthful. Jeffrey DeWilde followed behind his ex-wife, his face wreathed in a smile as broad as hers.

Grace gave the pair of them a faintly amused glance, then she crossed the room and swept Michael into a warm embrace. "Michael, how nice to see you on this side of the Atlantic. And Julia, my dear, thank you. I understand from Jeffrey that you're the person who told him to track me down so that I could come and visit my new grandbaby."

"Yes, that was me. How are you, Mrs. DeWilde?"

"We're both wonderful." Jeffrey took his wife's hand and tucked it around his arm. "We've just come from the hospital," he announced proudly. "Lianne gave birth to a baby girl just after midnight. Grace and I are grandparents."

"Congratulations!" Michael and Julia spoke in unison.

"I'll get some champagne," Michael said. "This deserves a toast."

"Lianne must be thrilled," Julia said. "I know she and Gabe were both hoping for a daughter. Have they decided on a name for her yet?"

"Elizabeth Gabrielle," Jeffrey said. "It seems a good mix of plain and fancy, don't you think?"

"It's a lovely combination," Julia said. "Have you seen the baby yet?"

"Of course. But only a quick glimpse before the nurses shooed us out and told us to come back tomorrow," Grace told her. "She's six pounds, two ounces, and utterly beautiful."

"She's bald as a coot," Jeffrey said. "However, based on past experience with our three, I'm optimistic that the condition isn't permanent."

"Her skin is very fair, not red at all," Grace said. "I think she's going to look a lot like Gabe."

Jeffrey chuckled. "Trust me, that's a likeness only a new grandmother could spot. Personally, I think she bears a startling resemblance to Winston Churchill."

Michael came back carrying a tray with four brimming glasses of champagne. "How's Lianne doing?" he asked, handing the glasses around. "Is she exhausted? More to the point, maybe, how's Gabe holding up?"

"We left him incoherent but edging toward sanity," Jeffrey said dryly.

"Lianne's sleeping," Grace said. "She had a C section in the end, and she was pretty groggy when we saw her, but there were no complications and the doctor expects her to be out of the hospital in five or six days." Her face lit up. "Isn't it wonderful to think we have a new person to welcome home within the week? This is so exciting."

"It certainly is." Jeffrey raised his glass. "Here's to Elizabeth Gabrielle," he said. "The first of the new generation of DeWildes."

"May her life be long and full of love." Grace touched her glass to Jeffrey's, then looked quickly away.

"And here's to Lianne and Gabe," Michael added. "The proud parents."

Julia smiled and lifted her glass. "Not forgetting the new grandparents."

"I'll drink to all of the above," Grace said happily.

The four of them drank their champagne, and Grace sighed contentedly as she put down her glass. "This has been such a good night," she said. "But I suppose we should get to bed if we're going to drive back to the hospital tomorrow morning."

"Why don't you two take Gabe and Lianne's bedroom?" Michael suggested. "That room has its own bathroom and it's at the back of the house, where it's quieter. You'll rest better if your room faces away from the road. Not that this lane gets much traffic."

Jeffrey and Grace looked at each other, then both seemed suddenly fascinated by their shoes. Grace was blushing, and Jeffrey appeared as thoroughly embarrassed as a sophisticated, mature man can manage to appear.

Julia was horrified by Michael's gaffe. How could he have forgotten that Grace and Jeffrey were divorced? "Of course you don't have to share—"

Michael stepped firmly on her toes. "Why don't you two go on up?" he said, as if Julia hadn't spoken. "We'll take care of locking up and turning off all the lights down here."

"That's very good of you," Grace said faintly.

"Well, good night, then." Jeffrey cleared his throat. "I'll get your overnight bag from the hall, Grace."

"Thank you." Without looking at either Michael or Julia, Grace made her way to the staircase. She walked upstairs, gaze fixed rigidly ahead. Jeffrey followed, a bag in each hand. The sound of footsteps along the upper hallway was followed by that of a door closing.

Julia stared wide-eyed at Michael. "They were divorced three months ago!" she exclaimed. "Michael, what in the world is going on here?"

He gave a small smile. "A reconciliation?"

"But according to Lianne and Gabe they've spent the past year making each other's lives totally miserable!"

Michael's smile became rueful. "True love," he said wryly. "Ain't it grand?"

CHAPTER SIX

Jeffrey supposed that he had endured more embarrassing situations in his life than walking upstairs to bed with his ex-wife under the fascinated scrutiny of a man and a woman young enough to be his children. Right at the moment, however, he couldn't recall one. Intellectually, he realized there was something comic about feeling so wicked at the prospect of sharing a bedroom with Grace. Emotionally, he was incapable of appreciating the manifold ironies of the situation. The truth was, at this moment he could think of nothing beyond the fact that Grace had publicly agreed to spend the night sleeping in his bed. That simple fact left him torn between lust and panic. He'd blown every previous chance for reconciliation by his own stupid behavior. What if he blew it again? God knew, he had no clever or sophisticated plan for wooing her back. Telling her how much he loved her and begging for her forgiveness was the best he could come up with, and he had a dreadful fear it wouldn't be enough.

He cleared his throat. Damn! Grace was going to think he'd developed defective vocal chords if he did that one more time. "Gabe and Lianne have done a splendid job with the remodeling of this cottage, haven't they? This room looks very comfortable." Trying not to stare with too much interest at the rather small four-poster bed, he put their overnight bags on the window seat and looked around for a suitable place to hang his clothes.

Yawning, Grace kicked off her shoes and dropped her linen jacket onto a chair. She turned around and gave him a glance that appeared equal parts affection and amusement. Not quite what he yearned to see, but a lot better than the hurt and angry glares of their recent past. "Briarwood Cottage is lovely, Jeffrey. In some ways it reminds me of Kemberly, although a much smaller version, of course." She opened her overnight bag. "The bed isn't very big, is it? Still, it looks comfortable."

"Very comfortable," Jeffrey said stiffly. He hadn't realized men of his age could blush at the mere mention of the word *bed*. In the nick of time, he remembered not to clear his throat. "Would you like to use the bathroom first, or shall I?"

Grace gave another yawn. "You go first. I'll finish unpacking while you're in the bathroom."

She sounded so matter of fact. The appalling thought struck Jeffrey that perhaps she intended to spend the entire night sleeping.

She couldn't possibly be planning to lie next to him for seven hours and just sleep. Or could she? Was that why she was yawning? To warn him she was tired?

Grace shook out the folds of a silk robe before dropping it onto the bed. "Would you like me to unpack for you, too, Jeffrey?"

He winced. Thirty-plus years of marriage suggested he should decline, but Jeffrey decided to be brave. How much damage could she do to a pair of slacks and a blazer? "Thank you, if it's not too much trouble. Perhaps you could find a spare coat hanger or two in the wardrobe. I'll take my shaving kit and dressing gown into the bathroom and leave everything else to you."

They might have been two polite strangers, he thought gloomily as he brushed his teeth. He combed his hair, relieved that although it was rapidly turning gray at the sides, at least he hadn't gone bald since Grace left him. He splashed on after-shave and peered in the mirror, hoping Grace would think his new gray hairs looked distinguished. Thank goodness his three-times-weekly squash games kept him fighting fit and he still had a few muscles to be proud of.

When he realized that he was actually standing in front of the bathroom mirror flexing his biceps, Jeffrey recovered his sense of humor. He reached for his dressing gown, smiling ruefully. Love, it seemed, could always find new ways to make sensible men behave like fools.

He walked back into the bedroom and paused in midstride, his breath catching in his throat when he saw Grace. In his absence, she had kicked off her shoes and climbed onto the bed, where she sat cross-legged in the middle of a heap of pillows, reading a magazine. She glanced up at the sound of the bathroom door opening and smiled at Jeffrey as she took off her glasses and put them on the bedside table.

For a few seconds, he would have sworn his heart literally stopped beating. He wondered what Grace would say if he told her that of all the things in their marriage that he missed, the familiar sight of her perched in the middle of his rumpled bed, reading, was the one he missed most.

Her smile was replaced by a look of concern. "Jeffrey? Is something wrong?"

"Nothing," he said hoarsely. "The bathroom's all yours."

"Thank you. I'll shower later, I think."

Later? But it was already past one o'clock in the morning. Jeffrey wondered what the hell he was supposed to do next. Climb into bed still wearing his robe? Discard it casually somewhere in the ten feet separating him from the bed? The etiquette of sharing sleeping quarters with an ex-wife entirely defeated him.

Grace twisted around so that they were facing each other. "Actually, Jeffrey, I was sitting here wondering if you'd remembered about the bet we made earlier this evening."

He'd been thinking of little else ever since they left the hospital. "I remember. I believe you said our new grandchild would be a girl. I predicted the baby would be a boy."

"Which means I won the bet." Grace looked contemplative. "As I recall, that means you owe me two hours of...service. That is what we agreed, isn't it?"

The way she said "service" was so heavy with innuendo that Jeffrey managed, just barely, to refrain from choking. "Er...yes, I believe two hours is what we wagered."

Before the divorce, their finances had been so intermingled that betting for money had seemed pointless. Over the years, they'd developed a system where they staked time instead of cash, with the loser having to do whatever the winner specified for the stipulated number of hours. Sometimes that had meant Grace agreeing to watch one of Jeffrey's beat-'em-up movies, or Grace dragging Jeffrey to one of the avant-garde art shows she loved and he hated. Once Jeffrey had been condemned to prune the roses at Kemberly, and in retribution the next time he won a bet, he'd forced Grace to balance their quarterly household accounts. Quite often, though, the bet had turned into a sexual game, with the loser required to make love in whatever way the winner commanded. On those occasions, by the time the bet had been paid, it was difficult to remember who had been the winner and who the supposed loser. Jeffrey hardly dared to hope that Grace was going to claim payment of their recent bet by demanding sexual favors from him. That seemed like rewarding him for losing with every fantasy of the past year rolled into one giant gift package.

Grace examined him thoughtfully. "Since we're here together, this seems like a good time to claim my payment."

"Er...yes. I suppose now is as good as any other time."

She smiled, a slow, sexy smile that had his stomach doing handsprings. "It's one-thirty," she said. "You realize that under the terms of the bet, you have to do exactly what I say until three-thirty?"

He shoved his hands into the pockets of his dressing gown to prevent himself running to the bed and grabbing her. "Yes. Until three-thirty." He rocked back on his heels, pretending reluctance. "Not a minute longer, mind."

"Of course not." She slid off the bed. "Come here, Jeffrey."

Somehow, he managed to control his eagerness and walk toward her without stumbling over his own feet. "Gracie," he murmured, reaching out his arms. "Gracie, I've missed you so much."

She quickly stepped backward, eluding him. "The first rule is that you're not allowed to talk."

He drew in an uneven breath. "All right."

She shot him a disapproving look. "No talking means no talking, Jeffrey."

He nodded.

She smiled. "And the second rule is that you're allowed to move only if I give you permission."

He stared straight ahead.

"Very good," she murmured. "Make sure you remember those two simple rules."

Jeffrey wanted to ask what would happen if he broke the rules, but Grace reached up and drew her hand across his cheek in a slow, intimate caress, so he decided to postpone his question. When she reached his mouth, she hesitated, then stroked across his lips, parting them so that she could slip her finger into his mouth. By the exercise of supreme self-control, Jeffrey obeyed orders and refrained from responding with his tongue to the erotic thrusting of her forefinger.

When he was almost at the point of moaning in frustration, Grace changed her form of torment, trailing her hands down his chest until she reached the belt of his dressing gown. "Is there anything you'd like me to do right now, Jeffrey?" she murmured.

He closed his eyes and clenched his fists.

She frowned. "Hmm. I'll consider that an attempt on your part to obey my rules." She didn't untie the belt of his robe, but she did at least part the lapels and rest her head against his chest. Before he even realized what he was doing, he'd fastened his arms around her, one hand on her hips, the other tangled in her hair.

For about twenty tantalizing seconds she allowed herself to be crushed against him. Then she twisted out of his embrace. "Four minutes," she said in mock reproach. "Goodness, Jeffrey, you're even worse at honoring your bets than you used to be."

He bit back his protest that he was a man, not a block of stone, and that he wanted her so desperately tonight that he was amazed he'd lasted four minutes without tumbling her onto the bed. She smiled, as if she knew how badly he wanted to speak, and dropped a quick kiss in the center of his chest before moving away and positioning herself on the other side of the room.

Pretending not to have noticed that he was staring at her with almost hypnotic fascination, Grace began to unfasten the leather belt at her waist. She slid the belt from the loops of her slacks with a seductive skill that would have done a professional stripper proud, playing with it for a couple of seconds before tossing it in the direction of the old-fashioned wardrobe. Sweat broke out on Jeffrey's forehead. If this was her way of punishing him for breaking the rules, he wasn't sure that it was succeeding. She was tormenting him, all right, but some torments were fiendishly enjoyable.

Her gaze locked with his, and her eyes gleamed with the satisfied knowledge of precisely what she was doing to him. She unfastened the button at the waistband of her slacks, lowered the zipper and shimmied out of them with a sinuous sway of her hips.

Jeffrey drew in a gasping breath and realized two things simultaneously. First, that he didn't have a hope in hell of surviving two more minutes of this crazy bet, let alone two more hours. And second, that for a woman who'd recently divorced him, Grace seemed delightfully willing to seduce him.

To hell with caution and restraint, he decided. This was the woman he loved, and he was starving for her. In a few quick strides, he covered the distance between them, sweeping Grace into his arms, tilting her head back and kissing her with blind, hungry passion. Oh, God, she felt so wonderful in his arms after months of harrowing abstinence.

She returned his kiss with all the fire he'd dreamed of, rubbing against him, her body lithe and still marvelously supple. Her arms came around him, stroking his shoulders, linking her hands with his, urging him backward onto the bed.

Jeffrey couldn't have been more willing to follow her lead. He tumbled onto the mattress, pulling Grace on top of him. He started to roll over, to reverse their positions so that he would be on top, when he realized that he couldn't move his right arm. Grace scrambled off him, and he sat up, staring in disbelief at his wrist.

"You've handcuffed me to the bedpost!" he said, gazing incredulously at the velvet-lined, stainless steel manacle that he'd seen once before, when Grace delivered the DeWilde jewels to his office.

She grinned mischievously. "Honestly, Jeffrey, you promised not to speak for two hours, and now you're not only speaking, you're shouting."

"I didn't expect to be chained to the bedpost!" he yelled.

"It's punishment for breaking the terms of our bet. You know I always take our bets very seriously."

"For God's sake, Gracie, how could you expect me to stand there like a statue? You were deliberately driving me crazy!"

Grace appeared unrepentant. "I hope this bedroom has thick walls," she said. "Otherwise Michael and Julia are going to think we have a very kinky relationship."

"They'd be dead right! We do have a kinky relationship, or at least a totally ridiculous one!" Jeffrey drew in a deep breath, wriggling his wrist to no avail. "Come on, Grace, be reasonable. Undo the handcuff."

She eyed him coolly. "No."

He lunged for her ankle, but she moved, swift as quicksilver, tucking her feet under her.

"This is insane," he said, struggling to control his frustration. "Grace, if you don't want me to make love to you, you don't have to lock me up. You just have to tell me. I'll be disappointed, of course, but I'm not about to force you against your will. For God's sake, what do you think I've turned into? Some kind of monster?"

"I don't think you've turned into anything, Jeffrey. I think you're just what you've always been, a proud and stubborn man."

"I'm not in the least stubborn, and pride isn't necessarily a flaw!" Jeffrey said hotly. He moved instinctively toward her, but was brought up short by the handcuff. "All right, Grace, I'll beg if you want me to. Please, let me out of this damned thing."

"If I do, are you going to try to make love to me?"

It took him a while, but finally he managed to say it. "No, I already told you that. Not if you don't want me to."

"I don't know if I want you to. It depends." She dangled the silver key chain from her index finger, waving it gently back and forth.

"On what?"

"On you, as it happens. Have you any idea how much heartache you've put me through over the past nineteen months, Jeffrey? Do you even begin to fathom how badly you hurt me?"

He didn't have to stop and think about his answer,

even for a moment. "Yes," he said, his voice hoarse with regret. "I know how much I hurt you, Gracie, because I hurt myself every bit as much. If there were some way to unravel time and go back to before this whole mess started, I'd do everything differently, I swear. But there isn't a way, and all I can do now is tell you how sorry I am and ask you to forgive me for destroying our marriage."

She continued to wave the key. "I left you. I was the one who flew off to San Francisco."

"To outsiders it may have seemed that way. We both know the truth. You didn't leave me, Grace, I drove you away."

"Nineteen months ago—six months ago—I'd have given my right arm to hear you admit that. But now apologies for the past aren't enough, Jeffrey."

He felt sick, and the pain was even worse because he knew he had no right to expect a different answer. "Enough for what?" he asked harshly.

"For us to build a future on." Her voice shook slightly, and Jeffrey realized her composure was nowhere near as complete as it seemed. "I guess this is the big moment, the point where we both have to make a decision about our respective futures. Tonight is the last time I'm ever going to ask you this question, Jeffrey. Are we going to spend the rest of our lives together or apart?"

"I want us to be together," Jeffrey said, clinging to the frail hope that she would show him a way to redeem himself, a way out of the quagmire he'd created. "God, Gracie, you can't even begin to imagine how much I want that."

"You want us to be married again. Is that what you're saying?"

Married again to Gracie. Jeffrey shut his eyes. He wanted that with such fierce intensity that he could barely respond. "Yes."

"Why?" she asked. "You have to tell me why you want us to be married, Jeffrey. I need you to give me the words."

Grace knew him too well, he thought. She knew how hard it had always been for him to express his feelings, to lay his vulnerability on the line, to run the risk of being rejected by the person he cared about most in the entire world. She knew how much easier it would be for him to make passionate love to her, then glide back into their relationship without ever verbalizing how much he loved and needed her, how much he regretted his past failures. But she didn't recognize yet how much he'd changed during the months of their separation. Losing Grace, suffering through their divorce, had taught him many things. Not least the lesson that love, freely given, was never wasted, and that whether Grace accepted or rejected his feelings for her, he would be richer for having expressed them.

He looked at her, the words flowing easily from his tongue, because they came straight from his heart. "I want us to be together again because I love you," he said. "You're my delight, my joy, my friend, and the best part of everything that I am. I don't deserve your forgiveness, but if you'll agree to marry me again, Gracie, I shall be the happiest man on God's earth."

To his absolute horror, Grace began to cry.

"Gracie! Don't! Please, don't cry! I didn't mean to upset you. If you don't want to marry me, you don't have to." He scrambled onto his knees and discovered that by stretching out his left hand, he could just manage to touch her cheeks. He tried to stem the flow of tears.

"Gracie, please don't be sad. I can't bear it if I've hurt you again."

She took his hand and held it against his cheek. "You haven't hurt me." She sniffed. "Goodness, Jeffrey, have you forgotten so much about me already? I always cry when I'm happy."

She was happy! Relief left him limp. "You cry when you're sad, too. How is a mere man supposed to tell the difference?"

She reached for a tissue from the box standing on the bedside table. "I don't know. A woman would never be in the least bit confused, but men are so hopelessly inadequate—" She broke off. "Jeffrey what are you doing?"

"Unlocking this damned handcuff," he said, freeing himself. He held up the key he'd stolen, dangling it just out of her reach.

She lunged for him. "Jeffrey DeWilde, stealing that key while pretending to console me was not the behavior of a gentleman."

He let her momentum topple him backward, so that she lay straddled along the entire length of his body. "Gracie, darling, chaining me to the bedpost was not exactly the behavior of a perfect lady."

She wriggled, pretending she wanted to get away and actually making not the slightest effort to escape his grasp. He put his arms around her and rolled sideways, capturing her firmly beneath him. "Are you going to ravish me?" she asked.

He looked down at her, smiling. "Yes, I believe I am."

"Thank God." She linked her hands behind his head and pulled his mouth down to hers. "It's about time."

CHAPTER SEVEN

JULIA SLEPT UNTIL AFTER nine the next morning, and woke to the sound of the village church bells ringing outside her open window. When she came downstairs, Michael was in the kitchen with charts and flow sheets spread over the table, the *Sunday Times* unopened at his elbow and the smell of brewing coffee permeating the air.

"Good morning." She headed for the coffeepot. "You look as if you've been up for a while. And working, too."

"Yeah." He rubbed his hand over his unshaven chin. "I woke at five and couldn't get back to sleep. Jet lag catching up on me, I guess."

He looked exhausted, Julia thought, and she'd bet good money that his insomnia had been caused by more than jet lag. Having spent the past year tied in knots over Gabriel DeWilde, she recognized the symptoms of someone wrestling with problems that refused to go away. "It's really annoying when you can't sleep," she said, keeping her voice casual. "You lie there wondering how you can feel so tired, and yet not be able to doze off."

He shrugged. "Insomnia's inevitable when you fly across the Atlantic as often as I do. Eventually your body goes on strike and decides it's sticking to San Francisco time regardless of where it happens to be."

"At least you don't have to work today." She gestured to the charts and flow sheets arrayed in daunting piles in front of him. "That's the great thing about papers filled with columns of figures. You know they'll still be there tomorrow."

Michael's answer was a noncommittal grunt while he swiftly collated the papers and stashed them into his briefcase. Julia sighed and poured herself a cup of coffee. She'd woken up feeling totally confused about what had happened between her and Michael, and his attitude was doing nothing to clarify things. She'd enjoyed his company last night more than she would have believed possible. She'd sensed a camaraderie between the two of them, almost as if they understood each other without needing to find the words to verbalize their feelings. This unexpected sense of intimacy would have been mystifying enough, even if he hadn't kissed her. But he had kissed her, twice. And on both occasions his kisses had aroused instant desire. Julia was still trying to come to terms with that startling fact. She couldn't understand why she'd responded so strongly to a man she wasn't sure she approved of. How could she fantasize about making love to a man who'd abandoned his own child? Wasn't she the woman who'd always considered a man's attitude to fatherhood as the litmus test of his true character?

Julia stirred milk into her coffee and delivered herself a quick lecture. Having fallen out of love with Gabriel DeWilde, she had no desire to tumble into a doomed relationship with Michael Forrest. Quite apart from her own ambivalence about what was going on between them, the kisses that left her in turmoil had probably created no more than a minor blip on Michael's emotional radar. At this point, the smart course of action would be to stop trying to strengthen a bond that existed only in her imagination.

Fortunately, in the aftermath of her affair with Gabe, she'd become highly skilled at chattering brightly about nothing in particular. "Have Grace and Jeffrey gone to the hospital already?" she asked, carrying her cup of coffee to the kitchen table.

"No, there hasn't been a sound out of them." Michael's eyes gleamed. "I'm guessing they had a long and active night. I think they may sleep for quite a while yet."

"An active night? Do you mean they...? Surely they can't have..." Julia realized Michael was laughing at her and she grinned reluctantly. "All right, so I'm being ridiculous. Of course they did. But, Michael, they're divorced."

He leaned across the table, lowering his voice to a conspiratorial whisper. "If you don't tell anyone, I won't, either."

She laughed, although she was bothered by the fact that she'd been so caught up in her own feelings last night that she'd been oblivious to Grace and Jeffrey's. "I was horrified when I heard you suggest that they should share Lianne and Gabe's bedroom. How in the world did you know they wanted to sleep together?"

"It wasn't exactly an inspired guess, Julia. The pair of them might as well have carried a twenty-foot banner."

"But they barely glanced at each other!"

"That was my first clue," he said dryly.

Julia shook her head. "All right, I admit I don't understand what's going on. The DeWildes were married for half a lifetime, and then they spent a year hurling legal hand grenades at each other. Finally, less than four months ago, they got a divorce. And now you're telling me they arrived here last night dying to sleep together. Michael, that makes no sense at all. None."

"Why would you assume that sexual relationships have to make sense?"

In view of the way she'd responded to Michael last night, Julia realized she had no valid answer to that. "If we were talking about my students, I wouldn't be so surprised. I don't expect people falling in love for the first time to behave rationally, not in the beginning when there's so much to discover—about yourself as much as about the other person. But since Grace and Jeffrey DeWilde managed to stay married for more than thirty years, you'd think they'd have worked out whether or not they actually love each other *before* they filed for divorce."

Michael got up and poured them both more coffee. "Sometimes people get carried away in a situation, and they have to reach some kind of closure before they understand that they've galloped off at full speed in the wrong direction."

Julia stirred her coffee without drinking it. "It's really hard to imagine Grace and Jeffrey DeWilde having such a...such a torrid relationship. They always seemed settled, as if they had every detail of their lives under control. Especially Jeffrey. I can't imagine him galloping off anywhere, let alone in the wrong direction. He's so calm and sophisticated, and he has that wonderful ironic wit, as if nothing anybody did would ever surprise him."

"A dangerous man to get close to," Michael said softly. He shoved the newspaper to one side with unexpected force. "Here's some advice for you, Julia. Beware of men who hide their feelings behind a facade of indifference. Too much cool and witty sophistication usually means there are hot and powerful emotions churning behind the mask."

Michael should know, because he and Jeffrey DeWilde were two of a kind. Julia felt a moment of astonishment that she'd taken so long to recognize something so obvious. Michael was less urbane and more cynical than Jeffrey DeWilde, more provocative and less dignified, but he played the same game. He'd learned how to protect his privacy not by hiding, but by stepping forward and deliberately thrusting a false image into the glare of the media spotlight. For whatever reason, this weekend Michael had allowed her to catch a few glimpses of the real man behind the public image, and Julia realized that she was hungry for more.

She looked up at him. "Are you warning me that you're a dangerous man to know, Michael?"

He hesitated a fraction too long, and she realized he wasn't going to let her step any further behind the mask, at least for a while. "I thought we were talking about Jeffrey," he said. With a skill she'd come to recognize, he segued into one of his ever-ready anecdotes. "I guess I was one of the few people who wasn't surprised when Grace and Jeffrey broke up. The hotel business teaches you that people are endlessly amazing, in good ways and bad. Our flagship hotel in Chicago just hosted a wedding reception for a seventy-five-year-old groom and his seventy-eight-year-old bride. Their most recent divorce had lasted for six years and this was their third wedding."

She knew he was deliberately distracting her, but he made it so entertaining to be diverted. "It was their third wedding to each other?" Julia said.

"Yep, it sure was. They had both their other wedding

receptions at our hotel, too, the first one in 1947 and the second one in 1965." He grinned. "Maybe next time I should give them a discount for being such loyal repeat customers."

"Michael, don't say that, even in fun! Heavens, I hope it's third-time lucky for them."

"The groom is very optimistic. I stopped and chatted with him for a few minutes while he was paying his bill. He informed me that the difference in their ages had always been a problem, but that he believed this time they had it licked." Michael managed to look solemn. "He felt he finally had a more mature attitude, and he planned to ignore snide comments about the age gap from his pals."

"How old did you say they were? Seventy-eight and seventy-five?" Julia shook her head.

"Yep. One of my grandmothers was an immigrant from Poland and she was full of wise peasant sayings. Her favorite was that we grow too soon old, and too late smart. I guess she had a point."

She laughed. "All right, Michael, you win. Obviously it's completely unreasonable of me to expect the DeWildes to have their act together just because they were married so long. By this reckoning, they've got at least another quarter century to go before wisdom strikes."

Michael leaned back in his chair, twisting a gold pen between his fingers. "While we're on the subject of Grace and Jeffrey, we should make plans for the day. They might be pleased to have the house to themselves this morning, don't you think? Why don't we clear up here as quickly as we can, then drive into Winchester and see Lianne and Gabe and the new baby?"

"I'd like that. We can leave a note for Grace and

Jeffrey to let them know what we're doing.'' Julia smiled at Michael, realizing that despite her confusion, she felt lighthearted, anticipating the day ahead in a way that had been foreign to her for much too long.

Michael stared at her for a long, silent moment. Then he pushed back his chair, the movement abrupt. "I'll see to things upstairs. Why don't you take care of cleaning the kitchen?"

"All right. I've packed my case, so I can be ready inside thirty minutes. How about you?"

"Sounds good to me," he said. "Meet you in the front hallway."

HIS PARENTS' MARRIAGE had not inspired Michael with any fondness for the institution, or any respect for the idea, fashionable in some quarters, that staying in a failed marriage was a more responsible choice than getting out. As for love and passion, his experience with Cherie Lockwood had convinced him that human beings would be far happier if they could take a lesson from amoebas and learn how to clone themselves without benefit of a partner.

Storm's birth had confirmed his opinion that long-term relationships carried penalties that far outweighed the dubious benefits, and he'd been careful in the past three years never to get seriously involved. He didn't lead the wild sexual life that the tabloids suggested, but he never dated a woman who might want more from him than the little he was prepared to give. Where relationships between the sexes were concerned, Michael was very much in favor of keeping things shallow—and therefore painless.

Julia Dutton tempted him to break all his own rules. He wasn't quite sure why her naive sexuality should be such a turn-on. He hoped like hell that he hadn't reached the point where he was so jaded that he needed innocence to spark a response in his cynical soul. If ever he'd heard a game plan for disaster, that was it. He couldn't risk getting sexually involved with a woman too unsophisticated to understand what sort of person she was dealing with.

Frowning, Michael unlocked the car. He'd been in a strange mood ever since Julia's arrival at Briarwood Cottage yesterday evening, and he'd found this morning's visit to Lianne and Gabe unsettling, to say the least. His brief encounter with their new daughter had brought back memories of Storm's birth that he would have preferred to keep safely buried. Damn! He thought it was women who were supposed to get sentimental over helpless infants, not men who had no intention of adding any offspring to the already overburdened planet.

"Wasn't Elizabeth Gabrielle beautiful?" Julia slid into the passenger seat and gave him a smile that made his heart race. Her cheeks glowed, her eyes sparkled, and the sun struck flashes of fire from her hair. Looking at her made his throat ache.

The fact that she seemed oblivious to the effect she was having on him only made her appeal more powerful. He watched, torn between self-mockery and fascination, as Julia shook her hair out of her eyes and adjusted the shoulder strap so that it lay more comfortably between her breasts. He'd noticed from the first that she was a restful person to be with, not someone who needed to fidget. As soon as the seat belt was in place, she clasped her hands lightly in her lap and turned to him with another smile.

"I agree with Grace, don't you? Elizabeth definitely

looks like Gabe. And did you see her hands? They were so crumpled and perfect. I love looking at a newborn baby's hands."

She sounded wistful and he wanted like hell to kiss her. Right before taking her to a room with a large bed and twenty-four-hour room service. He was aware of an odd tenderness winding its way through his other feelings, hooking itself onto what had started out as a perfectly straightforward case of sexual desire. The sensation was alien enough to make him edgy, unwelcome enough to annoy him, and he leaned forward, turning on the ignition as an excuse to avoid responding to her smile.

Best to get the conversation onto neutral territory as quickly as possible, he decided, backing out of their parking space. "Lianne looked well, didn't you think?"

"Yes, she did, considering how exhausted she must be. And Gabe was back to normal, thank goodness."

Michael raised an eyebrow. "I guess you could call it normal. Providing you overlook the fact that he spent ten minutes debating whether Elizabeth should enroll at Oxford or Harvard. Personally, I think it would be great if the kid got to open her eyes and look around the room before her parents started obsessing about her college applications."

She laughed. "You're forgetting how precocious our godchild is. According to Lianne, she's not only opened her eyes, she's already smiled. Remember?"

"No, I forgot. That improbable gem must have been dropped right around the same time Gabe told me that he was sure Elizabeth recognizes the sound of his voice."

"Perhaps she does." Julia patted him on the knee. "You're just a cynical old grouch, Michael."

He wanted to take her hand and guide it straight to the zipper of his slacks. He gripped the steering wheel and took a deep breath. "You're right," he said. "I'm a grouch. I guess hunger's making me bad-tempered."

"No wonder. You only had a sandwich for dinner and neither of us ate breakfast. We should find somewhere to have lunch. There's a restaurant not far from the motorway that isn't too bad."

He had enough phone calls and faxes waiting to occupy every minute of the afternoon and most of the night, not to mention the fact that he had arranged to spend at least three hours with Clive Browne to discuss hotel business. Michael hesitated for a second, then realized he had better things to do than waste time pretending to debate something that was already decided. The truth was, he'd been planning ever since last night to take Julia with him to Ashby Hall.

"There's somewhere I'd like to take you for lunch," he said. "Somewhere special, but it's out of our way. Are you in a hurry to get back to London?"

She shook her head. "I have no plans for tonight, and my first class isn't until ten tomorrow. It's the last week of school, so I'm basically wrapping up the year's work and suggesting some summer reading assignments, so I don't have any real preparation to do."

Michael doubled back the way he'd come, negotiated a busy traffic roundabout with the flair of a native Brit, and took the road that was signposted for Weyhill.

"Where are we going?" Julia asked. "Although, it's such gorgeous weather that almost anywhere with trees and a view of the sky would be great."

"I'm taking you to a place called Ashby Hall. It's about fifteen miles from here."

"Is it a restaurant?"

"A hotel, converted from an eighteenth-century country mansion."

"Oh, lovely! My favorite sort of place to eat. How did you hear about it? This road's pretty, but it's definitely off the beaten track."

"Grace brought me here a couple of years ago. The gardens at Ashby are famous among rose enthusiasts, and she wanted to see a particular variety of antique rose growing here that has been lost almost everywhere else. I believe it was called Autumn Damask. She was hoping the owners might agree to give her a cutting for the garden at Kemberly."

"And did they?"

"The head gardener decided she was worthy enough to be put on the waiting list. Grace said that was the gardening equivalent of winning an Olympic medal. After her split from Jeffrey and their divorce, I don't know whether she actually got the rose in the end."

"Isn't it unusual for a hotel to be cultivating rare and antique roses?"

"They don't just cultivate roses. Wait until you see the place. The gardens are amazing. The house has an interesting history, too. It was originally built for the local lord of the manor, who had no children, so it was inherited by a cousin, who also had no children, and that continued for another two generations, until the place began to acquire the reputation of being cursed. In 1860, when it came on the market, nobody would buy it until a man came along called Blodget, who'd made a fortune manufacturing decorative tins and canisters, and he snapped at the bargain. He already had ten children, so I guess he decided a sudden attack of sterility might not be all that bad."

She chuckled. "Blodget—what a great name! It

sounds like something out of Dickens. Did the family move in and live happily ever after? Please don't tell me all the Blodget children died, or something horrid like that."

"As far as I know, the ten little Blodgets lived long and happy lives, but their parents didn't have any more children, which means either Mr. Blodget failed to break the curse, or Mrs. Blodget got smart and locked him out of her bedroom."

"Or they discovered the miracle of family planning," Julia suggested.

"In the 1860s? I doubt it. Anyway, the moment Mr. Blodget's name was on the Ashby Hall deeds, he started to go through the house 'improving' it with artistic additions."

Julia pulled a face. "Let me guess. He added mock turrets to all the chimneys—"

"Sure." Michael grinned. "Not to mention a central Gothic tower with a striking clock, fake vaulted ceilings in the drawing room, and enough stained glass windows to decorate a small cathedral."

"Oh, Lord."

"You haven't heard the best. For his final flourish, Mr. Blodget brought an artist over from Italy to paint cherubs on every available ceiling and Chinese landscapes on all the door panels."

"He had an Italian artist painting the Chinese scenes?" Julia asked.

"I guess so. Mr. Blodget probably had the typical Victorian attitude and considered one foreign country interchangeable with another. Italian, Chinese, what's the difference?"

"None, obviously. They both eat noodles, don't they?"

Michael laughed, and realized he'd laughed more with Julia over the past twenty-four hours than with anyone else in the preceding six months. "Let's not be too hard on poor Mr. Blodget. To give credit where credit's due, the guy also overhauled the drains and modernized the plumbing. He even installed a bathroom in the attic for the servants, which was quite an innovation for his time."

"The bathroom was a nice touch, but isn't it strange how entire generations can suddenly lose their collective taste? It's horrifying to see what happened at the end of the last century. Aristocrats were tearing down magnificent old buildings and spending millions of pounds to build houses we can hardly look at today without flinching."

"Some of what they did was close to vandalism," Michael agreed. "But fortunately for posterity, Mr. Blodget ran out of money before he could totally wreck Ashby Hall, and his descendants were too strapped for cash to do any more damage. They continued to live in the house until the end of World War II, at which point they were done in by inheritance taxes, so the land was sold off to various enterprises and the house was turned into a hotel. And that's what it's been ever since."

"An interesting history. Is the hotel owned by one of the mega-corporations?"

"Until five months ago, it was run by the same family partnership that bought it right after the war. They never made much money, but they didn't seem to care. They were fanatically keen gardeners, so they chugged along, enjoying the gardens and not trying to do much more than keep their heads above water as far as the hotel proper was concerned. Then last year, the three original partners died in quick succession and the rest of the family decided they'd lost the heart to continue running the place. When I heard it had come on the market, I decided to buy it."

"You mean you bought the property on behalf of the Carlisle Forrest Corporation?"

He shook his head. "No, it wasn't a Carlisle Forrest deal. I've gone out on a limb and bought the place personally." He smiled wryly. "And in fifteen years or so, if all goes well, I shouldn't owe the bank a penny more than a million bucks."

Michael had expected her to be interested in his plans for Ashby Hall, but he hadn't anticipated the expression of intense longing that flickered across her face. "I envy you," she said huskily. "If your renovation project is successful, it'll be a wonderful way of giving new life to a house that's steeped in local history. What a terrific project! You must be so excited."

Excited? It was a word he would never have used to describe his own feelings, but Michael realized she was right. He did feel excited, although his enthusiasm was tempered by frustration. His obligations as president of the Carlisle Forrest chain consumed a minimum of fifty hours a week, which didn't leave him much time for moving ahead with his plans for Ashby Hall. He'd reached the point where he needed to block out a month where he could stay in England and get the project off the ground, instead of nibbling at the problems piecemeal during harried three-day trips, punctuated by jet lag. At the moment, however, finding such a month seemed about as likely as finding an honest man among his mother's coterie of lovers.

"I'm excited," he said finally. "But mostly I'm scared as hell." Which was a truth he wouldn't have admitted to another living soul.

"You? Scared?" Julia's expression changed from interest to astonishment. "But you've been so successful with your hotels, and this project seems more of the same. Right up your alley, in fact."

"I'd say it's more like taking a flying leap across the alley with a strong chance that I'll land flat on my backside in a heap of garbage."

She grinned. "You need to borrow a parachute from one of your Dallas cheerleader pals. You wouldn't look good sitting in garbage, Michael. Slapstick's not your style."

She surprised another laugh out of him. Then he sobered. "I can't afford to fail, Julia, and the truth is, this project's a huge gamble."

"You've developed a winning strategy before. You can do it again."

His mouth turned down. "I was a lot younger when I seized control of Carlisle Forrest, and too ignorant to know what enormous risks I was taking. Now, unfortunately, I'm a lot smarter. Smart enough to be worried. In some ways, the hotel industry is an incestuous community. If I screw up with my plans for Ashby Hall, it won't be long before there are rumors all over the place about my failure. And the rumors won't just affect me personally, they'll have an impact on my position as CEO of Carlisle Forrest, too. Nothing succeeds like success, and nothing drags you down quicker than failure. Before you know it, our stockholders will be invading the annual general meeting to ask questions about my competence—"

"What would they find to complain about? Everyone agrees you've done a brilliant job."

Her confidence was touching—and totally unrealistic. "You don't run a major corporation without making enemies, Julia, so everyone doesn't agree that I've done a brilliant job. Besides, you can be sure that stockholders who are looking for trouble will find something legitimate to complain about, because every president of every corporation screws up occasionally. If you make a hundred decisions a week and get ninety-nine of them right, I believe that's better than making fifty correct decisions and letting the other fifty issues slide into oblivion because you're afraid of being wrong. But every incorrect decision leaves you exposed when someone wants to cause trouble. If Ashby Hall goes into bankruptcy, there are enough hostile board members remaining from my father's day that you can bet one of them will want to know why I'm the president and CEO of ten giant Carlisle Forrest hotels when I can't even run a rinky-dink little English inn like Ashby Hall at a profit.''

"So this really is a high-risk venture for you." Julia stared straight ahead. "Now I envy you even more."

"Why?"

"For the same reason I admire Lianne. For having the courage to chase your dream even though you know in advance that you may be a spectacular failure."

"I'm not sure I'd call that courageous. Try stubborn."

Julia smiled. "All right, then. Stubborn and courageous, how's that?"

"Flattering." Until Julia's queries, Michael hadn't realized how much he'd begun to question the wisdom of his decision to buy Ashby Hall. And in responding to her comments, he was reminded of all the reasons why he wanted to tackle the challenge of developing a hotel from scratch, and strictly to his own specifications. "Now, to return to really important subjects, if you're as hungry as I am, you'll be delighted to know that once we turn the next corner, we're on Ashby property."

He heard the faint rasp of her indrawn breath as Ashby Hall came into sight, but she said nothing. She simply looked around her in wide-eyed silence until he'd parked the car in the new, tree-scaped lot he'd had built at the side of the hotel. Without waiting for him, she got out of the car and walked to the canopied front entrance, standing with her back to the hotel so that she could look out over the stretch of private road they'd just driven along.

He joined her, not breaking the silence.

"It's literally breathtaking," she said at last. "Those horse chestnut trees lining the driveway are spectacular. They must be eighty feet tall."

"Or more. They're old, too. So are the oaks around the eastern perimeter. Some of them are approaching their hundredth birthday. The copper beeches are newer. They were mostly planted in the fifties and sixties."

"You said the gardens were famous among rose lovers, but I didn't imagine anything this...grand. I don't think I've ever seen such perfect landscaping anywhere. And the flower beds! The colors in those terraced beds are almost unimaginable."

"Wait until you see the lily pond in the back, and the gazebo across the stream from the weeping willow tree. Not to mention our famous rose garden, of course. The grounds were laid out by Capability Brown for the original owner, and even Mr. Blodget had enough sense not to mess with the fundamental design."

"How in the world are you going to maintain the gardens without bankrupting the hotel?"

"An excellent question."

Julia looked at him in alarm. "You are planning to

keep them up, aren't you? It would be almost criminal to let a garden like this get overgrown and neglected. Although, I'm afraid to ask how many full-time gardeners you need to maintain the place to such a high standard."

"Less than you'd think. The landscaped area looks bigger than it is because the hotel is set on a hillock, creating the illusion that acres of gardens slope away and melt into the horizon. So far, we're managing with just two full-time gardeners, with a lot of the heavy-duty work contracted out to specialists. The gardeners don't waste time cutting the grass or lopping tree branches or applying weed-killer. They concentrate on caring for the decorative shrubs and the flower beds."

"Still, those are costs that most hotels don't have to carry. I'm beginning to understand why taking this place on is such a challenge."

"On the plus side, the gardens are a strong selling point as well as an expense. And I hope I've come up with a concept for marketing the hotel that will justify the high costs."

"What's that?"

"We'll talk over lunch." Michael put his hands on her shoulders and turned her toward the hotel entrance. "I'm going to start eating the delphiniums if I don't get some food soon. Let's go inside."

Julia's comments about the decor and layout of the entrance lobby showed Michael that Lianne hadn't been exaggerating when she claimed that Julia knew more about interior design than many professionals. He watched as she bent down and inhaled the scent from a bowl of cream-colored roses set on a console table near the window. She straightened, smiling when she realized he was looking at her, then stood admiring the view of the garden in contented silence. Michael felt a sudden surge of intense pleasure that Julia was with him, allowing him to see Ashby Hall through her eyes. His overall tension decreased a couple of notches. He still had a briefcase stuffed full of urgent company business to deal with, but so what? If he could make a success of Ashby Hall, a few more eighty-hour work weeks wouldn't seem so bad.

He recognized the woman at the reception desk, and remembered that her name was Jean and that she coached the local girls' swimming team. Her last name escaped him. He made a mental note to have all employees wear name badges, a standard practice in the States.

The receptionist greeted him with a crisp, professional smile. Clive Browne had his staff well trained. "Welcome back to Ashby Hall, Mr. Forrest."

"Thanks, it's good to be here," he said. "How have you been keeping, Jean? Won any good races recently?"

Her smile became warmer, less professional. "The county championship," she said proudly. "Last year the team came in fourth, so the girls are thrilled to have moved up so fast."

"Congratulations. You must have worked hard, all of you."

"We did." The receptionist picked up the phone, dialing as she spoke. "I'll page Mr. Browne to let him know you're here. He's been expecting you."

Clive Browne didn't keep them waiting long. A short, stout man with thinning hair and ruddy cheeks, he'd been hired as a stopgap manager a few weeks before the previous owners decided to sell out. Clive was in his early fifties, and Michael had originally kept him on simply because he'd been too busy to hire a replacement. In this case, dumb luck seemed to have worked better than brilliant planning. Clive had no college degree, and he'd never run a big hotel, but Michael was fast reaching the conclusion that the guy was the most astute general manager he'd ever dealt with.

"Michael, good to see you." Clive shook hands, his manner friendly but not effusive. "How was the drive down from London? Heavy traffic, I expect. The sunshine always brings out the weekend drivers."

"We didn't come from London," Michael said. "Julia and I spent the night in Winchester." He knew exactly what impression he'd create by saying that, and yet he said it, anyway. And then was annoyed when Clive directed a swift, speculative glance toward Julia.

Clive was much too savvy to let his curiosity become blatant, even though Michael had never before brought a friend—male or female—to Ashby Hall. Turning his assessing glance into a polite nod, Clive gestured toward the dining room. "I have a table saved for you in the Terrace Room, if you'd like to have lunch before we start work."

"We'd definitely like to eat right away. We're both starving." Michael put his arm around Julia's waist and drew her forward. The proprietary gesture felt good, too good considering he'd just decided that he didn't want Clive speculating about their relationship.

"I should introduce you two," he said abruptly. "Julia, this is Clive Browne, the general manager of Ashby Hall. Clive, this is Julia Dutton." He added no explanatory tag to her name, chiefly because he had no idea how to describe her. As an acquaintance? A friend? The woman he lusted after but didn't dare sleep with?

Clive extended his hand. "Nice to have you with us, Miss Dutton."

She shook hands, wrinkling her nose. "Please call me Julia. Otherwise I'll feel as if I'm back at school with my students."

"You're a teacher?" Clive asked, leading the way to the Terrace Room.

"Yes. I teach French at Kensington Academy in London."

"French was one of the many subjects I failed at school," Clive said. "Funny that, because when I went to work in France for a couple of years, I picked up more than enough of the language to get by. I still remember a lot of it, too."

Julia rolled her eyes. "Don't get me started on the subject of how foreign languages are taught in our schools. I promise you, Clive, that's a two-hour lecture you don't need to hear."

"If someone as attractive as you had been my French teacher, I might have paid a bit more attention." Clive honored her with one of his rare smiles. "Then again, I might not. I was a bit of a lout as a teenager. Now, if you'll follow me through this crowd, I'll show you the table we saved for you. I hope you'll be pleased with the way the decorating turned out, Michael."

"Were you satisfied?" Michael asked.

"More than satisfied. And the restaurant's already stirring up attention in local circles. Mostly word of mouth from customers, which is the best advertising you can get, of course."

When Michael last visited the hotel in June, the Terrace Room had been shrouded in drop cloths. Now the shabby wallpaper left over from the fifties had been replaced by an elegant Regency stripe in burgundy, gold and ivory. The marble cherubs had been removed from the fireplace, revealing the clean lines of the original structure and the superb craftsmanship of the carved wooden panels directly above the mantel. A thick, close-pile burgundy carpet deadened the inevitable noise of the busy dining room, and rose pink table linen added a frivolous touch to a room that might otherwise have seemed too formal.

Michael had found the heavy velour draperies that originally covered the triple French doors especially ugly, but these had been replaced with lighter ones made of chintz, in a pattern of summer wildflowers against an ivory background. Right now, the drapes stood open to take advantage of the sunny view across the lawn, but at night, or in winter, they could be drawn tight to block out the damp and chilly darkness.

The decorative changes were successful beyond his hopes, but as far as Michael was concerned, the best change of all was the crowd of customers who filled the room. At least thirty men and women of varying ages, in couples and larger groups, all seemed to be enjoying their meals. He let out a sigh of profound relief. His first gamble, hiring a talented younger chef full of enthusiasm and innovative ideas, seemed to be paying off.

"This is great, Clive. You told me the restaurant renovations had gone well, but the photos you sent didn't do the room justice."

"I'm glad you approve."

"And the chef's working out? From your point of view, as well as the customers?"

"He has to be the least talkative person I've ever met, but his cooking speaks for itself, and he's excellent at the administrative side of things. Not so good at explaining what he wants done to the line cooks. But, yes, he's working out very well. That was a good hire, Michael.''

Clive directed them to a table near the French doors and handed them menus. ''I'll send a waiter to take your orders. Have someone page me when you're ready to start work, Michael. I'll be waiting.''

CHAPTER EIGHT

Clive pushed his chair back from the computer. "Good Lord, Michael, look at the time! Julia will be furious that I kept you so long."

"What?" Michael tore his gaze away from the spread sheet on the computer screen and struggled up from the subterranean dungeon in which he'd been wrestling with the problem of expanding the client base for Ashby Hall. He stared bleary-eyed at the clock on the wall of Clive's office. Seven-thirty. Almost dinnertime.

"Seven-thirty!" He shot out of the chair. "My God, why didn't you say something? We've been working for five and a half hours straight."

"I didn't say anything because I didn't notice." Clive pulled a contrite face. "Sorry, Michael. It's no use setting one workaholic to keep track of another. That's worse than expecting the cat to guard the bird sanctuary."

Michael shut off his computer program and closed his laptop, wondering how in hell he was supposed to explain to Julia that he'd started outlining a promotional strategy for Ashby Hall and had totally forgotten the time. Julia was going to be madder than hell, and she had every right to be. It was one thing for him to spend an hour catching up on urgent business while she took a leisurely stroll through the gardens with one of the staff. It was quite another to have ignored her for the best part of six hours.

"We'll get back to this first thing tomorrow morning," he told Clive. "The restaurant is a bright spot in the financial gloom, but the room occupancy rate is still way too low. We need to come up with a marketing concept that boosts reservations on a year-round basis, and that's a tough sell. Ashby Hall has no golf course, no tennis courts, and not enough space for conference rooms, which means we're not going to make up our occupancy shortfall with business meetings."

Clive rubbed his forehead. "I'm brain-dead at the moment. We'll come back to it on Monday. Maybe a good night's sleep will bring some inspiration." He hesitated for a moment. "Are you and Julia going to spend the night here? If you are, you can take your pick of rooms. Unfortunately, we have at least fifteen vacancies."

"No, Julia and I will be going back to town." Michael slipped his computer disks into a carrying case. "I'll be ready to start work at seven tomorrow morning, if that's okay with you."

"Certainly." Clive didn't probe Michael's plans. He picked up his briefcase, which bulged at the seams with papers. "If you don't need me anymore, Michael, I'll call it a day. I should go home and try to make peace with my wife. I've just remembered we were supposed to be playing bridge with the neighbors."

"Good luck," Michael said. "Explaining how you forgot that could be quite a job." He sorted rapidly through faxes and printouts, deciding what to take with him to deal with tonight after he drove Julia home. "Tell me something, Clive, how do you keep the hours you do and stay married?"

"I've no idea." The manager's smile contained little humor. "Christine's my fourth wife," he explained.

"Oh."

Clive's smile tightened. "Yeah, there's not much else to say, is there. The only thing I did right was I never had kids."

Clive's laconic words just about summed up the situation, Michael reflected, heading toward the lobby in search of Julia. When you worked sixty hours a week and spent most of your remaining waking hours obsessing about the work you'd supposedly left behind, something had to give. And usually what gave was the person's marriage. He'd seen the pattern with his grandparents, who hadn't divorced but had led separate lives while supposedly sharing the same household. To this day, Michael had only to visualize his grandparents' living room in order to feel a tangible chill. He could never remember an occasion when he'd seen his grandparents actually touch each other, except by accident. And the pattern of isolation-without-divorce had been repeated in a much more destructive form in his parents' marriage, where his father had alternated between excessively hard work and equally excessive contrition, while his mother filled her empty hours with affairs, punctuated by hysterical reconciliations with his father.

As a teenager, Michael had found his father's guilty attempts to patch up his marriage and relate to his wife and children almost more unbearable than the lengthy periods of neglect. He'd been even more alienated from his mother, whose clandestine affairs had never been clandestine enough to remain undiscovered, but had still left her far too busy covering her tracks to have time for him and his sister.

For a while, Michael had hoped to break the patterns

of the past in his own relationships, but ever since his affair with Cherie Lockwood, he'd decided that the Forrest men weren't cut out for marriage, and he'd come to consider loneliness a small price to pay in order to avoid creating his own sick variation on his parents' destructive marital theme. Like his father and grandfather before him, Michael had a flair for choosing precisely the wrong woman when it came to serious relationships.

He passed the bar and library, poking his head into both. No Julia. It was possible she was in such a snit that she'd called a cab, gone to the station and caught a train back to London. He stopped at the reception desk and forced himself not to snarl. God knows, it wouldn't be the clerk's fault if Julia had left. "I'm Michael Forrest," he said to the young man on duty. "I'm looking for a friend of mine, Julia Dutton. Do you have any idea where she is?"

"Yes, sir." The clerk referred to his notepad. "She left word at four-fifteen that when you were ready to go back to London, she would be waiting for you in the Salisbury suite."

Four-fifteen. Three and a half hours ago. He hoped to God someone had pointed out the library and that she'd helped herself to a book. He had no one to blame but himself if a member of staff had simply dumped her in the Salisbury suite and left her to twiddle her thumbs. In retrospect, he couldn't understand how he'd become so wrapped up in his work that he'd made zero effort to see that she was entertained. Feeling uncomfortably guilty, Michael took the key offered by the clerk and headed for the guest rooms.

The Salisbury suite had been made over from Mr. and Mrs. Blodget's bedrooms, and it was the largest in the hotel. At least Julia hadn't been stuck in one of the small back rooms on the third floor that hadn't yet been refurbished. Ignoring the elevator, he raced up the curved staircase two steps at a time, inserting the key in the lock at the same time as he called out to let Julia know he was coming in. Prepared to grit his teeth and apologize even if she threw a mega-fit, he walked into the room.

She was sitting in a chair with her back to the window, a giant pad propped on her knees. About twenty balls of scrunched-up paper lay scattered around her feet. She had one pencil in her mouth, another behind her ear and a third in her hand. Whatever she was doing had her sufficiently absorbed that she didn't seem to register his presence.

He spoke softly. "I'm sorry to have kept you waiting, Julia, honey." The endearment sneaked out inadvertently, and he clamped his mouth shut, irritated by the slip.

He needn't have worried that she'd misinterpret the sappy way he'd said her name. She spoke around the pencil, her voice vague to the point of abstraction. "Hello, Michael."

Another few seconds passed before she truly absorbed the fact that he'd come into the room. "Michael!" she repeated, taking the pencil from her mouth and smiling in the way that always made his stomach somersault. "You're back!"

"Yes," he said, his voice sounding tight and strange even to his own ears. "I'm back. I thought you'd be waiting impatiently for me. It's almost eight o'clock."

"Heavens, I had no idea it was so late." She sprang to her feet, hurriedly gathering the crumpled balls of paper and stuffing them into the wastebasket. "Sorry,

Michael, I didn't mean to keep you waiting. I got carried away—"

Julia was apologizing to him. If her reaction hadn't been so unexpected, Michael might have found it comic. At best, he'd expected to be met with icy politeness, at worst, a full-scale tantrum. It had never occurred to him that she wouldn't even have noticed how long he'd been gone. He supposed there was an ego-crushing lesson somewhere in all this.

"Don't apologize," he said. "I'm the one who should be doing that. I'm glad you kept busy, Julia, but I should never have left you alone for the whole afternoon and half the night. I'm sorry, really sorry. Clive and I started brainstorming, and time just ran away from us."

"But you explained at lunch that you had a lot of work to get through, and I'd already told you that I was in no rush to get back to town, so I'm not sure what you're apologizing for." She found a second wastebasket and tossed in a few more paper balls. "If I hadn't been willing to wait for you and Clive to finish your work, I'd have asked you at lunchtime to arrange for someone to drive me to the station so that I could catch the train back to London. I stayed because I wanted to."

She sounded genuinely puzzled, as if she couldn't imagine anyone reacting differently to his hours of unexplained absence. If only she knew how unique her behavior actually was, Michael thought wryly.

"How did you entertain yourself for the whole afternoon?" he asked. "Did Brenda give you a tour of the gardens?"

"Yes, and the house, too. I saw everything, even the kitchens. Ashby Hall is wonderful, Michael. I've fallen in love. Quite desperately, I'm afraid."

He shot her a quizzical glance.

"With the house," she explained.

"Lucky house." There was no reason for him to have said something so suggestive. Why was it that with Julia his tongue always seemed to be racing two beats ahead of his common sense?

"Or lucky me." She gave him a rueful smile. "I've a suspicion that love affairs with houses tend to work out a lot better than love affairs with people."

"I'm sure you're right," he agreed, straight-faced. "Of course, the sexual aspect of the relationship can be a bit challenging."

She flashed a grin. "But enduring once you work out the kinks. Houses respond so well to a bit of loving care and attention."

If ever he'd heard an opening for a witty comeback, that was it. But when he looked at her, every wisecrack he'd ever known vanished from his head. He touched a curl that lay against her cheek, then brushed his thumb along her cheekbone. "You have a black smudge on your face. Hold still." He licked his finger and rubbed gently at the mark. "There, now it's gone."

"Thank you." She turned her head away. "I can never draw anything without getting pencil all over my face."

She'd just provided him with an easy out. He could ask what she'd been drawing when he came into the room and effectively break the tension building between them. Better yet, he could suggest going downstairs for dinner, where they could talk in the well-lit public safety of the Terrace Room. Hanging around with Julia in a room equipped with a large four-poster bed was a seriously dumb idea, leading to other, even more foolish ideas. Like canceling the trip back to town and spending the entire night making love under the stern gaze of Mrs. Blodget's portrait.

That would be seriously dumb, all right. Off the top of his head, he could come up with approximately thirty-seven reasons why he would regret having sex with Julia the minute the deed was done. And that was before he started counting the reasons why it would be a terrible idea from her point of view. All things considered, it was definitely time to get the hell out of Mrs. Blodget's bedroom.

He slid his hand from her hair to cup her chin and tilt her face to his. What he saw in her eyes set his heart pounding. The logic circuits of his brain sent out one final warning, then went into total shutdown. "Are you hungry?" he heard himself ask.

"Yes," she said, and her voice sounded as husky as his.

His thumbs shaped her lips, emphasizing the ambivalence of what they were talking about. "I'm hungry, too. Very hungry."

"We could order something from room service." Her cheeks flushed and her breath came quicker.

Odd, how something as ordinary as the heat of her breath against his fingers could be such a turn-on. "Yeah, I guess we could," he said, and closed his mouth over hers.

This was the third time he'd kissed her in the space of two days, and he should have been ready for the kick. He wasn't. Each time they kissed, he felt a jolt that squeezed his lungs, seared his gut and scrambled any small part of his brain that was still functioning. His mental guard down, Michael acknowledged that he hadn't forgotten about Julia this afternoon; he'd deliberately shut her out of his mind. He'd worked late because he'd wanted to offend her. He'd wanted to flaunt his bad habits in her face, to make her angry, to make her see how unsuited they were.

But his ploy hadn't worked. Inexplicably, she wasn't mad at him. She was yielding and passionate, and she felt so damn good in his arms that it was scary. Michael pushed his tongue against her teeth, finding his way into her mouth, drawing the taste of her deep inside him. She kissed him back, eyes closed, hips thrust hard against his body. Her kisses weren't sweet and demure; they were hot, and dark, and sent visions of fierce, stormy sex ripping through his head.

He couldn't stop thinking about the damned bed. It was right there next to them, a four-poster, piled with down pillows. He twisted his fingers in her hair, closing his eyes, shutting out his view of the bed. His mental image of the two of them lying together, naked and entwined, immediately became twice as vivid.

Michael gave up lying to himself. What was happening between them wasn't going to stop at a few hot kisses. He dragged her head back, kissing her throat, his knee thrust between her legs. Julia shuddered as his body slammed against hers. Her shudder was all pleasure and zero resistance.

Michael groaned. Julia was everything he wanted, and everything he knew he would later regret. Her kisses forced a response from him that was something more than passion, something more intense than desire. They were close, but he wanted to be closer yet, inside her, part of her. Her heart was pounding, her skin dewed with sweat, and he could smell the faint perfume of crushed rose petals on her skin. He imagined her walking through the gardens, the sun hot on her skin, and a rose tucked into her blouse. He breathed in the heady scent, too impatient to wait while she fumbled with the buttons of his shirt. Unable to bear the suspense, he ripped off his shirt, then tore apart her blouse, yanking it from her shoulders and tossing it onto the floor.

Her breasts were perfect, full and firm, filling his hands. He bent low and suckled. Julia made a small, incoherent sound and reached for the zipper of his slacks. Her hand slid inside. Sweat beaded on Michael's forehead. This must be what purgatory was like. The promise of heaven, not quite fulfilled. The threat of hell if she stopped touching him.

The posts of the bed loomed like giant sentinels at the corner of his vision. He imagined breaching their stern guard and sinking onto the bed with Julia in his arms. Sinking into those soft down pillows. Sinking deep inside Julia.

He reminded himself that there were thirty-seven good reasons not to have sex with her, but right now, he'd be damned if he could remember what a single one of those reasons might be. Her nails dug into his shoulders, and her body rocked in rhythm with his.

"I want you," he said.

"I want you, too. Make love to me, Michael," she murmured.

Her husky request snapped the last thread of his control. He reached for her, carrying her to the bed, tumbling onto the mattress, the primitive drumbeat of desire pounding in his ears and pulsing beneath his skin.

Together they scrambled out of their remaining clothes. He'd always assumed that making love to Julia would be sweet and tender. Until this moment, he hadn't understood that it was possible for sweetness and savagery to be wound so tightly together that the strands couldn't be pulled apart. There was a wildness in her that fed his hunger and increased his need, an urgency that swept away softer emotions. And yet, through it all, there was an aching tenderness, a yearning to feel the sort of closeness that he had never felt with another woman.

He trailed his mouth over the skin of her belly, and her shivers of pleasure quivered against his tongue. It was Julia's pleasure that had him gasping for air. Her pleasure that was sending him over the edge. Her face was turned sideways, half buried in the pillow, and he pulled her around so that he could see her expression.

"Look at me," he said harshly, although he had no idea why it was so important that she should. "I want you to look at me."

She opened her eyes. They were hazy with arousal, blurred with need. And full of trust, Michael realized. Damn it, she didn't even have the smarts to know that he would inevitably betray her.

It hurt to look at her, so he brought his head down and kissed her instead. His kisses were savage, ravenous, devouring. She gave him back all that he was demanding, and added a passion entirely her own. He plunged into her. Arching up, she welcomed him into her body, opening herself so that she could take more of him, wrapping herself around him, holding him tightly as her body convulsed, propeling him to his own climax. He collapsed on top of her, gasping, spent and—for a few seconds—ridiculously happy.

Julia stirred lazily, her body relaxed and boneless beneath him. Her face was flushed, her hair tangled, her gaze indolent and sated. Michael found her so beautiful that it made his throat ache.

And that was the thirty-eighth reason why he should never have made love to her.

Michael was still lying next to her, but Julia could feel the emotional distance he was putting between them as clearly as if he'd stood up and walked away. It was strange that she could divine Michael's feelings with relative ease when she wasn't at all sure what she herself was feeling. But then, nothing about her relationship with Michael was easy to understand. How long had she secretly been wanting to go to bed with him? For months, probably, given the way her body had reacted the moment he started to make love to her.

Julia sat up in the bed and wrapped her arms around her knees. The silence around them thickened, squeezing the air out of her lungs. She drew in a deep breath and spoke into the silence. "One of us probably needs to say something."

"Yeah." He gave her a brooding look. "We need a volunteer to go first and I pick you."

She was too shaken by the intensity of what had happened to be able to invent a face-saving lie. "I'm not sure what you want to hear, Michael. What should I say? That everything between us felt...right? That making love has never been like that for me before?"

He took her hands and turned them palms up, rubbing his fingers over the pulse in her wrist in a restless circle. "Julia, I'm the wrong man for you. You're warm, and generous, and easy to get along with. I'm egotistical, compulsive, driven, and where relationships are concerned, I'm unreliable and a hundred percent selfish. I should never have made love to you tonight, and I'm sorry."

Anger deadened some of the hurt his words might otherwise have caused. It was painful to hear him apologize for something she'd found so wonderful. "You're right about being egotistical," she snapped. "Why are you acting as though what happened here was entirely your choice? I'm not some inflatable sex doll, you know, programmed only to say yes. We both chose to make love, Michael, not just you."

"Then we both made a mistake," he said quietly.

"For a mistake, it felt pretty damn good."

At least that provoked a reluctant grin. "Mistakes often do."

Julia wanted to protest that what they'd experienced was an intimacy and a passion too special to be labeled a mistake. And yet part of her acknowledged that he was right. There was no future for the two of them, so what they'd started tonight had nowhere positive to go. Which was just another way of saying it had been a mistake. She was a teacher, living in a London suburb and dreaming of a husband and children of her own. How could she possibly fit into Michael Forrest's jet-setting life-style? Their sexual encounter had been spectacular, beyond anything she could have imagined. But sizzling sex was hardly a sensible basis on which to build her life's dreams. Right now, she was still floating in the afterglow of their lovemaking. When that glow faded, she'd be left to confront the fact that hot sex didn't take the place of shared values and a genuine liking for each other.

Now that she knew Michael better, she didn't believe that he'd casually abandoned his son. But she could easily imagine Cherie and Michael deciding that since their relationship was over, Storm would be better off growing up with his step-father, without confusing visits from his birth father. Storm was just one small example of the chasm between how she wanted to lead her life and how Michael had chosen to lead his.

What she'd tried to do tonight was to use sex to

bridge the chasm, a doomed move from the start. More than doomed, it had been arrogant. She'd accused Michael of being egotistical, but she was guilty of the same fault. She'd been unforgivably conceited to assume that she could make love to Michael and he would instantly realize that he needed to reconsider the whole way he ran his life.

She should stick to falling in love with houses, Julia thought, then went cold. She hadn't fallen in love with Michael. God, no. She refused to condemn herself to another year of pining for the unattainable. She swung her feet off the bed, her legs not quite steady. She found her blouse lying on the floor and shoved her arms into the sleeves, pulling the two sides over her breasts, keeping her back toward Michael. When they'd made love, she'd felt no inhibitions. Now it was uncomfortable to be naked in front of him.

"Julia, I'm sorry." He spoke from behind her, close enough for her to feel the touch of his breath on her neck.

She took a jerky step forward, afraid that she might cry, even more afraid that she might lean back and fall into his arms. "For heaven's sake, stop apologizing, Michael. If you recall, I didn't ask you for any promises or any commitments. We had sex. You seem to wish we hadn't. Personally, I enjoyed it. And before you say another word, you might like to know that at the moment I'm not feeling in the least sweet or easy to get along with, so you'd be wise to shut up."

She picked up her trail of discarded clothes and marched into the bathroom. "I'm going to take a shower. While I'm gone, maybe you can decide how I'm going to get back to town tonight. I assume you don't want to drive me."

When she came out of the bathroom, Michael didn't appear to have followed her instructions. He was sitting on the side of the bed, half dressed, the sketches she'd drawn that afternoon spread out over the rumpled surface of the bedspread.

"You can throw those away. I was just amusing myself by playing with some ideas." Julia crossed to the bed and started to bundle the drawings together. Her emotional state was too raw to sit and listen to Michael explaining how impractical and cost-inefficient her designs were.

He gripped her wrist. "No, leave them. They're very interesting. Where did you learn to draw?"

She shrugged. "Different places. I've taken a few adult education courses, quite a lot actually, but it's just a hobby, nothing serious." She sat down on the bed, absently reexamining the window treatments she'd drawn. "That's how I met Lianne. We were both at the London School of Design. Of course, she was enrolled full-time."

"But you were in the same drawing class?"

"From the school's point of view, drawing is drawing. They divide you according to ability, not according to your specific area of study."

"And the instructors considered you and Lianne to have equal ability?" Michael held a sketch in each hand. "What course were you taking?"

"Interior design." Julia frowned, not at all satisfied with her window treatments now that she looked at them again. Something was wrong, although she'd be damned if she could see what.

"How many courses did you take? Were you thinking of making a career change?"

Julia was only listening to Michael with half an ear.

"I studied for quite a few years, although just at night and on the weekends. I got my diploma as a certified interior designer about a year and a bit ago, a few months before Gabe and Lianne were married."

She propped the drawing against the headboard and squinted at it to get perspective. The filmy curtains and draped satin side panels that she'd envisioned were a vast improvement over the heavy cretonne monstrosities currently hanging at the windows, but something was lacking. Gold! That was it. No Regency interior was complete without livening touches of gilt paint or gold tassels to break up the potentially lifeless elegance. She reached for the pencil by the phone.

Her reach was blocked by the sudden intrusion of Michael's torso between her and the bedside table. "You'd forgotten I was here, hadn't you?" His voice sounded amused.

She blinked and sat back. "Well, not exactly forgotten. I just realized that I'd made a mistake with the design for the window treatments in this room and I wanted to correct it before you saw—"

She shot him an embarrassed grin when she heard what she was saying. "All right, Michael, you can stop smirking. Yes, I'd forgotten you were here. I admit that when I get started on redecorating a room, I can get a mite obsessive."

"What's wrong with the decor of this room?" he asked, sitting next to her and propping a selection of drawings across her knees and his. "And before you waste time being polite, I'll tell you that I already knew something was wrong with the furnishings in here, so wrong, in fact, that I fired the decorator before she could move on to any other bedrooms. Unfortunately, I don't know exactly what's wrong, and neither does Clive."

"The design concept's fundamentally flawed," she said flatly. "I'm guessing the designer got cold feet and mixed two radically different styles in an effort to make the room look more welcoming. Is this the same person who worked on the Terrace Room?"

"No. The man who worked on the Terrace Room died in a boating accident before he'd given us more than a couple of preliminary sketches for the bedrooms."

"That explains the difference. The designer working on the Terrace Room had the courage of his convictions, and the result is something striking and wonderful. This bedroom is just a mishmash."

"Does mixing styles matter so much?"

"Not always. But the basic elements in this room have been refurbished in classic Regency style. You have rectangular plaster panels on the walls, a vine-and-leaf medallion on the ceiling, and off-white woodwork."

"I asked for that. We've tried to return the house to its original eighteenth-century form."

"Well, you made a wise choice. The simple Regency style is perfect for the proportions of the room."

"So what went wrong?"

"It isn't the furniture. Most of that is modified eighteenth-century reproductions. So far so good. But then the designer's added a floral carpet in a William Morris design, a heavy Victorian counterpane for the bed and draperies that match the carpet."

"Okay, enlighten me. What's wrong with William Morris?"

"Nothing at all. He's the artist who invented the whole concept of arts and crafts in the latter part of the nineteenth century. You know, the idea that you can have something that isn't a piece of great art like Michelangelo's *Pieta,* but is still something much more than a mass-produced plastic margarine tub. The problem is that the carpet and draperies in this room are potentially magnificent, but they don't belong here. They're almost a hundred years out of date for the rest of the room."

"So you think they're wrong because they're from the wrong period?" Michael asked. "I doubt if many of our guests would know that."

"No, I don't care that the date on the carpet's wrong, that's not the point. We're talking hotel decor, not an exhibit in a museum. Besides, you can easily mix antique and contemporary styles if you do it right. What's wrong with this room is that the exuberance and flamboyance of William Morris is clashing with the Regency desire for subdued, classical elegance. The end result is that everything in here ends up looking... diminished. Even Mrs. Blodget's portrait."

Michael glanced up at the oil painting on the wall opposite the bed. "I thought poor old Mrs. Blodget looked so stern because of all the goings-on in her bedroom. Are you telling me it's something more?"

Julia smiled. "Well, the goings-on in her bedroom may be part of the problem. But her portrait should be a focal point for the room. Instead, she looks out of place, don't you think? Like an aquarium in a dentist's office. You know it's meant to be soothing and take your mind off what's ahead. Instead, you keep looking at all those tropical fish and wondering what the dentist is going to do that's so bad he needs to divert you with swordtails and gourami. Mrs. Blodget looks as if she's been stuck on the wall to divert your attention from the curtains."

"A humiliating fate for a mother of ten and pillar of the British Empire." Laughing, Michael turned toward her, but his laughter died abruptly when their eyes met.

No, Julia thought frantically. No, she wouldn't let this happen. She edged backward on the bed. One mistake she could chalk up to experience. The second mistake she wouldn't be able to dismiss so easily.

"Julia…" Michael murmured her name and she stopped moving off the bed. And when he kissed her, she clung to him instead of pushing him away. His hands cupped her breasts and she felt the same helpless arousal as before. Her body burned with heat, consuming her from the inside out, making her writhe and twist at his lightest touch. How could she want him again with this fierce, aching intensity, when they'd only just finished making love?

"Julia." He said her name again, holding her chin so that she was forced to look at him.

"What?" she whispered.

"Spend the night with me."

She closed her eyes, fortifying herself against temptation. "I can't. I have a French class to teach at ten."

"I'll hire a limo to take you straight there."

The problem wasn't really her French class in the morning, and they both knew it. When she hesitated, Michael kissed her again, with passion and the merest hint of tenderness.

It was the tenderness that was Julia's undoing. "Yes," she said, cursing herself for a fool. "I'll stay with you tonight, Michael."

CHAPTER NINE

AFTER FOUR DAYS of glorious weather, heavy clouds had rolled in from the Atlantic. Jeffrey looked out of his window at the slate rooftops awash in rain, remembering another rainy morning, when his spirits had been grayer than the skies. Propping his feet on the sill, he watched the raindrops stream down the window in silver ribbons, washing away the summer dust.

A lot had happened in the fifteen months since that terrible Monday when he'd had to tell the world that Grace had left him, and although he would always regret the way he'd torn apart his marriage, this morning he felt the sort of joy that could only be experienced after living through months of real sorrow. Happy and a little scared, he felt like a young man standing on the brink of an exciting journey into new and unexplored terrain. He and Grace would soon be together again, but—for good or ill—Jeffrey doubted if he would ever again be able to take the comfortable routines of his marriage for granted.

A knock sounded at the door of his office, and he put his feet on the floor, swinging his chair around. "Come in."

Gabe walked into the room, his arms full of computer printouts. "Monica said that you needed to see me urgently."

"Yes, I do." Jeffrey smiled and gestured to a chair.

"Sit down for a minute, Gabe. This isn't something we can discuss on the run."

"What's up?" Gabe put the printouts on the floor and settled into the chair. "I hope this is only a minor crisis. I promised Lianne I'd be back in Winchester by midafternoon."

"It's not even a minor crisis. In fact, I was surprised when Monica told me you were in the office. There's no reason why you shouldn't take the rest of the week off, Gabe. This is a time for you to be with Lianne and the baby, not worrying about next year's merchandising budget."

"Yeah, thanks, that's what I plan to do. I only came in today because I need to check on a few major projects before Lianne and the baby come home from the hospital."

"When is that going to be?" Jeffrey asked. "You must be looking forward to having the whole family at home."

Gabe smiled broadly. "Lianne should be able to leave the hospital by tomorrow, certainly by Thursday. I can't wait to see Elizabeth sleeping in her own crib, and I know Lianne's longing to be home."

Jeffrey raised an eyebrow. "That's rather early to leave hospital, isn't it, since Lianne had a cesarean? It's only three days since Elizabeth was born."

"Yes, but she's fine, not losing weight, and Lianne's recovering really well." Gabe grinned. "Besides, I think the doctor will be glad to get rid of her. My wife is a wonderful woman, but she isn't exactly what you'd call a docile patient."

Jeffrey chuckled. "Ah, yes, I've had experience with that sort of wife myself. When you and Megan were born, hospitals scarcely let mothers hold their own babies, much less change them or play with them. Grace lasted four days, and then she insisted on checking herself out, which was unheard of in those days, especially for a woman who'd just had twins.''

"Did you and Mom ever wonder if you were doing the right thing? Lianne's impatient to be home, and yet we're both a bit afraid that we're jumping the gun. We've read dozens of child-care manuals, and I can tell you all the stages of development for the baby's first year, but it's one thing to read about newborns in a book, and it's a completely different thing when it's your very own baby, and her head flops and her arms flail, and she's so scrunched up, you wonder if her legs will snap if you try to straighten them." Gabe's forehead creased in worry. "Elizabeth looks so fragile, I have to remind myself that she won't break if I don't hold her in exactly the correct position."

"Welcome to fatherhood," Jeffrey said dryly. "Of course your mother and I wondered if we were doing the right thing—parents spend a lot of nights lying awake second-guessing themselves. It's only adolescents who know they're right. Parents are generally a bit more humble."

"You mean I'm always going to feel this uncertain?" Gabe sounded appalled.

"It gets marginally easier as time goes on. At least until your angelic child turns into a teenager, and then you're back to square one." Jeffrey got up and gave his son a reassuring clap on the shoulder. "You're going to make mistakes because every parent does, but Elizabeth will thrive, anyway. Don't try so hard to be a perfect father that you forget to have fun."

Gabe grimaced. "I'm not shooting for perfect. Competent would suit me fine."

"You'll be much better than competent, Gabe, I'm sure. You love her, that's the most important thing by far." Jeffrey sat down again at his desk. "Keep in mind that children grow up much too fast, which everybody told us when you and Megan were born, and which we thought was nonsensical at the time, of course. And then one morning your mother and I woke up, looked around the house and realized it was just the two of us. Alone. Not a noisy, annoying teenager in sight. Somehow, while we weren't paying attention, you'd all three grown up and left us."

"Touching sob story, Dad." Gabe grinned. "But it would work better if I didn't know for a fact that you and my mother went out and celebrated your freedom with a luxury vacation in the Bahamas the week after Kate left for college."

"That was a case of drowning our sorrows."

"Sure, Dad."

"It's the inevitable fate of parents to have their sincerity questioned," Jeffrey said with mock solemnity. Although Gabe was right, of course, at least to a certain extent. He and Grace had relished the return of freedom and privacy to their marriage. Seeing three kids through the perils of adolescence was exhausting, physically and emotionally. Still, their vacation in the Bahamas had been only eighty percent celebration of the fact that they now had all their children successfully launched into adulthood. The remaining twenty percent had been consolation for their loss, and nostalgia for the years of parenthood that—in retrospect—had flashed by much too fast.

And now, with Elizabeth's birth, the generational cycle was starting over again, and Jeffrey was finding the experience far more satisfying than he would have anticipated. No wonder everyone said that being a grandparent was one of life's sweeter rewards. He stretched out his legs beneath the desk and smiled at his son, thinking how good life sometimes felt.

"When I pointed out that children grow up too fast, I wasn't asking for sympathy, Gabe, just advising you not to sweat the little things. Enjoy Elizabeth's company on a day-to-day basis, and try not to spend each stage of her babyhood wishing she'd move on to the next. When she's crawling, don't wonder how soon she'll start walking, and when she's playing peekaboo, don't wish it was chess." He shook his head, smiling ruefully. "And I swore I wasn't going to start passing on sage snippets of grandfatherly wisdom at least until Elizabeth's first birthday."

Gabe laughed. "Well, we both know that was a lost cause, Dad. You've been sitting us down on the other side of your desk and dishing out homilies ever since we were old enough to listen. We three kids have actually grown rather fond of them in a perverse kind of way. Now, if I'm going to get out of here today, we need to get back to business. What was it you wanted to see me about?"

"It's about your mother." Jeffrey steepled his fingers and tried to look casual. "Actually, about me and your mother." He could feel his smile grow stiff as he considered his son's probable reaction. Gabe had found the separation and divorce more troubling than either Kate or Megan, perhaps because he and his mother had once been especially close. "We're...um...getting married again, Gabe. Some time quite soon, I hope. We're both...delighted...to be together again."

"Are you serious?" Gabe's head snapped up. Then

he shook his head, looking bemused. "Lianne warned me this was going to happen."

"A woman of perspicacity," Jeffrey murmured.

Realizing something more positive than shock and disbelief was called for, Gabe got to his feet and crossed the room to pump his father's hand. "Congratulations, Dad. I hope you and my mother will be very happy."

In the old days, before his split from Grace, Jeffrey would have taken Gabe's words at face value and ignored the stiffness with which they were delivered. Not anymore. He leaned back so that his son was forced to meet his eyes. "You don't sound very enthusiastic, Gabe, given that you've spent the past year complaining about our separation. What's your problem?"

"Nothing, Dad." Gabe's body was rigid. "I'm very happy for you both. I guess."

"Never try to make your living as an actor, Gabe. You'd starve." Jeffrey turned around to stare out of the window, fighting the temptation to let the conversation slide into a comfortable pretense that everything was fine. The rain provided a sharp reminder of the dreary Monday morning when he'd been forced to tell Gabe that Grace had left for San Francisco and wasn't coming back. Gabe had been furious and Jeffrey had been mute with pain. He'd always understood that his son's angry bluster that day had been caused by hurt and feelings of abandonment at least as much as by genuine resentment, but he'd been too distraught to offer Gabe any help. This time, Jeffrey knew he owed his son something more.

He turned around to face the man who was his son. Strong, smart, and too handsome for his own good, Gabe would never find it easy to admit to the vulnerability of the child that still lurked within his aggressively masculine outer shell. But Jeffrey knew from personal experience how long it could take for that bewildered inner child to grow up. In his own case, it had taken fifty-odd years and the destruction of his marriage before he finally came to his senses and accepted that his own father, Charles DeWilde, had left him to fight a terrible war, not because he found his son unworthy. Now it was time to help Gabe accept at the deepest level that his mother had run away from the anguish of an intolerable marriage, not from her children.

Hard as it was for Jeffrey to give voice to his feelings, even to his son—or, perhaps, especially to his son—he forced himself to explain. "Fifteen months ago you stormed into this office and told me that Grace couldn't possibly have left me. You said that you knew we loved each other, that we'd been happily married for more than thirty years, and it was crazy for the two of us to split up."

"That was a long time ago," Gabe muttered. "A lot's happened since then."

"Yes, it has, but you were right about us, Gabe. Grace and I do love each other, we always have, and we always will. It was crazy for us to split up, and, thank God, we've finally worked everything through to the point where we can put our lives together again."

"Have you?" Gabe asked with barely concealed sarcasm. "And exactly how are you proposing to put everything together again, Dad? The two of you didn't just move into adjoining flats, you know. In case you've forgotten, my mother relocated five thousand miles to the other side of the Atlantic."

"That's a logistical problem, Gabe, nothing more." Jeffrey hoped like hell that was going to prove true.

"Since Grace and I are confident we can make our marriage work again, frankly I'm not sure why you need to worry."

"I'm not talking about your personal life, although that's going to be hard enough to reconstruct. I'm talking about putting things together professionally, which for sure isn't something you can resolve just between the two of you."

"Why not?"

"My mother used to work for DeWilde's. She doesn't anymore. She hasn't worked at DeWilde's for more than a year—and if either of you thinks she can come back and pick up where she left off, then you're badly mistaken. People have been promoted to take care of the projects she abandoned. We have a totally new reporting structure. Ask Megan and Ryder how happy they'll be to start filtering their decisions through Grace again. Ask Sloan DeWilde if he's anxious to have Grace second-guessing his activities in New York now that he's finally taking a real interest in the store and showing a profit—"

"And how about you, Gabe?" Jeffrey leaned across his desk. "Let's not leave you out of the discussion, because that's what this is really all about. Do you want to step down from your position as vice president and have Grace supervising your decisions again?"

"No, of course I don't," Gabe said curtly. "I understand that the breakup of your marriage had many complex causes, and just because my mother left you, doesn't mean she's the person who was at fault—"

"*Do* you understand that?" Jeffrey asked. "Or are you simply mouthing the words?"

Gabe drew in a deep breath. "I'm not just mouthing the words. Mother and I had a long phone conversation when she was in Nevada waiting for the divorce to come through. She helped me to realize that the breakup wasn't simply a case of her waking one morning and deciding she was bored and wanted out of the marriage. But your marriage and my mother's relationship with this company are two different things. Whatever problems the two of you were having, in my book that doesn't excuse her attitude toward this store. Damn it, she left this company in the lurch and she doesn't *deserve* to be taken back."

Jeffrey barely hung on to his temper. "It's bloody fortunate for you that I'm in such a cheerful mood, Gabe. That means there's a fifty-fifty chance we'll get through this discussion without me throwing a punch straight at your nose. In the first place, your mother didn't leave DeWilde's in the lurch. My behavior forced her away from this company every bit as much as from our marriage. In the second place, you obviously don't know your mother very well if you think she has the remotest intention of swanning back into DeWilde's and taking up where she left off, totally ignoring the feelings of her colleagues in the process. Even if I were stupid enough to propose such a thing, Grace is intelligent enough to refuse."

"I'm sorry." Gabe strode up and down the room, breathing hard, visibly struggling for control. "Okay, Dad, I'm sorry. My comments were out of line."

"Yes, they were. Grace would be the first person to acknowledge that she can't step back into DeWilde's as if she'd never been away."

Gabe said nothing and his mouth was set in a stubborn line. With a pang of regret, Jeffrey realized that despite his son's protestations, he still hadn't forgiven his mother. On a rational level, Gabe understood that

Grace hadn't deserted her children and left DeWilde's in the lurch. On a deeper emotional level, he hadn't been able to reconcile his intellectual knowledge with his gut feeling.

Jeffrey sighed. He'd spent a lot of time over the past year wondering if he should tell his son the truth about what had precipitated Grace's flight to San Francisco. Until today, he'd always decided against revealing the sordid facts—and not just because it showed him in such a bad light. Jeffrey had felt that it somehow dishonored Grace to discuss his adultery with their children. Now he reached the reluctant conclusion that confessing the truth to Gabe was one more price he would have to pay if he wanted to heal the wounds he'd inflicted on his family.

He spoke quickly, before his courage could fail him. "Gabe, for reasons that will be self-evident, this is a conversation I never wanted to have with you, but I can see it's time for me to tell you the truth."

Gabe's head jerked up. "About what?"

"About the reason Grace left me and flew to San Francisco so suddenly." Jeffrey tried to meet his son's gaze and found that he couldn't. What if he redeemed Gabe's relationship with Grace only at the cost of destroying his own relationship with his son? He was making the unpleasant discovery that his sins seemed twice as black and three times as foolish when they had to be explained to one of his children.

He forced himself to speak the ugly truth. "Your mother left me because after several months of appalling behavior on my part, she discovered that I was sleeping with...that I was having an affair with...a woman young enough to be one of your sisters."

Gabe said nothing. The silence grew and deepened,

until Jeffrey finally found the courage to turn around and look at his son. Gabe was white-cheeked. "Do I know the woman?" he asked.

"No."

"I can't believe you did something so...tawdry. After all those years together."

"You can't begin to guess how much I wish it hadn't happened," Jeffrey said, reflecting that words had rarely been so inadequate for expressing what he felt. He had never wished more fervently that he could go back in time and eliminate those disastrous weeks of adultery. Even on the terrible night when Grace had caught him in his own tangle of lies, he hadn't felt much more ashamed of his behavior.

"There's nothing I can say, Gabe, that makes what I did seem less dishonorable. All I can offer you by way of justification is the feeble excuse that marriage is a complicated relationship, and it sure as hell doesn't get any easier as time goes by."

Gabe's voice shook. "I've spent fifteen months condemning the wrong person for the breakup of your marriage."

"Yes, I believe you have." Jeffrey spread his hands in a gesture of appeal. "I didn't keep silent in order to pass the blame onto your mother, Gabe. I kept silent because it seemed to me that this was a confession that would hurt the people who heard it more than it would hurt me to make it."

"Why did you change your mind?" Gabe asked harshly. "I'm not sure this is something I wanted to know."

"Because I couldn't think of any other way to make you understand—really understand—how badly you've misjudged your mother."

"I've misjudged you, too."

Gabe's unspoken accusation was more painful than a blow. "Perhaps," Jeffrey said. "Or perhaps you're finally accepting the fact that your parents are human, both of us. I don't know if I'll ever be able to climb back onto the pedestal where you had me, Gabe, but that may not be such a bad thing. In the long run, I believe I'd prefer you to see me as I really am, warts and all."

Gabe spoke slowly. "If my mother's able to forgive you for what happened, then I guess it's not my place to pass judgment." He shook his head. "No wonder Mom left so abruptly."

"Yes." Jeffrey wasn't sure whether he felt relief that Gabe's opinion of his mother was clearly changing, or chagrin that he'd now effectively cast himself in the role of bad guy. For the moment, at least, he missed the familiar comforts of his pedestal.

Gabe stood up and paced across the room. "I guess this proves that nobody can tell what's going on inside a marriage except the two people involved." He clenched his fists. "My God, when I remember all the accusations I hurled at Mom! I don't know how she tolerated me."

"She loves you, and she's a very generous woman—as I know from firsthand experience."

Gabe swung around. "You're damn lucky she's taking you back."

"Yes, I am. Incredibly lucky." Jeffrey held his son's gaze. "But I hope I'm not going to lose you, Gabe, in the process of regaining Grace."

Gabe expelled a quick breath. "No, of course you're not going to lose me, Dad. Your halo may have been knocked out of alignment, but you're still the man I admire most in the world. Not least because I know you'd never have told me about your...affair...if you hadn't been so determined to make things right between Mom and me."

Jeffrey felt a hot spurt of relief race through his veins. Gabe looked and sounded almost like his old self. It would take a while for all the tangled strands of the relationship between him and Gabe and Grace to be worked out, but at least they were now heading down the right track. "Thank you for trying to understand," he said. "Your good opinion is very important to me, Gabe."

"You have it," Gabe said quietly. He ran his hand through his hair, visibly gathering his thoughts and trying to lighten the mood. "Well, Dad, if you're through with the day's quota of startling announcements, could we get back to the issue that prompted all these revelations?"

"I think I may have forgotten what that was," Jeffrey said wryly. "Do you mean your mother's future role at DeWilde's?"

"Yes. If Mom isn't going to rejoin the London store when you two get married again, what is she going to do with her free time? Somehow I can't imagine her retiring to a life spent planning charity balls and heading up volunteer committees."

"The choice isn't just between taking up her old job at DeWilde's and embarking on a life of leisure. You seem to have forgotten that your mother has a heavy financial and emotional investment in a store of her own."

"You mean Grace?"

"Yes. After we're married, she's planning to continue running Grace, more or less as she's doing now."

Gabe stopped pacing and stared at Jeffrey. "But how can she run a store that's in San Francisco when your home is here in England? I assumed she'd sell Grace now that the two of you are getting married again."

He'd made the same rash assumption, Jeffrey thought with a touch of chagrin. Grace had swiftly corrected his error, with several pithy side comments on the arrogance of men who, thirty years after the start of the feminist revolution, still seemed to think that women only played at their careers while marking time between husbands. Still, his rashness hadn't been without its rewards. Grace's demand for an abject apology had led to one of the more amazingly wonderful half hours they'd spent in a night filled with stupendous memories.

Afraid that he might actually be blushing, Jeffrey walked over to the bar and poured himself a glass of mineral water. "Your mother is proposing that Grace should become the sixth DeWilde store," he said, dropping a few ice cubes into his glass and stirring. "She's suggesting that in exchange for surrendering her personal holding of DeWilde stock, the DeWilde Corporation should take over the start-up debt of her San Francisco store. Fortunately, the store is privately owned by Grace and her backers, so we can make the acquisition without going through a complicated public bid for shares. Financially, it seems a good deal for DeWilde's, so I shall probably recommend that the board accept her proposal."

Gabe rocked back on his heels, hands shoved deep in his pockets. "It's an interesting solution," he said. "What would you call the store? DeWilde's San Francisco?"

"No, we've already decided to keep the name Grace. It's too soon after the opening of the store to risk confusing the customers with a name change. After we complete the acquisition, the only immediate change we'll make is to ensure that the DeWilde signature product line is added to the merchandise the store already carries."

"But how is Mom going to continue personally running Grace after the two of you get married again? You need to be here in London, and she would need to be in San Francisco. In practical terms, I don't see how that's going to work out."

"Let's just say that this is an area of intense prenuptial negotiation," Jeffrey said dryly. He shrugged. "Grace's answer is that we'll spend a lot of time flying between San Francisco and London. My answer is that we'll appoint a general manager to cope with the day-to-day running of the store and Grace can act as a consultant. Fly out to San Francisco for a week or ten days every couple of months, that sort of thing."

"Have you suggested that compromise to Mom yet?"

This time, Jeffrey was quite sure he was blushing. "Er...yes. Suffice to say, negotiations continue."

Gabe grinned. "Somehow I think I know how this one's going to work out. My guess is that you and Mom are going to be racking up a lot of frequent-flier miles."

"Well, San Francisco has always been one of my favorite American cities."

Gabe actually chuckled. "I have a suspicion that watching you two get together again is going to provide some memorable moments of family entertainment."

"You could be right. Just don't place any bets with Lianne on the details of the outcome. Take it from me, Gabe, she'll win every time."

"Good Lord, Dad, it didn't take me a year of marriage to work that one out." Gabe put his arm around his father's shoulders, and Jeffrey sighed with relief. He didn't think their discussion would have passed muster with some psychologists, but at least it was several steps higher up the evolutionary scale than his earlier attempts to communicate with Gabe about the subject of his marriage. And although there were a lot of regrets to go along with his confession about his affair with Allison Ames, he was confident that he'd done the right thing in telling Gabe. His mother's seemingly inexplicable flight had created a canker of resentment in Gabe's heart that could only be cured by drastic measures.

Gabe gave Jeffrey's hand a final squeeze. "I'd better get out of here or Lianne will have left the hospital in search of me." He paused in the doorway and tipped his hand in salute. "See you next Monday, Dad. Unless you and Mom can make it for dinner over the weekend?"

"I wish we could, but I think we'll be in San Francisco," Jeffrey said. "I need to see the store before I recommend buying it, and we also have to decide what to do about your mother's apartment. She thinks we may want to keep it so that we have a permanent pied-à-terre in the States. I'll call you before we leave, of course, and Monica will fax you a copy of my schedule."

"Speaking of which, where is Mom right now?"

"In Paris, with Megan and Phillip. She'll be back tomorrow night."

"I'll call her at the flat." Gabe drew in a visible breath. "I'd like to tell her how happy I am you two are getting together again."

"Actually, Grace isn't going to be staying with me. She's going to be staying at the Goreham."

"The new hotel in Knightsbridge? Why in the world is she staying there? Why not in your flat?"

Precisely because over the past fifteen months it had become *Jeffrey's* flat, not *their* flat anymore, although Gabe hadn't even noticed how he'd referred to it. "We have a few issues to iron out before Grace moves back in with me." The ice rattled as Jeffrey put down his glass of mineral water. He smiled bleakly. "In case you and Lianne ever decide to get divorced, Gabe, I advise against it. You were right in one thing you said earlier. Putting all the pieces of our marriage together again is proving complicated."

THAT WAS AN understatement of epic proportions, Jeffrey thought later that evening. He took off his jacket and hung it neatly on the valet stand in his dressing-room, then wandered into the bedroom and checked the messages on his answering machine. Grace had called to confirm that she would be catching an afternoon flight home from Paris tomorrow, and that she'd be waiting for him at the Goreham. She would arrange for dinner to be served in her suite at eight-thirty. "I love you," she'd said before hanging up. "I can't wait to see you again, Jeffrey."

He played that message three times before reluctantly moving on. The next message was from the interior designer, who wanted to know if he'd made any decisions about the swatches of curtain material she'd left behind. Jeffrey made a note to call her to apologize and say he was no longer planning to redecorate. The final message was from his mother, announcing that she assumed he was dead and the *Times* had forgotten to print an obituary. She could think of no other reason why she hadn't heard a word from him for the best part of three weeks.

The message was vintage Mary. Jeffrey would have felt considerably more guilty if he hadn't spent much of the past two weeks attempting to discover where his mother was. When last they'd spoken, she'd been in Boston, staying with friends. Where she'd gone next had been anyone's guess. He still wasn't quite sure where she was, since she hadn't done anything as helpful as leaving a phone number. However, since she talked about the *Times,* Jeffrey decided to try the phone number for her London flat.

Mary answered on the third ring. "Hello."

"Hello, Mother. This is Jeffrey. How nice to have you back in England again."

"And how nice to know that you aren't dead," she retorted. "Not that I expect you to telephone me with any degree of regularity, of course, even though I'm your mother—your frail, seventy-nine-year-old mother, I might add—"

"We both know you're eighty-one, and strong as a horse," Jeffrey said. His voice softened. "How have you been, Mother? More to the point, where have you been?"

"I went to Alaska," Mary said. "On a cruise, which was definitely a mistake. I've decided that people who go on cruises are either senile or prepubescent. Both of which are equally tedious when one is neither."

"I hope the scenery made up for the boring company."

"Oh, yes, it was very splendid, but I believe I shall spend the rest of the summer in London. I woke up one morning on the cruise ship and realized that I was yearning quite horribly for a brisk walk along an English country lane. I took two aspirin and reminded myself that I loathe walking anywhere that I might see cows, but the yearning didn't pass, so here I am. It's a melancholy thought, Jeffrey, but I believe that as I grow older, I'm becoming incurably sentimental. The other day I found myself reminiscing at tedious length about the man who used to deliver milk to the house when I was a child. He brought the milk in big metal cans, with no refrigeration, on the back of a horse-drawn cart, and we used to dip a ladle into the cans to pour the milk into our own milk jugs. As far as I can recall, in the entire time I was growing up, the same man delivered the milk every day. I've no idea if he ever took a holiday. And I've absolutely no idea why I started talking about all this."

"Because you're glad to be home," Jeffrey said. "And I'm delighted to hear you're going to stay for the summer." He realized that his mother didn't know yet that Lianne had given birth to Elizabeth Gabrielle and that she was now a great-grandmother. She would be thrilled to hear that the first member of a new generation of DeWildes had been born, even though she would pretend otherwise.

On the point of telling her about the baby's arrival, Jeffrey decided this was something too special to recount over the phone. Besides, if he had dinner with his mother, it would be easy to find the right moment to mention that he and Grace had decided to get married again. Mary was likely to have some trenchant opinions to express about that—Lord knew, she had trenchant opinions about everything—and the advantage of combining the news of his remarriage with news of Elizabeth's birth was that he could always redirect the conversation to the new baby if the going got too rough on the subject of his marriage.

"Mother, if you don't have any special plans for this evening, I'd like to have dinner with you. You haven't eaten already, have you?"

"What a splendid suggestion! Are you planning to take me out on the town and wine and dine me? You know, I adore that new French place in Knightsbridge—"

"I was thinking of something a little more intimate and low-key," Jeffrey said. "Let me pick up some Chinese food and bring it over to your flat. I have some important news for you, Mother. Good news that I know you'll be happy to hear."

"Which we're going to celebrate by eating unidentifiable objects, coated in batter, out of paper cartons." Mary sighed, and for once her voice sounded thin and a little old. "Sometimes, Jeffrey, I really do miss your father almost unbearably. Now, there was a man who knew how to enjoy life in style."

"I miss him, too," Jeffrey said gently. "But I want us to be able to talk without running into half a dozen acquaintances or having the head waiter hovering at our shoulders all night long. And since neither of us can cook, we'll have to put up with Chinese take-away. The alternatives are fish and chips or Indian curry. Take your pick, Mother."

"Chinese," she said, and he could visualize her delicate shudder as clearly as if they'd been together. She sighed. "You know, Jeffrey, at moments like this, I almost wish I knew how to cook."

"No, you don't," he said cheerfully. "I'll see you in about forty minutes, Mother."

"I LAID THE TABLE in the dining room," Mary said, tilting her head to the side so that Jeffrey could kiss her cheek. "I though we might as well eat from real plates, even if we're not eating real food."

"Good idea." Jeffrey walked into the dining room and set boxes of rice, steamed vegetables and spicy, Szechwan-style seafood on the platters his mother had arranged on the table. He removed the bottle of chilled champagne from its insulated bag and put it on a place mat. Then he took Mary's hands and drew her into his arms for a quick hug.

"You're looking wonderful, Mother. The Alaskan cruise seems to have agreed with you."

"It probably did. One doesn't need to live for seventy-nine years to reach the conclusion that things that are boring and disagreeable are almost invariably good for one."

Jeffrey laughed. "I'm going to cheer you up despite your determination to spend the evening sounding like a curmudgeon." He popped the cork on the champagne and poured each of them a glass. "Here you are, Mother. I propose a toast to the newest member of the DeWilde family. Elizabeth Gabrielle DeWilde, born early Sunday morning, weighing in at six pounds, two ounces, and sporting a fuzz of decidedly red hair."

Mary turned swiftly, her face wreathed in smiles. "Lianne and Gabriel had their baby? Oh, Jeffrey, how exciting! Everything's all right, I'm assuming?"

"Everything's wonderful. Lianne had a cesarean, but she's recuperating well. And, in the way of newborn babies, Elizabeth has everyone convinced that she's totally adorable."

"I can't wait to see her." Mary put down her glass. "Heavens, Jeffrey, I'm a great-grandmother. That sounds such a dignified thing to be. I'm not sure I'm up to the task."

"I have every confidence that you'll rise to the occasion in your own inimitable fashion."

Jeffrey drew out a chair for his mother, and she sat down, her cheeks flushed with pleasure and excitement. "When did you say Lianne and the baby are coming home? I must send them a hamper of goodies from Fortnum and Mason's so that they can indulge themselves for a few days. And then I shall go to Harrods and buy an exquisitely impractical dress. Something in organdy with silk ribbons, don't you think?" She was so busy making plans to go and see the baby that she helped herself to rice and seafood without a murmur of complaint.

The trouble with his ploy was that it had been too successful, Jeffrey thought half an hour later. Talk about Lianne and Gabe had led almost inevitably to talk about Kate and Megan and their recent marriages, and Mary's desire for more great-grandchildren before she was too old and dotty to appreciate them.

Finally, his mother leaned back in her chair, lighting up her cigarette in its long jeweled holder. She inhaled luxuriously, closing her eyes. "You've no idea how good that tastes now that I only smoke five a day," she said.

"Yes, I'm sure it does," Jeffrey said absently.

Mary shot him a glance laden with suspicion. "Are you quite well, Jeffrey? I can't remember any meal I've eaten with you for the last ten years when you haven't lectured me about how I need to stop smoking."

"Since ten years of lecturing has produced no results, I've obviously decided to save my advice for more receptive listeners."

"From anyone else, that explanation might be credible. From you, knowing how stubborn you are, it seems entirely unbelievable."

Jeffrey pushed his empty plate to the side. "All right. The truth is, Mother, that I have something else to tell you. It's wonderful news, and I'm very happy—"

"You're making me exceedingly nervous, Jeffrey. Please dispense with any further preamble."

He drew in a deep breath. "Grace and I are getting married again," he said baldly.

His mother didn't move or speak for a full five seconds. Then her face broke into a huge smile. "Thank God," she said. "Oh, thank God! I was so afraid you wouldn't come to your senses in time to keep her."

"Mother, are you crying?"

"Of course not." Mary dabbed the corners of her eyes with her linen table napkin. "Oh, Jeffrey, you truly couldn't have brought any news that would have made me happier." She frowned. "But where is Grace? Why isn't she with you?"

"She's in Paris. She went to see Megan and Phillip, but she's coming back to London tomorrow."

"Wonderful. And when are you going to get married again? Quite soon, I suppose."

"That hasn't been decided yet." Jeffrey repositioned the half-empty champagne bottle between the steamed vegetables and the leftover seafood. "A lot of things have happened in the past year and a half," he said. "In many ways, my life stood still while I came to terms with the havoc I'd wreaked. But Grace's life moved on. She made new commitments, carved out a different role for herself." Jeffrey looked up. "For one thing, she discovered that she likes living in San Francisco. That much as she's grown to love England over the years, there's a part of her that misses the town where she was born and raised."

"I can certainly understand that," Mary said, stubbing out her cigarette. "Of course, if the divorce hadn't happened, she probably would never have acknowledged her homesickness, even to herself."

"But it did happen," Jeffrey said quietly. "And now we have to accept that although we want to be married again, Grace and I aren't quite the same people who were married to each other before. A lot of the issues we have to resolve appear purely practical, but when we start to scratch a little bit deeper, beneath the surface, we realize that the practical problems all have emotional issues underpinning them. Grace wants to be sure—we both want to be sure—that we don't solve the issue of what to do with her San Francisco apartment without solving the emotional problem it represents. And so on, down the line."

"Of all the astonishing things you've said to me tonight, Jeffrey, I believe that is the most astonishing. It inspires me to hope that you and Grace will eventually be even happier in your second marriage than you were in your first. I never expected to live long enough to hear you acknowledge that emotional issues can defy the logic of a situation."

Jeffrey gave his head a rueful shake. "I'm getting quite good at mouthing the right words, Mother. I'm not so good at feeling as generous and understanding as I sound." He stood up and walked over to the window, looking out into the rain-soaked darkness. "I want Grace back, Mother, and to hell with her need for terms and conditions. I want her to move back into our flat first, and then we can iron out the details of how we're going to rebuild our marriage later."

"And Grace doesn't agree with that timetable?"

"She says she's from the wrong generation to live in sin, even with an ex-husband." Jeffrey leaned his forehead against the cool pane of the window. "I think the truth is, she's afraid that if she moves in with me, I'll sweep away all her objections and force her back into the lives we were leading before the divorce."

"You're a very powerful man, Jeffrey, and not easy to resist. I can see why she might be worried."

Jeffrey's features tensed. "She has no cause to be. I just want her back, that's all. I'm not in the least interested in bargaining to make sure I come out as the partner with more power in the relationship."

"It seems to me that the answer to your problem is quite simple, Jeffrey. By implication, you've told me that Grace is the most important person in the world to you, and that you want whatever will make her happy. Tell her that, and I have a strong suspicion that she'll be more than willing to start making plans for your wedding."

"Do you think so?" Jeffrey felt a surge of hope. "We're flying to San Francisco this weekend so that I can meet the executives running Grace's store. Perhaps before we leave, I could persuade her to slip out to Kemberly with me." He gave a small smile. "If the rose garden at Kemberly can't melt her heart, then I don't think anything will."

"Have you asked her to marry you?" Mary asked.

Jeffrey frowned. "Well, of course... I just told you that we've agreed to get married again."

"I wasn't talking about that. I was asking if you'd proposed. You know, gone down on one knee, put your hand on your heart, offered her your undying love and devotion, that sort of thing."

Did Grace expect a formal proposal from him? Surely she must realize that extravagant gestures like that weren't his style. Jeffrey shuffled from one foot to the other. "In the circumstances, Mother, don't you think that might be a little...excessive?"

She sent him a pitying glance. "Obviously, Jeffrey, your transformation into a man of sensitivity is not yet total. No, I wouldn't consider a formal proposal excessive. And in the circumstances, I think you'd be wise to make it as sincere and passionate and romantic as you possibly can."

"You haven't thought through what you're suggesting," Jeffrey protested. "Men traditionally hand over shiny new engagement rings when they propose to a woman, but what am I supposed to do? Grace still has the ring I gave her the first time I proposed, and it symbolizes everything that was good about what we shared for thirty-two years. I don't think either of us wants to put that aside and start our second marriage with new rings. So how do I set about making this romantic proposal you're advocating? Ask Grace to lend me her engagement ring for the night, so that I can put it in a box and give it back to her?"

"I will concede that you might have a small problem." Mary tapped her cigarette holder against the ashtray. "Wait here for a moment. I believe I may have the perfect answer to your problem sitting in my bedroom safe."

She returned carrying a worn leather jewelry box. "You've probably never seen this piece of jewelry before, and I don't believe Grace has, either. It might be the perfect gift for you to offer when you ask Grace to marry you again."

Jeffrey opened the lid and saw a gold, heart-shaped

brooch, Victorian in style, open in the center, with diamonds at the point and two cherubs perched on either side of the elaborately decorated heart. The design was executed with exquisite craftsmanship, but the piece wasn't especially valuable, and the style struck Jeffrey as rather sentimental, not at all what he would have expected to appeal to Grace.

"Is this a piece of your own jewelry?" he asked, careful not to indicate by his tone of voice that he couldn't imagine why his mother counted on this pin to melt Grace's lingering resistance.

"I inherited it," Mary said. "This used to belong to Anne Marie DeWilde, your great-grandmother. As you know, most of her jewelry was lost or destroyed during the Second World War, so this has a unique value."

Jeffrey looked at the piece with increased interest. "Mother, thank you for the thought, but if I'm remembering family legend correctly, Anne Marie and Maximilien hardly had a happy marriage, so I'm not sure if this is quite the right piece to offer Grace when I'm trying to persuade her to marry me as quickly as possible."

"Like many family legends, the one about Anne Marie and Maximilien being miserably unsuited is only half true. In some ways, they had a very great love for each other."

Jeffrey had forgotten that his mother had actually known Anne Marie, although only briefly, since his great-grandmother had been killed by a bomb in the early years of the war. "Mother, I've just had a wonderful idea. Wouldn't this brooch be the perfect christening gift for Elizabeth Gabrielle? After all, Anne Marie was her great-great-great grandmother, and no doubt Elizabeth would treasure it as she gets older."

"I believe Grace would appreciate it more," Mary said. She looked at her son intently. "I'm gathering from what you're saying that Grace hasn't yet mentioned that while she was in Nevada, waiting for the divorce, she spent some time reading the personal diaries of Anne Marie DeWilde."

"No, Mother." Jeffrey had a sudden vivid image of how he and Grace had spent most of their time together since their reconciliation—and it was a far cry from talking about the personal diaries of a DeWilde ancestor. He turned a gasp into a discreet cough. "I'm sure you understand that Grace and I have had a great deal to discuss."

"Yes, indeed. No doubt most of it prone and in a state of undress." Mary ignored her son's strangled murmur of protest. "I'll leave Grace to tell you more about what Anne Marie wrote in her diaries. Or if you should happen to find your curiosity piqued, I'd be happy to loan you the translation. Grace returned the diaries and translation to me with some nonsensical message to the effect that I was the family matriarch and the appropriate guardian of DeWilde history. I believe you'll find some of the information about your DeWilde ancestors quite—startling."

"If you say so, Mother. But what has any of this got to do with proposing to Grace and giving her that brooch?"

"Apart from the intriguing light they shed on the family history, the diaries also contain a moving story of Anne Marie's enduring love for Maximilien. I know Grace was profoundly affected by what she saw as parallels between her own situation and Anne Marie's. I'm confident that if you told her this was the brooch Maximilien gave to Anne Marie on their first wedding anniversary, at a time when their love was almost perfect, she would be deeply touched."

Jeffrey closed the box with a snap and put it into his pocket. "Then, thank you, Mother. I'll trust your judgment on this one and give this to Grace when I ask her to marry me."

"A wise decision." Mary touched his cheek in a quick, gentle caress that belied the briskness of her manner. "And your idea of giving Elizabeth Gabrielle a piece of family jewelry was an excellent one, which I shall take care of at once. Come and help me choose a christening gift for my new great-granddaughter. My goodness, hasn't this been a splendid evening?" She linked her arm through Jeffrey's. "We wouldn't have had nearly as much fun if we'd gone to a restaurant. I'm so glad I insisted that we should eat dinner at home."

CHAPTER TEN

SHE DIDN'T WANT TO GET UP, even though her alarm was ringing. Eyes closed, Julia groped for the snooze button. The buzz stopped for a few seconds, then started again. Resisting the urge to pull a pillow over her head, she cracked open an eye. The neon red digits on her clock informed her that it was 5:47 a.m.

She sat up in bed and tried to remember why in the world she needed to get up at such an ungodly hour when it was the last week of the school year and her Wednesday classes didn't start until the afternoon. Absolutely no reason came to mind. In fact, it was frightening to contemplate how empty the days ahead seemed when she contrasted them with the color and excitement of the weekend she'd just spent with Michael Forrest. Closing her eyes, she slid back beneath the covers, unwilling to face reality this early in the morning.

The buzz started again and Julia finally realized the sound was coming from her front doorbell, not from her alarm clock. Stomach churning, she grabbed her dressing gown and hurried to the door. She could imagine few reasons for anyone to pay a surprise visit at the crack of dawn, and the ones that came to mind were all bad. On the verge of drawing back the safety bolts, she remembered to check the peephole.

Michael Forrest stood outside, leaning on her doorbell. Wearing running shorts, a T-shirt and a heavy layer of sweat, he managed to look sexy even through the distorting lens of the peephole.

Julia rested her forehead against the door, trying to summon the willpower to turn around and go back to bed. Ten seconds was all it took to convince her that she was coming up seriously short in the willpower department. Her stomach was churning again, but this time it wasn't with fear.

She opened the door, her heart pounding and her pulse racing. Since she had no intention of sending him away, there didn't seem any point in pretending to be annoyed that he'd woken her, even less in pretending that she wasn't glad to see him. He was breathing hard, as if he'd run almost to the point of exhaustion, so she smiled and held the door wide open. "Hello, Michael. Come in and catch your breath."

He didn't answer, but stared at her for a long, silent moment, seemingly hypnotized by the sight of her smile. His eyes, normally alight with self-mockery, appeared dark and unfathomable. Only minutes earlier, Julia had been groggy with sleep. Now, just looking at Michael, she felt aroused.

He stepped into the flat, kicking the door shut behind him. Still without speaking, he took her into his arms, tipping her head up as his descended, kissing her hungrily, claiming her mouth with a fierce, deep thrust of his tongue.

Julia arched against him, shivering as the cool dampness of his flesh pressed against hers. He was soaking wet, with rain as well as with sweat, but the chill of his touch had the strange effect of making her feverishly hot. She moved restlessly against him, letting out a tiny sigh of relief when he untied her robe and shoved it from her shoulders. His hands explored her body, skimming her breasts, sliding down her belly, making her throb. She clung to him, too uncoordinated to stand without his support. How odd it was that her body felt weak, when inside she felt strong, alive, vibrant—exhilarated by her power to arouse him, to make him want her. She was trembling, but so was Michael. The knowledge excited her.

He finally spoke, his mouth against hers. "Where's your bedroom?"

She pointed behind her, down the hallway, and he took her hand, pulling her along the corridor, kissing her as they went. Julia tumbled backward onto the bed, gasping and greedy, already on the brink of climax. Michael followed her down onto the bed, imprisoning her beneath the weight of his body, driving his tongue deep inside her mouth until she felt drugged and heavy with need. The gasp of her breath changed into a long, low moan, a primal sound that she would have controlled if she could.

Michael stared down at her, tense and unsmiling, his eyes glittering, the skin taut over his cheekbones. Then he bent down again, covering her mouth with his, drinking in the sounds of her desire. Her pleasure built and crested, teetering on the edge of pain, making her captive to his slightest movement, aching for his lightest touch.

She arched her hips off the bed in a silent plea for release, and he plunged into her, sending her soaring, setting her free. And capturing her heart more completely than before.

THE SILENCE HAD STRETCHED out much too long when Michael spoke to the ceiling of her bedroom. "I came to invite you to have breakfast with me. You owe me a breakfast."

Julia spoke to the same section of ceiling. "You have a...novel way of issuing breakfast invitations."

"I didn't want to phone." Michael rolled onto his side, resting his head on his hand so that he could look at her. "I was afraid you might refuse."

"I still might. Especially if you're planning to carry out your threats and make me eat syrup and sausages."

"Don't refuse," he said huskily. "Have breakfast with me, Julia. Let's spend the whole day together."

She pulled away from him and sat up, hugging her knees. "I thought you were supposed to go back to America today. We already said our goodbyes on Monday morning."

"I postponed my return to the States for one day."

"Why?" She finally turned and gave him a long, steady look. "Because of your work?"

"Because of you." Michael sounded almost angry. "I've missed you like hell these past two days."

"I've...missed you, too." Her voice softened. "We had a good time last weekend, didn't we?"

He drew in a harsh breath, linking his hand with hers. "Come back to Chicago with me, Julia. I want to show you my hotels, and hear what you think of the interior design. I want you to see how beautiful Lake Michigan looks from my living room window. I want to go to bed and wake up with you lying beside me. I want to know that I have to quit work at a reasonable hour because you're waiting to have dinner with me." His voice thickened. "Say you'll come, Jules. I really need you to stay with me for—a while."

For a while. In other words, until he got tired of her. Which might be next week, or not for several months if she was lucky. Desire and longing washed over her. Oh, God, she wanted to say yes! And knew that because she was a sensible woman she would have to say no.

Julia untangled her hand from his and gripped the sheet, forcing herself to speak calmly, to behave rationally. "Thanks for the offer, Michael, but I can't accept." She tried to smile. "I'm too demanding to make good mistress material."

He laughed at that. "Julia, honey, you're the least demanding woman I've ever met."

"In the little things, perhaps. But not in the big things."

"What do you define as the big things?"

She looked down at his hand resting possessively on her thigh. "Everything you're not willing to give to a relationship, Michael. I want love, faithfulness, commitment and enough freedom to spread my wings and fly, knowing that the man in my life will be proud of me if I succeed and supportive of me if I fail."

He looked at her broodingly. "I can give you creative freedom," he said. "I can give you more career opportunities than almost any other man, in fact. Our hotels would be the perfect place for you to start your career as an interior designer."

In some ways, he knew her too well, which meant that he understood exactly how to tempt her. Julia shivered with excitement as she contemplated the possibility of walking into a world-class hotel like the Chicago Carlisle Forrest, knowing that she had Michael's permission to redecorate the famous lobby or to refurbish a suite that had housed presidents and kings. She wanted the chance his offer represented so badly that she felt sick with anticipation. Her chest tightened and her stomach cramped. Did it really matter that Michael hadn't offered love or commitment if he was willing to provide her with such a fabulous chance to change the course of her life?

When Julia realized what she was thinking, she understood for the first time how fatally easy it could be for an honest person to succumb to a bribe. Anyone was vulnerable—providing the lure was tantalizing enough. She spoke quickly, before she could yield to his enticement. "It's tempting, Michael, but the answer is still no. People don't start their careers at hotels as prestigious as yours. Not unless they're on an inside track and sleeping their way to the top."

He scowled. "You're a damn good designer."

"Perhaps. But I have no experience that would justify your decision to hire me. If I'm going to sell my body in exchange for a job, at least let's be honest about what we're doing."

A trace of color flared along his cheekbones. "By all means, let's be honest. Does that mean you'll accept now?"

"No." She let out a shaky breath. "It means I'm not willing to turn into a whore, even for you, Michael."

His expression became shuttered. Then he made a quick, dismissive gesture. "All right, let's leave your career aside for the moment. There are other ways I'd make your stay memorable, Julia. Chicago is a fabulous city, much underrated in this country, and you wouldn't regret coming with me, I promise. We'd have...fun... together."

If she didn't go with him, she was throwing away the chance to discover how their relationship might develop. Was she crazy to believe that he might gradually come to understand that they shared something special?

That beneath their superficial differences, they had a unique compatability?

Julia pushed away the beguiling temptation. She reminded herself to deal with reality, not fantasy. Michael had spent his entire adult life in a succession of short-term relationships with beautiful, brilliant, successful women. Women like Tate Herald and Cherie Lockwood. She would have to be delusional to imagine she could convince him to change the habits of a lifetime when those women had failed. After a week, or two weeks, or two months, Michael would inevitably become bored with her. He would move on to a new and more exciting mistress, and she'd be left to cope with the emotional devastation of her shattered dreams.

"What happens when you get tired of having me around?" she asked, the effort to keep her voice steady making her question sound caustic. "What's your standard severance package for mistresses, Michael? Do I get a gift certificate for a week at the Carlisle Forrest hotel of my choice and a plane ticket home to England?"

His eyes darkened with frustration, and perhaps with hurt. "You presumably don't expect me to make a serious response to that."

She sighed. "No, probably not. But I still can't come to Chicago with you, Michael."

"This is a no-risk proposition for you, Julia. I'm inviting you as a...friend, that's all. I'm not asking you to commit to anything serious or long-term."

She could tell him that far from being no-risk, from her point of view, his proposition was spring-loaded with hazards, chief among them the fact that he wasn't asking her to commit to anything serious. His feelings might be friendly, but hers were already something dangerously more. She could tell him that she wasn't quite foolish enough to put herself in a situation that guaranteed a major case of broken heart. Or she could tell him a half truth, and keep this conversation slightly less devastating to her ego.

She opted for the half truth. "Michael, I'm a schoolteacher brought up in a traditional family, with a strictly practical outlook on life. I can't throw away a solid career to fly halfway around the world on a whim."

"Why not?" he asked tersely. "You have no real obligations keeping you here. Isn't it time you stopped leading the life your parents want you to lead and let yourself do what you want? Have you ever even dared to sit down and ask yourself what your own goals might be?"

She hesitated. "If I had worthwhile ambitions, I think I'd have done something about them before now. Lianne and I are the same age, and look at what she's achieved—"

"Yes, she's achieved a lot—but with all the help and encouragement her parents could possibly provide! You, on the other hand, have heard nothing but warnings about the importance of keeping a steady job and finding yourself a husband and settling down. Why are you teaching French when you have more talent than ninety percent of the interior designers I've ever worked with? Why did you date a man like Edward Hillyard when you have nothing in common with him? No reason I can think of, except that your family thinks it's what you should be doing."

His assessment was too accurate for comfort. "Whatever influence my parents may have had in the past, I'm an adult now, and responsible for my own decisions."

"Then make your own decision, instead of letting

your family decide for you. Come with me to Chicago tomorrow."

"Michael, we're not going to get anywhere with this discussion." She couldn't tell him that the reasons for her refusal had almost nothing to do with her family and almost everything to do with the fact that she was dangerously close to falling in love with him. She started to get off the bed, but he grabbed her wrist, pushing her down against the pillows, leaning over her, kissing the hollows of her throat, his body so close to hers that she could almost feel his simmering frustration.

"Julia, you're smart, fun to be with and stunningly attractive. If you really wanted nothing from life except to be married and a mother, you could have fulfilled that ambition ten times over by now—"

On the point of protesting, Julia was brought up short by the realization that Michael was right. Odd that he should have seen straight through to her restless core, even though it had been buried by years of submission to her parents' conservative views. Whatever it was she did want from life, Julia acknowledged that it was nothing as straightforward as marriage to a kind man, followed by the birth of 2.5 children and the purchase of a cocker spaniel. Edward was simply the last in a long line of worthy, honorable men whom she'd held at arm's length, refusing to allow them the chance to develop a closer relationship. In her own quiet way, she'd been running as hard and fast as she could from the future her family wanted to impose on her. In retrospect, Julia wondered if some of her attraction to Gabe might actually have been the subconscious knowledge that he didn't love her and wasn't going to marry her, so he was safe to get involved with.

When she married—if she married—it wasn't going to be because her husband was a worthy man who would make a reliable father. She wanted to marry a man she loved with all the passion she was capable of, a man who loved her just as passionately in return. She wanted a man who expanded her horizons, challenged her creativity, tantalized her with new possibilities, made love to her with a fire that burned away her inhibitions and sent her spirits flying.

What she wanted was to be married to Michael Forrest.

The recognition of her feelings for Michael brought almost no sense of shock in its wake. On the contrary, she felt as if she were acknowledging truths her subconscious had known for months. Pining over her abortive affair with Gabriel DeWilde had been an effective way to distract her attention from the fact that she was so attracted to Michael that it literally hurt to be in the same room with him. But nothing about her feelings for him fitted into the existing framework of her life, so it was small wonder she'd been terrified to admit to what she felt.

He framed her face with his hands. "What is it?" he said. "You're looking sad."

"Not sad," she lied. "I was only thinking that you were right. I'm not ready to settle into a house in the suburbs with a nice man and wait around to get pregnant."

Relief flared in his eyes. "I'm glad you understand that. So now we have that out of the way, say you'll come to Chicago with me. Take a chance, Julia, and let yourself live a little."

It was suddenly painful to breathe. "Michael, coming to the States with you isn't just taking a chance. It's the emotional equivalent of diving off the Golden Gate Bridge and hoping someone has remembered to tie the bungee cord.''

''I promise to make sure the cord is secure,'' he said, lying down next to her and turning her to face him. ''You can count on me, Julia.''

''Can I? Like Cherie Lockwood and Storm counted on you, Michael?''

Julia realized that she'd tossed Cherie's name into the conversation more to remind herself that loving Michael was a high-risk proposition than for any other reason. But once she'd spoken, there was no way to call back her words. The sound of the two names vibrated in the space between them, impossible to ignore.

Michael eased himself away from her, barriers almost visibly falling into place. ''I've told you before, Julia, that Cherie and I parted by mutual consent. And I keep away from Storm because Brad Stein prefers it that way.''

''And did Storm sign onto this agreement?''

''No,'' he said tightly. ''Storm got shafted for the convenience of the adults in his life. Children often do, as you pointed out to me not so long ago. I regret that.''

She bit her lip. ''I'm sorry, Michael. I have no right to question the custody arrangements you and Cherie have worked out for Storm.''

Michael pulled on his shorts and shirt, then knelt to lace up his sneakers, his back turned to her. ''My relationship with Cherie was finished three years ago, and it has nothing—absolutely nothing—to do with you and me. I asked you to come with me to Chicago. I'm still waiting for your answer, Julia.''

She closed her eyes, unable to look at him when she refused. ''My answer is no,'' she said. Strange that something she knew was right should feel so horribly wrong.

Michael finished tying his shoes. He straightened and started walking toward the front door, his reaction to her rejection masked behind an expression of slightly bored indifference. "Then I guess this really is goodbye."

At least she was no longer foolish enough to assume he felt nothing simply because his face betrayed no particular emotion. She swallowed over the outsize lump in her throat, fumbling to pull on her robe so that she could follow him to the door. "Yes, I guess so."

"Take care of yourself, Jules." He brushed his fist gently across her cheek, the merest flicker of emotion in his eyes. "Look me up if you're ever in Chicago."

"Yes, of course." Easy to promise, since she was unlikely ever to be within a thousand miles of Chicago.

"Quit your job, Jules. Have faith in your own talents. There's no point in being a second-rate teacher when you could be a first-rate designer." He kissed her, swiftly and with unexpected tenderness. "Lock the door after me."

"Yes, I will. Goodbye, Michael—"

But he was already gone.

CHAPTER ELEVEN

SMILING IN WELCOME, Grace opened the door to her hotel suite. "Hello, Michael, come in. I didn't expect you to get here for another twenty minutes or so."

"I took the tube—it was quicker than a taxi. Thanks for agreeing to see me on such short notice." Michael glanced across the room and saw the remains of a meal spread out on a table beside the window. "I'm sorry, Grace, have I arrived so early that I interrupted your lunch?"

"No, I'd already finished. Jeffrey's taking me out to dinner tonight, and somehow he always persuades me to have dessert, so I decided to eat lightly and save some calories."

Grace spoke with studied nonchalance, but even in his current mood, Michael wasn't quite self-absorbed enough to miss hearing the lilt of happiness in his cousin's voice. "Grace?" he said, spinning around to look at her. "Did it work, then? Are you and Jeffrey officially reconciled?"

Her blush deepened, but her eyes sparkled with merriment. "If you mean, did your outrageous ploy of locking Jeffrey into the bedroom with me at Briarwood Cottage have the desired effect...? Well, I would have to say the answer is a resounding yes. We're going to be married again, Michael. Quite soon, I think."

He swept her into his arms and whirled her around,

before kissing her on both cheeks and setting her back on her feet. "That's wonderful news, Grace. Fantastic! Jeffrey doesn't deserve you, of course, but the poor guy's really been suffering these past few months. And I think you've endured a couple of fairly bleak patches yourself."

"Too true," Grace said cheerfully. "I was so furious with Jeffrey that I couldn't stand to be near him, and I was so miserable without him that I could hardly bear my own company." She laughed. "It's amazing how difficult it can be to understand what we want out of life, isn't it?"

He'd never thought so, Michael reflected. He'd always believed his goals and desires were crystal clear, leaving no room for doubt and ambiguity. From the time he was an adolescent, he'd craved success in business, and the wealth and power that went with it. He realized that rage at his father's neglect fueled much of his ambition, but recognizing the lash that drove him did nothing to lessen the relentless, self-imposed pressure to succeed. Equally, he understood it was his parents' unhealthy relationship and his mother's constant adultery that had given him such an aversion to marriage. But understanding the cause of his feelings didn't change them. Love was a destructive emotion that Michael had no desire to experience. His relationship with Cherie Lockwood had merely reinforced every cynical, self-protective impulse he'd adopted as a teenager.

All of which made his current black mood difficult to explain. Julia fitted into none of his plans, so he ought to be delighted that she'd called a halt to their affair before they both ended up in a place where they didn't want to be. He ought to be rejoicing in his narrow escape from an entanglement that would only complicate his future. Instead, the knowledge that he might never see Julia again—that he would never again laugh with her, talk to her, make love with her—lodged in his gut like a throbbing wound. All in all, the way he felt right now was irrational, inexplicable—and downright disconcerting.

Grace led the way to two chairs, set on either side of a fireplace filled with fake logs. "May I get you something from the minibar?" she asked. "Or I could order a pot of coffee, if you like."

"No, thanks, I'm fine." Michael sat down next to the fireplace, thinking that Julia would have a field day diagnosing all the problems with the Goreham's design schemes. Picturing Julia, he started to smile, then frowned with annoyance when he realized what he was doing. The reason he'd arranged this meeting with Grace was precisely so that he'd stop obsessing about Julia until his flight left tomorrow morning for Chicago.

He brought his attention back to his cousin. "I'm really glad you and Jeffrey have worked things out," he said with complete sincerity. "The two of you belong together, you really do."

"We've both known that all along, I think. But human emotions are strange creatures, Michael, and I've come to the conclusion that the fear of being hurt by someone we love can be the most powerful emotion of all. From an outsider's point of view, my behavior over the past eighteen months must sometimes have seemed crazy, but there was always a horrible, twisted logic to what I was doing."

Michael grinned. "Okay, Grace, I'll admit you've got me stumped. If there was any logic to what you and Jeffrey were doing this past year, I'll be damned if I can see what it was. Unless you're about to tell me the pair of you were taken over by aliens and you've just now reclaimed possession of your bodies."

"Trust me, I had moments when I wondered if that's what had happened. But in my saner moments, I knew I was lashing out at Jeffrey because I couldn't bear to give him the power to hurt me anymore. So every time he made a tentative gesture toward reconciliation, I'd sabotage his efforts."

"You wanted to hurt him before he could hurt you," Michael suggested.

"Exactly. Once I realized he was probably doing the precise same thing, it was relatively easy to find the way back to each other."

Michael leaned forward and took her hands. "Is it going to work this time, Grace? You and Jeffrey have both changed quite a bit. Are you going to be able to put the pieces back together again?" He made an abrupt gesture, dropping her hands. "I'm sorry—forget I asked that. It was way out of line."

"Actually, it's a question I need to answer, at least to myself." Grace's gaze turned inward. "I guess what I've learned from this debacle is that if a relationship is worth saving, you have to confront your fear of rejection and move past it. After the divorce was finalized, I realized life without Jeffrey was so miserable that the risk of laying my heart on the line and being rejected was no worse than the daily grind of carrying on without him. Sounds simple enough when you say it, but it's amazingly difficult to reach the point where you accept that you have nothing to lose except your pride. Jeffrey and I know now that we love each other, and we want to spend the rest of our lives together. We can build whatever partnership we want on that foundation."

Nothing that she said should have been threatening, yet Michael felt an uncomfortable flash of self-awareness. The truth was that in thirty-six years of living, he'd never confronted his own fear of rejection. In fact, he'd constructed an entire life-style to minimize the chances of getting hurt. He chose to date women who weren't willing to commit to a serious relationship, and then, with cynical hypocrisy, turned around and claimed that love and long-term commitment were myths. Of course love and commitment were myths—for him. If he wasn't prepared to take any emotional risks, how could he ever hope to reap the rewards? For the first time, he found himself wondering if he was really willing to grant his parents such a stranglehold on his emotions that he allowed their failures to dominate his life. Okay, so Cherie Lockwood had screwed him over. That didn't mean every other woman in the world would do the same. And in all honesty, hadn't Cherie become involved with him in the first place precisely because his reputation and attitude suggested he wasn't likely to get hurt?

He got up and paced, too tense to sit. "You and Jeffrey had such a great relationship, Grace. You're both good people—wise people. What I don't understand is where it all went wrong in the first place." He tried to smile and found he couldn't. "My God, Grace, if the two of you couldn't make your marriage last, what hope is there for the rest of us messed-up folks?"

Grace's hands knotted in her lap. "Jeffrey and I made one big mistake," she said after a slight pause. "We tried to patch over a hole in our relationship without first acknowledging that the hole was there. Eventually the hole got bigger, and the patch strained at the seams, until it ripped wide open. Jeffrey and I found ourselves staring at this massive rent in the fabric of our marriage—knowing that neither of us had any idea how to mend it. We would never have found a path back to each other if we hadn't separated for a while and forced ourselves to decide what we truly wanted from our relationship. After thirty-two years of marriage, I'd forgotten how to think about myself as an individual person. When I finally crawled out of my depression and looked around at the shambles of my life, I knew I couldn't start to move forward until I found out who I was when I wasn't being Mrs. Jeffrey DeWilde. And it wasn't until I'd proved to myself that I could make it entirely on my own that I was ready to go back to Jeffrey. So simple once I realized it. So damn difficult to grasp when I was still floundering around in the dark." She smiled ruefully. "Does what I've just said make any sense at all, Michael?"

"Yes, of course it does." Michael astonished himself by getting up and hugging her. "I love you, Grace," he said. "You know I wish you and Jeffrey every possible happiness. I sincerely hope I'm around to celebrate when they put your picture in the papers as the longest-married couple in England."

"Dear Michael." Grace touched him lightly on the cheek, her eyes misty. She sniffed. "Damn, we're about to find out if that new mascara I bought is really waterproof."

Michael's hug tightened momentarily. "You know, for two people who were supposed to be discussing a business proposition, we're becoming appallingly sentimental."

"You're right, we are." Grace drew back and searched her pockets for a tissue. "All right, Michael. Enough about my marriage, my remarriage and my ruminations on the meaning of life. Let's get back to business. Why was it that you wanted to see me? Something about a promotional scheme of benefit both to you and to my store?"

"Yes, although I may be approaching the wrong person at the wrong time. I assume if you and Jeffrey are getting together again, you won't be running Grace anymore?"

Grace raised an eyebrow. "You know, Michael, I find that there are certain depressing similarities in the functioning of the male brain. Or perhaps I should say the nonfunctioning of the male brain. For the past year, I've spent twelve hours a day, seven days a week, struggling to make Grace a success. I can't think of a single good reason why marrying Jeffrey should suddenly mean that I want to close the store, or sell it, or do anything except continue to run it. Preferably at a healthy profit. Did you listen to a single word I said just now about the difficult year I've spent learning to be an independent, self-sufficient person?"

Michael chuckled, genuinely amused for the first time since leaving Julia's apartment that morning. "Ah," he said. "Let me guess. I believe I've just stuck my finger smack bang on top of one of the sore spots you and Jeffrey have been attempting to resolve."

Grace sighed. "Actually, it was a sore spot, but we've partially resolved the issue. I've agreed that it's only sensible for my store to become part of the DeWilde Corporation, subject to a suitable financial settlement, of course. But we're still debating exactly who is going to manage Grace, and how active a role I can play given that I'm not going to be living full-time in San Francisco anymore."

"Are you sure you want to listen to a promotional pitch at this point?"

Grace shot him a searching glance. "You're sounding unusually hesitant, Michael. Based on my past acquaintance with you where business is concerned, I'd have expected you to pitch a promotional idea at a funeral, if that was the only time you could get your quarry in your sights."

Michael winced. "I hope to God you're joking, Grace. I'm not quite that obsessive."

"Perhaps not quite. Anyway, relax, Michael, and tell me what you're proposing. Your ideas are always worth listening to."

"It's about Ashby Hall," he said. "I know the hotel has enormous potential, but we're struggling to establish a client base for overnight accommodations and losing money hand-over-fist while we wait for people to discover us."

Grace's forehead wrinkled in thought. "The location of the hotel isn't in its favor. You're not going to attract many people by chance. I'm assuming you've advertised in the obvious places and made some renovations so that the interior isn't quite so dreary?"

"Yes, that's all been taken care of. We've totally redesigned and reequipped the kitchens and offices, and we found a designer who did a magnificent job of refurbishing the main public rooms on the ground floor. Unfortunately, he died before he could complete the redecoration of the guest bedrooms, but I'm working on finding a replacement designer, so the bedrooms should soon be as appealing as the public rooms and the gardens."

"It's an exciting project," Grace said. She smiled. "I'm guessing you're having as much fun trying to make Ashby Hall a success as I've had with my store in San Francisco. There's something incredibly exciting about developing a business where your personal reputation is pinned right on the line. And the more success you've had in the past, the more closely you know everyone is watching and waiting for you to fail—and therefore the greater the challenge."

"You're so right about that, but the truth is, I find the challenge energizing. Licking Ashby Hall into shape has been more fun than anything else I've worked on in a couple of years."

"That surprises me, given how hard you've worked to restore the profitability of the Carlisle Forrest chain."

"Don't get me wrong, I've enjoyed that, too. But the Chicago hotel was built in 1892, and the chain has been world-famous for at least three-quarters of a century, so I wasn't exactly starting from scratch. Then there were shareholders to answer to, as well as a very demanding board of directors and a dozen senior management members. That's not quite the same as working to build the reputation of a new hotel from the ground up, especially when the money that's at stake is your own." He grinned ruefully. "And the bank's, of course."

"You can't tell me anything about the agony and the ecstasy of getting a financing package together," Grace said wryly. "So you're hoping I can help with a cross-promotional idea you have for Ashby Hall and Grace?"

Michael nodded. "Ashby Hall is ideally suited for wedding receptions, so I'd been thinking along the lines of advertising a wedding package in some of the trade journals—a reception in the Terrace Room or on the south lawn, accommodation for out-of-town guests who don't want to drive home after drinking too much champagne, and a suite for the bridal couple before they fly off on their honeymoon."

"It's a very workable concept."

He pulled a face. "Workable, but neither exciting nor in the least original. However, Julia came up with quite an intriguing proposal—"

Grace looked up. "Julia Dutton? Have you taken her to Ashby Hall?"

"Yes. We went there on Sunday, after our visit to the hospital." Michael had a dreadful suspicion that he might be blushing. Grace knew that he never took his dates to any of his hotels, let alone Ashby Hall, and she must be wondering why Julia was the exception. Michael kind of wondered that himself. He cleared his throat. "Anyway, Julia and I were tossing a few ideas around over lunch and she suggested expanding my wedding package concept to include anniversary celebrations. She pointed out that although newlyweds tend to want a beach and guaranteed sunshine for their honeymoon, a couple celebrating their wedding anniversary might be delighted to settle for a luxurious weekend at a hotel that promises excellent service, wonderful food and magnificent gardens."

"An anniversary package," Grace said, getting up and taking a notebook and pencil from the desk. "Interesting. It certainly seems an idea worth exploring. The great thing about the English climate is that a well-planned garden like Ashby Hall can support flowers and blooming shrubs nine months of the year, so you'd have something to serve as a focus—"

"And in December when there are no flowers, we can offer a nostalgia package that ties in with the Christmas holiday theme and plays up the idea of Ashby Hall as the local manor house," Michael concluded. "But here's where Grace comes in. I'm eager to publicize Ashby Hall in the States, and it occurred to me that this wedding anniversary concept could easily be linked to a promotion in your store. From the beginning, you've made sure that Grace carries products that meet the needs of nontraditional couples, so you already stock clothing and jewelry that's geared to older men and women. How about developing an advertising campaign that would target couples celebrating an anniversary as opposed to a wedding? You could announce that you've gathered together a collection of diamond eternity rings and other jewelry that's particularly suitable for anniversary gifts, and invite all your customers to participate in a draw for the Grand Anniversary Prize. Which would be two round-trip first-class plane tickets from San Francisco to London, and four nights, all expenses paid, at Ashby Hall."

Grace stopped writing. "But no matter how massive an advertising blitz we ran, most of the customers coming into our store wouldn't be married couples celebrating an anniversary. They'd be engaged couples, or people shopping for wedding gifts for friends—"

"That's no problem, because we can make the prize transferable to family members. The only condition would be that the couple who actually comes to Ashby Hall would have to be celebrating their wedding anniversary."

"It could work," Grace said cautiously.

"It will work. Handled right, this is something that could generate a lot of local media coverage—a bridal store that remembers there are years of marriage to come after the wedding day. For argument's sake, let's say that a young couple shopping for an engagement ring wins the prize. No problem. They can give it to her parents as an anniversary gift. Or his parents. Think of the positive publicity that could generate for Grace—not to mention my hotel.''

''I'm thinking,'' she said dryly. ''I'm also imagining the family squabbles as our young couple tries to decide whether her parents or his get to go on vacation. I'm visualizing broken engagements and hurt feelings all around.''

''Don't be a cynic, Grace, that's my role. Think positively and visualize lots of human-interest media stories. You could have posters throughout the store displaying the full glory of the Ashby Hall gardens at different times of the year, which would benefit the hotel a great deal, but would also be a fabulous focal point for in-store displays if you chose to devote a month to the idea that couples can come to your store not just to plan a great wedding but also to arrange a wonderful anniversary celebration.''

Grace was scribbling furiously. ''You're setting off a whole chain of possibilities in my mind, Michael. We'd have to be very careful not to lose our focus and reputation as San Francisco's major upscale bridal store. On the other hand, I've been thinking for a while that we're missing out on a significant potential market. For all the marriages that end in divorce, there are far more that last a lifetime, and if we can come up with goods and services that are appealing to a couple celebrating a special anniversary, I believe we'd be tapping into an important new market.''

''Of course, my hotel would cover the full cost of the grand prize,'' Michael said. ''If you want to throw in a few consolation prizes of gold lapel pins or something, those costs would be up to you. We could split the promo budget.''

"What sort of timetable are you looking at?" Grace asked. "I can tell you that our plans are locked in tight for the next six months."

"The sooner the better, obviously, but I'm flexible on timing. And we shouldn't get bogged down with the details, Grace. If you agree in principle, we both have competent people to work on the specifics. All I want is exposure for my hotel."

Grace scribbled a few more notes, then closed the folder with a snap. "You're right, Michael. I can see the scope here for a good deal of valuable cross-promotion. Send me a formal proposal, and if it lives up to my expectations, I'll hand it over to my marketing people with a strong recommendation to go ahead. You came up with such innovative ideas for the start-up of my store, I'm glad to know we might be able to return the favor."

"Great." Michael rose to his feet, conquering a ridiculous urge to take a cab straight to Julia's flat and share the news of how he'd implemented her suggestion. He reminded himself that she hadn't been willing to accompany him to Chicago, and that since there was nowhere for their relationship to go, he needed to forget her.

He took Grace's hand and kissed the tips of her fingers, not with any of his usual subtle mockery, but with respect and affection. "Goodbye, Grace. When you see Jeffrey tonight, don't forget to tell him that I think he's an exceptionally lucky man."

Grace chuckled. "I'll certainly tell him, since I feel on principle that it's wise to keep husbands properly humble, but at the moment, I confess I feel rather lucky myself. I'm in the sort of benevolent mood where I want to recommend love and marriage to everyone. Even you, Michael."

He flashed a practiced smile. "Grace, my sweet, I'm a hopeless case. I'll just have to resign myself to being a bachelor."

Instead of smiling, Grace scrutinized him with uncomfortable intensity. "You know, Michael, I've often remarked to myself that in many ways you remind me of Ian Stanley. You've met my friend Ian, haven't you?"

"Yes, several times." Michael wondered where this conversation was leading. "Ian's very entertaining company," he added.

"He is indeed. He's charming, good-looking, intelligent, hard-working and successful. He's the sort of man who gets invited to the most interesting parties, and no matter who else is there, he always seems to be escorting the most attractive woman in the room."

"Lucky man," Michael said.

"I wouldn't say so." Grace's gaze remained fixed on Michael's face. "Despite his amazing popularity, I've always suspected that Ian is one of the loneliest men I know."

"Are you trying to tell me something, Grace?"

"Yes, I am, and I'm not going to waste time being subtle. You're every bit as attractive, intelligent and hard-working as Ian Stanley. I hope that you're not going to wake up one day and realize that you're also every bit as lonely."

Michael forced himself to smile. "Not everyone is as lucky as you and Jeffrey. If I remember correctly, your friend Ian has been married three times. Seems to me he might have felt less lonely if he'd stayed single."

"Perhaps. But I had the impression when I saw you

with Julia Dutton this weekend that the two of you felt something rather special for each other."

"Special?" Michael managed a shrug. "I find Julia attractive," he said curtly. "What man wouldn't? In a week or two, I'm sure I'll find some other woman equally attractive. You may think I'm like Ian Stanley, but I've always thought I take after my father. I find it a lot easier to commit to my work than to a woman."

"Don't make the mistake of comparing yourself to your father," Grace said. "I can't think of a father and son who had less in common than you two. And for God's sake, don't judge all marriages on the basis of what happened between your parents. They were one of the most tragically unsuited couples I've ever known."

Michael had no intention of prolonging a difficult conversation by pointing out the long and dreary roster of couples he knew whose marriages were every bit as gruesome as his parents'. "Send me an invitation to your wedding, Grace, and I promise to come and dance the night away. I think that's as close to marriage as I'm going to get this year."

Grace gave him a hug goodbye. "You never know what life holds around the corner," she said, then smiled sheepishly. "And you don't have to say it, Michael. I know that's one of those trite clichés people produce when they have nothing sensible to say."

He paused at the entrance to her room. "Stop over in Chicago on your way home from San Francisco," he said. "I'd like to take you and Jeffrey to my favorite restaurant for a celebratory dinner. Le Perroquet, do you know it?"

"It's one of my favorites, too," she said. "Thank you, Michael. If we can squeeze an extra night away from London, we'll definitely do that. Take care, and have a safe trip home.''

There was no danger in flying across the Atlantic, Michael thought as he hailed a cab and gave the name of his hotel. The only danger he faced at this moment was the risk that he might extend his stay in London and see Julia again. The longing to do just that was fierce enough to keep him locked in his hotel room, drowning in papers, faxes, memos and phone calls until it was time to leave for the airport. Thank God for work. It was such a good way to avoid confronting disturbing feelings.

CHAPTER TWELVE

UNTIL GRACE LEFT HIM, Jeffrey had never appreciated how much of his enjoyment of life came from the pleasure of doing small, everyday things in the company of his wife. Driving to Kemberly after work on Friday evening, he was seized by a burst of happiness simply because she was there, in the seat next to him. They weren't discussing anything important in the grand scheme of things, just chatting about inconsequential snippets of news culled from Kate's latest phone call, Megan's plans for a trip to Hong Kong with Phillip, and Elizabeth Gabrielle's three-ounce weight gain in her first three days home from the hospital. In one way, Grace's presence at his side felt so absolutely right that it was as if she'd never been gone. In another way, it felt like several lifetimes since he'd been this content.

Overcome by a rush of emotion, he slowed the car and parked it on the side of the road, drawing Grace into his arms the moment he'd put on the brakes. He kissed her long and hard, only releasing her when another car drove past, honking loudly to indicate the driver's displeasure at finding half the narrow road blocked by a parked car.

"What was that all about?" Grace asked rather breathlessly, returning to her side of the car and adjusting her seat belt. "Not that I'm complaining, mind you."

"Making up for lost time, I think." Jeffrey squeezed her hand before resuming the drive. "Or maybe sheer unadulterated relief that you're here with me. The flat in London has felt empty without you, but visiting Kemberly has been like forcing myself to spend weekends in a barn built on a stretch of Arctic tundra. Your absence from Kemberly has been almost unendurable. I'm so glad we put off our trip to San Francisco so we could come here together."

"You know, Jeffrey, you've become so eloquent at expressing your feelings since I left that I may have to fly away on an annual basis, just to inject some poetry back into your soul."

His hands clenched the steering wheel. "Don't joke about leaving me, Gracie. That's one subject where I have absolutely no sense of humor."

"I can only joke about it because I know it won't happen." She turned to look out of the window as they turned off the road and onto the lane that led to the house. "I thought I'd remembered how green the fields around Kemberly are, but I hadn't. Oh, Jeffrey, it feels so good to be coming home."

"Nowhere near as good as it feels to have you here," he said. He managed to get the Rolls as far as the front courtyard before taking her into his arms again. "Welcome home, my love."

He had no idea how many times the housekeeper coughed and cleared her throat before he finally noticed she was there. What was even more astonishing, Jeffrey decided he didn't care. "Good evening, Mrs. Milton," he said, getting out of the car and making no effort to smooth his ruffled hair. "And how are you on this fine summer night?"

"Very good, thank you, and all the better for seeing

you here again, Mrs. DeWilde. We've missed you at Kemberly, and that's a fact."

Grace gave the housekeeper a hug. "I've missed you, too, Mrs. M. Not to mention how much I've missed those wonderful dinners you always cooked for me. Nobody makes pastry like you."

Mrs. Milton beamed. "Then you'll enjoy the rhubarb tart I made for dinner tonight. I made a salmon mousse, too, because I know that's one of your favorites."

"Thank you," Grace said. "It all sounds delicious, but you shouldn't have gone to so much trouble for the two of us. You're spoiling me."

"And happy to do it, Mrs. DeWilde. The meal's all ready, so I can serve it right away if you're hungry."

"Sorry, Mrs. M. I'm afraid I need to ask you to hold dinner for an hour. Grace and I have some important business to attend to first." Jeffrey held out his hand. "Coming, Gracie?" He ignored Mrs. Milton's scandalized expression and headed straight for the stairs—and the master bedroom.

Half an hour later, lying in his arms, Grace lay back against the pillows and chuckled. Jeffrey rested his hand possessively on her thigh. "A lesser man might find that giggle intimidating, my dear. What's so funny?"

"Mrs. Milton. You. I'm not sure which of you was more shocked when you instructed her to hold dinner and marched me upstairs."

"Definitely me," he said wryly. "She's intimidated me for years. It was quite astonishing to realize that if I wanted to make love to you, the housekeeper had no right to tell me that I couldn't."

Grace laughed again, then stretched lazily and got off the bed. "If we don't want to offend her for life, however, we'd better get dressed and go downstairs to eat.

We'll have to lavish praise on her salmon mousse as compensation for keeping her waiting."

"That won't be a problem. At the moment, I'm feeling benevolent enough to lavish praise on boiled shoe leather."

As it turned out, Jeffrey had no need to be generous. Mrs. Milton's dinner was delicious, and had survived the delay without any noticeable damage. After they'd eaten, it was Grace who suggested they should skip their usual cups of coffee and take a stroll through the garden to see how her roses were doing.

They wandered through the grounds, taking a meandering route to the rose garden, holding hands but not talking very much. Jeffrey's thoughts drifted back to the first time he'd proposed to Grace. It had been in midafternoon, after church on a hot Sunday, when the air was filled with the scent of fallen rose petals and the bees buzzed drowsily among the blossoms. He'd been young, superficially sure of himself, and heady with the certainty of his love. Carried away on a flood of emotion—not to mention youthful hormones—he'd proposed in grand style. Grace had been seated on a white wooden bench in the arbor, and he had gone down on one knee to slip the heirloom DeWilde sapphire ring onto her finger.

During the dark days of his separation from Grace, he'd examined his memories of that scene with a mixture of contempt and self-pity. The rift between him and Grace—which had precipitated his affair and ultimately led to their divorce—had started when Grace had confessed to him that she had accepted his proposal that day without being truly in love with him.

Now he saw the scene in the rose garden from yet another perspective, not as a moment of deception on

Grace's part and foolish romanticism on his, but rather as the start of a marriage that had united him with the woman he loved, brought him the gift of three wonderful children, and filled thirty-two years of his life with more happy moments than he would ever be able to count. The fact that Grace had not yet fallen in love with him when she agreed to marry him seemed supremely irrelevant in light of all that had since followed.

With her hand tucked into his arm, he led her across the flagstoned walkways of the rose garden to the same bench where he'd first proposed to her. In the moonlight, Grace looked impossibly young for a woman who'd just become a grandmother. Impossibly young, and impossibly beautiful. Jeffrey's heart swelled with quiet joy at the knowledge that she was his and they were together again, not just for a special occasion, but for every day. They sat without speaking for a few minutes, letting the nighttime scents and sounds of the garden fill their senses. A bird called out a brief song, and a breeze jousted with the leaves of a nearby beech tree.

"Do you think that's a nightingale?" Grace asked, leaning her head against Jeffrey's shoulder.

"I haven't the faintest idea." He smiled at her in the darkness. "You've only been gone a little over a year, Gracie. I haven't turned into a completely new man, you know. I still can't tell a starling from a cuckoo."

She closed her eyes, reaching up to stroke his face. "I'm glad. I'm kind of fond of the old tin-eared Jeffrey."

Since his conversation with his mother, he'd planned the moment when he would formally ask Grace to marry him a hundred times, but none of his plans had involved proposing to her when she was half asleep, drowsy from too much of Mrs. Milton's rhubarb tart. Somehow, though, it seemed easy and natural to disentangle himself from her arms and kneel in front of her, clasping her hands between his.

She looked down at him, and what she read in his eyes seemed to make the breath catch in her throat. "Jeffrey?" she whispered

"I love you, Grace," he said hoarsely. "A thousand times more today than I did when I first asked you to marry me. I want to share the rest of my life with you, waking and sleeping, the good times and the bad. You're my heart and soul, Gracie, everything that gives color and warmth to my life, but I realize now there's nothing I can offer you that you can't earn for yourself—except my love, and that's already yours. So I'm not sure why you'd say yes, but will you please do me the honor of becoming my wife?"

"Of course I will," she said. She leaned forward and kissed him, her eyes misty with tears. "I love you, Jeffrey DeWilde, and I can't imagine anything I want more than to be married to you again."

He reached into the pocket of his jacket and pulled out the worn leather box that contained the brooch his great-grandfather Maximilien had given to his wife, Anne Marie, on their first wedding anniversary. After the conversation with his mother, Jeffrey had grown curious about his great-grandmother's diaries, and he'd asked Mary to let him read the translation she'd commissioned. Shocking as he'd found the revelations in the diaries, he understood why Grace felt such an affinity for Anne Marie and why Mary believed that the brooch would be the perfect engagement gift.

"This is for you," he said, handing her the box. "It used to belong to Anne Marie DeWilde, and it's one of the few pieces of her personal jewelry that survived the Second World War. Maximilien gave it to her on their first wedding anniversary, way back in 1871. He wasn't very rich in those days, and he must have saved for months to be able to afford it. He gave it to her with love, Grace, and I pass it on to you with all that love, and my own, too."

Grace pressed the latch and the lid sprang open. She stared at the heart-shaped pin. A tear trickled from the corner of her eye and splashed onto the back of her hand, but she didn't seem to notice. "He loved her so much when they were first married," she said huskily.

"I know. I've read her diaries."

Startled, Grace turned to look at him. "You've read all of them?"

"Yes, just during the past few days. I know now that the DeWildes aren't really DeWildes at all, which I dare say would have been quite a scandalous piece of information if it had come to light seventy years ago. Today, it seems interesting but unimportant. We are who we are. From my personal point of view, I was more impressed by what a fool Maximilien DeWilde actually was beneath all that self-righteous bluster of his, and how he threw away his own chance for happiness."

"Anne Marie committed adultery," Grace pointed out. "Not once, but twice. In her day, everyone would have agreed she was the guilty party."

"She was wrong in what she did, whatever the justification, just as I was terribly wrong to betray our vows." Jeffrey was grateful when he felt Grace's hand tighten reassuringly around his. Thank God his sins had been judged by a loving, forgiving woman like Grace, and not a proud, intractable man like Maximilien.

"Anne Marie's diaries had a tremendous impact on

me, Grace. Reading her outpourings, I realized that being proud and self-righteous is no compensation at all for being warm-hearted and forgiving. Anne Marie loved Maximilien, despite all his faults, and she waited an entire lifetime for him to see that by refusing to forgive her, he condemned both of them—and their children—to years and years of needless suffering."

He took the brooch and pressed it into Grace's hand, closing her fingers around the cherubs. "Take the brooch, Gracie, and when I get into one of my highfalutin' moods, remind me that I don't want to spend the rest of my life being a pompous ass like Maximilien DeWilde."

She pinned the brooch to her lapel, then cradled her hand against his cheek. "Trust me, Jeffrey, you may have moments when you're a touch pompous, but you're nothing like Maximilien. You're far more honorable and much too loving—more like your real ancestor, in fact."

"Thank you," Jeffrey said, and got up, brushing the dust from his trousers. He pulled a face. "I have to tell you, Gracie, my arthritic knee is killing me. If you ever want me to propose on bended knee again, we'll have to bring a cushion."

She laughed, tucking her arm through his. "Let's stroll for five minutes and then go back to the house. I've enjoyed my apartment in San Francisco, but I have to admit that I spent a lot of evenings this past year longing for the Kemberly gardens."

"Gracie, my dearest, try to remember that flattery will get you everywhere. You should have said that you've spent a lot of nights longing to walk with me in the Kemberly gardens."

Her eyes gleamed in the moonlight. "But of course!

Isn't that what I said? It's definitely what I meant.'' She stopped to pick a spray of night-blooming jasmine and tucked it into his lapel. "We have to talk about when and how we're going to get married again, Jeffrey. Do you have any ideas at all about how you want to do this?"

"By special license, the day after tomorrow," he said promptly.

"In a way, that's what I'd like, too. But we have to think of the family, especially the children. Our separation was a devastating experience for them, and we might need to have a family celebration so that they can be convinced that we've truly managed to put our marriage together again."

Jeffrey sighed. "I see what you're saying, Grace, but it's a daunting prospect. I'm beginning to understand why Gabe and Lianne decided to elope. Between the two of us, we have an enormous family. Where do we draw the line? Do we invite just our three children and their spouses and Mother? But what about Ryder? In some ways, he's almost as close as a son. And if we invite Ryder and Natasha, how can we ignore Dev and Maxine? Lord knows, now that we've finally found Dirk's descendants, it seems a shame not to include them in major family get-togethers. Then there's your brother, Leland, not to mention Mallory, who's your godchild as well as your niece, and her husband. And she might have had her baby by then—"

"Stop!" Grace laughed. "All right. I get the picture. Either we elope or we have an 'intimate' family wedding with a guest list that starts at two hundred and works its way up."

Looking at her, Jeffrey knew there was no way in hell he was willing to wait while they put together a family wedding with a guest list two hundred strong. Even for the DeWildes, that meant a minimum of six weeks to allow time for guests to make travel arrangements, if for no other reason. Determined not to wait longer than a few days, he racked his brains for a compromise.

"I've got it!" he said, turning to her with a triumphant grin. "We'll get married as soon as we can in a small private ceremony at the church here in Kemberly. Then, sometime in September, we'll throw a huge party and invite the whole family and as many of our friends as want to come. We could really go to town, Gracie."

"That's a wonderful idea," Grace said, her eyes lighting up. "And I know just the place to throw the party. At Michael's new hotel. It's a wonderful old mansion with beautiful gardens, and you know if Michael's in charge of arranging the catering, he'll do a bang-up job."

If she'd wanted to throw the party in a submarine, Jeffrey would have said yes, just so long as she agreed not to delay their wedding ceremony more than a few days. "Ashby Hall sounds the perfect place. And I'll see if the vicar's willing to marry us next weekend. Since we're not inviting any guests, it shouldn't take more than fifteen or twenty minutes, so he can't claim he's too busy."

She hesitated for a moment. "Even if we don't invite any guests, we'll need two witnesses for the actual wedding ceremony, Jeffrey."

They might have been separated for a while, but after thirty-two years he didn't have any trouble identifying the reason for her hesitation. "I guess I get to choose one witness, and you get to choose the other," he said. He stopped and turned her to face him. "My choice is easy. Ian Stanley was best man at our first wedding, and we've been friends ever since. I can't imagine anyone I'd rather have to stand beside us when we renew our vows."

Grace laid her head against his chest. "Thank you, Jeffrey," she whispered. She looked up, smiling again. "And my choice is easy, too. I would like to invite your mother to be our second witness. Maybe if she stands right next to us, some of her wisdom will brush off on us."

"More likely her bad habits," Jeffrey said, and grinned cheerfully. They turned and strolled at a leisurely pace toward the house. "Is that agreed, then? Next week we're going to San Francisco, but we'll fly home in time to be married on the weekend. Is Ian going to be in town, do you know?"

"He's not leaving for China until the end of the month, so we should just be able to squeeze in our wedding before he goes."

Jeffrey chuckled, and Grace turned to him. "What is it?"

"Mrs. Milton," he said in a low voice. "She's peeking at us from behind the drawing-room curtains."

Grace's expression became mischievous. "Then we should give her something worthwhile to look at, don't you think?"

"Definitely." Jeffrey folded Grace into his arms and tilted her head back, looking into the sparkling depths of her eyes. "Let's give her a real show," he said, and bent his head to kiss his once and soon-to-be wife with fierce, loving passion.

The drawing room curtains twitched and Mrs. Milton gasped, but by the time they finally walked back inside the house, they'd both forgotten all about the housekeeper.

CHAPTER THIRTEEN

JULIA HAD FELT pathetically sorry for herself when Gabe broke the news that he didn't love her. She'd moped around the flat, playing the role of brave but tragic heroine and generally indulging herself in a wallow of self-pity. In the wake of Michael's return to Chicago, her mood was radically different. She didn't feel in the least sorry for herself, and the pain of his absence was far too acute to be eased by role-playing. Instead of self-pity, what she felt was rage—at Michael for being such an idiot that he expected her to toss aside everything in order to become his mistress, and at herself for being such a hidebound fool that she'd lacked the courage to accept his offer and take a chance on love. She'd been brought up to believe that avoiding risk was always the prudent thing to do. More and more lately, she'd begun to wonder if avoiding risk wasn't a symptom of cowardice rather than good sense. What was life worth if you marched straight through it, never daring to explore any of the most enticing byways for fear of running into a patch of brambles?

The final two days of the school year kept her busy, and on Friday evening she celebrated eight weeks of upcoming vacation with some of her fellow teachers and managed not to think about Michael for three whole hours. But when Saturday afternoon rolled around and the household chores were done, she discovered that she couldn't knuckle down to sketching a design for the wall hanging she intended to embroider as a christening gift for Elizabeth Gabrielle. She'd found a wonderful reproduction of a Renaissance painting of the Archangel Gabriel at the National Gallery bookstore, but the fourth time she ruined the powerful line of Gabriel's arm, she gave up for the day.

Unable to settle, she wandered over to the old electric typewriter set up in a corner of her bedroom and scrolled in a sheet of heavy white bond paper. She'd typed her letter of resignation to the headmistress of Kensington Academy, effective immediately, before she had any conscious idea that this was what she'd spent the past several days planning to do.

Stunned, she stared at the letter for several minutes before she finally pulled out the page and read through the brief, formal paragraphs and the courteous tag line thanking the headmistress for her advice and encouragement over the past five years. Ignoring the slight tremor of her hands, she signed her name, folded the letter into an envelope and sealed it before she could change her mind.

In September, when school reconvened, she wouldn't be there. Her stomach lurched at the thought, but as much with excitement as with trepidation. Walking across the road to the corner pillar-box to post the letter, she could already hear the lectures her brothers would deliver at the next family gathering, and see the pitying looks she'd get from her sisters-in-law as they discussed this latest evidence of her failure to take life seriously. To her astonishment, she discovered that she didn't give a damn.

She knew her parents would be worried sick that she had done something so rash, but watching the letter slide down into the dark depths of the pillar-box, Julia felt as if she'd been released from an intolerable burden. Michael might have been wrong to expect her to give up everything at a moment's notice and fly to Chicago with him, but he'd been absolutely right to say that she needed to change her job. She was willing to work hard, and she had no dependents. If she couldn't afford to take a risk, who could? The mortgage on her flat was no good reason to put a mortgage on her soul, which was what she'd been doing for the past several years. It was time to stand up for herself and begin living the life she wanted to lead, instead of the life her well-meaning family had mapped out for her.

Julia's burst of self-confidence lasted until she got back into the house and began to read through the Situations Vacant column of the daily newspaper. Unfortunately, the four pages of job listings contained no mention of any company in need of an interior designer with no practical experience and a fascination with the techniques of antique fabric restoration. By the time she'd read the job listings for a second time, the old Julia would have been on the phone, begging the headmistress to pay no attention to her letter of resignation. The new Julia swallowed hard, wiped her sweating palms on her jeans and doggedly began to reread the list of openings. If she couldn't get a position as an interior designer, she'd work as a sales assistant in a home furnishings store or a paint-and-wallpaper shop. However limited the scope for exercising her creativity, she would be employing her talents more usefully than teaching French. She could match curtain material with carpets and bedspreads better than anyone she knew, whereas she'd met at least a dozen French teachers who were more inspiring at their jobs than she was. As for paying the mortgage on her flat out of a shop assistant's salary—well, she had some savings, and the rent from her flat mate, who would soon be returning from a short sabbatical in South Africa. If she lived economically, she could hold out for at least a year before she seriously depleted her small nest egg.

The phone rang, and she was tempted to ignore it. Her mother usually called at this time on a Saturday afternoon, and Julia didn't want to have to deflect questions about Edward Hillyard or risk letting it slip quite yet that she'd resigned from her job. Just as the answering machine was about to take the call, she screwed up her courage and grabbed the receiver. No use avoiding the inevitable.

"Hello," she said.

"Julia? This is Tate Herald. You sound busy, I hope I haven't called at a bad time."

"Not at all." Julia's spirits perked up at the unexpected call. "As a matter of fact, your timing's terrific, Tate. I was looking through the Situations Vacant columns and deciding that my skills are in terrifyingly short demand. I definitely needed the distraction."

Tate laughed sympathetically. "Believe me, I know the feeling. But I would have thought a teacher with your qualifications would have no trouble finding a job."

"I'm not looking for a teaching position," Julia said. "It's the end of the school year, so this seemed a good time to start a new career as an interior designer."

"How interesting. Michael mentioned that you had some very creative ideas for refurbishing some of the rooms at Ashby Hall."

Julia's grip tightened around the phone. "You've spoken to Michael since he went back to Chicago?"

"Mmm...yes, we're old friends, you know. He called me a couple of days ago. Your name came up in our conversation a few times."

Julia wanted to ask what Michael had said about her, but she couldn't find the words to form the question without sounding overeager. She hung on to the receiver and waited, hoping for she wasn't sure what.

"Do you have plans for tonight?" Tate said. "My date had to fly to L.A. for a last-minute audition, so I've been stood up. Would you be interested in joining me for dinner? If you wouldn't mind going somewhere quiet and out of the way, that is."

"I'd love to join you, Tate, and somewhere off the beaten track is fine."

"Thanks. You know, most of the time I love being recognized by my fans. Never believe an actor who tells you that he or she doesn't like fame—we're all hungry for it. But there are occasions when I really empathize with Greta Garbo, and tonight I'm having one of my 'I want to be alone' moods."

"Then why don't you come here to my flat so that you don't have to spend all evening signing autographs on paper napkins? I could cook us something simple. A cheese soufflé, maybe."

"Simple? A soufflé?" Tate gave an appreciative gurgle. "Julia, you're a marvel. I can be there by seven. Is that too early?"

"It's perfect timing," Julia said, relieved to have something to occupy her mind other than the twin problems of her nonexistent affair with Michael Forrest and her equally nonexistent job as an interior designer. "I'll look forward to seeing you in a couple of hours, Tate."

TATE ARRIVED PUNCTUALLY at seven. "What a lovely room," she said, following Julia into the living room.

"The colors are so restful, and that sofa in front of the fireplace is gorgeous."

Julia smiled. "If I didn't know she's been too busy fussing over her baby to think of anything else, I'd suspect Lianne of coaching you on what to say. That sofa's my pride and joy. It's a 1920s piece that I bought from a junk shop on the Portobello Road, and then I spent weeks searching for material to reupholster it. I'm glad you like it."

Tate ran her hand along the back of the sofa. "Are you telling me that you recovered this yourself?"

Julia shrugged. "Well, yes, but it's easy to do once you know how. There's nothing skilled or high tech about it. Restoring the wood on the armrests was much harder than the actual upholstering."

"Lianne told me once that you were intimidatingly talented. Looking around this room, I realize that she wasn't exaggerating."

Julia blushed. "You know Lianne, she's much too generous about her friends. But thanks for saying all the right things, Tate. I'm still trying to convince myself that I'm not crazy to have thrown away a perfectly good teaching position in pursuit of a dream that may never succeed."

"You're not crazy, you're talented. There is a difference, although there will be plenty of days when you'll find yourself wondering. Trust me on this, Julia—I've been where you are now, and you're never going to be happy until your work reflects the woman you really are."

"When times get tough, I'll remind myself that you and Lianne both believe I can make it." Julia grimaced. "I suppose the worst that can happen is that I fall flat on my face and provide my family with endless opportunities to say they told me so."

"Then pick yourself up, dust yourself off and tell them to butt out." Tate gave the sofa a final appreciative stroke before sitting down. "You know, if I'd listened to my parents, I'd probably be slogging away at some desk job in a huge conglomerate, thoroughly miserable with life. But I'm lucky enough to have a grandmother who's my greatest fan. When I was starving my way through drama school—not to mention waiting tables for several years afterward—Gran would remind me that when you're born with a special talent, you have an obligation to develop it. She was more thrilled than I was when I finally landed a job as the model in an advert for women's underwear." Tate grinned. "To listen to Gran, you'd have thought I'd been signed for a world tour with the Royal Shakespeare Company instead of an agreement to be photographed in my bra and knickers."

Julia laughed, but she could hear a wistful note in her own laughter. Her parents were good people, so were her brothers, but they no more understood her hopes and dreams than they understood the motivations of a tribal chieftain in the Brazilian rain forest. She envied Tate her sympathetic grandmother. "She must be thrilled now that you're a genuine star."

"She is, but she helps me keep my success in perspective. As soon as I'd made it within sniffing range of the big time, she stopped telling me how wonderful I was and started to remind me that I can't afford to keep my nose stuck up so high in the air that I fall over my own feet. A wise woman, my gran."

"You're lucky to have her." Julia glanced at her watch. "The soufflé should be ready in a couple of minutes. Why don't you come into the kitchen while I check on it? The people who owned this flat before me knocked out the wall between the dining room and the kitchen, so it's one big room and you have to eat where you cook. Now that I'm used to the idea, I like it a lot better.''

''Much more practical now that nobody has squads of servants to serve the meal,'' Tate agreed.

Dinner was a successful meal, and not only in terms of the soufflé and accompanying salad of baby greens. Tate turned out to be a fascinating guest, and Julia felt a genuine rapport growing between the two of them. If only she'd been able to find some tactful way to bring Michael's name into the conversation, she would have considered the evening almost perfect.

Finally, when they'd carried a tray of after-dinner coffee into the living room, Julia swallowed her pride and abandoned any pretense of subtlety. ''How did you first get to know Michael Forrest?'' she asked, pouring a cup of coffee and handing it to Tate.

''It was strictly an arranged match,'' Tate said. ''We were hooked up by my PR consultant. I needed some publicity in the States to coincide with the launch of 'Grosvenor Square' on American network television. Michael and I both happened to be using the same PR firm, and they decided that pretending to have an affair with Michael was one of the easiest ways to get my name splashed across the front pages of the tabloids.''

''How did you manage to persuade Michael to cooperate?'' Julia asked. ''I'd have thought he generates enough affairs of his own, without needing a PR firm to set him up with dates.''

''You'd be surprised at how many of Michael's dates are actually business arrangements,'' Tate said. ''In my case, the PR firm brokered a deal between Michael and the producers of 'Grosvenor Square.' The cast of the show stayed at his hotels during our publicity tour, and the producers threw their launch parties at the Los Angeles Carlisle Forrest. In exchange, Michael agreed to partner me to enough high-profile events to generate a media buzz about our torrid romance. In reality, once the cameras turned off, our relationship was about as torrid as Ma and Pa Kettle's. Although, as it happened, we did become good friends."

Julia stirred her coffee, although she was too preoccupied to have put in any cream. "I can understand why the publicity might be valuable for you, since you're very photogenic, and getting your picture on TV, or in the tabloids, might persuade an American audience to watch your show. But I still don't understand why Michael would find the media attention worth his time. People don't choose a hotel because the company president leads a glamorous life."

"In fact, that's not entirely true. Michael's discovered that convention business can be influenced by adding an aura of glamour to a hotel's reputation. But Michael doesn't have the luxury of keeping out of the limelight, even if he wanted to. He became interesting to the media when he wrested control of the Carlisle Forrest empire from his father. He was still in his twenties at the time, his mother was already notorious for her succession of famous lovers, and his father chose to make a dramatic, public appeal to shareholders to side with him. When Michael won the battle and was appointed president, the media wouldn't leave him alone. His affair with Cherie Lockwood sealed his fate, because she chose to publicize their relationship in every way she could. After Storm was born, Michael learned the hard way that once you're in the spotlight, journalists will generate gossip about you, one way or another. He decided to make sure they generated the gossip he wanted people to read."

Julia returned her cup to its saucer with special care. "But Michael's affair with Cherie Lockwood wasn't a media invention, was it? Storm exists, and Michael's acknowledged he's the father."

Tate took a few moments to answer. She finally looked up, her gaze locking with Julia's. "Michael was royally screwed over by Cherie Lockwood, and I personally wish like hell that he hadn't allowed the story of their affair to be played out as if he were the bad guy. But my personal feelings don't give me the right to betray his secrets, or Cherie's, either, much as I despise the woman. If he hasn't told you the truth about his affair with Cherie, then it's not my place to do so. Besides, if you aren't smart enough to realize that Michael's the soul of honor, then you aren't the right woman for him. Which is a shame, because I thought when I saw you two together that he might finally have found the woman who would make him happy."

It amazed Julia how calm her voice sounded when her stomach was turning cartwheels and her heart was hammering hard enough to burst. "I first met Michael over a year ago," she said. "Ever since then, I've used his relationship with Cherie and Storm as an excuse not to acknowledge how I feel about him."

"Is it so difficult for you to admit that you've fallen in love?" Tate asked quietly.

Julia didn't bother to deny that she was in love. "I've always believed that people should be friends before they become lovers. With Michael, I seem to be doing everything backward. I fell in love first, now I'm trying to get to know him."

Tate shot an uncomfortably shrewd glance in Julia's direction. "It's pretty damn difficult to get to know a man when he's on one side of the Atlantic and you're on the other, wouldn't you say? Personally, I'd have thought it would be a hell of a lot easier to find out exactly how you feel about Michael if you were at least within shouting range."

TATE'S LOGIC WAS irrefutable, Julia thought after Tate had gone and she was alone again. There was no reason in the world for her to be sitting here in London, aching for Michael's company, when she could be with him. On Wednesday, when Michael had asked her to go to Chicago with him, she'd instinctively retreated into the habits of a lifetime. Instead of reaching for the chance of happiness and grabbing it with both hands, she'd drawn back in a futile attempt to protect herself from hurt. In retrospect, she wondered why in the world it had seemed sensible to send away the man she loved. How had she protected herself by turning her back on the most interesting, exciting and attractive man she'd ever met? How had she made herself less vulnerable to hurt by ignoring the fact that she was deeply in love?

It was suddenly so easy to see what she needed to do that Julia couldn't understand why it had taken her so long to work it out. She picked up the phone and called British Airways. Ever since Michael left, she'd felt incapable of performing routine tasks without a massive effort at concentration. All at once, with the decision made, her brain felt nimble again, her body light and coordinated. She tapped her fingers on the counter, doodling hearts on the message pad by the phone as she waited for someone to answer.

A clerk, sounding bored, asked how he could help her. Julia drew in a deep breath, calming her reckless sense of anticipation. "I'd like to book a ticket on your next direct flight to Chicago," she said. "How soon would that be?"

JULIA HAD TRAVELED throughout Europe, so she wasn't prepared for the sensation of foreignness that greeted her when she landed at O'Hare Airport on Sunday afternoon. Almost everyone around her was speaking English, but the unfamiliar accent and pitch of their voices meant that she had to focus all her attention just to understand what they were saying. The cavernous space of O'Hare struck her as profoundly alien. She knew that London's Heathrow airport was the busiest in the world, but its flights were divided among four separate terminals, so that the scale of each individual terminal appeared relatively cozy and intimate. By contrast, O'Hare gathered everything under one roof, as if flaunting its dominant position at the center of the vast North American continent. To Julia's eyes, its futuristic design, exposed pipes and shimmering laser lights all pulsed with the hurried beat of the twenty-first century.

The immigration officer viewed her passport with every appearance of intense suspicion, and Julia's confidence wasn't bolstered by having to ask him to repeat everything he said before she understood his questions. Whoever perpetrated the myth that Americans drawled had obviously never listened to the rapid-fire speech of the officials at O'Hare airport. Julia felt that she'd accomplished something major when she survived Customs inspection and managed to follow the overhead signs to a point outside the terminal building where she could get herself and her suitcase into a cab.

"The Carlisle Forrest, please," she instructed the driver, pushing her hair out of her eyes and wondering if she'd ever feel cool again. Her long-sleeved English summer dress was sticking to her all over. Thank God she hadn't worn panty hose!

"Carlisle Forrest? That's on Lake Shore Drive."

"Yes, that's what the address says."

The cabbie started his meter. "Humidity's a real killer today," he commented. "Heard on the radio it's ninety-four degrees, hundred percent humidity. That's Chicago for you. If it ain't freezin' you to death, it's fryin' you." He sounded rather proud of his city's demanding climate. He eased into the flow of traffic. "You gotta cute accent," he said. "Where did you fly in from?"

"London," Julia said, adjusting her mind to the interesting concept that she spoke with a foreign accent. "I'm English, and this is my first trip to America."

"I like the way you folks talk over there. My wife and me, we went to London last summer. Nice place. Expensive, though. That your hometown?"

When she nodded, he launched into a detailed account of his visit, during which he'd seen the changing of the guard at Buckingham Palace, visited the chamber of horrors at the Tower of London and enjoyed an afternoon at Madame Tussaud's. He was very upset that he'd been unable to catch a personal glimpse of either the queen or Princess Diana, and he informed Julia that the British royal family was missing out on a considerable source of profit by not agreeing to pose for photographs with visiting groups of tourists.

"My wife woulda paid fifty bucks, maybe more, to

get her picture taken with one of the royals," he said. "Ten people at a time, that's five hundred bucks a pop, and it wouldn't take more'n a coupla minutes of their time. Diana wouldn't have to keep worrying about her divorce settlement, then, would she? She could earn plenty just posing for photos."

Amused by this evidence of the famed American entrepreneurial spirit, Julia agreed that this might be a good way to make money, although she didn't hold out much hope that the royal family would be jumping on the suggestion anytime soon.

The nine-hour flight had left her tired enough that she was quite glad to have the cab driver do most of the talking, but when they reached downtown Chicago, her fatigue vanished as she became lost in admiration of the spectacular architecture and spacious plazas. Most of what she knew about the town was limited to gangster movies featuring Al Capone, or documentaries recounting the horrors of the blighted South Side. Nothing had prepared her for the splendor of Lake Michigan or the magnificence of the city's towering skyscrapers, aglow in the late-afternoon sun.

The cab driver drew to a halt in front of an imposing thirty-story building standing right by the lake. Michael had mentioned that this flagship hotel of the Carlisle Forrest chain was more than a hundred years old. It was astonishing to think that in the 1890s, architects in Chicago had already been able to safely design buildings as tall as this one. Energized by the sheer vitality and elegance of her surroundings, Julia paid the cab driver and walked into the hotel.

The lobby was such a perfect example of art deco at its best that she could only stare in silent awe at the sweeping arches, the gleaming chrome fixtures and the polished walnut counters. The very idea of her making suggestions on how to improve the decor in a hotel this splendid would have been funny if it hadn't been so absurd. It was mind-boggling to realize that Michael was the president and manager not only of this grand hotel, but of nine more just like it. She'd recognized his leadership abilities and ambition from the first moment she met him, but having seen him only when he was in the company of friends, or against the relatively small-scale setting of Ashby Hall, she hadn't begun to grasp the full size and scope of his position as CEO of the Carlisle Forrest Corporation. Just standing in the lobby of his flagship hotel was enough to put his responsibilities into a whole new perspective.

A nagging voice, the legacy of her parents, warned Julia that she was about to make a first-class fool of herself. How was it possible that a man like Michael Forrest could have any lasting feelings for her? The two of them had been thrown together by force of circumstance, and they weren't in the least suited to each other. If Elizabeth Gabrielle hadn't decided to arrive a month early, they would never have discovered how many interests they shared. And from Michael's point of view, the lovemaking that she'd found so spectacular probably hadn't been anything out of the ordinary. Carried away by the heat of the moment, he had suggested she should fly back with him to Chicago. Now that she was here, he'd most likely be embarrassed that she'd taken his invitation seriously.

With a supreme effort of will, Julia shook off years of negative thinking. She knew what she was doing. God, she hoped she knew. The ache of yearning she felt for Michael made everything else irrelevant. In the last resort, what did it matter if Michael rejected her? If she didn't take this chance, she would always regret what might have been, and she was sick to death of leading a life based on avoidance of risk. Squaring her shoulders, she made her way to the registration counter.

"I'd like to speak to Michael Forrest if he's in the hotel," she said to the clerk. "I'm a personal friend of his and I've just arrived from London. My name's Julia Dutton."

The clerk's expression became simultaneously super-polite and totally inscrutable. "Is Mr. Forrest expecting you, miss?"

"Not exactly. Not today, at least."

If possible, the clerk's expression became even more bland. "I'll dial his office number, Miss Dutton, but it is Sunday, and I doubt if he's in the hotel this afternoon."

"I have his home number, but somehow I expected him to be here."

The merest flicker of interest sparked in the clerk's eyes at the information that she had Michael's home phone number. "I'll call Mr. Forrest's office for you now, miss." He dialed a series of numbers and the phone was apparently answered almost at once, although Julia could only hear the clerk's side of the conversation.

"Mr. Forrest, this is David at the front desk. A friend of yours is downstairs at reception and would like to speak with you. Her name is Julia Dutton—"

The clerk got no further. "Yes, sir," he said, obviously in answer to a question. "She's right here at the check-in counter." He paused again. "Yes, sir. I'll make sure that she waits right here."

The clerk hung up the phone and looked at Julia again, this time with undisguised interest. "Mr. Forrest says he's coming down immediately. He asked you to wait for him here, Miss Dutton.''

The elevators weren't visible from where she was standing, so Michael was only a few yards away from her when she saw him striding across the lobby, devastatingly handsome in a formal business suit. His gaze locked with hers, and suddenly she was running toward him, arms outstretched, the dozens of other people in the lobby entirely forgotten.

His arms clamped around her waist. Her hands clasped around his neck. "You told me to come and see you next time I was in the neighborhood," she said.

"Yeah, so I did." He pulled her against his chest, his smile crooked. "I'm glad you happened to be passing by."

"I came to pay off my debts," she said. "If you remember, I'm supposed to eat a real American breakfast. Something gross about pancakes, syrup and sausages." Her fingers raced across his face, absorbing the shape and texture of him, reminding herself of how wonderful the stubble of his beard felt beneath her fingertips.

"I remember." His hands wound possessively in her hair, tilting her head back so that he could look deep into her eyes. His smile faded. "God, Jules, I've missed you. This has been a hell of a week."

His mouth came down on hers with passionate, seeking demand, and she surrendered herself to the kiss, sinking deeper and deeper, lost to the world until a polite male voice thrust her back to awareness of her surroundings. "Michael, sorry to intrude, but there was a photographer from the *National Investigator* here in the lobby just a few minutes ago. You might want to take your…friend…into my office so that you can both have some privacy."

Julia leaned against Michael, her breath coming fast and jagged, her legs too shaky to allow her to move. The man who'd spoken wore a dark suit and a discreet name tag bearing the inscription Thomas Burdine, Assistant Manager. She supposed she ought to feel ashamed of having made a spectacle of herself. How she actually felt was deliriously, gloriously happy.

Michael released his hold on her waist, but he kept his hand locked with hers. "Thanks for the warning, Tom." He grinned. "I'm sorry if we lowered the tone of the lobby."

The assistant manager permitted himself a small smile. "I'd say you raised the interest level rather than lowered the tone."

Julia glanced around and saw that, without exception, every employee in the place was staring at her and Michael with an identical expression of hypnotized fascination. She was just beginning to feel embarrassed when a uniformed bellman came in from the sidewalk. He looked at his fellow workers in puzzlement, then shrugged and made his way over to Michael's side.

"Your limo's here, sir. The driver says that traffic out to the airport is unusually heavy this afternoon, so you need to leave as soon as possible or you'll miss your flight."

Michael smiled. "Thanks, Ron, but I won't be going to the airport today, after all. Tell the limo driver to bill my personal account, will you?"

"Yes, sir. I'll let him know right away." The bellman was well trained, and he allowed himself only one quick glance at Michael and Julia's linked hands before turning smartly on his heel and returning to the canopied portico.

"You shouldn't have canceled your flight for me," Julia said. "I know how busy you are, Michael, and I could have gone with you wherever you were going. Or waited till you got back."

He looked at her, his eyes glinting. "I was going to London," he said.

"Oh." She felt a smile begin to play around her lips. "Not more problems at Ashby Hall, I hope?"

"No," he said. "I'd decided it was time to take care of some pressing personal problems."

"What a coincidence," she said. "That's exactly why I came to Chicago. What a good thing we didn't cross in mid-Atlantic."

"Julia." Her name came hoarsely from his throat. He moved toward her again, caught the eye of the hotel manager and stepped back, drawing in an unsteady breath. "You know, I'll bet if we went up to my suite, we'd be able to take care of each other's personal problems in a heartbeat."

She managed to keep a straight face. "You know, Michael, I'll bet you're right."

THEY LAY TOGETHER on the bed in Michael's private suite, their limbs tangled, breath gradually slowing to normal, hands stroking each other's backs in a sated, sleepy caress. Julia only realized that she'd drifted into a light doze when she woke up and found Michael looking down at her, watching her intently in the encroaching dusk.

He saw that she was awake, and his hand reached out to splay against her rib cage in a gesture of mingled tenderness and possession. "What made you decide to come to Chicago?" he asked.

"I wanted to be with you."

His hand tightened over her breast. "Why?"

She wrapped her hand around his, feeling the heat of her own flesh beneath his fingers. "Because I love you and because everything else suddenly seemed trivial in comparison to that."

She was so accustomed to seeing his emotions shuttered behind a mask of self-mockery that it was almost shocking to see the naked relief and happiness that swept across his face.

"God, Julia, I love you." His voice cracked as if the words had been dragged out of him, the awkward confession of a man who'd been given too many reasons in the past to keep his emotions tightly guarded.

She brushed her lips over his before drawing back just enough to smile into his eyes. "If you practice saying that every day, I promise it'll soon be no more painful than having a root canal without anesthesia."

"I love you," he said again.

"See?" She cradled his face between her hands, her gaze tender. "That time you didn't even wince."

He smiled, but she could feel his tension. "We have a lot to talk about, Jules. We both know this isn't going to be an easy relationship to work out. And living on opposite sides of the Atlantic is almost the least of our problems."

"The best relationships are never easy. Look at Grace and Jeffrey DeWilde. I'm sure they love each other to distraction, but their marriage is still a work in progress thirty-three years after it started!"

He frowned, contemplating. "Grace gave me some advice last time I was in London. She said that you should never try to stitch a relationship together without acknowledging the problems that you're facing. So maybe that's what we should do. I want to give us a fighting chance, Jules, but it's hard for me to talk about commitment and marriage and happily ever after. My parents had the sort of marriage that gives divorce a good name, and the only time I fell in love before I met you, I got badly burned."

"By Cherie Lockwood," she said tentatively.

"Yes."

"You don't have to talk about her if you'd prefer not to." Julia leaned closer, holding his hand. "Is she really important to us? We're neither of us teenagers, Michael, and we'd be pretty boring people if we didn't have any relationships in our past."

"It's not as simple as that," Michael said. "I need to explain about Cherie so that you'll understand why, even though I love you, it's difficult for me to make the sort of commitment another man might find easy. I associate marriage more with broken promises and betrayals than with anything positive."

"But you were never married to Cherie, were you?"

"No, I've never been married, but from what I've seen, marriage has never been a beneficial partnership. My parents' marriage made me gun-shy until Cherie came into my life and I imagined myself deeply in love. I was already thirty-three years old when we met, and accustomed to thinking of myself as cynical and sophisticated and wise to all the angles, but in reality, I guess I was still naive enough to be an easy mark. Cherie seemed sweet and exotic and loving, a beautiful bundle of conflicting needs and temptations. She was also elusive, which had the immediate effect of sending me chasing after her in a big way. Which was exactly what Cherie had counted on, of course. She'd chosen her sucker well."

Julia looked up. "But why were you a sucker just because Cherie Lockwood chose to pursue you? She was attracted to you, presumably."

"Not in the least." Michael's smile contained no mirth. "Cherie arranged to meet me because she'd discovered she was three weeks pregnant and she was desperate to provide a father for her baby. She selected me because of my reputation as a bachelor who lived life in the fast lane, and also because I had approximately the same hair and eye coloring as her baby's real father. I'm sure the fact that I wasn't a Hollywood insider counted for a lot, too. I wasn't about to recognize great acting when I saw it up close and personal."

Julia frowned. "I'm not getting this. Why couldn't Cherie Lockwood name the true father of her child? Or if she didn't want to do that for some obscure reason, why did she need a father at all? She's an actress, not a nun or a candidate for public office. Lots of female stars in Hollywood have had babies without identifying the father. What did she need you for—or any father, for that matter?"

"Cherie was terrified that some enterprising journalist would put two and two together and come up with the name of her baby's real father, and that's what she was frantic to avoid. Storm's father was—is—a man who couldn't afford to be caught out in an adulterous affair. So to protect her lover, she had the most public and torrid love affair with me that she could manage to devise. What I really resent is that when she started to become visibly pregnant, she told me I was the father of her baby."

"Oh, no!"

Michael gave a cynical shrug. "I had no reason to disbelieve her, since at that stage, we'd been living in each other's pockets for almost four months. We'd used birth control, of course, but birth control fails, I knew that, and I was more than willing to take responsibility for my actions and learn to be the best parent I could. For the next two months, I kept asking her to marry me, and she kept inventing excuses as to why she couldn't say yes. Finally, she had the locks changed on her house and refused to meet with me or take my phone calls. She had her lawyers threaten me with a suit for harassment. It was only because a nurse called me anonymously to say that Cherie had gone into labor that I knew she was delivering the baby I still thought was mine. I flew back from New York, where I happened to be, and arrived at the hospital in L.A. a couple of hours after Storm was born."

"My God, Michael, how could she do something as cruel as letting you think Storm was your son when he wasn't? And why did she do it?"

"I don't think she meant to be cruel. To be fair, I think Cherie misread me on the question of how I'd feel about having a child. Based on my reputation, she assumed I would dump her the minute she announced she was pregnant. She didn't expect me to keep insisting that I wanted to play a major role in Storm's upbringing."

"The fact that she understood nothing about your character doesn't excuse what she did, Michael. In fact, it makes it worse that she could set out to use somebody she hadn't bothered to learn anything about."

Michael smiled faintly. "Thank you for sounding so indignant on my behalf."

Julia flushed. "I keep remembering all the times I

needled you about your neglect of Storm. I feel so guilty, Michael."

He took her hand and kissed the tip of her fingers. "You have nothing to feel guilty for, Jules. You believed exactly what everyone else believed, and why wouldn't you? You'd never even met me when the stories about Storm's birth and my neglect of Cherie started to surface in the tabloids."

"How long did it take Cherie before she finally got around to telling you Storm wasn't your son? And once you knew the truth, why didn't you broadcast it to the world?"

"She told me right after he was born, when I came to the hospital in L.A. I threatened to take legal action to get access to Storm on a regular basis, and so Cherie delivered her ultimate zinger. She informed me Storm wasn't my son, that she'd already been pregnant when she met me, and that she was willing to have blood tests done to prove the baby wasn't mine."

Julia rested her head against Michael's chest. "Did she tell you who the father was?"

"Yes, because I threatened to turn the tables on her and tell the media Storm wasn't mine. She begged and pleaded with me to let everyone continue believing that Storm was my son. And in the end, I agreed. Ironically, if she'd told me the truth in the first place, I might have agreed to help her out without any need for all the deception."

"But why?" Julia exclaimed. "Why would you agree to let yourself be used like that? Who in the world were you protecting?"

"Not Cherie," Michael said. "And certainly not her lover. I kept silent because of the other woman in the triangle. Terri was dying of muscular dystrophy, and she didn't need to hear that her husband had committed adultery and fathered the child with Cherie that she'd never been able to give him.''

"Oh, my God!" Julia finally understood. "Storm's father is Brad Stein."

"Yes," Michael confirmed. "The man famous throughout the movie industry for his devotion to his first wife, Terri. And now adding to his reputation as a good guy by marrying Cherie Lockwood and taking care of the son I supposedly walked out on."

Julia shuddered. "How can you bear to know that Brad Stein's so respected when he's got all the moral integrity of a cockroach?"

"I'd have destroyed Brad's legend in a heartbeat, but at the time Storm was born, Terri was in the terminal stages of her illness, and I didn't want to be responsible for hurting her when she was struggling to enjoy the last few months of her life. And much as I loathe the hypocrisy of what Brad and Cherie did, I honestly believe they were far more concerned about Terri than they were about anything else. Cherie genuinely liked Terri, and she was desperate to protect her from finding out the truth about Brad being Storm's father. She really needed to be able to point an accusing finger in my direction."

"Cherie might have genuinely liked Terri, but she wasn't concerned enough about her to refrain from having an affair with her husband," Julia said hotly. "And the same goes for Brad Stein. He didn't love his wife enough to remain faithful to her when she was dying. You're kinder to both of them than I would be, Michael, a lot kinder."

He finally gave her a genuine smile. "I've had three years to work on my charitable feelings. Besides, in retrospect, I keep thinking how damn grateful I am that Cherie Lockwood isn't the mother of my firstborn son. Because, you know, the kicker in all this is that by the time Storm was born, I realized that I'd never been in love with Cherie at all. She'd dangled an intriguing package in front of my nose, and I'd chased after it. I'd made no more of an attempt to get to know the real Cherie Lockwood than she did to get to know me."

Julia moved closer, nuzzling her cheek against him. "That sounds like the story of my relationship with Gabe," she said. "He's good-looking, intelligent and the heir apparent to the DeWilde empire, so I convinced myself I was in love with him. The truth is, I never tried to get to know the real Gabriel DeWilde. I was too busy enjoying the image he projected to waste much time bothering about the fact that there was absolutely no spark between us, no genuine intimacy."

Michael held her tight. "I guess we have plenty of spark," he said.

She smiled. "Yes, I guess we do. And even some excess sizzle."

For a man who normally radiated self-confidence, he looked remarkably unsure of himself. "When two people love each other, the logical next step is for them to get married," he mumbled.

Her laughter was tinged with a note of sadness. "Well, yes, that's true as a general rule. But not when they look as terrified of the idea as you do, Michael."

He drew in a shaky breath. "The *idea* of marriage still terrifies me, but this past week I realized how crazy it was to throw away the chance of having something wonderful with you just because my parents were unhappy and Cherie Lockwood screwed me over. Ever since that morning in your flat when you sent me away,

I've been trying to think of all the reasons why you were wrong to refuse to come and live with me. Last night, I finally quit blaming you and faced the fact that I was the one who'd behaved like an idiot."

He stroked her hair away from her forehead, holding her gaze. "I was flying to London to ask you to marry me. I know now that I want you to be the person who shares my life, the woman who'll be the mother of my children, my friend as well as my lover. Will you marry me, Julia? Please?"

She must have said yes, because next thing she knew, she was in Michael's arms and he was kissing her passionately, in between murmuring promises about how he was going to love and cherish her forever. When they finally broke apart, he held her head cradled against his chest.

"Did I mention that I'll expect you to sign a prenuptial agreement?" he said casually.

She jerked away, but he tightened his hold and pushed her head back against his chest. "There are only a couple of clauses in the agreement," he said. "The first is that you have to guarantee that all our children will look like you."

She blinked. "*All* our children? How many do you plan on having?"

"The precise number is subject to negotiation. The pre-nup will merely state that they all have to look like you."

She let out a tiny breath of laughter. "Well, that sounds entirely reasonable. I agree."

"There's one other clause. You must offer your services as an interior designer exclusively to corporations run by me."

"Mmm...I don't know, Michael. That might be a

deal breaker. I already promised Tate Herald that I'd act as her decorator for the house she's just bought in London.''

"You did?" Michael looked delighted rather than chagrined. "Congratulations," he said softly. "I'm sure you'll do a great job for Tate."

"Thanks, I hope so. I've taken your advice, Michael, and resigned from Kensington Academy, so I have plenty of time on my hands." She sent him a provocative glance. "In fact, for the right sort of fee, I'm sure I could be persuaded to work two design jobs at once. Say, refurbishing the bedrooms at Ashby Hall at the same time as I do Tate Herald's house."

"It's an interesting offer. What sort of a fee did you have in mind?"

She waved an airy hand. "Oh, several million pounds at least."

His eyes gleamed. "I'm a tough negotiator, sweetie. How about giving me a hundred thousand pounds' discount for every night we spend together in Mr. and Mrs. Blodget's bedroom?"

"A hundred thousand a night?" Julia collapsed against the pillows, laughing. "Good Lord, Michael, you place a pretty high value on your services."

"And I'm worth every penny." He leaned over her, arms braced on either side of her body. "Do you want me to show you how I'll earn my hundred thousand?"

Desire burned suddenly in her throat. "Yes," she said huskily. "Show me now, Michael."

His smile contained tenderness along with predatory male satisfaction. "My pleasure, sweetheart," he said, and closed his mouth over hers.

CHAPTER FOURTEEN

FOR THE PAST SEVERAL DAYS, relatives, friends, colleagues and well-wishers had been arriving at Ashby Hall from all over the world, and, finally, the gala dinner celebrating the remarriage of Grace and Jeffrey DeWilde was about to begin. Outside, the October night was cold and dark, but inside, the hotel reverberated with warmth, light and the hum of voices. Waiters circulated carrying trays of champagne and hors d'oeuvres, and guests admired the attractive table settings and the superb arrangements of chrysanthemums and dahlias plucked from the hotel's famous gardens.

In the Salisbury Suite, Jeffrey paced up and down, elegant in black tie and dinner jacket. He tried not to watch the ormolu clock, ticking reproachfully on the mantelpiece. Many things had changed over the past months, he reflected wryly, but one thing had remained the same. Grace—who was never so much as a minute late for a business appointment—still couldn't manage to get ready on time for her own parties.

She hurried out of the bedroom, breathless, flushed and ravishingly attractive in a strapless gown of midnight blue satin. The Dancing Waters necklace shimmered at her throat, the only jewelry she wore tonight other than her engagement and wedding rings. She sent him a smile that was both shy and rueful. "I know I'm late, but you're not to scold me, Jeffrey. I wanted to look beautiful for you tonight. Unfortunately, that takes considerably longer to achieve these days than it did the first time we celebrated our marriage."

Jeffrey remembered how beautiful he'd thought Grace was thirty-three years ago when she'd floated down the aisle in her white bridal gown embroidered with pearls, her features misty and enticing beneath her fluttering lace veil. He knew beyond any possibility of a doubt that she was a hundred times more beautiful to him tonight than she'd been then, just as he knew that the love he had felt for her that day was no more than a flickering shadow of the love he felt for her now.

"You look breathtaking, definitely worth waiting for, and I love you to distraction. Your dress is perfect with that necklace." He took her into his arms and kissed her, taking care not to muss her hair or ruin her lipstick. Along with all the big lessons, years of marriage had taught him some of the little things, too. He held out his arm. "Well, Mrs. DeWilde, shall we go downstairs and greet our guests?"

Over the past year, she had never expected her son to look as happy as he did tonight, Mary thought as Grace and Jeffrey came downstairs to the accompaniment of a round of applause. Grace looked radiant, too, and—as usual—more elegant than any other woman in the room, her sense of style impeccable, and her happiness adding a soft glow to her complexion.

"Hello, Mother." Jeffrey bent to kiss her cheek, and Mary hugged Grace before falling into step at her son's side. Ian Stanley, recently returned from a trip to China, excused himself from a conversation with Sloan DeWilde and came to bow low over Grace's hand. Mary was saddened to see that the tan Ian had picked up during his travels couldn't disguise either his underlying pallor or his continuing weight loss. He'd definitely lost ground since the last time she'd seen him, when she and Ian had been the witnesses at Grace and Jeffrey's remarriage.

But the smile he gave Grace and Jeffrey was vintage Ian—dashing, debonair and faintly wicked. He bowed to Mary with a flourish and kissed the tips of Grace's fingers. "Darling Grace, you really ought to take pity on the rest of the women in the room and try not to look quite so stunningly beautiful. No wonder Jeffrey is wearing that infuriating look of smug self-satisfaction."

"You're misinterpreting my expression," Jeffrey said, giving his friend's arm a gentle squeeze. "I'm merely displaying delight that you decided to bring all three of your ex-wives to our party. That was certainly an unexpected pleasure."

Ian grinned. "Thought you might appreciate a graphic reminder that it's much simpler to keep marrying the same woman."

"Thank you for your thoughtfulness," Jeffrey said dryly. "But Grace and I have already decided that two weddings in a lifetime are about all we can handle."

"Grace! Jeffrey!" Leland Powell hurried across the room and kissed his sister's cheek, then turned and shook Jeffrey's hand. "I only wish Liam and Mallory could be here to celebrate such a joyous occasion with the family. But the baby's too small to travel. Did I tell you they're calling her Catherine? Isn't that a lovely name? Mallory decided to name her after our mother, you know."

Grace hugged him, obviously delighted to see how thrilled her brother was about his new granddaughter. "I love the name Catherine!"

"Now we're both grandparents," he said, beaming smugly.

"Welcome to the club," Grace replied, smiling. "How are Mallory and Liam coping?"

"Mallory's fine, and Liam's over the moon." Leland sobered for a moment. "I'm glad they had a girl. This way, Liam will be able to fall in love with his new daughter without feeling disloyal to the memory of the son he lost."

Michael Forrest came up and asked Jeffrey a question about the wine being served with the first course of the dinner, and Grace left to circulate among her guests. Michael was a handsome devil, Mary thought. Good-looking in any circumstances, he was almost lethally attractive in evening dress. He reminded her in some ways of her late husband. They both had that aura of intense, controlled sexuality that women found so compelling. Mary smothered a spurt of silent laughter. By Jupiter, if she were forty years younger, she'd give Julia Dutton a run for her money.

She tapped Michael on the arm, snagging his attention. "Jeffrey tells me your fiancée is responsible for the way the bedrooms in this hotel have been redecorated."

"Well, yes, that's right—"

"She's a talented gel." Mary looked across the room to where Julia was talking and laughing with Lianne and Gabe. "She's pretty, too. You should marry her before she has a chance to slip through your fingers, Michael."

He smiled. "Don't worry, Mrs. DeWilde, I intend to marry her as soon as possible. Her family wants a traditional ceremony, though, so we're going to have to wait until Christmas."

"Christmas weddings can be delightful. Where are you going to have the ceremony?"

"Here in England, probably London, because Julia's family are all here, and she has two little nieces that are going to be flower girls. And you'll have to excuse me, Mrs. DeWilde. I see my manager over there, trying to send me signals. I believe he's anxious to start serving dinner."

"Of course, you must go to him. We don't want to ruin the meal." Mary walked through the crowded lounge, avoiding people she knew, content to be an observer. That couple in the corner with Ryder Blake must be DeWilde Cutter and his wife, Maxine. She'd have to meet them later and get to know them. One of the compensations of getting old was that one could ask questions that cut right to the heart of things without being told that one was being impertinent. Cutter didn't look much like a DeWilde, but Mary detected a definite hint of the family arrogance in the thrust of his jaw and the way he carried himself, shoulders squared, spine straight, ready to take on the world. Ryder's wife, Natasha, had exactly the same bearing and the same proud tilt to her head—a more compelling and enduring legacy from Dirk DeWilde than the stolen jewelry she'd inherited.

Megan and Phillip Villeneuve were talking to Kate and her new husband, Nick Santos. Kate still looked all fine-drawn lines and bundled energy, but Mary was pleased to see how close she stood to her husband, and how willingly she accepted the touch of his hand on her shoulder. She smiled to herself when she saw Nick's hand slide up and down his wife's bare back. Even across the room, Mary could feel the sexual tension between the two of them. And the same was true of Megan and Phillip, who were having a hard time keeping their hands away from each other.

Of all her grandchildren, Mary considered that Megan had undergone the greatest transformation in the last year. For some reason, despite her achievements, Megan had always been unsure of herself and her place in the world, but once she realized that Phillip was willing to give up everything in order to make her his wife, she'd blossomed with self-confidence. For that, if for nothing else, Mary would have been more than willing to bury the decades-old feud with Phillip's father. She smiled to herself as Megan emphasized the point she was making to Nick Santos with an expressive and uniquely French gesture. The DeWildes had always been international mongrels, despite the fact that Charles had struggled to perpetuate the myth that they were solid British citizens. Mary found it oddly satisfying to know that Anne Marie's descendants were scattered on three continents and in five different countries. Megan and Phillip's children would undoubtedly be intriguing people to know.

The crowd was thinning as Michael Forrest, with Julia Dutton at his side, ushered the hundred or so guests into the dining room. This seemed to be the year for weddings, Mary mused, making her way to the table where Grace and Jeffrey were already sitting with their children and spouses. She hoped with all her heart that this generation of newlyweds would find as much joy in their lives as she had found with Charles.

Mary waited until the guests were all seated, then she rose to her feet and held up a glass of champagne. "I claim the dubious privilege of being the oldest person in the room," she said. "Which gives me the right to make a speech, giving you the benefit of my wisdom, whether you want it or not." She smiled and waited for the ripple of laughter to die down.

"Fortunately for all of us, I have only a few words to say, but they come from my heart. This has been an amazing year for the DeWilde family. My three grandchildren have married, we've welcomed Elizabeth Gabrielle, the first member of the next generation, into the world. We've discovered a new branch of the family in Australia and New Zealand, and reconciled long-standing feuds that had their origins in events that took place before most of the people in this room were born. Best of all, Jeffrey and Grace have found their way back to each other. The path may have been twisted at times, but I believe the two of them have discovered how sweet love is when it's finally reclaimed. And now, before I'm overcome with embarrassing sentimentality, I ask all of you to join with me in drinking a toast to my son and his wife, Mr. and Mrs. Jeffrey DeWilde. Grace, Jeffrey, may the next thirty-two years of your marriage be even happier than the first thirty-two."

Mary sat down to a thunderous burst of applause and hugs from her grandchildren. Jeffrey lifted his glass and touched it to his wife's. "Welcome home, Grace. It's wonderful to have you back."

"It's wonderful to be home again." Grace touched her glass to her husband's. "Here's to us, Jeffrey," she said softly. "Here's to us."

Available for the first time in almost twenty years, a classic story...

New York Times **bestselling author**

Stella Cameron

Torn apart by past troubles, Laura Fenton and Mark Hunt are reunited years later... and soon discover that even old hurts and guilt cannot erase the incredible love they share.

Faces OF A Clown

Coming to stores in April!

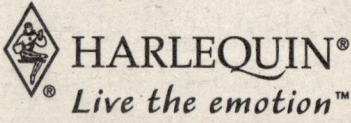

Visit us at www.eHarlequin.com

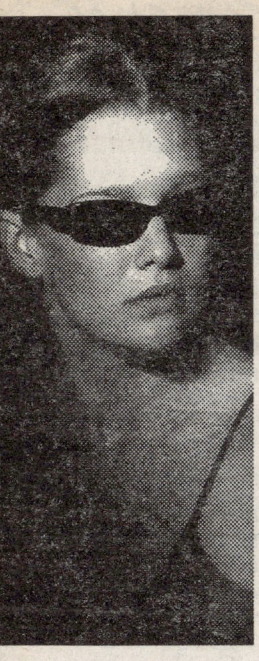

New York Times bestselling author

TESS GERRITSEN

Brings readers a tantalizing tale of romantic mystery in her classic novel...

IN THEIR FOOTSTEPS

Also featuring two BONUS stories from

Kay David
Amanda Stevens

A dramatic volume of riveting intrigue and steamy romance that should be read with the lights on!

Available in May 2004 wherever books are sold.

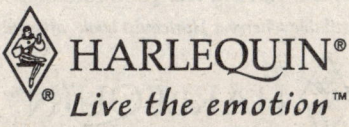

Visit us at www.eHarlequin.com

PHGDS621

Harlequin Romance

What happens when you suddenly discover your happy twosome is about to be turned into a...family?

Do you panic? Do you laugh? Do you cry? Or...do you get married?

The answer is all of the above—and plenty more!

Share the laughter and the tears as these unsuspecting couples are plunged into parenthood! Whether it's a baby on the way, or the creation of a brand-new instant family, these men and women have no choice but to be

When parenthood takes you by surprise!

Look out for the next story in this miniseries: *Her Boss's Baby Plan* (#3797) by Jessica Hart

On sale May 2004 in Harlequin Romance® Fresh, vibrant, feel-good romance!

Available wherever Harlequin books are sold.

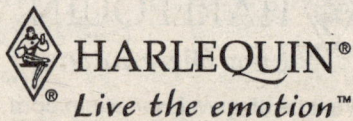

Visit us at www.eHarlequin.com

If you enjoyed what you just read,
then we've got an offer you can't resist!

Take 2 bestselling novels FREE!
Plus get a FREE surprise gift!

Clip this page and mail it to The Best of the Best™

IN U.S.A.	IN CANADA
3010 Walden Ave.	P.O. Box 609
P.O. Box 1867	Fort Erie, Ontario
Buffalo, N.Y. 14240-1867	L2A 5X3

YES! Please send me 2 free Best of the Best™ novels and my free surprise gift. After receiving them, if I don't wish to receive anymore, I can return the shipping statement marked cancel. If I don't cancel, I will receive 4 brand-new novels every month, before they're available in stores! In the U.S.A., bill me at the bargain price of $4.74 plus 25¢ shipping and handling per book and applicable sales tax, if any*. In Canada, bill me at the bargain price of $5.24 plus 25¢ shipping and handling per book and applicable taxes**. That's the complete price and a savings of over 20% off the cover prices—what a great deal! I understand that accepting the 2 free books and gift places me under no obligation ever to buy any books. I can always return a shipment and cancel at any time. Even if I never buy another The Best of the Best™ book, the 2 free books and gift are mine to keep forever.

185 MDN DNWF
385 MDN DNWG

Name _____ (PLEASE PRINT) _____

Address _____ Apt.# _____

City _____ State/Prov. _____ Zip/Postal Code _____

* Terms and prices subject to change without notice. Sales tax applicable in N.Y.
** Canadian residents will be charged applicable provincial taxes and GST.
All orders subject to approval. Offer limited to one per household and not valid to current The Best of the Best™ subscribers.
® are registered trademarks of Harlequin Enterprises Limited.

BOB02-R   ©1998 Harlequin Enterprises Limited

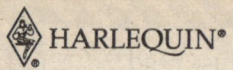

INTRIGUE

presents

THE SEEKERS

an exciting new miniseries by

SYLVIE KURTZ

These men are dedicated to truth, justice...
and protecting the women they love.

Available in April 2004:

HEART OF A HUNTER
(HI #767)

U.S. Marshal Sebastian Falconer's devotion to his job had nearly cost him his marriage—and put his wife in grave danger. When a vicious attack robbed her of her memory forever, Sebastian had to choose between being a hero, or pursuing the fugitive who tried to kill her.

**Don't miss the next book in this thrilling miniseries:
Mask of the Hunter (HI #773) On sale May 2004**
Available at your favorite retail outlet.

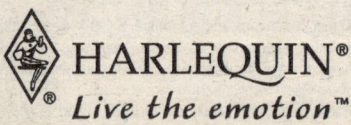

HARLEQUIN®
Live the emotion™

www.eHarlequin.com

HITSEEK

Experience two super-sexy tales from national bestselling author

A collector's size volume of HOT summer reading!

Two extraordinary women explore their deepest romantic desires in Mallory's famously sensual novels, *Love Game* and *Love Play*.

Catch the sizzle…in May 2004!

"Ms. Rush provides an intense and outrageously sexy tale..."
—*Romantic Times*

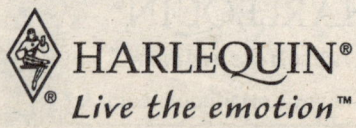

Visit us at www.eHarlequin.com